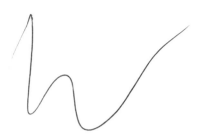

WP

POSTSCRIPT

It's been seven years since Holly Kennedy's husband died — six since she read his final letter, urging her to find the courage to forge a new life. When a group inspired by Gerry's letters, calling themselves the PS, I Love You Club, approaches her asking for help, she finds herself drawn back into a world that she worked hard to leave behind. Reluctantly, Holly begins a relationship with the club, even as their friendship threatens to destroy the peace she believes she has achieved. As each of these people call upon Holly to help them leave something meaningful behind for their loved ones, Holly will embark on a remarkable journey — one that will challenge her to ask whether embracing the future means betraying the past, and what it means to love someone forever . . .

Books by Cecelia Ahern
Published by Ulverscroft:

PS, I LOVE YOU
HOW TO FALL IN LOVE
THE YEAR I MET YOU
LYREBIRD

CECELIA AHERN

◆

POSTSCRIPT

Complete and Unabridged

CHARNWOOD
Leicester

First published in Great Britain in 2019 by
HarperCollins*Publishers*
London

First Charnwood Edition
published 2020
by arrangement with
HarperCollins*Publishers*
London

The moral right of the author has been asserted

A catalogue record for this book is available
from the British Library.

ISBN 978-1-4448-4479-5

Published by
Ulverscroft Limited
Anstey, Leicestershire

Set by Words & Graphics Ltd.
Anstey, Leicestershire
Printed and bound in Great Britain by
T. J. International Ltd., Padstow, Cornwall

This book is printed on acid-free paper

For fans of *PS, I Love You*, all around the world, with heartfelt gratitude

Prologue

Shoot for the moon and even if you miss you'll land among the stars.

It's engraved on my husband's stone at the graveyard. It was a phrase he often used. His optimistic, cheery inflection oozed positive self-help phrases as though they were fuel for life. Positive words of reinforcement like that had no effect on me, not until he died. It was when he spoke them to me from his grave that I really heard them, I felt them, I believed them. I clung to them.

For a full year after his death, my husband Gerry continued his life by giving me the gift of his words in surprise monthly notes. His words were all I had; no more spoken words, but *words*, written from his thoughts, from his mind, from a brain that controlled a body with a beating heart. Words meant life. And I gripped them, hands clasped tightly around his letters until my knuckles went white and my nails dented my palms. I hung on to them like they were my lifeline.

It's 7 p.m. on 1 April, and this fool is revelling in the new brightness. The evenings are stretching and the short, shocking, sharp sting of winter's slap is being nursed by spring. I used to dread this time of year; I favoured winter when everywhere was a hiding place. The darkness

1

made me feel that I was concealed behind gauze, that I was out of focus, almost invisible. I revelled in it, celebrating the shortness of the day, the length of the night; the darkening sky my countdown to acceptable hibernation. Now I face the light, I need it to prevent me from being sucked back.

My metamorphosis was similar to the instant shock the body experiences when dipped into cold water. On impact there's the overwhelming urge to shriek and leap out, but the longer you remain submerged, the more you acclimatise. The cold, like the darkness, can become a deceptive comfort you never want to leave. But I did; feet kicking and arms sweeping, I pulled myself up to the surface. Emerging with blue lips and chattering teeth, I thawed and re-entered the world.

Transitioning day to night, in transitional winter to spring, in a transitional place. The graveyard, considered a final resting place, is less peaceful beneath the surface than above. Below the soil, hugged by wooden coffins, bodies are altering as nature earnestly breaks down the remains. Even when resting, the body is perpetually transforming. The giddy laughter of children nearby shatters the silence, unaware of or unaffected by the in-between world they stand on. Mourners are silent but their pain is not. The wound may be internal, but you can hear it, you can see it, you can feel it. Heartbreak is carried around bodies like an invisible cloak; it adds a load, it dims eyes, it slows strides.

In the days and months after my husband's

death, I searched for some elusive transcendental connection to him, desperate to feel whole again, like an insufferable thirst that needed to be quenched. On days when I was functioning, his presence would creep up behind me and tap me on the shoulder, and suddenly I'd feel an unbearable emptiness. A parched heart. Grief is endlessly uncontrollable.

He chose to be cremated. His ashes are in an urn slotted into a niche behind a Columbarium Wall. His parents reserved the space beside his. The empty space in the wall beside his urn is for me. I feel as though I'm staring death in the face, which is something I would have embraced when he died. Anything to join him. I would have gladly climbed into that niche, folded myself up like a contortionist and cradled my body around his ashes.

He's in the wall. But he's not there, he's not here. He's gone. Energy elsewhere. Dissolved, besprinkled particles of matter around me. If I could, I would deploy an army to hunt down his every atom and put him together again, but all the king's horses and all the king's men . . . we learn it from the beginning, we only realise what it all means in the end.

We were privileged to have not just one but two goodbyes; a long illness from cancer followed by a year of his letters. He let go secretly knowing that there would be more of him for me to cling to, more than memories; even after his death he found a way to make new memories together. Magic. Goodbye, my love, goodbye again. They should have been enough. I

3

thought that they were. Maybe that's why people come to graveyards. For more goodbyes. Maybe it's not about hello at all — it's the comfort of goodbye, a calm and peaceful, guilt-free parting. We don't always remember how we met, we often remember how we parted.

It's surprising to me that I'm back here, both in this location and in this frame of mind. Seven years since his death. Six years since I read his final letter. I had, *have* moved on, but recent events have unsettled everything, rattled my core. I should move forward, but there's a hypnotic rhythmic tide, as though his hand is reaching for me and pulling me back.

I examine the stone and read his phrase again.

Shoot for the moon and even if you miss you'll land among the stars.

So this must be what it's like then. Because we did, he and I. We shot straight for it. We missed. This right here, all that I have, and all that I am, this new life that I've built up over the past seven years, without Gerry, must be what it's like to land among the stars.

1

Three Months Earlier

'Patient Penelope. The wife of the King of Ithaca, Odysseus. A serious and diligent character, a devoted wife and mother, some critics dismiss her as a symbol of marital fidelity, but Penelope is a complex woman who weaves her plots as deftly as she weaves a garment.' The tour guide leaves a mysterious pause while his eyes run over his intrigued audience.

Gabriel and I are at an exhibition in the National Museum. We're in the back row of the gathered crowd, standing slightly away from the others as though we don't belong, or don't want to be a part of their gang, but aren't too cool to risk missing what's being said. I'm listening to the tour guide while Gabriel leafs through the brochure beside me. He will be able to repeat what the guide has said later, word for word. He loves this stuff. I love that he loves this stuff more than the stuff itself. He's somebody who knows how to fill time, and when I met him that was one of his most desirable traits because I had a date with destiny. In sixty years, max, I had a date with someone on the other side.

'Penelope's husband Odysseus goes to fight in the Trojan War, which is fought for ten years and it takes him a further ten years to return. Penelope is in a very dangerous situation when one hundred and eight suitors in total begin demanding her hand in marriage. Penelope is clever, and concocts ways to delay her suitors, leading on each man with the promise of possibility but never submitting to any one.'

I suddenly feel self-conscious. Gabriel's arm draped loosely over my shoulder feels too heavy.

'The story of Penelope's loom, which we see here, symbolises one of the queen's cunning tricks. Penelope worked at weaving a shroud for the eventual funeral of her father-in-law Laertes, claiming she would choose a husband as soon as the shroud was completed. By day, she worked on a great loom in the royal halls, at night she secretly unravelled what she had done. She persisted for three years, waiting for her husband to return, deceiving her suitors until they were reunited.'

It grates on me. 'Did he wait for her?' I call out.

'Excuse me?' the tour guide asks, eyes darting to find the owner of the voice. The crowd parts and turns to look at me.

'Penelope is the epitome of conjugal fidelity, but what about her husband? Did he save himself for her, out there in the war, for twenty years?'

Gabriel chuckles.

The tour guide smiles and talks briefly about the nine other children Odysseus had with five other women, and his long journey to return to Ithaca from the Trojan War.

'So, no then,' I mumble to Gabriel as the group move on. 'Silly Penelope.'

'It was an excellent question,' he says, and I hear the amusement in his voice.

I turn again to the painting of Penelope while Gabriel flicks through the brochure. Am I Patient Penelope? Am I weaving by day, unravelling by night, deceiving this loyal and beautiful suitor while I wait to be reunited with my husband? I look up at Gabriel. Gabriel's blue eyes are playful, not reading into my thoughts. Amazingly deceived.

'She could have just slept with them all while she was waiting,' he says. 'Not much fun, Prudish Penelope.'

I laugh, rest my head on his chest. He wraps his arm around me, holds me tight and kisses the top of my head. He's built like a house and I could live inside his hug; big, broad and strong, he spends his days outdoors climbing trees as a tree surgeon, or arborist to use the title he prefers. He's used to being up at a height, loves the wind and rain, all elements, an adventurer, an explorer, and if not at the top of a tree, he can be found beneath one, with his head in a book. In the evening after work, he smells of peppery watercress.

We met two years ago at a chicken wing festival in Bray, he was beside me at the counter, holding up the line behind him while he ordered a cheeseburger. He caught me at a good moment, I liked the humour, which was his intention; he'd been trying to get my attention. His chat-up line I suppose.

Me mate wants to know if you'll go out with him.

I'll have a cheeseburger, please.

I'm a sucker for a bad chat-up line, but I've good taste in men. Good men, great men.

He starts to move one way and I pull him in the opposite direction, away from Patient Penelope's gaze. She's been watching me and she thinks she recognises her type when she sees one. But I'm not her type, I'm not her and I don't want to be her. I will not pause my life as she did to wait for an uncertain future.

'Gabriel.'

'Holly.' He matches my serious tone.

'About your proposition.'

'To march on the government to prevent premature Christmas decorations? We've just taken them down, surely they'll go up again soon.'

I have to arch my back and crane my neck to look up at him, he's so tall. His eyes are smiling.

'No, the other one. The moving in with you one.'

'Ah.'

'Let's do it.'

He punches the air and makes a quiet stadium-sized-crowd-cheering sound.

'If you promise me that we'll get a TV, and that every day when I wake up you will look like this.' I stand on tiptoe to get closer to his face. I place my hands on his cheeks, feel his smile beneath the Balbo beard he grows, trims and maintains like a pro; the tree man who cultivates his own face.

'That is a prerequisite of being my flatmate.'

'Fuck-mate,' I say and we laugh, childishly.

'Were you always so romantic?' he asks, wrapping his arms around me.

I used to be. I used to be very different. Naïve, perhaps. But I'm not any more. I hug him tightly and rest my head on his chest. I catch Penelope's judgemental eye. I lift my chin haughtily. She thinks she knows me. She doesn't.

2

'Are you ready?' my sister Ciara asks me quietly as we take our positions on bean bags at the head of the shop while the crowd hums, waiting for the show to begin. We're sitting in the window of her vintage and second-hand shop, Magpie, where I've worked with Ciara for the past three years. Once again, we've transformed the shop to an event space where her podcast, *How to Talk about . . .* , will be recorded in front of an audience. Tonight, however, I'm not in my usual safe place, servicing the wine and cupcake table. Instead, I have given in to the persistent requests of my beleaguering yet adventurous and fearless little sister, to be a guest on this week's episode, 'How to Talk about Death'. I regretted my yes as soon as the word left my lips and that regret has reached astronomical intensity by the time I sit down and am faced by the small audience.

The rails and display stands of clothing and accessories have been pushed to the walls and five rows of six fold-up seats fill the shop floor. We cleared the front window so Ciara and I could sit at an elevated height while, outside, people racing home from work throw passing glances at the moving mannequins sitting on bean bags in the window.

'Thanks for doing this.' Ciara reaches out and squeezes my clammy hand.

I smile faintly, assessing the damage control of pulling out this minute, but I know it's not worth it. I must honour my commitment.

She kicks off her shoes and pulls her bare feet up on to the bean bag, feeling perfectly at home in this space. I clear my throat and the sound reverberates around the shop through the speakers, where thirty expectant, curious faces stare back at me. I squeeze my sweaty hands together and look down at the notes I've been furiously compiling like a frazzled student before an exam ever since Ciara asked me to do this. Fragmented thoughts scribbled as inspiration seized me, but none of them make sense at the moment. I can't see where one sentence begins and another one ends.

Mum is sitting in the front row, seats away from my friend Sharon who is in the aisle seat, where she has more space for her double buggy. A pair of little feet, one sock hanging on for dear life, one sock off, peeks out from beneath a blanket in the buggy, and Sharon holds her six-month-old baby in her arms. Her six-year-old son Gerard sits on one side of her, eyes on his iPad, ears covered by headphones, and her four-year-old son is dramatically declaring he's bored and has slumped so low in the chair only his head rests against the base of the back of the chair. Four boys in six years; I appreciate her coming here today. I know that she's been up since the crack of dawn. I know how long it took her to leave the house, before entering it again three more times for something she forgot. She's here, my warrior friend. She smiles at me, her

11

face a picture of exhaustion, but ever the supportive friend.

'Welcome, everybody, to the fourth episode of the Magpie podcast,' Ciara begins. 'Some of you are regulars here — Betty, thank you for supplying us all with your delicious cupcakes; and thanks to Christian for the cheese and wine.'

I search the crowd for Gabriel. I'm quite sure he's not here, I specifically ordered him not to attend, though that wasn't necessary. As someone who keeps his private life to himself and has a firm check on his emotions, the idea of me discussing my private life with strangers boggled his mind. We may have strongly debated it but right now, I couldn't agree with him more.

'I'm Ciara Kennedy, owner of Magpie, and recently I decided it would be a good idea to do a series of podcasts titled *'How to Talk about . . . '* featuring the charities that receive a percentage of the proceeds of this business. This week we're talking about death — specifically grief and bereavement — and we have Claire Byrne from Bereave Ireland with us, and also some of those who benefit from the wonderful work that Bereave do. The proceeds of your ticket sales and generous donations will go directly to Bereave. Later, I'll be talking to Claire about the important, tireless work they do in assisting those who have lost loved ones, but first I'd like to introduce my special guest, Holly Kennedy, who just so happens to be my sister. You're finally here!' Ciara exclaims excitedly, and the audience applaud.

'I am,' I laugh nervously.

'Ever since I started the podcast last year, I've been pestering my sister to take part. I'm so glad you're doing this.' She reaches across and takes my hand, holds it. 'Your story has touched my life profoundly, and I'm sure that so many people will benefit from hearing about the journey you've been on.'

'Thank you. I hope so.'

I notice my notes quivering in my hand and I let go of Ciara's hand to still it.

' 'How to Talk about Death' — it's not an easy topic. We are so comfortable with talking about our lives, about how we are living, about how to live better, that often the conversation about death is an awkward one, and not fully explored. I couldn't think of anyone else that I would rather have this conversation about grief with. *Holly*, please tell us how death affected you.'

I clear my throat. 'Seven years ago I lost my husband Gerry to cancer. He had a brain tumour. He was thirty years old.'

No matter how many times I say it, my throat tightens. That part of the story is still real, still burns inside me hot and bright. I look quickly to Sharon for support and she rolls her eyes dramatically and yawns. I smile. I can do this.

'We're here to talk about grief, so what can I tell you? I'm not unique, death affects all of us, and as many of you here today know, grief is a complex journey. You can't control your grief, most of the time it feels like it's in control of you. The only thing you can control is how you deal with it.'

'You say that you're not unique,' Ciara says,

13

'but everybody's personal experience *is* unique and we can learn from one another. No loss is easier than another, but do you think because you and Gerry grew up together that it made his loss more intense? Ever since I was a child, there was no Holly without Gerry.'

I nod and as I explain the story of how Gerry and I met, I avoid looking at the crowd, to make it easier, as if I'm talking to myself exactly as I rehearsed in the shower. 'I met him in school when I was fourteen years old. From that day on I was Gerry *and* Holly. Gerry's girlfriend. Gerry's wife. We grew up together, we learned from each other. I was twenty-nine when I lost him and became Gerry's widow. I didn't just lose him and I didn't just lose a part of me, I really felt like I lost *me*. I had no sense of who I was. I had to rebuild myself.'

A few heads nod. They know. They all know, and if they don't know yet, they're about to.

'Poo poo,' says a voice from the buggy, before giggling. Sharon hushes her toddler. She reaches into a giant bag and emerges with a strawberry-yoghurt-covered rice cake. The rice cake disappears into the buggy. The giggling stops.

'How did you rebuild?' Ciara asks.

It feels odd telling Ciara something she lived through with me and so I turn and focus on the audience, on the people who weren't there. And when I see their faces, a switch is flicked inside me. This is not about me. Gerry did something special and I'm going to share it on his behalf, with people who are hungry to know. 'Gerry helped me. Before he died he had a secret plan.'

14

'Dun, dun, dun!' Ciara announces to laughter. I smile and look at the expectant faces.

I feel excitement at the reveal, a renewed reminder of how utterly unique the year after his death was, yet over time its significance has faded in my memory. 'He left me ten letters, to be opened in the months after his passing, and he signed off each note with 'PS, I Love You'.'

The audience are visibly moved and surprised. They turn to each other and share looks and whispers, the silence has been broken. Sharon's baby starts to cry. She hushes him and rocks him, tapping on his soother repetitively, a faraway look in her eyes.

Ciara speaks up over the baby's grumbling. 'When I asked you to do this podcast, you were very specific about the fact you didn't want to concentrate on Gerry's illness. You wanted to talk about the gift he gave you.'

I shake my head, firmly. 'No. I don't want to talk about his cancer, about what he had to go through. My advice, if you want it, is to try not to fixate on the dark. There is enough of that. I would rather talk to people about hope.'

Ciara's eyes shine at me proudly. Mum clasps her hands together tightly.

'The path that I took was to focus on the gift he gave me, and that was the gift that *losing* him gave me: finding myself. I don't feel less of a person, nor am I ashamed to say that Gerry's death broke me. His letters helped me to find myself again. It took losing him to make me discover a part of myself that I never knew existed.' I'm lost in my words and I can't stop. I

15

need them to know. If I was sitting in the audience seven years ago, I would *need* to hear. 'I found a new and surprising strength inside of me, I found it at the bottom of a dark and lonely place, but I found it. And unfortunately, that's where we find most of life's treasures. After digging, toiling in the darkness and dirt, we finally hit something concrete. I learned that rock bottom can actually be a springboard.'

Led by an enthusiastic Ciara, the audience applauds.

Sharon's baby's cries turn to screams, a high-pitched piercing sound as though his legs are being sawn off. The toddler throws his rice cake at the baby. Sharon stands and throws an apologetic look in our direction before setting off down the aisle, steering the double buggy with one hand while carrying the crying baby in the other, leaving the older two with my mum. As she clumsily manoeuvres the buggy to the exit, she bumps into a chair, mows down bags sticking out into the aisle, their straps and handles getting caught up in the wheels, muttering apologies as she goes.

Ciara is holding back her next question until Sharon has gone.

Sharon crashes the buggy into the exit door in an effort to push it open. Mathew, Ciara's husband, rushes to assist her by holding the door open, but the double buggy is too wide. In her panic, Sharon crashes time and time again into the doorframe. The baby is screaming, the buggy is banging and Mathew tells her to stop while he unlocks the bottom of the door. Sharon looks up at us with a mortified expression. I mimic her earlier expression and roll my eyes and yawn. She smiles gratefully before fleeing.

'We can edit that part out,' Ciara jokes. 'Holly, apart from Gerry leaving letters for you after his death, did you feel his presence in any other way?'

'You mean, did I see his ghost?'

Some members of the audience chuckle, others are desperate for a yes.

'His energy,' Ciara says. 'Whatever you want to call it.'

I pause to think, to summon the feeling. 'Death, oddly, has a physical presence; death can feel like the other person in the room. The gaps that loved ones leave, the *not* being there, is visible, so sometimes there were moments when Gerry felt more alive than the people around me.' I think back to those lonely days and nights when I was caught between the real world and trapped in my mind. 'Memories can be very powerful. They can be the most blissful escape, and place to explore, because they summoned him again for me. But beware, they can be a prison too. I'm grateful that Gerry left me his letters, because he pulled me out of all those black holes and came alive again, allowing us to make new memories together.'

'And now? Seven years on? Is Gerry still with you?'

I pause. Stare at her, eyes wide, like a rabbit caught in the headlights. I flounder. No words come to me. Is he?

'I'm sure Gerry will always be a part of you,'

Ciara says softly, sensing my state. 'He will always be with you,' she says, seeming to reassure me, as if I've forgotten.

Dust to dust, ashes to ashes. Dissolved, besprinkled particles of matter around me.

'Absolutely.' I smile tightly. 'Gerry will always be with me.'

The body dies, the soul, the spirit lingers. Some days in the year following Gerry's death, I felt as though Gerry's energy was inside me, building me up, making me stronger, turning me into a fortress. I could do anything. I was untouchable. Other days I felt his energy and it shattered me to a million pieces. It was a reminder of what I'd lost. I can't. I won't. The universe took the greatest part of my life and because of that I was afraid it could take everything else too. And I realise that all those days were precious days because, seven years later, I don't feel Gerry with me at all.

Lost in the lie I've just told, I wonder if it sounded as empty as it felt. Still, I'm almost done. Ciara invites the audience to ask questions and I relax a little, sensing the end is in sight. Third row, fifth person in, tissue squashed and rolled up in her hand, mascara smudged around her eyes.

'Hi, Holly, my name is Joanna. I lost my husband a few months ago, and I wish he had left letters for me like your husband did. Could you tell us, what did his last letter say?'

'I want to know what they all said,' somebody speaks out, and there are murmurs of agreement.

18

'We have time to hear them all, if Holly is comfortable with that,' Ciara says, checking with me.

I take a deep breath, and let it out slowly. I haven't thought about the letters for so long. As a concept I have, but not individually, not in order, not exactly. Where to start. A new bedside lamp, a new outfit, a karaoke night, sunflower seeds, a birthday trip away with friends . . . how could they understand how important all of those seemingly insignificant things were to me? But the last letter . . . I smile. That's an easy one. 'His final letter read: Don't be afraid to fall in love again.'

They cling to that one, a beautiful one, a fine and valiant ending on Gerry's part. Joanna isn't as moved as the others. I see the disappointment and confusion in her eyes. The despair. So deep in her grief, it's not what she wanted to hear. She's still holding on to her husband, why would she consider letting go?

I know what she's thinking. She couldn't possibly love again. Not like that.

3

Sharon reappears in the emptying shop, flustered, with the baby asleep in the stroller and Alex, her toddler, holding her hand, red cheeks and flushed.

'Hello, buster.' I lean towards him.

He ignores me.

'Say hi to Holly,' Sharon says gently.

He ignores her.

'Alex, say hi to Holly,' she growls, channelling the voice of Satan so suddenly that both Alex and I get a fright.

'Hi,' he says.

'Good boy,' she says ever so sweetly.

I look at her wide-eyed, always amazed and perturbed by the double personality that the mother role brings out in her.

'I'm so embarrassed,' she says quietly. 'I'm sorry. I'm a disaster.'

'Don't be sorry. I'm so happy you came. And you're amazing. You always say the first year's the hardest. A few more months and this little man will be one. You've almost made it.'

'There's another one on the way.'

'What?'

She looks up, tears in her eyes. 'I'm pregnant again. I know, I'm an idiot.'

She straightens up, trying to be strong, but she looks broken. She's deflated, all wiped out. I feel nothing but sympathy for her, which is an emotion that has increased with each pregnancy reveal as the celebration levels have reduced.

As we hug we speak in unison. 'Don't tell Denise.'

I feel stressed just watching Sharon as she leaves with the four boys. I'm also exhausted after the nervous tension of today, the lack of sleep last night and from discussing a personal story in depth for an hour. It has wiped me out, but Ciara and I must wait until everybody has left to return the shop floor to the way it was and lock up.

'That was nothing short of wonderful,' Angela Carberry says, interrupting my thoughts. Angela, a great supporter of the shop who donates her designer clothes, bags and jewellery, is one of the main reasons Ciara can keep Magpie going. Ciara jokes that she thinks Angela buys things for the sole purpose of donating them. She's dressed stylishly as always, a jet-black bob with a blunt fringe, a bird-like frame, and a set of pearls around her neck over the pussy bow tie on her silk dress.

'Angela, so good of you to come.' I'm taken aback when she reaches for me and hugs me.

Over her shoulder, Ciara's eyes widen at the surprising display of intimacy from this usually austere woman. I feel Angela's bones beneath her clothes as she hugs me tightly. Not one for impulsive behaviour or physical contact, she's always seemed quite unapproachable on the occasions she personally delivered boxes of her clothes to the shop, shoes in their original boxes, bags in their original dust covers, telling us

21

exactly where we should display them and how much we should sell them for without expecting a cent in return.

Her eyes are moist as she pulls away from me. 'You must do this more often, you must tell this story to more people.'

'Oh no,' I laugh. 'This was a one-off, more to silence my sister than anything else.'

'But you don't realise, do you?' Angela asks, in surprise.

'Realise what?'

'The power of your story. What you have done to people, how you have reached in and touched every single heart in this room.'

Embarrassed, I look to the queue that has formed behind her, a queue of people who want to talk to me.

She grabs my arm and squeezes it, too tightly for my liking. 'You must tell your story again.'

'I appreciate your encouragement, Angela, but I've lived it once and told it once and I'm finished with it all.'

My words aren't harsh but there's a toughness to me that I didn't expect. An edgy, prickly outer layer that springs into existence in an instant. As though my thorns have pierced her hand, she immediately loosens her grip on my arm. Then, remembering where she is and that there are others who want to speak with me, she reluctantly lets go.

Her hand is gone, my prickles disappear, but something of her pinching grip stays with me, like a bruise.

* * *

I crawl into bed beside Gabriel, the room spinning after drinking too much wine with Ciara and Mum in Ciara's flat above the shop until far too late.

He stirs and opens his eyes, studies me for a moment and then grins at my state.

'Good night?'

'If I ever have any notions to do anything like that again . . . don't let me,' I murmur, eyes fluttering closed and trying to ignore the head spins.

'Agreed. Well, you did it. You're sister of the year, maybe you'll get a pay rise.'

I snort.

'It's over now.' He moves close and kisses me.

23

4

'Holly!' Ciara shouts my name again. Her tone has gone from patience to concern to sheer shrill anger. 'Where the hell are you?'

I'm in the stockroom behind boxes, perhaps crouched down behind them, perhaps with some clothes draped over the top like a little den. Perhaps hiding.

I look up and see Ciara's face peering in.

'What the fuck? Are you hiding?'

'No. Don't be ridiculous.'

She throws me a look; she doesn't believe me. 'I've been calling you for ages. Angela Carberry was looking for you, she was insistent that she speak to you. I told her I thought you'd stepped out for a coffee. She waited for fifteen minutes. You know what she's like. What the hell, Holly? You made me look like I didn't even know where my own staff member was, which I didn't.'

'Oh. Well now you do. I'm sorry I missed her.' It's been a month since we recorded the podcast and Angela Carberry's advocacy for me sharing my story has developed into stalking, in my opinion. I stand up and stretch my legs with a groan.

'What's going on with you and Angela?' Ciara asks, worried. 'Is it something to do with the shop?'

'No, not at all. Nothing to do with the shop,

24

don't worry. Didn't she just deliver another bag full of clothes?'

'Vintage Chanel,' Ciara says, relaxing, relieved. Then she's confused again. 'So what is going on? Why are you hiding from her? Don't think I haven't noticed — you did the same thing when she came by last week.'

'You're better with her on the floor. I don't know her. I find her very bossy.'

'She is very bossy, she has a right to be: she's giving us thousands of euro worth of stuff. I'd display her necklace on my own naked body on a mechanical bull, if that's what she wanted.'

'Nobody wants that.' I push past her.

'I'd like to see that,' Mathew calls from the other room.

'She asked me to give you this.' She holds out an envelope.

There's something about this that makes me uncomfortable. Me and envelopes have a history. It's not the first time in six years that I've opened an envelope, but there is a sense of foreboding about this one. I expect it to be an invitation to speak about grief at a ladies' lunch or something like it, organised by Angela. She has asked me several times if I'd continue my 'talk', or if I'd write a book. With each visit to the shop she has given me a phone number for a speaking events agent, or a contact number for a publishing agent. The first few times I politely thanked her, but on her last visit I shut her down so directly I wasn't sure if she'd ever come back. I take the envelope from Ciara, fold it and shove it into my back pocket.

25

Ciara glares at me. We have a stand-off.

Mathew appears at the door. 'Good news. Download statistics reveal 'How to Talk about Death' was the most successful episode to date! It had more downloads than all the others put together. Congratulations, sisters.' He enthusiastically lifts his two hands for high-fives from both of us.

Ciara and I continue to glower at each other; me angry because her podcast has made me the target of Angela's almost obsessive attention, her angry that I'm annoying her greatest donator for reasons unknown.

'Ah, far out, don't leave me hanging.'

Ciara slaps his raised palm half-heartedly.

'Not what I was expecting,' he says, looking at me with concern and lowering his hand. 'I'm sorry, was that insensitive of me? I wasn't high-fiving Gerry, you know — '

'I know,' I say and offer him a smile. 'It's not that.'

I can't celebrate the podcast's success; I wish nobody had listened to it, I wish I hadn't done it. I never want to hear or speak of Gerry's letters ever again.

★   ★   ★

Gabriel's house in Glasnevin, a single-storey Victorian terraced cottage that he patiently and lovingly restored to life himself, is a cosy eclectic home that, unlike mine, oozes with character. We lie on the floor, on a monstrous velvet bean bag atop a comfortable shagpile rug, drinking red

26

wine. The living room is an internal room and so light, albeit dull February light, streams down on us from the roof light. Gabriel's furniture is a mixture of antique and contemporary, whatever he liked and collected along the way. Every item has a story, even if it's not a moving one, or has any value, but everything's come from somewhere. The fireplace is the focus of the room; he doesn't have a TV, and instead entertains himself with obscure music on his record player, or reads from his copious book collection, the current read being the art book *Twenty-Six Gasoline Stations*, made up of black-and-white photographs of gasoline stations in the US. The music mood is Ali Farka Toure, a Malian singer and guitarist. I stare up at the evening sky through the skylight. It's wonderful, it really is. He's what I need, when I need it.

'When is the first house viewing?' he asks, growing impatient at how slowly things have been progressing since we made the decision well over a month ago. My distraction since the podcast has knocked me off course.

My house hasn't officially gone on the market yet, but I can't bring myself to own up to that, so instead I tell him, 'I'm meeting the estate agent at the house tomorrow.' I lift my head to sip my wine and then return to resting on his chest, as strenuous a duty as this day commands. 'Then you will be mine, all mine,' I laugh maniacally.

'I am already. By the way, I found this.' He puts his glass down and retrieves a crumpled envelope from between a messy pile of books by the fireplace.

'Oh yes, thanks.' I fold it over and squeeze it behind my back.

'What is it?'

'A guy heard me speak at the shop. Thinks I'm a sexy widow and gave me his number.' I sip my wine, serious.

His frown makes me laugh.

'A woman in the audience at the podcast recording wants me to continue telling my story. She keeps pestering me to do more events, or to write a book.' I laugh again. 'Anyway, she's a pushy rich woman that I don't know very well and I told her I'm not interested.'

He looks at me with interest. 'I listened to it in the car the other day. You spoke very movingly. I'm sure your words helped a lot of people.' This is the first time he's spoken positively about the podcast. I suppose my words were nothing he didn't already know — our early days and months were spent in respective intimate soul-digging as we got to know each other — but I want to leave it all behind me.

'I was helping Ciara.' I shut his compliment down. 'Don't worry, I'm not going to start talking about my ex-husband for a living.'

'I'm not worried about you talking about him, it's what constantly reliving it could do to you.'

'Not going to happen.'

He squirms on the bean bag and wraps his arm around me, I think for a hug, but his hand goes down beneath me and he grabs the envelope instead. He pulls it free.

'You haven't opened it. Do you know what's inside?'

'No. Because I don't care.'

He studies me. 'You do care.'

'I don't. Otherwise I would have opened it.'

'You do care. Otherwise you would have opened it.'

'It can't be important anyway, she delivered it to me weeks ago. I forgot I had it.'

'Can I at least see?' He rips the top.

I attempt to grab it from him and instead I spill my wine on the rug. I clamber up out of his arms, pull myself up from the bean bag on the floor with a groan and hurry to the kitchen to retrieve a damp towel. I can hear him ripping the envelope open while I run the cloth under the tap. My heart is pounding. The prickles are rising on my skin again.

'Mrs Angela Carberry. The PS, I Love You Club,' he reads aloud.

'What?!'

He raises the card in the air and I move closer to him to read it, the damp cloth drips and trickles on his shoulder.

'Holly,' he moves, agitated.

I take the card from his hand. A small business card with elegant print. 'The PS, I Love You Club,' I read aloud, feeling curious and furious at once.

'What does that mean?' he asks, wiping the sloppy mess from his shoulder.

'I have no idea. I mean, I know what PS, I Love You means, but . . . is there anything else in the envelope?'

'No, just this card.'

'I've had enough of this nonsense. It's like

stalking.' I grab my phone from the couch and move away from him for privacy. 'Or plagiarism.'

He laughs at my abrupt change of mood. 'You'd have to have written it down somewhere for it to be remotely so. Try to tell her to fuck off nicely, Holly.' He turns his attention to his art book.

It rings for a long time. I drum my fingers on the counter, impatiently constructing a firm dialogue in my head about how she needs to leave this alone, back off, fuck off, kill it immediately. Whatever this club is, I will have nothing to do with it, and I insist that nobody else does either. I was helping my sister, and all I felt afterwards was exhausted and used. And those words belong to my husband, in my letters; they are not hers to use. My anger intensifies with each new ring, and I'm about to hang up when a man finally answers.

'Hello?'

'Hello. Could I speak with Angela Carberry, please?'

I feel Gabriel's eyes on me, he mouths *be nice.* I turn my back to him.

The man's voice is muffled as though he's moved his mouth from the mouthpiece. I hear voices in the background and I'm not sure if he's talking to them or me.

'Hello? Are you there?'

'Yes, yes. I'm here. But she's not. Angela. She's gone. She passed away. Just this morning.'

His voice cracks.

'They're here with me, the funeral people. We're planning it at the moment. So I have no

30

information for you as yet.'

I brake hard, career into a ditch, anger crashed and burned. I try to catch my breath.

'I'm sorry. I'm so sorry,' I say, sitting down, noticing as I do that I have Gabriel's full attention. 'What happened?'

His voice is coming and going, weak and strong, wobbly, away from the receiver, back again. I can sense his disorientation. His world is upside down. I don't even know who this man is and yet his loss is palpable and like a weight on my shoulders.

'It was very sudden in the end, took us by surprise. They thought she had more time. But the tumour spread, and that was . . . well.'

'Cancer?' I whisper. 'She died of cancer?'

'Yes, yes, I thought you knew . . . I'm very sorry, who is this? Did you say? I'm sorry I'm not thinking very clearly . . . '

He talks on, confused. I think of Angela, thin and needy, holding on to my arm, squeezing me so tightly it hurt. I thought she was odd, I found her irritating, but she was desperate, desperate for me to visit with her — and I didn't. I didn't even call her. I barely gave her time. Of course she was moved by my talk, she was dying of cancer. She was holding on to my arm that day as though she was clinging to life.

I must be making a noise, I must be doing something because Gabriel is down on his knees beside me and the man on the other end of the phone is saying, 'Oh dear, I'm sorry. I should have worded it better. But I haven't had to . . . this is all very new and . . . '

31

'No, no,' I try to keep it all together. 'I'm very sorry for disturbing you at this time. My sincere condolences to you and yours,' I say quickly.

I dissolve the call.

I dissolve.

5

I did not kill Angela, I know that, but I cried as if I did. I know that a phone call, a visit to Angela or an agreement to take part in one of her events would not have prolonged her life, and yet I cried as if it could have. I cried for all the irrational beliefs that stampeded through my head.

As Angela had been a generous contributor to the shop, Ciara feels obligated to attend her funeral and, despite Gabriel disagreeing, I feel I have even more reason. I had been hiding from Angela in the weeks before her death, I had shut her down so many times. We don't often remember how we meet, we mostly remember how we part. I didn't give Angela the best impression when we met, I want to say goodbye to her properly.

Her funeral is in Church of the Assumption in Dalkey, a picturesque parish church on the main street opposite Dalkey Castle. Ciara and I pass through the lingering crowds outside and go directly into the church and sit near the back. The funeral attendees follow the coffin and the family inside and the church pews fill. Leading the procession is a lone man, her husband, the man I spoke with on the phone. He is followed by crying family and friends. I'm satisfied to see he is not alone, that people are sad, that Angela is missed, that her life contained love.

It's clear the priest didn't know Angela very well, but he does his best. He has collected the core information about her, like a magpie drawn to shiny items, and he has a kind delivery. When it's time for the eulogy, a woman takes to the podium. A TV screen is wheeled into the old church, wires and all.

'Hello, my name is Joy. I would love to say a few words about my friend Angela, but she told me I couldn't. She wanted to have the last word. As was usual.'

The congregation laughs.

'Are you ready for this, Laurence?' Joy asks.

I can't see or hear Laurence's response but the screen comes to light anyway and Angela's face fills the screen. She is thin, clearly this was filmed in her final weeks, but she is beaming.

'Hello, everybody, it's me!'

This draws gasps of surprise, and the tears flow around me.

'I hope you're all having an awful time without me. Life must be dreadfully dull. I'm sorry I'm gone, but what can we do. We must look forward. Hello, my darlings. My Laurence, my boys, Malachy and Liam. Hello, my little babies, I hope Grandma isn't scaring you. I hope to make things a little easier for you. Well, let's move it on. Here we are in my wig room.'

The camera turns around, held by her, to survey her wigs. Wigs of various shapes, colours and styles sit on mannequin heads on shelves.

'This has been my life for some time, as you all know. I thank Malachy for bringing this one home from a recent music festival,' she zooms in

34

on a Mohawk. She lifts it off and places it on her head.

Everybody laughs through their tears. Hankies flying, tissues being taken out of handbags and passed along the pews.

'So, my darling boys,' she continues, 'you three are my most precious people in the whole entire world and I'm not ready to say goodbye to you. Beneath these wigs I've taped envelopes to every head. Each month I want you to remove a wig, place it on your head, open these envelopes, read my notes, and remember me. I'm always with you. I love you all and thank you for the happiest, most blessed beautiful life a woman, wife, mother and grandmother could wish for. Thank you for everything.

'PS,' she blows a kiss, 'I love you.'

Ciara grabs my arm and slowly turns to look at me. 'Oh my . . . ' she whispers.

The screen goes black and everybody, everybody is crying. I can't imagine how her family feel after this. I can't look at Ciara. I feel sick. I feel dizzy. I feel like there's no air. Nobody is paying the slightest attention to me but I feel self-conscious, as if they all know about me, and what Gerry did for me. Would it be rude for me to leave? I'm so near to the door. I need air, I need light, I need to get out of this claustrophobic suffocating scene. I stand and steady myself on the back of the pew then walk towards the door.

'Holly?' Ciara whispers.

Outside, I suck in air, but it's not enough. I need to move away, get away.

35

'Holly!' Ciara calls, hurrying to catch up with me. 'Are you OK?'

I stop walking and look at her. 'No. I'm not OK. I'm definitely not OK.'

'Shit, this is my fault. I'm so sorry, Holly. I asked you to do the podcast, you didn't want to and I practically forced you, I'm so sorry, this is all my fault. No wonder you were avoiding her. It all makes sense now. I'm so sorry.'

Her words somehow manage to steady me, it's not my fault for feeling like this. This happened to me. It's not my fault. It's unfair. She's offering sympathy. She hugs me and I rest my head on her shoulder, back to feeling weak and vulnerable and sad. I don't like it. I stop myself. My head snaps up.

'No.'

'No what?'

I wipe my eyes roughly and charge towards the car. 'This is not who I am any more.'

'What do you mean? Holly, look at me please,' she pleads, trying to meet my eye as I look around wildly, desperate to sharpen my focus, desperate to get things in perspective.

'This is not happening to me again. I'm going back to the shop. I'm going back to my life.'

★　★　★

The skill I discovered when I began working with my sister, after the magazine I worked for folded, is that I'm good at sorting. While Ciara is a magnificent creature when it comes to dealing with the aesthetic, beautifying the shop and placing each item in a place of importance, I could happily, and do quite happily, spend long days in the stockroom emptying boxes and bin liners of the things people no longer want. I get lost in the rhythm of it. These actions are particularly therapeutic in the days that follow Angela Carberry's funeral. I empty everything on to the floor, sit down and go through the contents of handbags and pockets, sorting the precious from the trash. I polish jewellery until it sparkles, shoes until they shine. I dust off old books. I discard anything that's not appropriate: dirty underwear, odd socks, used handkerchiefs and tissues. Depending on how busy I am, I can be nosy and get lost in studying receipts and notes, trying to date the last use of the object, understand the life of the person who lived with it. I run the clothes through a rinse wash, I use a steamer to smooth wrinkled fabric. I treasure anything of value: money, photographs, letters that should be returned to their sender. As far as possible, I make detailed notes of who owns what. Sometimes the possessions will never be reunited with their owner; those who have dropped boxes and bags off without contact details are just happy to be rid of their clutter. But sometimes I manage to matchmake. If we don't feel we can sell the product, if it's not right for Ciara's vision, then we repackage them and give them to charities.

I take what's old and make it new and I'm rewarded by the belief that there is value in my work. Today is a good day to get lost in a cardboard box filled with possessions that became objects as soon as they were dropped into the bag. I lift a box of books from the stockroom and carry them to the shop floor. Again I sit on the floor, wiping covers, folding back dog-eared pages and flicking through the pages for bookmarks of value. Sometimes I find old photographs that are used as bookmarks; mostly I don't find anything, but every find is important. I'm lost in this world of sorting when the bell rings above the shop door.

Ciara is across the other side of the shop battling with a disarmed and beheaded mannequin as she tries to squeeze a polka-dot tea dress onto its body.

'Hello,' she greets the customer warmly.

She is better with customers than I am. I focus on the products when given the choice and she focuses on the people. She and Mathew opened the shop five years ago after they bought it as a house on St. George's Avenue in Drumcondra, Dublin. The front of the house already had a floor-to-ceiling window built in, from its former life as a sweet shop. They live upstairs in a flat. As a second-hand shop on a quiet terraced street, we don't attract much in the way of passing trade, but people travel to get here, and the local university provides plenty of students as customers, lured by the cheaper prices and the cool factor that comes with wearing vintage. Ciara is the star of the shop, hosting evening events, attending trade fairs, contributing to magazines, and a sometime-TV-presenter of breakfast television fashion slots, displaying the latest arrivals to the shop. If she is the heart of this shop, Mathew is the brains who handles the accounts, runs their online presence and over-sees the technical side of the podcasts, and I'm the guts.

'Hello,' the customer, a woman replies.

I can't see her, I'm hidden behind a display unit, sitting on the floor. I'm already zoning out and allowing Ciara to do her thing.

'I recognise you,' Ciara says. 'You spoke at Angela's funeral.'

'You were there?'

'Yes, of course. Angela was a fantastic supporter of the shop. My sister and I were there. We'll miss her, she was a powerhouse of a woman.'

So now I'm listening.

'Your sister was there too, you say?'

'Yes. Holly, she's . . . busy at the moment.' Ciara uses her smarts and remembers that I will not wish to speak to this woman, as I have not wanted to speak about the entire funeral episode since it happened two weeks ago.

I did what I said I would do. I returned to the shop, I went back to my life, I tried not to think of what happened at the funeral for one second, but inevitably I did. I can't stop thinking about it. Angela was clearly inspired by my experience with Gerry's letters to do the same for her family in her final weeks, this I understand, but what I don't understand is her business card. What on earth was she intending on doing with the PS, I Love You Club? Over the past few weeks I've wanted to know and I didn't want to know and yet, here I am, not wanting to be seen but wanting to hear at the same time.

'Did Holly . . . ' The woman abandons her question. 'My name is Joy, pleased to meet you. Angela loved this shop. Did you know this is the house she grew up in?'

'No! She never mentioned it. Never, I can't believe it.'

'Yes. Well, it would have been like her not to say. She and I were school friends, I lived around the corner. We recently reconnected, but I know she would have enjoyed seeing her belongings in the place she grew up — not that we had such fine things back then. I still don't.'

'Wow! I can't believe this,' Ciara replies. Sensing this woman is not here to browse, she extends her usual wonderful and, in this instance, annoying, hospitality. 'Would you like a tea or coffee?'

'Oh, a tea would be lovely, thank you. With a small drop of milk, please.'

Ciara goes into the back rooms, and I hear Joy walk around the shop. I pray that she won't discover me but I know that she will. Her footsteps near me. They stop, I look up.

'You must be Holly,' she says. She has a cane.

'Hello,' I say, as though I hadn't heard a word her and Ciara had said.

'I'm Joy. A friend of Angela Carberry's.'

'I'm sorry for your loss.'

'Thank you. She went fast in the end. She declined so quickly. I wonder if she had a chance to speak with you.'

If I was polite I would stand up. Stop this woman on a cane from having to lean down and

40

talk to me. But I'm not feeling polite.

'About?'

'About her club.' She reaches into her pocket and retrieves a business card. The same one that Gabriel had shown me.

'I received the business card, but I have no idea what it's about.'

'She gathered — well, she and I both gathered a group of people who are fans of yours.'

'Fans?'

'We listened to your podcast, we were so moved by your words.'

'Thank you.'

'I wonder if you could meet with us? I want to continue the good work Angela began . . . ' her eyes fill. 'Oh, I'm very sorry.'

Ciara returns with the tea. 'Are you OK, Joy?' she asks when she sees the woman with a cane crying, while I'm still sitting on the floor with a book in my hand. She throws me a look of confusion and horror. Her cold-hearted sister.

'I'm fine. Yes, I am, thank you. I'm very sorry for the imposition. I think I'll just . . . gather myself.'

'There's no need to leave, take a seat over here.' Ciara guides Joy to an armchair beside the dressing room, a corner of the room with a mirror and dramatic draping, still in my line of vision. 'You stay here and rest until you feel right. There's your tea. I'll get you a tissue.'

'You're very kind,' Joy says, weakly.

I remain on the floor. I wait for Ciara to leave before speaking, 'What's the club about?'

'Did Angela not explain it to you?'

'No. She left the business card here for me, but we never talked.'

'I'm sorry she didn't explain it to you. So please do let me. Angela was shining like a light after she attended your talk; she came to me with her idea, and when Angela Carberry got something in her head she was bound to it. She could be very persistent, and not always in the right ways. She was used to getting what she wanted.'

I think of Angela's hand squeezing my arm, her nails digging into my flesh. The urgency that I misread.

'Angela and I were in school together but we lost contact, as you do. We met each other a few months ago and because of our illnesses I think we connected more than we ever had. After she heard you speak, she called me and told me all about it. I was as greatly inspired by your story as she was. I told a few others who I felt would benefit.'

As Joy takes a breath I realise I'm holding mine. My chest is tight, my body is rigid.

'There are five of us — well, four of us now. Your story filled us with light and hope. You see, dear Holly, we got together because we have something that bonds us.'

My fingers are clenching the book so hard it's almost bending.

'We have all been diagnosed with terminal illnesses. We joined together not just because of the hope that your story inspired in us but because we have a shared goal. We want to write letters for our loved ones as your husband did for you. We desperately need your help, Holly. We're running out of ideas and . . . ' she breathes in as if summoning the energy, 'all of us are running out of time.'

Silence as I pause, freeze, try to absorb that. I'm speechless.

'I've put you on the spot and I'm very sorry,' she says, embarrassed. She attempts to stand, with the cup of tea in one hand and her cane in the other. I can only watch her; I'm too stunned to feel anything but numb to the sadness of Joy and her fellow club members. If anything, I'm irritated that she would bring this back into my life.

'Let me help you,' Ciara says, rushing over to take the tea and hold her arm to assist her.

'Perhaps I'll leave my phone number for you, Holly. So that if you want to . . . ' She looks at me to finish her sentence but I don't. I'm cruel and I wait.

'I'll get a pen and paper,' Ciara says, jumping in.

Joy leaves her details with Ciara and I call goodbye as she makes her exit.

The bell rings, the door closes, Ciara's footsteps click-clack across the wooden floors. Her 1940s vintage peep-toe heels, worn with fishnet stockings, come to a halt beside me. She stares at me, studies me, and I'm quite sure she has eavesdropped and heard it all. I look away and slide the book on to the shelf. Here. Yes, I think it will look good here.

6

'Easy on the gravy, Frank,' Mum says, taking hold of the jug in Dad's hands. Dad clings to it, intent on finishing his gravy annihilation of his roast dinner, and in the tug of war the gravy glugs from the spout and drips on the table. He looks pointedly at Mum, then wipes the thick drips from the linen with his finger and sucks it in protest.

'There won't be enough for everyone,' Mum says, holding it out to Declan.

Declan catches the dribbles from the spout and licks his finger. Then goes for another swipe.

'No double-dipping,' Jack warns, stealing the jug from Mum's hands.

'I haven't had any yet,' Declan gripes, trying to steal it back, but Jack retains possession and pours it over his food.

'Boys,' Mum admonishes them. 'Honestly, you're behaving like children.'

Jack's kids laugh.

'Leave some for me,' Declan watches Jack. 'Do they not have gravy in London?'

'They don't have Mum's gravy in London,' Jack says, winking at Mum, before pouring a little on the kids' plates, and then passing it to his wife, Abbey.

'I don't want gravy,' one of the kids moans.

'I'll have it,' Declan and Dad say in unison.

'I'll make more,' Mum says with a sigh, and hurries back to the kitchen.

Everybody mills into their food as if they haven't eaten for days: Dad, Declan, Mathew, Jack, Abbey and their two children. My older brother Richard is delayed at choir practice and Gabriel is spending the day with his teenage daughter Ava. As she has wanted very little to do with him most of her life, these visits are precious to him. All are preoccupied by their meal apart from Ciara, who watches me. She looks away when I catch her eye and reaches for the salad spoon in the centre of the table. Mum returns with two jugs. She places one in the centre and another beside Ciara. Jack pretends to reach for it, like a false start, and it makes Declan panic, jump and grab the jug.

Jack laughs.

'Boys,' Mum says, and they stop.

The kids giggle.

'Sit down, Mum,' I say gently.

She surveys the table, her hungry family all greedily tucking in, and finally sits beside me at the head of the table.

'What's this?' Ciara says, looking into the jug.

'Vegan gravy,' Mum says proudly.

'Ahh, Mum, you're the best.' Ciara pours, and a murky watery substance flows all over the base of her plate like soup. She looks up at me, uncertain.

'Yum,' I say.

'I'm not sure if I made it correctly,' Mum says apologetically. 'Is it nice?'

Ciara takes a small taste. 'Delicious.'

'Liar,' Mum says with a laugh. 'Are you not hungry, Holly?'

My plate is practically empty and I haven't even begun eating. Broccoli and tomatoes are all I could bear to look at on my plate.

'I had a big breakfast,' I say, 'but this is fabulous, thank you.'

I sit forward and tuck in. Or try to. Mum's food, vegan gravy aside, really is delicious and on as many Sundays as possible she tries to gather the troops for a family meal, which we all adore. But today, as has been the case for the past few weeks, my appetite is gone.

Ciara eyes my plate, then me, worriedly. She and Mum share a look and I immediately sense that Ciara has spilled the beans about the PS, I Love You Club. I roll my eyes at both of them.

'I'm fine,' I say defiantly, before stuffing an entire broccoli floret in my mouth as proof of my stability.

Jack looks up at me. 'Why, what's wrong?'

My mouth is stuffed. I can't answer, but I roll my eyes and give him a frustrated look.

He turns to Mum. 'What's wrong with Holly? Why is she pretending she's fine?'

I grumble through my food and try to chew quickly so I can end this conversation.

'There's nothing wrong with Holly,' Mum says calmly.

Ciara pipes up in a fast-paced high-pitch volley: 'A woman who died of cancer started a PS, I Love You Club before her death, made up of people who are terminally ill, and they want Holly to help them write letters to their loved

46

ones.' She seems immediately relieved to have gotten it out of her system and then afraid of what will happen next.

I swallow my broccoli and almost choke. 'For fuck sake, Ciara!'

'I'm sorry, I had to!' Ciara says, holding her hands up defensively.

The kids laugh at my language.

'Sorry,' I say to their mum, Abbey. 'Guys,' I clear my throat. 'I'm fine. Really. Let's change the subject.'

Mathew looks at his tell-tale wife with disapproval. Ciara sinks lower.

'Are you going to help these people write their letters?' Declan asks.

'I don't want to talk about it,' I say, slicing a tomato.

'With who? With them or with us?' Jack asks.

'With anyone!'

'So you're not going to help them?' Mum asks.

'No!'

She nods. Her face is completely unreadable. We eat in silence.

I hate that her face is unreadable.

Frustrated, I give in. 'Why? Do you think I should?'

Everyone at the table, bar the kids and Abbey, who knows better than to get involved, answer at the same time and I can't decipher anybody's words.

'I was asking Mum.'

'You don't care what I think?' Dad asks.

'Of course I do.'

He concentrates on his food, hurt.

'I think . . . ' Mum says thoughtfully, 'you should do what feels right for you. I never like to interfere, but as you've asked: if it has you this . . . ' she looks at my plate, then back at me ' . . . upset, then it's not a good idea.'

'She said she ate a big breakfast,' Mathew says in my defence, and I throw him a grateful look.

'What did you eat?' Ciara asks.

I roll my eyes. 'A big dirty fry-up, Ciara. With pig's meat and pig's blood and eggs and all kinds of dirty animal products dripping in butter. Butter that came from a cow.' I didn't. I couldn't stomach breakfast either.

She glares at me.

The kids laugh again.

'Can I film it if you help them?' Declan asks, his mouth full of food. 'Could make a good documentary.'

'Don't talk with your mouth full, Declan,' Mum says.

'No. Because I'm not going to,' I reply.

'What does Gabriel think?' Jack asks.

'I don't know.'

'Because she hasn't told him yet,' Ciara says.

'Holly,' Mum admonishes me.

'I don't need to tell him about it if I'm not doing it,' I protest, but I know I'm wrong. I should have discussed it with Gabriel. He's not an idiot, he already senses something is up. Never mind Joy's reveal about the club, ever since I got off the phone with Angela's husband weeks ago, I've not been my usual self.

We all go quiet.

'You still didn't ask me,' Dad says, looking

around at everyone as though they've all individually hurt his feelings.

'What do you think, Dad?' I ask, exasperated.

'No, no. It's clear you don't want to know,' he says, while he reaches for the replenished jug of gravy and drowns his second helpings.

I violently fork another floret. 'Dad, tell me.'

He swallows his hurt. 'I think it sounds like a very thoughtful caring gesture for people in need, and it might do you good to do good.'

Jack appears irritated by Dad's response. Mum, again, is unreadable; she's thinking it all through, examining the angles before sharing her opinion.

'She can't eat as it is, Frank,' Mum says quietly.

'She's practically inhaling her broccoli,' Dad says, winking at me.

'And she put six chipped teacups out in the shop this week,' Ciara adds salt to the wound. 'She's distracted as it is, just knowing about it.'

'Some people don't mind chipped teacups,' I retort.

'Like who?'

'Beauty and the Beast,' Mathew replies.

The kids laugh.

'Hands up if you think it's a good idea,' Ciara addresses the table.

The kids put their hands up, Abbey quickly pushes them down.

Dad raises his fork in the air. So does Declan. Mathew looks like he's with them, but Ciara glares at him and he stares her down, but doesn't raise his hand.

'No,' Jack says firmly. 'I don't.'

'Me neither,' says Ciara. 'And I don't want it to be all my fault if it goes wrong.'

'It's not about you,' Mathew mutters, frustrated.

'No, I know. But she's my sister and I don't want to be the one to be responsible for — '

'Good afternoon, everybody,' Richard's voice calls out from the hall. He appears at the door. He looks around at us all, sensing something. 'What's going on?'

'Nothing,' we say in unison.

★ ★ ★

I'm alone in the shop, behind the desk. Sitting on a stool, staring into space. Ciara and Mathew have gone out to collect donations from a family nearby who are moving house. The shop is empty of customers, and has been for the past hour. I've emptied every bag and box I could, setting precious things aside and making phone calls to their owners to arrange for collection. I've tidied every rail, moved things an inch to the left or an inch to the right. There's nothing left to do. The bell rings as the door opens and a young girl, a teenager, steps inside. She's tall, wearing a striking black-and-gold turban on her head.

'Hello,' I attempt cheerily.

She smiles shyly and self-consciously, so I look away. Some customers want attention lavished on them, others like to be left alone. I watch her while she's not looking. She's carrying a baby in a baby carrier. The baby, who's only a few months old, is facing outward, pudgy legs squeezed into a pair of leggings that kick spontaneously. Her mother — if she is her mother, as she seems so young to have a child, but what do I know — has mastered the craft of standing sideways so that the child can't reach anything on the rails. The teenager keeps glancing at me and then back to the rails. She's looking at the clothes but not really looking, she's more intent on keeping an eye on me. I wonder if she's going to steal something; sometimes shoplifters have that look, checking out my whereabouts rather than the items. The baby cries out, practising her sounds, and the teenager reaches for the baby's hand; little fingers wrap around her finger.

I wanted a baby once. It was ten years ago and I wanted a baby so much my body was calling out to me every day to provide one. That longing vanished when Gerry became sick. It became a longing for something else: for him to survive. It put all its energy into making him survive, and when he was gone, the longing for a child died with him. I had wanted a baby with him, and he was no longer here. Looking at her beautiful bouncy baby, something chimes inside me, a reminder of what I once wanted. I'm thirty-seven years old, it could still happen. I'm moving in with Gabriel, but I don't think either of us are quite there yet. He's too busy working on the relationship with the daughter he has.

'I'm not going to steal nothing,' she says, snapping me out of my trance.

51

'Pardon?'

'You keep staring. I'm not going to steal nothing,' the teenager says defensively, annoyed.

'Sorry, I wasn't, I didn't mean to . . . I was daydreaming,' I say. I stand up. 'Can I help you with anything?'

She looks at me, a long stare as if deciding something, as if weighing me up. 'No.'

She walks to the door, the bell rings, it closes. I stare at the closed door and I remember, she's been in here before. A few weeks ago, maybe last week, perhaps a few times, doing the same thing, browsing with her baby. I remember because Ciara complimented her on her turban and then, fashion-inspired, wore a red and white polka-dot headscarf for a week. The girl has never bought anything. It's no big deal, people always browse through second-hand shops, people like to see what others once owned and gave away, how others once lived. There's an extra something attached to objects that have once had an owner. Some think they're more precious, others think used means dirty, and then there are those who have a desire to be around these things. But she was right, I hadn't trusted her.

Mathew and Ciara's van pulls up outside the shop. Ciara leaps out, wearing an eighties spangly jumpsuit and trainers. They open the back doors and start sliding out the goods.

'Hello, David Bowie.'

She grins. 'Man did we find some treasures over there, you're going to love them. Anything exciting happen here?'

'No. It's been quiet.'

Mathew races by with two rolled-up carpets under his arm, announcing in his thick Australian accent, 'We'll have more rugs than a bald man's house.'

Bald. I think of Angela's funeral, her display of wigs, the letters hidden beneath for her family.

She studies me. 'You good?'

'Yes, Ciara.' She asks me at least every ten minutes.

She waits for Mathew to disappear into the stockroom. 'I just wanted to say, I'm sorry. Again. I really feel responsible for everything that's happened.'

'Ciara, stop — '

'No, I won't. If I've set you back, if I've fucked up everything, I'm so so sorry. Please, tell me what I can do to fix it.'

'You didn't do anything wrong, things happened, and it's not your fault. But if Joy or anyone else from the club comes by, tell them I'm not interested, OK?'

'Yeah. Of course. I told that guy yesterday not to come back.'

'What guy?'

'He said he was from the club. His name was . . . doesn't matter what his name is. He's not coming back, I made it very clear to leave you alone, especially at your place of work, it's not right.'

My heart pounds with anger. 'So they are coming here.'

'They?'

'The club members. There was a girl earlier. She'd been in here before, she was looking at me oddly. Accused me of accusing her of stealing. She must be with them too.'

'No . . . ' Ciara studies me with concern. 'I mean, you can't think that everyone in here that looks at you is from the club.'

'The woman said they had five members, four members left. My ghost of Christmas past, of present and today of future have all paid me a little visit. They're never going to leave me alone, are they?' I ask, the anger pumping through me at this invasion of my nice normal stable happy moving-on life. 'You know what, I'm going to meet with them. I'm going to meet this little club and tell them in no uncertain terms to leave me alone. Where is that woman's number?' I start rifling through the drawers.

'Joy?' Ciara asks, concerned. 'Maybe you'd be better to leave it, Holly, I think they'll get the message eventually.'

I find the slip of paper and grab my phone. 'Excuse me a minute.' I hurry to the door, I need to make this call outside.

'Holly,' Ciara calls after me. 'Remember, they're sick. They're not nasty people. Be kind.'

I step outside, close the door and walk away from the shop, dialling Joy's number. I'm going to tell this club to leave me alone once and for all.

7

The PS, I Love You Club gather in Joy's conservatory, the 1 April morning sun heating the glass room. Her blond Labrador snoozes on the hot tiles, in the path of the sunlight in the centre of the room. We have to step around him to get anywhere. I look at the club members seated in front of me, feeling awkward and annoyed. I'd arranged to meet with Joy to deliver my well-rehearsed, polite but firm refusal to her invitation to be involved, but I hadn't bargained on everyone else being here. Clearly, she understood my request to meet as meaning entirely the opposite, and I wish now that I'd told her over the phone instead of opting to come here for an honourable face-to-face rebuff.

'He's a lazy lump, aren't you, my old friend,' Joy says, gazing fondly at the dog as she places a cup of tea and a heaped plate of biscuits on the table beside me. 'We got him when we first heard my diagnosis, thinking he'd be company, a distraction for everyone, and he's served us well. He's nine,' she says defiantly. 'I have MS. Multiple Sclerosis.'

Bert, a big man in his late sixties, oxygen being fed to him through a nasal cannula, goes next. 'Too handsome for my own good,' he says, winking.

Paul and Joy chuckle, Ginika rolls her eyes, the teenager caught amongst the bad dad jokes. I'd been right about the girl in the shop, I'm not paranoid after all. I smile politely.

'Lungs. Emphysema,' Bert corrects himself, laughing at his joke.

Paul next. He's younger than Bert and Joy, closer to my age. Handsome, deceivingly healthy-looking, and the second mystery person to have visited the shop, and turned away by Ciara. 'A brain tumour.'

Young man, handsome man, brain tumour. Just like Gerry. It's too close. I should leave, but when's a good time to get up and leave when a young man is telling you about his cancer?

'But my situation is a little different to the others,' he adds. 'I'm in remission.'

A slight weight lifts. 'That's great news.'

'Yes,' he says, not at all appearing like it's great news. 'This is my second time, in remission, it's quite regular for brain tumours to recur. I wasn't ready to go the first time round. If it recurs again, I want to be prepared for my family.'

I nod. My chest tightens a bit more; even in remission he is preparing for his death, in fear of the tumour recurring. 'My husband had primary brain cancer,' I feel the need to add, by way of conversation, but as soon as the words have left my mouth I realise it's not a great talking point. We all know my husband died.

I came here to put an end to this before my involvement began, but as soon as I walked in the door and saw the group, I felt the hourglass had been flipped. Now that the grains of sand are falling, I wonder if perhaps my being here this once will be all I need to do. I can ease my

56

guilt, try to be of help, then go back to my life. It will only take an hour.

I look to the teenager beside me, Ginika. Perhaps this visit will end their stalking of me. It will have to, because I will tell them in no uncertain terms to stop. Her baby, Jewel, is contently sitting on her lap, playing with the bangles around Ginika's wrist. Feeling the attention on her, Ginika speaks without lifting her gaze from the floor.

'Cervical cancer,' she says, firmly, her back teeth pushed together as she forces the words out. She's angry.

OK. OK. Tell them, get it over with. Tell them you don't want to be here, that you can't help them. A silence falls.

'As you can see we're all in various stages of our illnesses,' Joy, the voice of the group says. 'MS isn't a terminal illness but a life-long condition and lately my symptoms are advancing. Angela seemed to be responding well to treatment but then declined rapidly. Paul is in a great place, physically, but . . . none of us really know — we're all up and down, aren't we,' she says, looking around her comrades. 'I think I can speak for us all when I say I don't know how much *quality* time we have left. Still, we're here, and that's the main thing.'

They all nod to that, apart from Ginika, for whom being here now is not the main thing.

'Some of us have ideas for our letters, others don't. We would appreciate your insight.'

This is my window to extract myself. They are human, they will understand, and even if they don't, what is it to me if they don't care about my mental stability; I must put myself first. I sit forward. 'I need to explain — '

'I have my idea,' Bert leaps in. He's breathless as he speaks, though this doesn't seem to limit the amount of words he uses. 'It's a treasure trail for my wife Rita, and I could do with your help to place clues all around the country.'

'Around the *country*?'

'It's like a pub quiz. For example, question one: where did Brian Boru lose his life in his final battle? And so Rita goes to Clontarf and I'll have the next clue waiting for her there.' A fit of coughing takes over.

I blink. Not quite what I'd expected to hear.

'I think you're being a cheapskate,' Paul teases. 'You should send Rita to Lanzarote like Gerry did for Holly.'

'Get away out of that,' Bert snorts, and folds his arms high on his chest and looks to me. 'Why did he send you there?'

'It was their honeymoon destination,' Paul answers on my behalf.

'Ooh yes!' Joy closes her eyes dreamily. 'And that's where you saw the dolphins, isn't it?'

My head is spinning as they speak about my experience as though it was an episode of some TV reality show. Watercooler chat.

'He left the tickets with the travel agent for her to collect,' Ginika tells Bert.

'Ah yes,' he says, remembering.

'What was the connection to the dolphins? I don't think you said in the podcast,' Paul asks, reaching for a chocolate biscuit. Their eyes are on me and I feel peculiar, hearing them speak about Gerry's letters like this. I know I spoke about them briefly with Ciara, in a small shop in front of thirty people, but somehow I forgot about the fact it could go further, downloadable onto devices, to be listened to in people's homes like entertainment. The way they are so casually discussing one of the biggest, deepest, darkest moments of my life, makes me feel far away, like I'm having an out-of-body experience.

I look from one to the other, trying to keep up with the speed of their conversation. Questions fly at me as if I'm a contestant on a quiz show, under a timer. I want to answer them, but I can't think fast enough. My life can't be summed up in rapid one-word answers, it requires context, scene-setting, explanations and emotional responses, not quick-fire rounds. To hear them speak of the process of writing and leaving these letters in such a cavalier way feels surreal and makes my blood boil. I want to shake them all and tell them to listen to themselves.

'The letter *I* really want to know about is the one with the sunflower seeds. Is that really your favourite flower?' Joy asks. 'Did Gerry ask you to plant the seeds? I quite like that. I'd like to ask Joe to plant a tree or something, in my name, and then they'd look at it every day and they'd think of — '

'How many years you've been gone,' I interrupt, without thinking. My voice is sharper than I intend.

'Oh,' she says, surprised, then disappointed. 'I

59

wasn't thinking of it like that. Just something for them to remember me by.' She looks to the club for backup.

'But they will remember you. They'll remember you every second of every day. They won't be able to stop remembering you. Everything they say, everything they smell, taste, hear, absolutely everything in their lives is linked to you. In a way, you will haunt them. You will be constantly in their thoughts even when they don't want you there, because they'll need you gone so that they can get through, and then there are days when they'll need you there in order for them to get through. Sometimes they'd do anything to not think of you. They won't need extra plants and trees to see you, they won't need a quiz to remember you by. Do you understand?'

Joy nods quickly and I realise I've raised my voice. I've sounded angry when I haven't meant to. I check myself, reign myself in. I'm surprised by my reaction, by the harshness of my tone.

'Holly, you liked Gerry's letters, didn't you?' Paul asks, breaking the stunned silence.

'Yes, of course!' I hear the defensiveness in my voice. Of course I did. I lived for those letters.

'Only, it sounds a bit like — ' Paul begins, but he's interrupted by Joy's hand on his knee. He looks down at her hand.

'It sounds like what?'

'Nothing.' He holds his hands up defensively.

'You're right, Holly,' Joy says slowly, thoughtfully, studying me as she speaks. 'Maybe they would see it as a marker of my death rather than a way of celebrating my life. Is that how the sunflowers made you feel?'

I feel sweaty. Hot.

'No. I liked the sunflowers.' Again I hear my words, so carefully guarded they sound armour-plated. 'I plant them on the same day every year. Gerry didn't tell me to do that. I just decided it was something I wanted to continue.'

Joy is impressed by that idea, makes a note of it in her diary. I don't tell them that it was my brother Richard's idea, that he planted them and kept them alive. But I looked at them. I looked at them all the time. Sometimes I couldn't bear the sight of them, other times I was drawn to them; on the good days, I barely noticed they were there.

Joy continues to muse while I squirm uncomfortably. 'Plant something on the same date every year. Maybe the date of my passing — or, no — ' She stops and looks at me, biro pointed at my face. 'My *birthday*. More positive.'

I nod weakly.

'I don't have a good imagination for this kind of thing,' she sighs.

'I do,' Bert says; it's his turn to be the defensive one. 'I have it all planned out. I got the idea from my local. I love a table quiz. She'll have great fun, we haven't travelled for so long because of this thing,' he says, throwing a thumb at his oxygen tank.

'What if she doesn't know the answers?' I ask. They look at me.

'Of course she'll know. It will be a general knowledge quiz. Where was Brian Boru defeated? Which group of islands give their name to a

61

sweater? Where was Christy Moore from? And then off she'll go to Limerick for the next clue.'

'Christy Moore is from Kildare,' I say.

'What? No, he's not,' he says. 'Sure, I listen to him all the time.'

Paul gets on his phone to google it. 'Kildare.'

'For feck sake, Bert,' Ginika says, rolling her eyes. 'This isn't going to work if you don't know the answers to your own bleedin' questions. And which of the Aran Islands is she supposed to go to? And which building? Is she going to find your letter on the ground when she steps off the boat? Will it be bobbing up and down in a bottle on the beach? You have to narrow it down.'

Paul and Joy laugh. I can't. It's too surreal. How have I ended up deep in this conversation?

'Ah stop it, the lot of you,' Bert says, getting agitated.

'Thank God we have Holly here to guide us,' Joy says, looking away from them and to me with a perplexed frown. As if to say, *See? This is why we need you.*

She's right to be concerned. This is serious, they need to end these antics. I need to help them refocus. 'Bert, what if your wife doesn't know the answers? She will be grieving. It's a brain scrambler, believe me. She might feel under pressure, like it's a test. Maybe you should write the answers down and leave them with somebody for her.'

'Then she'll cheat!' he exclaims. 'The whole reason for this is to get her out there, thinking.' He breaks into racking coughs again.

'Give your answers to Holly,' Joy says. 'And if

62

Rita gets stuck on one, she can call Holly.'

My stomach heaves. Heart flips. I'm only here for the hour. One hour, nothing more. Tell them, Holly, tell them.

'Holly, you can be the guardian of our notes, if you will,' Bert says, saluting me. 'As we head off to war.'

This is not what I'd planned. I had convinced myself that I could sit with them for an hour, hear their ideas for their letters, guide them, and then extract myself from their lives. I don't want to be invested. If Gerry had had someone helping him with his letters, I would have besieged them with questions. I would have wanted to know more and more, pressing them for every last detail of his secret moments away from me. I'd practically invited the travel guide, Barbara, to my house on Christmas Day for drinks, trying to make her a part of my life, before I realised the imposition I was putting on her. She couldn't provide me with any more information, I was squeezing her dry of what had been a short experience, pleading with her to share it with me over and over again.

And here they are, making plans for me to be their gate-keeper after their deaths, these strangers. They'll be gone, and the advice I give them will affect their loved ones forever more. I should leave immediately, before I get too involved, before it's too late. I should stick to the plan. I came here to tell them 'no'.

'Oh, would you look at that,' Joy says, pouring the last of the tea into her cup, and filling it so that tea spills out over the rim and pools on her saucer. 'We're out of tea. Holly, would you mind?'

Taking the teapot in a dazed state, I step over the dog and leave the room. As I'm standing waiting for the kettle to boil, trying to figure out how to escape this nightmare, feeling trapped and panicked, I hear a door off the kitchen opening, a man coming inside and wiping his feet on the mat. He steps into the kitchen as I ready myself for our greeting.

'Oh,' the man says. 'Hello. You must be with the book club.'

I pause. 'Yes, yes, the book club,' I reply, putting the kettle down and wiping my wet hands on my jeans.

'I'm Joe — Joy's husband.'

'I'm Holly.'

He shakes my hand, studies me. 'You look . . . well . . . Holly.'

'I am very well,' I laugh, and it's a split second later that I catch his meaning. He may not know the real reason behind the supposed book club, but he has figured out that its members are not at all well.

'Good to hear it.'

'I was about to leave, actually,' I say. 'Just topping up the tea before I go. I'm late, for an appointment. I've cancelled it twice before and really can't again, or I'll never get another one,' I blather on.

'Well, off you go, can't have you missing it again. I'll make the tea.'

'Thank you.' I hand him the teapot. 'Do you

64

mind giving them my apologies that I had to leave?'

'Not at all,' he says.

I back away in the direction of the front door. I can easily make my escape. But something about his movements stops me and I watch him.

He opens a cupboard and then another. Scratches his head. 'Tea, you say?' he says, pulling open a drawer. He scratches his head. 'I'm not sure . . . ' he mumbles as he searches.

I step back closer to him, reach to the cupboard above the kettle and open the door, revealing the box of tea. 'Here it is.'

'Ah,' he says, sliding closed the bottom drawer containing pots and pans. 'That's where that is. Joy always makes the tea. They'll probably want the sugar bowl too.' He starts opening more cupboards. He looks back at me. 'Off you go now, don't want you missing that appointment.'

I open the cupboard again. It's beside the tea. 'Found it.'

He turns suddenly and knocks over a vase of flowers. I hurry to help him and mop up the water with a dishcloth. When I've finished, the dishcloth is unusable. 'Where's your washing machine?'

'Oh, I'd say that it's . . . ' he looks around again.

I open the wooden cupboard beside the dishwasher and find the washing machine.

'There it is,' he says. 'You know your way around here better than I do. Truth be told, it's Joy that does everything in here,' he admits guiltily as if I couldn't have guessed. 'Always said

65

I'd be lost without her.' It feels like something he's always said, and now it has real meaning. Life without Joy, as he knows her, is nearing. It's real.

'How is she doing?' I ask. 'She seems very positive.'

'Joy is always upbeat, to others anyway, but it's got harder for her. She went through a period where nothing changed, she didn't worsen. We thought that was it, but then it advanced — and it's when it advances that the body declines.'

'I'm sorry,' I say softly. 'For you both.'

He purses his lips and nods. 'But I do know where the milk is,' he says, perking up and pulling open a door.

A broom falls out.

We both start laughing.

'You'd best be off to your appointment,' he says again. 'I know how they can be. Waiting list after waiting list, life is one big waiting room.'

'It's OK.' I pick the broom up from the floor, the desire to run gone. I sigh to myself. 'It can wait.'

★　★　★

When I return to the group with the replenished tea, Bert has faded. Whatever burst of energy his medication gave him for the hour has worn off, leaving him exhausted. As if anticipating this, his carer has arrived to collect him.

'Why don't we talk about this in detail the next time we meet,' Bert taps his nose in a secretive but terribly obvious manner, and jerks his head towards the sound of his carer speaking with Joe in the hallway. His chin wobbles as he moves. 'And not in my house, because Rita will be suspicious.'

'Here,' Joy says. 'We can all meet here again.'

'That's unfair on you, Joy,' Paul says.

'I can take over from where Angela left off. I wouldn't have it any other way,' she says firmly, and it's clear, at least to me, that it suits Joy in more ways than one to remain in her home.

'Good for me,' Bert says. 'How about two days from now, same time? If we meet tomorrow, Rita will be jealous of Joy.' He chuckles and winks. 'Will you come back to us, Holly?'

Everyone looks at me again.

I should not get involved in this club. I do not want to get involved in this club. It can't be healthy.

But everyone is looking at me, hopeful and expectant. Ginika's baby Jewel lets out a sound, as if she's joining in, trying to convince me along with the group. She makes happy bubbling sounds. She is six months old, she could be a one-year-old when her mother dies.

I look around at them all, this motley crew. Bert is struggling to breathe, Joy is barely holding herself together. I've been here before, I know how short six months can be, how quickly everything can change, how health can deteriorate in two weeks, how twenty-four hours can change it all.

I read an article on how the clocks stand still to keep our time in sync with the universe. It's called the leap second: a one-second adjustment

67

applied to the coordinated universal time because the Earth's rotation speed changes irregularly. A positive leap second is inserted between second 23:59:59 and second 00:00:00 of the following date, offering an extra second in our lives. News articles and magazine features have posed the question, what can happen in a second? What can we achieve with this extra time?

In one second, almost two and a half million emails are sent, the universe expands fifteen kilometres and thirty stars explode, a honey bee can flap its wings two hundred times, the fastest snail travels 1.3 centimetres, objects can fall sixteen feet, and 'Will you marry me?' can change a life.

Four babies are born. Two people die.

One second can be the difference between life and death.

Their expectant faces peer up at me, waiting, hoping.

'Let's give her time to think about it,' Joy says softly, but her disappointment is obvious. They all back off.

8

Rage has returned and it rushes through me. I am angry, I am seething. I want to scream. I need to shout it off, cry it off, exorcise it before I cycle home. My bicycle could surely not take the extra weight, couldn't cope with the ever-shifting emotional imbalance. I cycle out of sight of Joy's home, dismount, lazily discard the bike on the ground, and hunker down, leaning against a painted white popcorn wall that digs into my back. The PS, I Love You Club are not Gerry but they do represent him, his journey, his struggles, his intent. I always felt in my heart that the point of Gerry's letters was to guide me, and yet the motivation for these people is fear of being forgotten. It breaks my heart and makes me furious. Because, Gerry, my love, how could you ever feel that I'd forget you, that I *could* forget you?

Perhaps the root of my rage is that I lied to Ciara about not still feeling his presence. I could never forget him, but Gerry *is* blurring. Though he lives on in the stories we share and in my memory, it is becoming harder to summon the vivid living, moving, fluid, animated Gerry to mind. I don't want to forget him, but the more I move on and the more new experiences I have, the more the old memories get pushed aside. Selling the house, moving in with Gabriel . . . Life won't let me stay still and remember.

No. I made a decision that I wouldn't allow myself to stay still and remember. Waiting ... waiting for what, a reunion in death that I don't even know will happen?

'Hi.' I hear a voice beside me and I jump to my feet, startled.

'Ginika, hi, you gave me a fright.'

She examines my bike, where I'm standing, the way I'm standing. Perhaps she recognises a hiding place when she sees one. 'You're not coming back, are you?'

'I said that I'd think about it,' I reply weakly. I'm pissed off, I'm agitated. I don't know what the hell I want.

'Nah. You're not. It's OK. It's all a bit weird anyway, isn't it? Us lot? Still, it gives us something to do. Something to focus on, thinking about our letters.'

I exhale slowly. I can't be angry at Ginika. 'Do you have an idea of what you want to do?'

'Yeah,' she adjusts her grip on Jewel's thigh as the baby sits on her hip. 'But it's not, like, smart the way the others' ideas are.'

'It doesn't have to be smart, just yours. What's your idea?'

She's embarrassed and avoids eye contact. 'It's a letter, that's all. One letter. From me to Jewel.'

'That's lovely. It's perfect.'

She seems to prepare herself to say something and I brace myself. She's firm, strong, shoots from the hip, a hip loaded with a baby she made.

'You weren't right in there, what you said, about everyone remembering us when we're gone. She won't remember me.' She holds her baby tighter. 'She won't remember anything about me. Not my smell or nothing of the things you said. She's not going to look at anything and think of me. Whether it's good or bad. Ever.'

She's right. I hadn't considered that.

'That's why I have to tell her everything. Everything from the start, all the things about me that she knows now but won't remember, and all the things about her as a baby, because there'll be no one to tell her. Because if I don't write it all down about her, then she'll never know. All she'll have of me is one letter for the rest of her life, and that letter has to be from me. About me and her. Everything about us that only we know and that she won't remember.'

'That's a beautiful idea, Ginika, it's perfect. I'm sure Jewel will treasure it.' These are feathery kinds of words in response to the weight of her reality but I have to say something.

'I can't write it.'

'Of course you can.'

'No, I mean. I can't write. I can barely read. I can't do it.'

'Oh.'

'I left school. I didn't, couldn't keep up.' She looks around, embarrassed. 'I can't even read that sign up there.'

I look up at the road sign. I'm about to tell her that it says *No Through Road* but I realise it doesn't matter.

'Can't read my baby bedtime stories. Can't read the instructions on my medication. Can't read the hospital paperwork. Can't read directions. Can't read buses. I know you're so

71

smart and all, you probably don't understand.'

'I'm really *not* smart Ginika,' I say, with a bitter laugh. If I had been smart I wouldn't have gone to Joy's house today, I wouldn't be in this position now. If I was smart, if I could think clearly through the mush and the fog, then I would know exactly what to do next, instead of standing here, feeling completely emotionally incapacitated, this supposedly experienced adult facing a teenager, unable to aid or guide. I'm reaching out and grasping for golden nuggets of advice and inspiration, but my hands flail uselessly in the emptiness. Too wrapped up trying to clean the shit off my own wings instead of helping a younger woman to fly.

'I don't ask for help,' Ginika says. 'I've always been able to do everything myself. Don't need no one else.' She shifts Jewel's weight to her left hip. 'But I need help writing the letter,' she says it as though she's pushing it out through her teeth, it's that hard for her to say.

'Why don't you ask somebody in the club to write the letter for you?' I suggest, trying to weasel myself out of the equation. 'I'm sure Joy would be wonderful. You can tell her exactly what you want to say and she can write it down, exactly as you want. You can trust her.'

'No. I want to write it myself. I want to learn how to write this letter for her. Then she'll know that I done something good for her, because of her. And I don't want to ask any of them. They mean well, but they haven't a clue. I'm asking *you* to help me.'

I look at her, feeling stunned, frozen, by the

72

magnitude of this request. 'You want me to teach you how to write?' I ask slowly.

'Can you?' she looks at me, her large brown eyes deep and pleading.

I feel that I should say yes; I know that I shouldn't.

'Can I . . . ' I begin nervously, then shut down my emotions, the desire to protect myself is too great. 'I'd like to take some time to think about it.'

Ginika's shoulders drop instantly, her demeanour slackens. She has swallowed her pride and asked for help and, selfish coward that I am, I can't bring myself to say yes.

I know it's prosaic, I know it's tedious to say this after so much time has passed, when everything is OK, when I am more than a woman in grief, but sometimes something sets me off and everything gets tilted. I lose him all over again and all I am is a woman in grief.

The smashing of his favourite *Star Wars* mug. Discarding our bedsheets. When his clothes lost his smell. The broken coffee machine, the sun we'd rotated every day like two desperate planets. Small losses but huge. We all have something that unexpectedly derails us when we are motoring smoothly, blissfully, ardently. This encounter with the club is mine. And it hurts.

My instinct is to move inward, recoil, curl in a ball like a hedgehog, but never hide or run. Problems are excellent hunters with their flaring nostrils and sharp teeth; their special sensory organs ensure there is no place they can't find you. They like nothing more than to be in

73

control, on top, predator to you the prey. Hiding from them gives them power, even feeds their strength. A face-to-face meeting is what is required, but on your own terms, in your own territory. I go to the place where I process and acknowledge what is happening. I ask for help; I ask it of myself. I know the only person who can ultimately cure me is me. It's in our nature. My troubled mind calls out to my roots to dig deep and steady myself.

I cycle away from Ginika, my heart pounding, my legs feeling shaky, but I don't go home. As if I'm a homing pigeon, an inner compass takes over and I find myself at the graveyard staring at a Columbarium Wall. I read the familiar words of one of Gerry's favourite phrases, and wonder just how and when the past started chasing me, when I started running, and the moment it caught me. I wonder how on earth all that I worked so hard to build up has so suddenly come crashing down.

Damn you, Gerry. You came back.

9

I watch the 'For Sale' sign being hammered into the soil in the front garden.

'I'm glad we finally got to do this,' the estate agent breaks into my thoughts.

I'd made the decision to sell the house in January, and it's now April. I'd cancelled our appointment a few times, a representation of the yin-yang pendulum swinging in my newly altered state of mind, though I told Gabriel it was because the estate agent kept cancelling. I had to arm-wrestle his phone to the floor when he threatened to give her a piece of his mind. My reluctance has not been because I've changed my mind, but because I seem to have lost the ability to focus my mind on ordinary tasks. Though as I watch the 'For Sale' sign's violent disturbance of the peaceful daffodil beds, I acknowledge this task is not ordinary.

'I'm sorry, Helen, my schedule kept changing.'

'I understand. We all lead busy lives. The good news is I have a list of very interested people — it's the ideal starter home. So I'll be in touch with you very soon to organise viewings.'

A *starter* home. I look out the window at the sign. I'll miss the garden, not miss doing the physical work which I delegated to my landscaper brother Richard anyway, but I'll miss the view and the escape. He created a haven for me, one that I could disappear to when I craved it. He will miss this garden and I will miss the connection we have because of this garden; it binds us together. Gabriel's house has a courtyard in the back, with a beautiful lone mature pink cherry blossom tree. I sit and gaze at it from his conservatory, captivated by it when in bloom and willing it on in winter. I wonder if I should grow new plants, how Gabriel will feel about a pot of sunflowers, in keeping with my annual tradition since Gerry sent me the seeds in one of his ten letters. If this is my starter home, does that mean Gabriel's house is the main event? Or is there a third course with him or another person that I have to look forward to?

Helen is staring at me. 'Can I ask a question? It's about the podcast. It was wonderful, incredibly moving, I had no idea what you'd been through.'

I'm put out, not ready for the sudden veering into my personal life and thoughts in the middle of a regular life moment.

'My sister's husband died. Heart attack, out of the blue. Only fifty-four.'

Twenty-four more years than Gerry had. I used to do that; a calculation of how many more years people had with their loved ones than I managed. It's cold but it used to help feed the bitterness that occasionally came to life and chomped at every hopeful thing around it. Apparently the gift has returned to me.

'I'm sorry to hear that.'

'Thanks. I was wondering . . . did you meet somebody else?'

I'm taken aback.

'In your husband's final letter, he gave you consent, his permission to meet somebody else. That seems so . . . unusual. I can't imagine my brother-in-law doing that. I can't imagine her with anyone else anyway. Xavier and Janine. Just rolls off the tongue, you know.'

Not quite, but that's the point, isn't it. People who don't fit together suddenly do and then you can't imagine anyone else fitting at all. Circumstance and happenstance collide to synchronise two people who until then repelled each other, so they find themselves pulled into a net electric field. Love; as natural as shifting tectonic plates with seismic results.

'No.'

She seems uncomfortable at having asked, starts to backtrack. 'I suppose there's only one real true love. You're lucky you had him at all,' she blurts. 'At least, that's what my sister says. OK, so I'll get this in motion, and I'll call you as soon as I have viewings arranged.'

It may seem like a lie, that I'm a Judas to my Gabriel, but I didn't mean to tell her that I haven't found love again. It was her paraphrasing of Gerry's final letter that I took issue with. I did not receive nor did I need Gerry's consent or permission to fall in love again; that human right to choose who I love and when I love has always lain with me. What Gerry did was provide a blessing, and it was this blessing that boomed the loudest in the scared, excited Greek chorus of my mind when I began dating again. His blessing fed a desire that already lived within me. Humans possess insatiable longings for wealth, status, and power, but are hungry, most of all, for love.

'Which room did it happen in?' she asks.

'His death?' I ask, in surprise.

'No!' she says, aghast. 'Where were they written, or discovered, or read? I thought that might help with the tour of the house. It's always nice to have a little story. The room where the wonderful PS, I Love You letters were written,' she says, grinning, her salesperson head on full blast.

'It was the dining room,' I say, making it up. I don't know where Gerry wrote the letters, I'll never know, and I read them in every room, all the time, over and over again. 'The same room he died in. You can tell them that too.'

★ ★ ★

His breath, hot, against my face. His sunken cheeks, his pale skin. His body is dying, his soul is still here.

'See you on the other side,' he whispers. 'Sixty years. Be there or be square.'

He's still trying to be funny, the only way he can cope. My fingers on his lips, my lips on his. Inhale his breath, inhale his words. Words mean he's alive.

Not yet, not yet. Don't go yet.

'I'll see you everywhere.' My reply.

We never speak again.

10

I study Denise for a hint of what to expect. She seems calm, but impossible to read, and that's always how Denise announces these things. I recall her face when she announced her engagement, her apartment, her promotion, coveted shoes bagged in a sale: any announcement of good news has been preceded by this solemn expression, to trick us into thinking she's going to deliver bad news.

'No.' She shakes her head and her face crumples.

'Oh sweetie,' Sharon says, reaching for her and embracing her.

I haven't seen the old bubbly Denise for a few years. She is tamer, quieter, distracted. I see her less often. She's exhausted, constantly putting her body under stress. This is the third course of IVF that has failed in six years.

'That's it, we can't do it any more.'

'You can keep trying,' Sharon says, in soothing tones. 'I know somebody who went through seven courses.'

Denise cries harder. 'I can't do this four more times.' There is pain in her voice. 'We can't afford one more time. This has wiped us out.' She wipes her eyes roughly, sadness turned to anger. 'I need a drink.' She stands. 'Wine?'

'Let me get it,' I say, standing.

'No,' she snaps. 'I'm getting it.'

I hurriedly sit.

'You'll have one too, Sharon,' I say in a tone that I hope she can decipher. I want her to order the wine, sit with it, pretend to drink it, anything to draw attention away from the fact Sharon currently has something growing inside her that is the only thing Denise wants. But Sharon isn't getting it. She thinks that I've forgotten. She's making ridiculous wide-open eyes in an attempt to secretly remind me, but Denise watches this pantomime act and knows at once that something is up.

'Sparkling water is fine,' Sharon says to Denise finally.

I sigh and sit back. All she had to do was order the damn thing. Denise wouldn't have noticed. Denise's eyes run over Sharon's body, as if she's carrying out her own ultrasound.

'Congratulations,' Denise says flatly, before continuing to the bar.

'Fuck,' Sharon says, breathing out.

'You should have just ordered the drink,' I sing. 'That's all you had to do.'

'I know, I get it now, but I couldn't figure out what you were doing — I thought you'd forgotten. Oh, for fuck's sake,' she says, holding her hand to her head. 'Poor Denise.'

'Poor you.'

Denise returns to the table. She sets down the glasses of wine and the sparkling water, then reaches over to hug Sharon. They hold each other for a long time.

I take a large gulp of wine that burns going down my throat. 'Can I run something by you both?'

'Sure,' Denise says, concerned and happy to be distracted.

'After the Magpie podcast, a woman from the audience was so moved by what she heard she set up a club, called the PS, I Love You Club. It's made up of people who are ill, and they want to write letters to their loved ones, the way Gerry did.'

'Oh my . . . ' Denise says, looking at me with wide eyes.

'They reached out to me and want me to help them write their letters.'

Sharon and Denise share a concerned look, each trying to figure out how the other feels.

'I *need* your honest opinions, please.'

'Do you want to help them?' Denise asks.

'No,' I say firmly. 'But then I think about what I'd be helping them with, I know the value of what they're doing and I feel slightly obligated.'

'You are *not* obligated,' Sharon says firmly.

They're both pensive.

'On the positive side,' Denise begins, 'It's beautiful that they asked you.'

The beauty of it we cannot deny.

'On the *realistic* side,' Sharon steps in, 'for you, it would be like reliving the entire thing. It would be going backwards.'

She echoes Gabriel's podcast concerns and half of my family's feelings on the matter too. I look from one to the other like it's a tennis match, my two best friends replaying the exact same conversation I've had in my head all week.

'Unless it would actually take her forward. She's moved on,' Denise defends it. 'She's a

81

different Holly now. She has a new life. She works. She washes herself. She's selling her house, she's moving in with the sexy tree-man.'

The more Denise speaks, the more nervous I get. These are all things I worked hard to achieve. They cannot become undone.

Sharon is studying me, concerned. 'How ill are they?'

'Sharon,' Denise elbows her. 'Ill is ill.'

'Ill is not ill. There's ill and then there's . . . ' she sticks her tongue out and closes her eyes.

'Ugly?' Denise finishes.

'They aren't *all* terminally ill,' I admit, attempting a hopeful tone. 'One guy, Paul, is in remission and Joy, has a life-long . . . deteriorating condition.'

'Well, isn't that a rosy picture,' Sharon says, sarcastically. She doesn't like it. She fixes me with one of her scary mummy faces that takes no nonsense. 'Holly, you need to be prepared. You'd be helping these people because they're sick and they're dying. You're going to have to say goodbye over and over again.'

'But imagine, how beautiful it could be,' Denise changes the tone, to our surprise. 'When they write the letters. When they die knowing they achieved it. When their loved ones read their letters. Think ahead to that part. Remember how we felt, Sharon, when Holly would open an envelope on the first day of every month? We couldn't wait to get to her. Holly, you received a gift from Gerry and you are in a position to pass it on. If you are able to, if you feel it's good for you, you should do it; if you think it will set you

82

back, then don't and don't feel guilty about it.'

Wise words but a straight yes or no would have been more helpful.

'What does Gabriel think?' Sharon asks.

'I haven't told him yet, but I already know what he'll say. He'll say no.'

'No?' Sharon says, huffily. 'You're not asking him for his permission.'

'I know but . . . I don't even think it's a good idea.'

'Well then, there's your answer,' Sharon says in a final tone.

So why am I still asking the question?

I tune out of the rest of their conversation, my mind racing back and forth as it chases the options, grasping for a decision. I feel as though I should, I know that I shouldn't.

We part, back to our lives, back to our problems.

To weave and unravel, to unravel and weave.

11

It's 2 a.m. and I pace the downstairs rooms of my house. There aren't many. Living room to dining room to small U-shaped kitchen that only has enough standing room for two people, a toilet and shower room under the stairs. Which is ideal for me because it's only me, and occasionally Gabriel. His house is nicer and we stay there more often. Mine and Gerry's was a starter home; a new build in the suburbs of Dublin for us to begin the rest of our life together. Everything was shiny and new, clean, we were the first to use our shower, the kitchen, our bathroom. How excited we'd been to come from our rented flat to our own home with stairs for the first time.

I walk to the staircase and look up.

'Holly!' Gerry calls me.

He was standing where I'm standing now, at the foot of the stairs, hand on the banister.

'Yes!' I yell from upstairs.

'Where are you?'

'In the bathroom!'

'Where? *Upstairs?*'

'Gerry, our only bathroom is upstairs.'

'Yes, but we have a toilet *downstairs*.'

I laugh, understanding. 'Ah yes but I'm in the bathroom *upstairs*. Where are you? Are you *downstairs?*'

'Yes! Yes, I'm here *downstairs!*'

'OK great, I'll see you in a minute when I come downstairs, from where I am upstairs!'

'OK.' Pause. 'Be careful on the stairs. There's a lot of them. Hold on to the banister!'

I smile at the memory, running my hand up and down the banister, touching all the places he touched, wanting to rub him on to me.

I haven't done this late-night room wandering for years, not since the months after he passed, but now I feel the house is owed my attentive farewell. My mind is whirring with ideas. Bert's quiz, Ginika's letter, Joy's trees and flowers notions; I didn't ask Paul what he wants to do. They had more questions for me than I for them, about the dolphins, the holiday, the sunflowers. Sunflowers. My October letter from Gerry. A sunflower pressed between two cards and a pouch of seeds *to brighten the dark October days you hate so much*, he'd written.

When Gerry was alive, I hated winters. When he died, I embraced them. These days, I simply take them at the natural rhythm they arrive. The seeds were included with Gerry's eighth letter. I'd told everyone it was because sunflowers were my favourite flowers. They weren't. I'm not really the type of person to have a favourite flower; flowers are flowers and they are mostly all attractive. But the sunflowers had a meaning, a story. They started a conversation. Gerry had managed to start a conversation from his deathbed, which was Gerry's gift.

The first month in our house, we had very little furniture. Most of the furniture in our apartment had belonged to the landlords and so we had to start afresh, which meant we couldn't afford to buy everything at once, but also we weren't the best at managing delivery times, expecting couches to be available the moment we chose them from the shop floor, all the usual beginner mistakes. And so we had three months in the house without a couch or coffee table. We sat in the TV room, on bean bags, drinking wine, using our unpacked moving boxes as side tables.

'Sweetheart,' I say one evening when we're snuggled on a bean bag with a bottle of red wine after eating steak and chips for dinner.

'Uh oh,' Gerry says, looking at me sideways, and I laugh.

'Don't worry, it's not bad.'

'OK,' he says, reaching to his plate on the floor to spear some left-over steak.

'When do you want to have a baby?'

His eyes widen comically and he immediately puts the steak in his mouth, chewing slowly.

I laugh. 'Come on. What do you think?'

'I think,' he talks through his chews, 'we need to start marinating our steak.'

'OK, if you're not going to be adult about it, I'll speak. We've been married for two years, and apart from one horrible summer, and the two weeks we broke up when I saw you kissing Jennifer O'Brien, we've been together — '

'I did not kiss Jennifer O'Brien.'

'She kissed you.' I'm smiling. I'm really over it by this point. We were fourteen years old at the time.

'She didn't even kiss me. She leaned in and *brushed* my lips, and the reason we brushed is

86

because I moved my head *away*. Let it go,' he besieges me, mockingly.

'Hmm. Anyway. Let me continue.'

'Please do.'

'We've been married for two years.'

'You said that.'

I ignore him, continuing: 'And we've been together twelve years. Give or take.'

'Give. Always give.'

'And we said as soon as we left the rat-infested apartment — '

'One mouse. One time.'

'And bought our first house, we would discuss when to have a baby. We have now bought a house, which we won't own for another one hundred years, but isn't it time for the discussion?'

'And no better time than right when Man United have just kicked off against Arsenal. No better time at all.'

I laugh. 'You have a stable job — '

'Oh, you're still talking.'

'And when I'm working, my jobs are stable.'

'Between the instability,' he agrees.

'Yes. But I currently have a job that I dislike intensely and won't miss while on maternity leave.'

'I don't think you get maternity leave in temp jobs. You're covering for somebody else's leave.' He looks at me, his eyes laughing at me.

'OK, so maybe I don't get maternity leave, but I do get *leave*,' I reason. 'So all I have to do is get pregnant and *leave* . . . '

He laughs.

'And you are beautiful, I love you, and you have powerful super semen that should not be kept away from the world, hidden away down there, in a dark place, all alone.' I make a sad face.

He chuckles harder.

'They're ready to create a super species. I sense it.'

'She's still talking.'

'And. I love you. And you'll be an amazing daddy.'

He looks at me, serious now. 'Are you finished?'

I think some more. 'And I love you.'

He smiles. 'I want to have a baby with you.'

I start to squeal and he kills it.

'But what about Gepetto?'

'No!' I move away from him and throw my head back, frustrated, and stare at the ceiling. 'Do not bring up Gepetto again.'

'Gepetto was a great beloved member of our family and you . . . frankly, Holly, you killed him. You took him away from us.'

'Gerry, can we have an adult conversation for once?'

'This is an adult conversation.'

'Gepetto was a plant.'

'Gepetto was a living, breathing life form that needed air, light and water, like us. He also happened to be a very expensive bonsai, exactly the same age as our relationship. Ten years old. Do you know how difficult it was to find that bonsai? I had to drive to Derry to get him.'

I groan and pull myself up out of the bean

bag. I carry the plates to the kitchen, half-irritated, half-amused by the conversation. Gerry follows me; eager to ensure he hasn't really annoyed me but unable to stop when he's in this zone, prodding, poking away like a stick at the fire.

'I think you're more annoyed that you had to drive to Derry to a dodgy bonsai dealer than you are at me for killing it.' I scrape the food from the plates into the bin. I put the plates in the sink. We don't have a dishwasher yet, the basis of most of our arguments.

'Ah! So you admit to murdering him.'

I raise my hands in surrender. 'Sure, I killed him. And I'd do it again if I had half the chance.'

Gerry laughs.

I swivel around for the full reveal. 'I was jealous of the attention you were giving Gepetto, how the two of you left me out. So when you went away for two weeks, I planned it. I left him by the window, the place that gets the most sun and . . . I didn't give him water.' I fold my arms and watch Gerry double over laughing. 'OK, seriously, if this conversation about Gepetto is a distraction because you're not ready for a baby, that's fine with me. I can wait. I was only bringing it up for discussion.'

He wipes his eyes and the smile off his face. 'I want to have a baby with you. There is no doubt in *my* mind.'

'I'm ready.'

'You change your mind a lot.'

'About what dress to wear, and whether I should get tinned chopped tomatoes or whole peeled plum. About work. About wall-paint colours and tiles for the bathroom floor. Not about babies.'

'You sent the dog back after one week.'

'He ate my favourite shoes.'

'You change your job every three months.'

'It's called temping. It requires that I must. If I stay longer they'll have me forcibly removed.'

He leaves a silence. The corners of his mouth twitch.

'I won't change my mind on this,' I say, getting agitated, finally, with this conversation, with having to prove myself — me a grown adult — to my own husband. 'In fact, I already waited three months to have this conversation.' Because he's right, I do always change my mind. Apart from a commitment to Gerry, pretty much any other decision that involves long-term change scares me. Signing the mortgage on this house was terrifying.

He reaches out to stop me from leaving, and pulls me back to him. I know he's not deliberately trying to wind me up. I know he's trying to ensure I'm serious, in the only way he feels won't cause an argument. We kiss tenderly and I feel this is the time for decision, a life-changing moment in our lives.

'But,' he says mid-kiss.

I groan.

'I still can't help but feel we need to prove it.'

'I need to prove shit to you. I want a baby.'

He laughs. 'First,' he holds his finger dramatically and I roll my eyes and try to move away from where he's pinned me against the counter. 'For Gepetto and for the future of our super child, you will do one thing. You must prove you can grow and keep a plant alive. Then and only then can we make a baby.'

'Gerry,' I laugh, 'I think that's what they tell people who are leaving rehab who want to start new relationships.'

'Yes, unstable people like you. It's good advice. In the name of Gepetto.'

'Why are you always so dramatic?'

'Why are you . . . not?' His lips twitch.

'OK,' I say, getting into the game. 'I want a baby, so I'll see your ridiculous dare and I'll raise you. We both have to plant and grow our own seeds to prove we can both care for a baby. I will surprise you.'

'Can't wait,' he grins. 'Game. On.'

★　★　★

'Mum,' I whisper, down the phone.

'Holly? Are you OK? Have you lost your voice? Do you want to me send over some chicken noodle soup?'

'No, my throat is fine,' I reply, then rethink it. 'But I'd still love the soup. I'm calling because Gerry and I are doing this thing. Kind of like a competition.'

'Honestly, you two,' she says, chuckling.

'What's the fastest seed, flower thing, I could grow?' I ask, making sure Gerry's out of earshot.

Mum laughs loudly.

★　★　★

91

I clear out a jam jar. Gerry watches me while he drinks a coffee before leaving for work. I stuff the jar with cotton wool, then place two butter beans among the cotton wool. I pour water inside, just enough to make the cotton wool damp.

Gerry roars with laughter. 'Seriously? If that's how you think you grow flowers, I'm worried about how you think babies are made.'

'You watch,' I say, carrying the jam jar to the windowsill. 'My little butter beans will blossom where Gepetto perished.'

He holds his heart as though he's been shot. 'I only hope the cow that you sold was worth these magic beans.'

'I'm winning already. Where's yours?'

'I'm surprised that you're so quick off the mark. Some of us have to buy *soil* and *seeds*. Even though I haven't planted anything, I'm still winning because all you did was plant beans in cotton wool,' he says, and doubles over laughing.

'You wait. I want to be a mother, I will grow these beans with sheer determination alone,' I say, grinning, loving the sound of the words aloud. *I want to be a mother!* Gerry is right, such certain words from me are rare, and it's exciting to be a person who knows what she wants for once. But I am also stubborn and often choose to stick to my side of the argument whether I believe it or not. But not in this case.

Two days later when I go downstairs in the morning, I notice that one of the beans has started to sprout a small root, which is visible against the glass. I grab the jar and race upstairs. I jump on the bed, waking him, annoying him, and bounce up and down with my prospering bean.

He rubs his eyes and stares grumpily at the jar. 'That's impossible, how the hell is it growing in cotton wool. Did you mess with it?'

'No! I'm not a cheat. I *watered* it.'

Gerry doesn't like to lose. That evening he returns from work with a packet of sunflower seeds, but he has forgotten to buy a pot and soil.

On the fourth day, when he has only planted the sunflower seeds, my bean root has little tendrils.

Gerry takes to talking to his sunflower seeds, he reads the seeds a book. He tells the seeds jokes. He carries out full-on conversations with the seeds while I laugh. Two more days on, while Gerry's sunflower seeds are still beneath the soil, my beans sprout shoots. Gerry carries the sunflower seed pot to the bean bags where he plays computer games with his pot, even going so far as to place a controller in front of the pot.

One morning I walk into the bathroom to find the sunflower pot sitting on the toilet seat lid, with an open dirty magazine.

After ten days of this carry on, I call it.

'OK, admit it: I've won.' My beans have sprouted and grown shoots, and there is a large network of shoots off the main root, with a sturdy stem growing straight upwards and out of the cotton wool.

But of course he won't give in.

The following morning, he gets out of bed and goes downstairs to make our morning coffee before I do, which is a rare and precious thing, and I know something is up. He starts yelling, frantically, and I think we've been burgled. I fall out of bed, stumble downstairs and find him dancing around in his boxers, holding his potted plant with a single two-foot-tall sunflower climbing high.

'It's a miracle!' he says, wide-eyed.

'You're a cheat.'

'I did it!' he dances around with the sunflower, following me to the kitchen, and points a finger at me accusingly. 'You thought you could bury me, you didn't know I was a seed.'

'Cute,' I nod. Game over. 'So now we can have a baby?'

'Definitely,' he says, serious. 'It's what I've always wanted.'

On a high from our decision, we drink our morning coffee, him from his *Star Wars* mug; we're grinning at each other like lunatics, as though we've made the baby already. The post lands on the hallway floor.

Gerry gathers the envelopes and brings them to the kitchen, flicks through them and one takes his interest. He tears it open and I watch him, grinning at my gorgeous husband who wants to make a baby with me in my new house with a staircase that brings you upstairs from downstairs and downstairs from upstairs, feeling like life couldn't be any more perfect.

I study his face. 'What is it?'

He hands me the letter. 'I got the appointment for the MRI.'

I read the letter and when I look up, I can see he's nervous.

'These things are standard procedure. It just rules things out.'

'Yeah, I know,' he says, kissing me quickly, distracted. 'Still hate it. I'm going for a shower.'

'Where? *Up*stairs? To our shower upstairs?'

He stops at the bottom of the stairs and smiles, but the light has gone out in him. 'The very one. You take care of Esmerelda. She likes porn and video games.'

'Esmerelda?' I look at the sunflower, and laugh. 'Nice to meet you, Esmerelda.'

Esmerelda doesn't live much longer; our collective sense of humour stalled somewhat after the results of the MRI. But we don't know that yet on that morning. That morning we're busy planning life.

Gerry runs up our new staircase and then I hear the shower water running.

He's twenty-seven years old.

⋆   ⋆   ⋆

I finish my walk through my rooms at the door to my bedroom. I scan the room. It's not the same at all. New bed, new headboard, new curtains, new paint. New large strong protective lump beneath the duvet. Gabriel stirs, and a hand reaches out for me in the bed. It feels around. He lifts his head from the pillow, scans the room and finds me at the door.

'Everything OK?'

'Yes,' I whisper. 'I was getting some water.'

He looks at my hands, which are glass-of-water free; he can't be fooled. I climb into bed and kiss him. He lifts his arm and I turn my back to him and reverse into his warm body. He closes his arm around me and I'm instantly cocooned. He can protect me from the past that's chasing me, build a bubble around me where memories and emotional backtracking can't penetrate me. But what happens when he lets go, when the streaming light of morning stirs him, and the safety of slumber slithers away revealing truth? Much as I want to, I can't hide in him forever.

12

Gabriel and I rise early to get ready for work. It's dark, the house is cold and damp, impossible to heat as it needs a new central heating system, and we're both tired. We don't speak very much, we shuffle around the tiny kitchen, bumping into each other while we try to make our coffees ourselves, just the way we like it, and our own porridge. I make mine with milk, Gabriel prefers his with water. Blueberries on mine. Honey on his. Gabriel is too drained by recent family events in his life and frankly I'm too exhausted to listen to the new drama created by Ava, his sixteen-year-old daughter, the source of his pleasure and pain. A self-confessed bad husband and bad dad, he has spent the last few years trying to reconnect with his daughter. He has been doing all the chasing. His daughter is his world, he is her self-appointed moon, and she knows it: the faster she spins the greater her gravitational pull. My brain is slowly whirring as it warms up for the day. Neither of us are morning people, we keep to ourselves, together.

I lean against the countertop, waiting for the first sip of coffee to help fuel my brain and I collect my thoughts to tell him about the PS, I Love You Club. It's a good time because it's a bad time. We both have to leave the house in a few minutes or we'll be late for work, and so it will leave little room for discussion or argument.

97

It will give me a sense of his mood so I can prepare myself for a longer discussion later. I try to practise an intro line that doesn't sound rehearsed.

'Why is this in here?' Gabriel asks, looking in the cupboard at the coffee mugs.

I already know what he's talking about but I feign ignorance. 'Hmm?' I turn around and see the cracked *Star Wars* mug. 'Oh yeah. I broke it.'

'I can see that,' he says, looking at it for longer than necessary.

Weirded out by his interest, I concentrate on blowing on my coffee and warming my hands on my mug.

The cupboard closes, thankfully, but he looks at me. For too long. 'Would you like me to fix the mug?'

I wasn't expecting that. 'Oh sweetheart, that's so thoughtful of you, thank you. But no, it's OK. I'll throw it out eventually.'

Pause for everything that should be said.

'OK.'

Pause again for all that won't be said.

I should tell him about the PS, I Love You Club. That I've met them. That I'm absolutely not going to help them. I should really tell him, now. He's waiting for something.

'Holly,' he says, 'if you're having second thoughts about moving in with me, please just say it.'

'What?' I reply, stunned, not expecting that. 'Absolutely not. No second thoughts at all. Why would you say that?'

He seems relieved, then confused. 'Because I

feel that you're . . . I don't know, holding back. You're distracted. It took you so long to put it on the market, for one.'

'I have absolutely no doubts about living with you,' I say firmly, and I mean it. 'I'm sorry I was slow to get it moving.'

Yesterday I'd planned to wait in the local café while the house was being shown. But I wanted to know who was in my home, so I watched through the windows, feeling like a spy and saw figures in the living room. It was so odd to see strangers in my own home, wandering around my rooms, assessing how they could change the foundations of my life and alter them to suit theirs. Knock down walls, wipe traces of me away, the proof of my existence a stain on their new beginning. But it made me sure that I was ready to do the same.

'So everything's OK?' Gabriel asks again.

'Yes,' I say brightly.

'OK,' he says, kissing me. 'Sorry, I misread. Ava's got me over-analysing everything.'

I close my eyes and hate myself for the deceit. I feel like I'm cheating on him with thoughts of my dead husband.

'Tonight at my place?' he asks, finally.

'Yes, perfect,' I say, overly relieved.

I'll tell him then. I just don't know what exactly I'm telling him.

* * *

It's the end of the day and I'm carrying my bicycle through the shop, from the storage room

99

to the front door, when Gabriel calls. I can instantly tell from his tone that something is not right.

'I'm sorry, I've to cancel tonight,' he says, sighing. There's shouting and banging in the background. 'Shut up!' he yells loudly, away from the mouthpiece but it's enough to give me a fright. I rarely see Gabriel angry. Grumpy and irritated, yes, but rage isn't something he exhibits often and never at me; he is usually measured, or keeps it to himself and lets rip on the days that we are not together. A proficiency in self-containment is a finesse you adopt after big relationship number one, a trickle-down strength.

'Sorry,' he returns to the phone.

'What's going on?'

'Ava. She's having problems with her mum. She came to me. Kate chased her here. They've decided this is the destination to argue their points.'

There is a screech from Kate, and a holler from Ava. And a door bangs.

'Jesus,' I say, eyes widening.

'I think it will be a long night.'

'Oh, Gabriel. I'm sorry.'

'I'm sorry too. But I'm glad she came to me. This is what I've wanted.'

I end the call. 'Be careful what you wish for,' I say quietly to my phone.

'Who's wishing for what?' Ciara asks. She's been hovering behind me, eavesdropping. I tuck my phone into my backpack.

'Nobody and nothing.'

100

'Stay with us for dinner?' she asks. 'Vegan chili con carne, if you can stomach the lack of the taste of tortured animal?'

'I'm barbecuing steak!' Mathew yells from the back room.

'Tempting.' I smile. 'Thanks, but I'll go home. I have to start decluttering anyway before I move, so this is a good opportunity.'

'Is everything OK between you and Gabriel? Did you tell him yet?'

'Everything is fine, I haven't told him, but I will soon.' I shudder at the thought of the conversation. 'Why am I so nervous about it?'

'Because . . . ' she sighs. 'You don't want him to say no.'

Her words strike me, because they're true.

Helmet on, visor on, I mount my bike and prepare to escape, not from the shop but from my head.

I began cycling after Gerry's death. Before, I could barely drag myself to the gym, though my more youthful body was better at coping with lack of exercise. Now I thrive on the exercise. I need it. It doesn't help me to think, it makes me stop thinking. Everything I could find to stop thinking was and is a gift. Pushing myself to the absolute maximum gives me a release I can't get anywhere else. Motion is lotion. I like that I can choose a different route each time, even when going to the same destination. I don't need to rely on traffic to get me there on time. My journey isn't dependent on anyone but myself, I am the author of my own destiny. I see statues and streets I never noticed when I was in a car, I observe the way the light hits buildings in a way I never did before. I can take stock of everything, feel the wind in my hair, the rain and sun on my skin. It's the kind of movement that helps me notice things, not one that stalls my mind and traps everything in there.

I feel free.

There is so much about me that Gerry wouldn't recognise. I am older than Gerry ever was, I know things that he never knew, that he will never know. And it's the little things that stop me in my tracks. He never lived to hear the word 'hangry'. Every time I hear the word I think of him, he would have loved it when his belly was full and hated it when it was empty. The invention of things he would appreciate. New phones. New technologies. New political leaders, new wars. Cronuts. New *Star Wars* movies. His football team winning the FA Cup. When he died, he gave me his thirst for knowledge of the things he loved, and in the early years after his death I wanted to discover them for him. I was always looking for new ways to connect with him, as if I was the middle person between his life and death. I don't do those things any more.

I outlived my husband, and now I've outgrown him. The beauty and challenge of long-term relationships is that you change and shift at different times in different directions, side by side under the same roof. Most often, these changes are subtle and you're subconsciously adapting all the time to the constant but gentle shifting of another human being that you're so connected to; like two shape-shifters battling to coincide, for better or worse. Remain who you are while they alter, or change with them. Inspire them to go in another direction, gently push, pull, mould, tear at, nurture. Wait.

If Gerry were alive, he might have adapted his form to accept and make space in his heart and mind for the woman I am today. But over the past seven years my shape has shifted without having to assent to the energy of another. If Gerry were to return and meet this woman seven years on, he would not recognise me. He would possibly not love me. I don't even know if this Holly would have the patience for Gerry. But despite the fact I know me now and I like me, I'll be forever sorry that Gerry didn't get to meet this me.

★ ★ ★

The following day Gabriel and I sit outside in a café. The weather is warmer but we're still bundled up in the May sun.

'What happened last night?'

'Ava was suspended from school for two days.'

'What for?'

'Smoking cannabis on school grounds. One more suspension and she'll be expelled.'

'Hopefully that will scare her off. The most trouble I ever got into was for kissing Gerry on school grounds,' I say with a smile.

He watches me. He usually never minds if I bring Gerry up, so perhaps I'm being paranoid. 'You were a good girl,' he says, eventually.

'I was. Were you like Ava at school?'

'Unfortunately, yes. I was hoping I'd see something of myself in her, but this isn't the part I was hoping for,' he says, rubbing his beard tiredly. 'But at least she's finally coming to me.'

'Hmm,' I say dubiously, and immediately wish I hadn't.

'What does that mean?'

I question Ava's timing. She didn't want anything to do with her dad until she started getting in trouble. As the arguments with her mother and step-dad increase, the more often Gabriel finds her on his doorstep. And he's gentler with her. So eager to please her, to be back in her life.

'I don't want her exploiting your good nature, that's all.'

'What's that supposed to mean?' He's a hunky chunk of anger today.

'It means . . . what it means, Gabriel. Back down.'

I wait a minute to change the subject.

'OK, I know you've noticed that I've been distracted recently and I have to talk to you about it.'

I have his full attention. 'The PS, I Love You Club,' he says.

'You know about it?'

'You changed the moment you saw the card. I wish I hadn't opened the damn envelope,' he says, and I can hear the irritation beneath his words.

'Oh.' His mood and tone is making this more difficult.

'So you found out what it is,' he says, pressing me.

'Yeah. It's a real club. There are four members who are battling illnesses, some terminal. What I said on the podcast about Gerry's letters gave them hope, and it gave them an idea. They want to write their own 'PS, I Love You' letters.'

'That's a bit fucked up, isn't it?'

I bristle. Payback for my comment about Ava, I'm guessing.

'I met with them.'

He leans forward, it feels intimidating, charged. 'When?'

'A few weeks ago.'

'Cheers for telling me.'

'I'm telling you now. I needed to figure it out in my own head first. Plus I was worried you'd react like this.'

'I'm reacting like this because you took so long telling me.'

Round and round in circles we go.

'They want me to help them with their letters. Guide them.'

He looks at me. Crystal blue eyes searing into me. I hold his stare.

'I was going to ask you what you'd think of me doing that, but I think I can guess.'

He downs his coffee and sits back in his chair. 'I thought the podcast was a bad idea, and I think this is a bad idea.' He seems ready to move.

'Are you in a rush? Can we talk about it? I need to talk it through. It clearly makes you angry, so tell me why you think it's a bad idea.'

'Because you've moved on and you shouldn't go back. I think that watching people die may take you back, to a time when you've told me you were so desperately unhappy you could barely get out of bed.'

I nod along, letting it sink in. I can understand his concern but I'm thrown by his anger. Perhaps it is difficult when the person you know becomes caught up with the person she was. We've been together for two years, two intense years during a profoundly transformative time in both of our lives, when everything around us was a big enough excuse for us to pull us away from each other, and yet we kept returning to each other for more. My heartache, my grief, his self-prescribed loneliness, our fears and trust issues. We overcame all of that, still do, to make each day work. Moving in together is something we both thought we would never do. Him because he never wanted to live with another woman again, me because I thought I could never love another man with the same intensity.

'You've spent the past few weeks creeping around like you're seeing someone else. I knew something was up — you should have told me, Holly.'

'I wasn't creeping around,' I say, annoyed. 'And fine, if it's going to agitate you so much, I won't help them.'

'Oh no no, don't put that on me,' he says, reaching into his pocket and searching through his money to pay the bill. 'You did the podcast for Ciara, and you're not helping this club, for

106

me. Take ownership of something, Holly.'

He throws the money on the table, and leaves.

★ ★ ★

Cycling home, the pressure has intensified. Choosing not to help the club would relieve me of the constant stress of thinking about the club, but I don't think I'd be able to stop thinking about Joy, Bert, Paul, and Ginika. I wouldn't be able to stop myself from wondering what they're doing, how they're getting on. And Jewel. Would Ginika swallow her pride again and ask for help from someone else to write her letter? I don't know.

There's a loud angry car horn. I feel a hard thud against my right leg and I can't control my bike. I'm forced over and crash to the ground.

Screams, shrieks, yells, a car horn long and loud, ringing in my ears. The car has stopped, the engine is still running. The car horn finally stops. I lie on the ground, my heart pounding, my leg throbbing. I see a lone shoe on the ground nearby. My trainer. There's a heaviness on top of me and I think it's the car, that it's above me and I'm trapped. It's a moment before I realise it's my own bicycle.

After the cacophony, there's a stunned silence.

A car door slams shut. The yelling begins again; angry this time. I brace myself. My body feels contorted, but I don't dare move. I close my eyes. My nose touches the cold concrete. I try to steady my breathing, try to stop my heart from ripping out of my chest, feeling crumpled.

I know death. Death knows me. Why does it keep following me around?

13

The taxi that hit me had suddenly veered dangerously to the left to avoid hitting the car in front, which had braked hard for a right turn, without indicating. He successfully managed to avoid hitting the car in front but hadn't checked his mirror to see me in the cycle lane. In my fall, I fractured my left ankle, and scored plenty of bruising to my body as I hit the ground. Helmet on, my head is fine. I also got my shoe back.

'I love you, I love you, I love you,' Gabriel murmurs in my ear in the hospital, comforting warm whispers over and over again, in my ear, on my lips, showering my face, my body, with butterfly kisses, as I fall into the deepest of exhausted sleeps into the same dream that has been in replay mode.

I'm lying on the hard concrete, around me is shattered glass, a battered car, a twisted and mangled bicycle. I somehow manage to stand up and the glass crunches beneath my feet. I find a single trainer. The road is filled with empty cars. Where has everyone gone? I circle car after car with a single shoe in my hand, trying to find its matching pair. Over and over again I find the same single shoe. I'm exhausted; I've been doing this for hours. I search again, going round and round the cars, one after another; it is dizzying, the trainers I find are identical, always for the same foot. But I cannot match a single pair of shoes.

I wake up sweating and panting, heart pounding, confused by my surroundings. Mum is beside me and starts talking to me, calmly, softly, but my mind is still half-trapped in my recent nightmare. I look around, trying to orientate myself. I'm home. It's my childhood home, where I grew up. I'm in my old bedroom, where I cried, and dreamed, plotted, planned and most of all waited, waited for school weeks to go by, for summers to begin, for boys to call me, for my life to begin. Mum and Dad had insisted I stay with them for a few nights after I was released from hospital.

'Are you OK?' Mum asks.

'I thought I was dead.'

'You're safe, sweetheart,' she says softly, gently brushing my hair back from my forehead, then her lips graze my skin.

'For a moment, when the driver came over to me, and was asking me over and over again if I was OK, I kept my eyes closed, like I was pretending to be dead,' I explain.

'Oh love.' She wraps her arms around me and I rest my head on her chest. There is only one way that I can lie in bed, with a cast on my broken ankle.

'Possum,' Dad says, out of nowhere.

I look up and see him standing at the door, with bedhead tousled hair that I haven't seen for so very long. He's wiping his glasses on the ends of his vest, before placing them over his sleepy eyes that get larger as soon as they're behind the lenses. He steps into the room and sits at the end of the bed. My parents, back at the same scene where they settled my childhood nightmares. There is something comforting about this, that no matter how much the world changes, no matter how much our relationships with others alter, they still are who they are to me and always will be.

'Playing possum, or apparent death, is a behaviour in which animals take on the appearance of being dead,' Dad goes on. 'It's a form of animal deception also known as tonic immobility, whereby animals become apparently temporarily paralysed and unresponsive. It occurs during an extreme threat such as being captured by a predator. The same thing can occur in humans undergoing intense trauma, whereby they freeze in response to life-threatening situations. I watched a documentary about it.'

'Oh.'

'Frank,' Mum says, annoyed by his response.

'What? It's perfectly natural, is all I'm saying,' he says.

'Well then why don't you just say that? I don't think she needs to be listening to a lecture on possums at a time like this.'

'All right, all right,' he says, hands up in defence.

I smile, then laugh, laying back on the pillow as I listen to them bicker.

But Dad might be on to something.

★ ★ ★

Even though I want to go straight back to work, Ciara gives me the week off. I'm a little woozy from the painkillers and as Gabriel has to work, Mum and Dad insist I stay on with them until the pain in my leg has lessened, I get to grips with my crutches, and my fear has subsided. I lie in bed some days, daydreaming, watching daytime TV. Other days I move to the couch to do the same. I spend time with my family: a painting session with my mum, watching nature and history documentaries with my dad, who narrates the entire thing, listening to Declan's new documentary ideas with time to guide and listen and advise, overseeing planting in Mum and Dad's garden with Richard, interrogating my nieces and nephews about their lives, playing Snap with Jack, being comforted by Gabriel.

I seek solace, I seek solitude, I seek company, I search for me. I long to go for a cycle and realise how much I had used movement and *doing* as a way to not think. I was the friend I avoided because I didn't like the topic of conversation; too close to the bone. It may have been necessary for a spell, to get myself out of my head, but for now I have to get inside my head, make myself comfortable. There are thoughts to be processed, actions to analyse and decisions to be made. For once, I can't run from me.

I descend the stairs on my bum on a Thursday morning, which since Dad has retired feels very much like a weekend in my parents' home. I reach for my crutches at the bottom of the staircase, and swing my way into the kitchen.

They're both sitting at the kitchen table. Mum is wiping her teary eyes, but she's smiling, and Dad's face is a picture of emotion.

'What's wrong?'

'Nothing's wrong.' Mum puts on her reassuring voice and pulls out a chair. 'Come sit with us. Your dad found something.'

I sit with them and notice an open shoebox on the table. Piles of folded pieces of paper fill each one.

'What are these?'

'Do you remember?' Dad begins, but his voice is shaking and he clears his throat. Mum places a hand on his cheek and they both laugh. 'Do you remember when you were younger and I had to travel for work?'

'Yes, of course I remember. You used to bring me back a bell, every trip. I had dozens of them.'

'I hated flying,' Dad says.

'You still do.'

'It's simply not natural,' he says firmly. 'Humans were made to be on the ground.'

Mum and I laugh at his deathly serious state.

'Well, every time I had to get on one of those awful things I was sure the plane would go down,' he says.

'Dad!' I say, surprised.

'It's true,' Mum says, grinning. 'It was more stressful dealing with your dad going away than it was with you all missing him.'

'Every trip where I had to get on a plane, I'd sit down the night before and write you all a note. In case the plane went down and I never got to speak to you again. I left it in the drawer

113

beside my bed with strict instructions to Elizabeth to give you the messages.'

I look at both of them in surprise.

'He didn't leave me any letters, mind you,' Mum says, teasing.

'It's not the same thing as Gerry did for you, not the same thing at all. I never equated my little notes with Gerry's letters. I didn't even use envelopes. But I kept them. I just needed to put in words all the things I would want to say to you if I wasn't here. Guiding words for your life, I suppose.' He slides a shoebox towards me. 'These are yours.'

'Dad,' I whisper, looking into the box. 'How many are there?'

'Fifteen or so. I'm sure I didn't write one for every trip. I didn't feel so scared going on short flights to the UK. But the longer letters were when I was getting on a propeller plane.'

Mum snorts with laughter.

As I lift the envelopes from the box and flick through them, Dad adds, 'I thought they might be helpful to you now. To help you make your decision.'

The lump in my throat is so enormous I can't speak. I stand up to reach over and hug him, but I put my weight on the wrong foot.

'Ow, fuck,' I groan, sitting down again.

'All these years, and that's the response I get,' he says, amused.

Crouched with Dad around the letters at the table, with a box of my collection of bells that Mum retrieves from the attic, I choose one at random. Dad opens it and inspects it. I can tell

114

he's enjoying the game of retracing his past.

'Hmm, let's see. Barcelona trip. Sales Conference with the horrifically foul-breathed Oscar Sheahy, who had more time for escorts than meetings.'

I laugh and search through the bells. A tiny porcelain black-handled bell with a cathedral and sunset sky. *Barcelona* is hand-painted in white around the base. I tinkle the bell and Dad hands me the letter. I read aloud:

Dear Holly,

You're six years old this week. I'll be travelling for your birthday and I just hate it. You'll have a clown party. I hope it doesn't scare Declan, he hates clowns and kicked one in the goolies for Jack's party. But you love them. You dressed as a clown for Halloween this year and insisted on telling a joke at every door we knocked on. 'What do you call a zoo with only one dog?' you asked Mrs Murphy. 'A shih-tzu.' You love telling that one.

I'm sorry I'll miss your birthday, this very important day of your life, but I'll be thinking of you all the time. I didn't want to leave you on this very special day but Daddy has to go to work. I will be with you all the time, even if you don't see me. And please remember to keep me some birthday cake.

Lots of love,

Daddy

'Oh Dad.' I reach across and take his hand. 'That's so lovely.'

Mum is standing by the kitchen sink, listening. 'That was the day Jack jumped off the roof of the shed and cracked his two front teeth.'

We look up at her in surprise.

'And I ate all the birthday cake,' she adds.

★　★　★

I stalled after Gerry's death. His letters got me back on my feet again. The following year I began to cycle and I'd been pedalling fast ever since. But now, I must be still, and learn to walk again. It is this simple quality of life and rhythmic functioning, almost like a production line, that gets me thinking: I'm equally terrified by life and ecstatic to be living it at the same time.

I selfishly thought after Gerry's death that the universe owed me. I experienced a great tragedy at a young age and I thought that was me done, I got it over and done with. In a world of infinite possibilities, I should have known there is no end to the loss that we can experience, but neither is there to the knowledge and growth that arises because of it and in spite of it. Now I think surviving the first prepared me for the second, for this moment, and for anything else that lays ahead. I can't stop tragedy from unfolding, I am powerless in the face of life's sleight of hand, but while I lick my wounds and heal, I tell myself that although the car knocked me off my perch, momentarily tore my confidence, ripped me raw and broke my bones, I'm healing and my skin is growing back thicker.

My mind sent an SOS to my roots. This is what my roots have come back with: my unravelling at this time could be the making of me. After all, it happened once before, so why can't it happen again?

Once upon a time I wanted to die.

When Gerry died, I wanted to be dead.

When he died, a piece of me did die, but a part of me was born too.

But in the midst of my grief, if I had been faced with a speeding oncoming car, I would have wanted to live. Perhaps it is not death that angers or scares us, it's the fact that we have no control over it. Life cannot just be taken away from us without our consent. Given time, and our permission having been granted, we would accept our fate and plot our own timely deaths. But we can't. All of which thinking brings me back again and again to the PS, I Love You Club.

Play dead to survive.

Play at living while dead.

We want to control our deaths, our goodbye to the world, and if we can't control it, we can at least control how we leave it behind.

14

Gabriel is quiet at breakfast. I arrived at his house late last night, just as he was going to bed, and I joined him, thankful there were no stairs to negotiate. At my parents' home I'd been going upstairs on my bum nightly like Gretl von Trapp singing 'So Long, Farewell'. We didn't talk, at least not about what we last argued about, and then I slept, Gabriel didn't. I could tell each time I opened my eyes and found him sitting up reading through his phone. Either my accident has affected him deeply, or our argument, or I'm being naïve and there's something else on his mind. He stands at the island, naked from the waist up, concentrating intently on his boiled eggs.

'Are you OK?'

He doesn't answer.

'Gabriel?'

'Hmm?' He looks up.

'Everything OK?'

'My boiled eggs are hard,' he says, studying them again. His toast pops. It's burnt. He sighs dramatically, joking, 'It's going to be this kind of day.'

I smile. He butters the toast, sending cremated crumbs all over the counter.

'You're going to help the PS, I Love You Club, aren't you?' he says, sensing my thoughts.

'Yes.'

He's silent. He moves his boiled eggs and toast to the breakfast bar at the edge of the island and sits on a high stool. Calm face, busy head. He picks up the toast that's been cut into neat soldiers and dips it into the egg. The toast bends. It doesn't dip into the yolk as he likes, doesn't send it oozing down the side of the shell and cup for his finger to wipe and lick.

'Fuck,' he says angrily, and drops the toast.

His outburst gives me a fright, though I was dreading this reaction from my usually cool-headed boyfriend.

'I have to get dressed,' he says, then makes his way to the bedroom.

'Don't you want to talk about it?'

He stops midway. 'You've already decided. I've figured you out. Long silences and not talking for months on end means you're making your own decisions. That's fine, that's how you and me will function from now on. Let's just do our own thing and let each other know after.'

He disappears into the bedroom. As I am breathing out slowly, he appears in the doorway to the living room, top still off. 'Not so long ago you got hit by a car, Holly, probably because you were thinking about this club and weren't paying attention to what you were doing. You shouldn't make rash decisions after something like that.'

'It's not rash. It was over a week ago, and sometimes frights make you think faster, with more focus. I can see it more clearly than ever. There is absolutely no reason why helping them would make me revert to who I was. It's an entirely different set of circumstances. I can help

119

them. And anyway, the accident wasn't my fault, the taxi pulled out, I couldn't have avoided it.'

'What did you tell me the night you came home from the podcast? If I ever decide to do this again, stop me. I remember that, you might not. You've been through enough. God knows what the hell you're thinking after what happened to you.'

'I think that this will help me.'

'You're doing this for you? Or for them?'

'For all of us.'

He throws his arms up. 'You almost got run over by a car!'

'It *bumped* me. I hurt my ankle, not my head! But at least my recuperation has given you more time to spend with Kate and Ava,' I snap.

My catty response is not quite how I wanted to mention the amount of time Gabriel has been spending with his daughter and ex-wife since the accident. I shouldn't throw it at him as a negative because I know time with his daughter is what he's been craving since I met him. Though it was my decision to stay with Mum and Dad for the week, it grated on my nerves a little bit more each time he was out with them.

'I'm not getting back together with Kate, if you're jealous.'

'And I'm not getting back with Gerry, if you're jealous.'

He calms and smiles at that. He runs his hand through his hair.

'But *why?*' he asks simply. 'Why do you choose to be surrounded by so much . . . death?'

'I'm not going to run away from it and

pretend that it hasn't affected me. I see this as a positive way of dealing with it. Gabriel, I'm not going to let this club affect us, if that's what you're worried about?'

'Yet we're arguing. Now. About us. Because of them.'

But an argument is never really over just one thing. It's the creature that feeds off its host, and it leaves me wondering what exactly we are arguing about.

15

Back at work, I move more slowly around the shop but I'm still able to function. Though I can't cycle, I'm able to drive, and I'm thankful that my car is automatic as my left foot is in a cast but I can still use my right on the pedals. I'm ready to get back to business. It's been over a month since I spoke to or heard from the PS, I Love You Club and I have the overwhelming urge to begin as soon as possible. It was Bert who had a clear idea of what he wanted to achieve with his letters and Bert in my opinion who was the most misguided. Hearing the kind of things he was going to do for his wife reminded me exactly what it was that Gerry did for me and it made me feel angry that he was getting it wrong. I feel if I have any chance of helping the club, Bert is first on my list.

I call Bert and nervously wait to see if the gang I cast aside when they needed me, are willing to take me back. I would pace, but the cast hinders me, it slows me down in so many different ways.

'Hi, Bert, it's Holly Kennedy.'

'Holly Kennedy,' he wheezes.

'From the podcast, I met your group some time ago.'

'PS, I Love You, Holly,' he says.

'How are you holding up, Bert?'

'So-so,' he wheezes. 'Had an . . . infection in

my lung . . . just home . . . for as long as . . . I can.'

'I'm sorry to hear that.'

'Better to be home,' his words are a raspy whisper.

'Did you write your PS letters?'

'Yes. We decided to continue.'

'I'm sorry that I let you down.'

'You have nothing to be sorry for.' He coughs. It's so loud and violent that I have to remove the phone from my ear.

'I wonder if you'd still like me to help?' I realise, as I wait, that I really really want him to say yes.

'You've had a change of heart.'

'Maybe I just grew one.'

'Now, now, don't be so hard on yourself,' he says breathlessly.

'I didn't express myself clearly when we met in Joy's house. I was out of sorts, uncomfortable with what was happening. I wasn't supportive and I apologise. I think I sounded defensive or that I wasn't happy with Gerry's letters. That's not true. So please allow me to redeem myself. Maybe I could cast my eye over your letters and offer some advice? I could think of it from the perspective of your loved ones.'

'I'd like that,' he whispers.

Relieved, I grow in confidence. 'Gerry's letters were special to me for many reasons. I've come to realise that what Gerry did for me was to create a conversation between us. Or more importantly, continue it. Even after he passed, we continued to have a relationship and a connection that went beyond revisiting memories. We were making new moments after his death. That's the magic. Perhaps that's what you should focus on. Your letters to Rita are not for entertainment purposes — well, not exclusively for entertainment purposes — and it's not a test of her love for you either. I'm sure that's not what you were planning on achieving.'

'No.'

'Does Rita like history?'

'History? No.'

'Do any of the questions for her relate to a private joke or hold a private meaning between you both?'

I wait.

'No.'

'OK. What you should do, if you would still like to take my advice, is ask her questions that relate only to you two, that only you could both know. Personalise your quiz so that it means something to her, so that it unlocks a special memory and then physically brings her to that place to make it even more intense. Bring Rita on a journey, Bert, make her feel like you're right by her side and you're doing it together.'

He's silent.

'Bert?' I stop pacing. 'You still with me?'

He makes choking sounds.

'Bert?' I panic.

He starts laughing, wheezy rasps. 'Just . . . joking.'

I curse his humour.

'Sounds like I'll have to start again.'

'I've to get back to work now, but I can drop

by your house later this week so we can plan it, is that OK?'

Pause. 'Tonight. Time is . . . of the . . . essence.'

★ ★ ★

I visit Bert's house after work as promised. His carer shows me into the house, and I share the obligatory story that follows the observation of my crutches and cast, and I sit on a chair in the hallway, as if I'm in a waiting room while the family gathers in the living room. As was the case in my house during Gerry's illness, it has been turned into a bedroom, so that Bert doesn't have to go up and down the stairs. It meant that I could be with Gerry at all times, even when preparing the food that he inevitably wouldn't eat, and he felt more connected to the world instead of hidden away in the bedroom, but he preferred to have a bath instead of the shower we installed downstairs. The bath was upstairs. We installed a stair chair. Gerry hated using it, but he hated leaning on me more and so he swallowed his pride. He would close his eyes and relax in the bath, while I sponge-cleaned him. Bathing him, holding him, drying him, dressing him, were some of the most intimate moments we ever had together.

The door to Bert's room is closed but I can hear that it is filled with people, young children being the loudest. The PS, I Love You Club is a secret to add to the element of surprise after death, and I don't know what Bert has told his family about me, if anything at all, but the idea of a book club is thankfully a good cover and so I've brought a sports memoir with me to pretend I'm recommending our next read.

Suddenly there's a rise of beautiful music as a choir of young voices sing 'Fall on Your Knees'. The sounds of his grandchildren to lift his spirits, they probably don't know that they're saying goodbye but their parents do. Bert does. He probably looks at them all one by one as they sing and wonders about their future, hoping they'll be OK, guessing who will become what, wishing he could see it. Or perhaps it's his own children he worries about, as they watch their singing children with strained smiles and pain in their hearts, and he feels their pain, their struggles, knows the hurdles they have overcome in life and worries about how they will cope in the future. Because he knows their characters, even on his deathbed as they're worrying about him, he's unable to stop worrying about them. Their dad, forever. And perhaps he thinks of Rita, who will be faced with it all alone when he's gone. I envisage it all as the sweet young voices drift through the walls.

The door opens and cries of 'Goodbye, Granddad,' 'We love you Granddad,' drift out the door. The grandchildren stream excitedly from the room, hopping and skipping, chattering happily; they're followed by children and in-laws, who smile at me as they pass and leave through the front door, pausing to hug Rita on the way. Bert's wife is a small woman in a pair of pink golf trousers and sweater, with a set of pearls and

126

lipstick to match her outfit. I stand as she closes the door behind the last of them.

'Sorry for the wait,' she says warmly. 'I'm afraid Bert didn't tell me you had an appointment. Oh goodness, you poor thing, what happened?'

She doesn't seem the slightest bit emotional after the scene I witnessed, not as moved as I am, but I remember the feeling of always being the strongest person in every room, because if you weren't, everything would be impossible. High emotions, goodbyes, and talk of the end becomes the norm and the soul builds up a super layer of armour when faced with it. When alone, it was a different matter; alone was when everything was free to come crashing down.

'Cycling accident,' I reply. 'It will be off soon, thankfully.'

'He's waiting for you,' she says, guiding me into his room. 'I'll put the kettle on. Tea or coffee?'

'Tea, please. Thank you.'

Bert is lying in a hospital bed in the living room. The couches have been pushed to one side. He's hooked up to his oxygen, and when he sees me he motions for me to close the door and sit beside him. I obey.

'Hi, Bert.'

He signals to the tubes in his nose and rolls his eyes. The energy from our first meeting in Joy's conservatory is gone, but there is life and a twinkle in his eye for our project.

'You look worse than me,' he gasps between words.

'I'll heal. Only four more weeks left. I brought you this book, for our book club.' I wink, and place it on the locker beside him.

He chuckles. Then coughs, angry coughs that rip him of life. I stand and move closer to him, hovering, as if that will help.

'I told Rita something else.'

'Oh God, do I want to know?'

'My feet,' he says, and I look to his toes that are wiggling at the end of the blanket his coughing has pulled up. Crusty flat feet with long tough yellow nails. I am not touching those feet for love nor money.

'Foot . . . massage . . . therapy.'

'Bert,' I look at him wide-eyed, 'we're going to have to come up with a better cover story.'

He chuckles again, enjoying this.

I hear cups and plates rattling in the kitchen as Rita prepares.

'OK,' I shake my head, 'let's get down to business. Have you thought about the new questions?'

'Under my pillow.'

I stand and help him lean forward. Laughing, I retrieve the papers from beneath his huge stack of pillows and hand them to him.

'Ever since I was a boy I've always wanted to plan a heist.'

'Well, you've certainly been busy scheming.'

'Nothing . . . else to do.'

He shows me a map with coloured circular stickers in the exact locations. To my absolute relief, all are Dublin-based but his writing is so erratic I can barely read it.

128

'It's rough. You'll have to write it again,' he says, possibly noticing my struggle.

The sound of a rattling tray and footsteps nears the door. I hide the papers under my coat on the chair and open the door for Rita.

'Here we are,' she says brightly.

I help her wheel the tray table closer to Bert. Pretty teapot and mismatching cups and saucers, with a plate of biscuits.

'Will this be in the way of your work?' she asks, concerned.

'Oh no, it's OK,' I reply, hating the lie. 'I can slide it across easily.'

We shuffle it around and she leaves us. I'm sure she's relieved to have an hour to herself. I remember that I did. In the depths of a difficult reality I would watch home make-over shows, transforming gardens, cooking shows, everything to do with transformation and crying, surprised guests. I got lost in their sorrow and then was lifted by their hope.

Bert chuckles. He loves the intrigue. I don't, but wonder if Gerry was the same, when his body and mind was being analysed and owned by everyone else, if he was enjoying keeping something to himself.

I retrieve the papers again and study them.

'You wrote poems?'

'Limericks. Rita is the poetry fan, she hates limericks,' he says, a look of devilment in his eyes.

'Bert,' I keep my voice low. 'One of the reasons I loved Gerry's notes was because they were handwritten. I felt like he'd left a part of him behind. His words, from his hand, from his mind, from his heart. I think it's best if you write these notes yourself.'

'Oh?' He looks up at me and it's impossible to think that this big man, with enormous hands and broad shoulders, could ever lose a battle against anything. 'Rita's always hated my handwriting, insisted on writing greeting cards herself. She has lovely handwriting. You should do it.'

'OK. Or I could print it out. So that it's not from me, exactly.'

He shrugs. He's not too bothered about how the message is relayed, so long as it is. I blink. I need to learn to take this into account: that each person will disregard what I felt was important and place great importance on an aspect that I never contemplated. There can be nothing generic about these letters; their desires and not mine must be accounted for.

'And we need nice paper. Do you have stationery?' Obviously he doesn't. 'I can get you that.'

He doesn't touch the biscuits, he doesn't touch his tea. There is a plate of sliced fruit beside his bed, also uneaten.

I look at his notes and the map, not seeing anything, but thinking fast in my head. It is too much to ask him to do this all again, he has done what he can, as quickly as he can.

'Bert. Just so I don't get any words wrong when I'm transcribing it, I need you to do one thing for me.' I take out my phone to record. 'Read them for me.'

He reaches for his glasses but the effort is too great. I go to the side table and hand them to him.

He looks at the page, breathes in and out, fast short breaths. He reads them quietly, his words whipped away by his breath. He stalls. His eyes go misty. Then he starts to weep as though he is a small boy. I stop the recording and I hold his hands tightly. As his cries intensify, I wrap my arms around him and this old man cries on my shoulder like a boy. He's exhausted when he's finished reading and weeping.

'Bert,' I say gently. 'I really don't want to say this, but have you got lotion?'

He wipes his wet eyes, confused.

'If we're going to keep up this cover story I'm going to have to leave those feet looking happier.'

He chuckles again. And in one second, sorrow can mutate to joy.

16

In the stationery shop, I stare at the shelves of writing paper. So many different types: coated, uncoated, laid, bond or woven. Gloss, silk, matt, patterned or parallel lines. Smooth or textured. Pastels or strong primary colours. Which size? My mind blurs. It's only paper, what does it matter? Of course it matters. It matters more than anything. Bert has six notes for Rita. One pack of fancy cards contains four. Why four? Why not five? So I need two packets. But will the extra four allow for enough mistakes? Perhaps I should buy three packets. The envelopes come in packs of seven. Why seven? And can I print on this paper?

My hands tremble as I scour the shelves, trying to find matching envelopes. Self-adhesive, or folded; two versions of myself. A challenge, a dare. Choose this and it defines you. Which is best? To stick myself together again, or fold and admit defeat?

Gerry would have done this. He would have gone shopping for the small cards that contained his notes and letters, knowing it was for me to read after his death. Did he choose just any paper or did he care? Was he pragmatic about it? Was he emotional? Did he request assistance or was he sure? Organised? Excited, or sad?

Suddenly my mind is full of questions I'd never considered before. Did he grab the first packet of notecards that he saw? Did he have a practice round? Did he make mistakes and rip them up angrily? Did he have other options that never made it to the final ten? Did he make a list? How long did he plan it? Was it all in one day? A spur of the moment decision, or did he take his time? There were no errors in his notes, he must have taken his time, or made a few attempts. I never did find the attempts. He wrote with blue pen, did he experiment with other colours? Did the blue mean something to him? Should it have meant something to me? Did he even care what colour or what paper he was using, did he know how much I would analyse every single part of his gifts?

Did he stand here, crying, a cane keeping him upright, as my crutches do now, feeling dizzy, scouring the shelves of paper, just fucking paper, trying to find a way to communicate to ensure he'll be remembered. Worrying about not being remembered. Grasping at every last straw to lengthen his life when he ran out of treatments, terrified of being forgotten. Thinking his whole life has come to this moment, choosing paper for his final words for a person he'll never see again.

'Are you OK?' asks the sales assistant.

'Yes,' I say, angrily, wiping my eyes roughly. 'Superglue. I also need superglue.'

★　★　★

I call Joy and apologise for deserting them. I reveal my change of heart. She is gracious and appreciative, despite my abandoning them for

133

such a long time when time of all things is most precious in their lives. I arrive early for the club in Joy's home, before everyone else turns up, and ask her to give me time alone so that I can set up the conservatory.

I remove the stationery from the shopping bags, discard the packaging and lay the paper, cards and envelopes out neatly and in line on the table. I place a bunch of fresh flowers and light some candles between the little piles of stationery. I sprinkle petals around the stationery. The room smells of fresh avocado and lime. When I'm finished, I step back. It's like a papyral sacrificial offering; a handwritten note for a life.

They've all arrived, minus Bert, while I've been working, and they wait patiently in the kitchen. It's taking me longer to set up than I expected. It's more of a moment than I ever could have imagined, and now that I'm feeling it, I want to make it as good as it can be. I call them all into the room, Joy leading the way. She halts when she sees the display.

'Oh,' she says, hand going to her chest, her open palm across her heart.

Paul folds his arms and his jaw works as the emotion takes over. His eyes survey the display. Ginika holds on tightly to Jewel in her arms.

Joy reaches out to touch the pages, she walks along the edge of the table, fingertips trailing the tips of the pages. She picks one up, feels it, places it down again. It's hypnotic, watching her. Paul and Ginika don't move, don't dare distract her. It's a moment. Then suddenly Joy lets out a sob and dissolves. We all rush to her and Paul

134

gets to her before I do, she falls against him, weak in his arms. I stand back, shaken. Then Ginika too steps forward and wraps her free arm around Joy. Paul widens his arm and welcomes them into his embrace.

Tears prick my eyes.

They're running out of time, but they're running out of time together.

When they break up, they wipe their eyes, laughing, embarrassed, and blow their noses.

Ginika moves closer to the table. 'Which one do you like, Jewel?' She lowers herself to a level where Jewel can reach the paper. Jewel looks at the table, at all the pretty colours and reaches her hands out, kicks her feet excitedly at something new. She reaches for the pink, bangs her hand on the surface as though playing a drum. Then she quickly grabs the paper and crumples it, raises it high in the air, shakes it up and down.

Ginika grins. 'You like that?'

Jewel lowers the paper from above her head and studies it, eyes wide. She crumples it in her hand, curiously feeling its texture.

'We've chosen ours,' Ginika says, confidently.

'Job done,' Paul says, 'Well done, Jewel.'

It's only paper, but it's not. They're only words, but they're not. We're only here for such a short time, the paper will outlive us all, it will scream, shout, roar, sing our thoughts, feelings, frustrations, and all the things that go unsaid in life. The paper will act as a messenger for their loved ones to read and hold; words from a mind, controlled by a beating heart. Words mean life.

17

I set up the books and papers that I have bought in preparation for Ginika's first reading and writing lesson. I'm nervous. I'm not a teacher. I have always felt I've absorbed more from others than I've given. I've researched as much as I could about adult literacy, and the best books to help teach the early stages of reading. But that advice is for a beginner, I know that Ginika may have dyslexia from her own personal explanation, and for that I am completely unqualified. I don't know the practices, tricks and tools to give her, and I would assume a test to learn her levels is the most responsible way to go. She has a year at most to learn what children learn over a few years, but I've given her my word.

My phone rings and I check the caller ID. I guess it's Ginika cancelling and I'm almost hoping for that. Instead it's Gabriel.

'Shit.'

I watch it ringing, consider ignoring it and then decide that will be worse.

'Hello?'

'Hi.'

Silence.

'It's been a week. I miss you. I don't like arguing, you and I never argue.'

'I know. I miss you too.'

'Can I come over?' he asks again.

'Oh. Um. Now?'

'Yeah. You at home?'

'Yes, but . . . ' I squeeze my eyes shut knowing this won't go down well. 'I'd love to see you, but I've made arrangements with someone, they're coming over in a few minutes.'

'Who?'

'You don't know her, her name's Ginika.'

'From the club?'

'Yeah.'

He's silent. 'OK,' he says tightly. 'Call me when you can.' He ends the call.

I sigh. One step forward, two steps back.

Ginika arrives at 8 p.m., with Jewel in her arms and a baby bag across her body. Jewel gives me a beautiful smile.

'Hello, gorgeous,' I say, taking her tiny soft fingers. I welcome them into my home, leading them from the hall, through the living room to the dining room, but Ginika stops in the living room.

'You have a nice house,' she says, looking around.

I stand at the table, hinting at her to sit, but she takes her time nosily looking around. Her eyes rest on the framed wedding photos of Gerry and me on the wall.

'It's not usually so tidy, but I'm selling the house. I've everything hidden away, so don't open a cupboard or my entire life will topple out.'

'That's Gerry,' she says.

'That's him.'

'He's handsome.'

'He was. And he knew it. Best-looking boy in

the class,' I say, smiling. 'I met him in school.'

'I know, when you were fourteen,' she says, continuing to study his photograph. Her eyes move to the single framed photograph of Gabriel and me, on the mantelpiece.

'Who's he?'

'My boyfriend, Gabriel.'

I stalled the house viewings during the two weeks while I recuperated but this week viewings have resumed. I usually remove all the photographs when prospective buyers are visiting the house. I'm private by nature, despite spilling my experiences of grief over a podcast, and prefer not to have people snooping through my personal items. If Ginika is this invasive before my very eyes, then I can't imagine what people do when I'm not here. I make a note to hide more things in better places.

'He's different,' she says, her eyes moving from Gabriel to Gerry.

'Polar opposites,' I agree, joining her in the living room, sensing she's going to take her time.

She examines Gabriel closely, then her eyes run slowly over Gerry. Comparison is natural, I suppose, I'm not the only one who does it.

'In what way?'

I'm not in the mood to analyse Gabriel right now. 'Gabriel's much taller,' I say with a sigh.

'That's it?' She arches an eyebrow.

'And older.'

'Moving.' Dissatisfied with my response, she looks around to continue her inspection.

'It's late,' I say, leading her to the dining table again. 'When does Jewel sleep?'

138

'When we get home.'

'That will be late,' I say, concerned.

'We always go to bed at the same time.'

'Do you want to put her down while we work? I can get a blanket. She's not crawling yet, is she?'

'No. I have a baby mat in my bag but she's OK for the time being.'

Gabriel noticed during our first dates that I kept my jacket on when I was nervous. He said he knew he could stop worrying about me leaving as soon as my jacket came off. I never noticed that, I always thought I was just cold, that my body needed a moment to adjust to the restaurant's temperature, but he was right, it was my need to adjust to the entire situation. We had to work towards that first reveal, which I suppose is how relationships go; at some point you both feel safe enough to remove a layer, reveal a little more. For Ginika, I can see that Jewel is her jacket, her security blanket. I don't think I've ever seen her without her in her arms and never with a buggy.

She expertly removes her baby bag from across her body while holding Jewel and walks slowly towards the dining table, eyeing it distrustfully as if it's a ticking time bomb. I can tell she's nervous, trying to put the moment off.

'Are you left-handed or right-handed?' I haven't been able to judge, Ginika has been so adept at managing everything with both hands as she switches a busy Jewel from one hip to the other.

'Right. Maybe I should try my left. Maybe that

was the problem.' She laughs, nervously.

I examine her for differences since I last saw her. I expected her to have lost weight but she is bloated, probably from the drugs.

'First off, the best advice I can give you is that I could help you find a tutor.' I'd looked into it. I'm far from having extras in my wallet but I could subsidise a lesson a week if I cut back on unnecessary online shopping spends. 'They'd know exactly what they're doing and could speed the process up.'

'No. I prefer you. I'll work really hard. I promise.'

'I don't doubt you at all, it's me I'm worried about.'

'Holly,' she says, wide-eyed, 'I only want to write a fucking letter. We can do this.' She claps her hands encouragingly.

I smile, buoyed by her enthusiasm.

Jewel imitates by clapping her hands.

'Good girl!' Ginika laughs. 'Clap handies!'

'Do you want to put her down?'

I can tell the answer is no by the look on her face.

'I bought her a little light reading too, to keep her occupied.' I hand her *My First Book*, a soft padded-page book for babies. Jewel takes it in her chubby hands, her eyes wide and immediately stimulated by the apple on the front.

'A-a-apple,' I say to Jewel.

'A-a-a,' she repeats.

Ginika's eyes widen. 'See? You can do it. I've always wanted to read her a book. I can only look at the pictures and make the stories up.'

140

'I think you'll find that's what most kids want. They like improvisation.'

'Did you want to have children?'

I pause. 'Yes. We did.'

'Why didn't you?'

'We were going to start trying just before they found the tumour.'

'Fuck.'

'What about you?'

'Did I want children?' she says, amused.

'I mean, was she planned or . . . ?'

'Did I plan to get pregnant at fifteen and have a baby at sixteen? No, Holly, I didn't. It was a one-night stupid mistake. When my ma and da found out, they wanted nothing to do with me. I brought shame on our family.' She rolls her eyes.

'I'm sorry.'

She shrugs. Whatever. 'They found the cancer when I was pregnant. They wouldn't give me treatment because it would harm her.'

'But you started treatment after she was born?'

'Radiation. Then chemo.'

'What about Jewel's dad? Is he around?'

'I don't want to talk about him,' Ginika says, turning to Jewel. Jewel responds by touching her mother's lips, and then pulling at them. Ginika pretends to gobble them and Jewel giggles.

I straighten the baby mat on the floor beside us. A quilted play rug with mirrors, zips, tags, squeezy things that squeak, and enough to keep her occupied. At the sight of the mat, Jewel becomes agitated.

'I told you,' Ginika says, nervously. 'Honestly,

she'll become a different baby as soon as I let her go.'

I wonder if it's more that Jewel is picking up on how Ginika's body has tensed at the idea of placing her down. As soon as Ginika sets her on the floor, the easy and happy-go-lucky beauty transforms into a bomb that instantly explodes and screams with such ferocity that even I want to pick her up, anything to stop the sound and her apparent pain.

I lift her and the crying continues, torture to my ears. Jewel wriggles and pushes, such strength for someone so small, arching her back and throwing herself backwards, practically out of my arms. As soon as Ginika takes her, she quietens, her shaking breaths and sniffles the only give-away to her ordeal. She buries her head in Ginika's chest, not looking anyone in the eye for fear she'll be moved again.

I look on in amazement.

'Jewel!'

Jewel ignores me. She knows what she's done.

'I told you,' Ginika says, consoling her. 'Possessed child.'

Which is putting it politely.

'OK,' I take a deep breath. 'So we do this with her on your lap.'

It's almost 9 p.m. and Jewel is content again but she yaps, babbles, reaches for the paper, the pens, pulls everything within reach to the floor. She rips a page from Ginika's notepad. But every time Ginika places her down on the mat, the legs-being-sawn-off sound starts up again and it doesn't stop even when we wait. Two minutes, three minutes, five minutes is our maximum, she is as stubborn each time. I'm no super-nanny but even I know that putting her down and rewarding her with cuddles to silence her is the wrong message. She's winning every time. She's a tough cookie, and as much as she's her mother's comfort blanket she's also her weakness. With someone pulling at her physically and emotionally, Ginika understandably can't concentrate. I can barely think. We finish at 10 p.m., further behind than even my most negative thoughts had forecast. I'm exhausted.

As I open the door into the dark night, I try to keep a positive spin on it.

'Practise everything we've done tonight and go over and over the sounds.'

Ginika nods. There are dark circles under her eyes; she can't look me in the eye. I'm sure she's about to cry as soon as I close the door.

It's late. It's dark. It's cold. The bus stop is a walk away. She has no buggy. I long to have a bath and go to bed, hide my head from the scene I've just lived. Cringe in private. If anyone had seen me — Gabriel, Sharon, anyone — they would have told me I was fighting a losing battle, nothing at all to do with Ginika's abilities and everything to do with own my lack thereof. But I can't close the door on them. I grab my keys and tell her I'm driving her home.

'Can you drive with that thing?' She looks at my cast.

'I've found a way to do everything with this thing,' I say with an irritated grimace. 'Except cycling. I miss cycling.'

143

I drive Ginika home to North Circular Road. It takes twenty minutes in light traffic at the late hour. Ginika would have had to get two buses, and be home after 11 p.m. Suddenly my plan of slotting other people in at a time to suit me seems less angelic and more selfish. I'm embarrassed that I've asked this trek of her. Though we all have to take responsibility for our own lives, I'm not sure I can allow a sixteen-year-old extremely ill young mother to make these decisions for herself.

I stop at a terraced house, minutes from Phoenix Park, minutes from Phibsboro village. It's a period-style house but it lost its glory a long time ago. It's dirty and damp-looking, the garden has an abandoned look, with grass rising so high the building seems derelict. A group of boys hang around the entrance steps.

'How many people live in there?'

'Don't know. There's four studio rooms and three single rooms. The council sorted it for me. Mine's the basement flat.'

I look to where the steps lead to darkness.

'Nice neighbours?' I ask hopefully.

She snorts.

'Are your family close by?'

'No and it wouldn't matter if they were. I told you: we've hardly spoken since the day I told them I was pregnant.'

I had been watching her in the rear-view mirror but now I turn around.

'They do know that you're ill, don't they?'

'Yes. They said that I made my bed and now I have to lie in it. My ma said it was

144

punishment for having a baby.'

'Ginika,' I say, utterly disgusted.

'I dropped out of school. Hung out with the wrong people. Got pregnant, got cancer. They think it's God's way of punishing me. You know Ginika means 'What can be greater than God?'' She rolls her eyes. 'My parents are very religious. They moved here twenty years ago to give me opportunities and they say I wasted them. I'm better off without them.' She opens the car door, struggles to pull herself out with the bag and the baby, and as I sit there, stunned, it occurs to me that I should have helped her, but she moves faster than I'm able to with my cast.

I open my door. 'Ginika,' I call out firmly and she stops. 'They're going to care for Jewel though, aren't they?'

'No,' she says, her eyes flat. 'They never cared for her from the second they knew about her, they're not going to start caring about her when I'm gone. They don't deserve her.'

'So who's taking Jewel?'

'Social have sorted a foster family. She goes to them when I'm in treatment. But you don't have to worry about that bit,' she says. 'You only need to worry about teaching me to write.'

I watch her walk across the courtyard to the steps. The gang part just enough for her to squeeze through and she pushes past them. Words are exchanged. Ginika has enough attitude to beat them away. I glare at the gang angrily, the best suburban middle-class idiotic scare that I can muster, and contemplate

145

attacking them with a crutch.

Then I quickly lock the doors.

★   ★   ★

It would be a lie to say that I did not lie in bed weighing up whether I should offer to take care of Jewel for Ginika, to promise her a life of love, comfort, support and promise of a safe future. I should have heroically made the gallant gesture of offering to be her guardian. But I am not that person. I am not that pure. I thought about it, entertained the notion and all of its possible angles for at least seven minutes in a detailed daydream where all versions were analysed comprehensively. But no matter how I altered the daydream, this terribly lucid daydream, my final decision was still no. I worry about Jewel, I worry about her future, who will care for her, who will love her, whether she will be placed in safe and loving arms or whether her life will be terribly impacted by a series of foster homes and a feeling of displacement in the world, a loss of identity, like a feather blowing in the wind with no one to lift or anchor her. These haunting thoughts dominate my mind far longer and with greater intensity than the daydream of caring for her myself.

But all thoughts lead to the same conclusion. Just because I've had my share of problems, I cannot become a fixer. Gabriel is right on one thing: that behaviour would be unhealthy. If my involvement in the club is to be a success, I can't become too involved. I have to rein myself in and

146

be realistic. I agreed to help the PS, I Love You Club with writing their letters, not their lives.

My mission — my gift to Jewel and Ginika — will be for Jewel to have a letter, handwritten to her, by her mother, to have and to hold, wherever in the world Jewel may end up.

18

Richard, my eldest and most dependable brother, arrives at my house twenty minutes early. We greet, awkwardly, as if we've just met, the only way you can ever greet my socially challenged brother. This half-hug is made awkward because of the large toolbox in his hand, weighing him down on one side, and even more so because I'm dressed in a bath towel, dripping with water from the shower that I had to abandon midway through to go down the stairs on my behind to answer the door because he's early, and with the cast on my ankle, showering is no easy feat. I've covered my cast with plastic wrap and sealed it at the top and bottom with elastic bands to prevent the water from dripping down my leg. The itching in my leg is intensifying and I wonder if I should have been more careful the past few weeks to protect the cast from water. To add salt to my wounds, my lower back is paining me from the pressure I'm placing on it with the crutches, and I can't sleep properly, though I don't know if that's solely because of my ankle or because of everything else going on.

Between avoiding banging the toolbox against my leg, and trying to avoid my wet body, Richard doesn't know which way to look or lean. I lead him to the living room, and start to tell him what I need him to help me with, but he can't focus.

'Why don't you . . . fix yourself first?'

I roll my eyes. Patience. It is true that we revert to the childhood versions of ourselves with family members. At least it's true of me. I spent most of my adolescence — and twenties, for that matter — rolling my eyes at my very particular brother. I hop back towards the stairs.

Dry and dressed, I meet him in the living room where he can look me in the eye properly.

'I want to take down these photo frames but they're, I don't know, screwed to the wall,' I explain.

'Screwed to the wall,' he repeats, looking at them.

'I don't know the terminology. They're not on a string, hanging on a nail like the others, is what I mean. The photographer hung them for me, like he was afraid they'd fall off in an earthquake, as if that would ever happen.'

'You know there was an earthquake twelve years ago, twenty-seven kilometres off the coast of Wicklow in the Irish Sea with a three-point-two magnitude, which was ten kilometres deep.'

He looks at me and I know that he's finished speaking. He mainly speaks in statements, and rarely opens these up for discussion. I don't think he realises this; he probably wonders why he doesn't get responses. His conversations work like this: I deliver some information, then you deliver some information. Any following of natural links away from the subject is liable to confuse him. To his mind, these digressions from the main topic of discussion are not valid.

'Really? I didn't know we had earthquakes in Ireland.'

'There were zero reports from the public.'

I laugh. He looks at me, confused, he didn't intend it as a joke.

'The largest earthquake to hit Ireland was in 1984, the Llyn Peninsula earthquake, which measured five-point-four on the Richter scale. It was the largest known onshore earthquake to occur in Ireland since instrumental measurements began. Dad says they woke up when their bed slid across the floor and hit the radiator.'

I snort with laughter. 'I can't believe I didn't know that.'

'I made you tea,' he says suddenly, pointing to the coffee table. 'It should still be hot.'

'Thanks, Richard.' I sit down on the couch and sip. It's perfect.

He studies the wall and tells me what screws are in and what he'll need. I listen but don't absorb any of it.

'Why do you want to take them down?' he asks, and I know that this is not a personal question; he's asking because he wonders about the wall, perhaps about the frame, something that will have a bearing on his taking them down. It's not a question about *feelings*. But I live and think more in feelings and less in function.

'Because people are viewing the house and I want to protect my privacy.' Despite having discussed my private life in front of an audience and allowing it to be made available online for everyone to hear.

150

'You've already had viewings.'

'I know.'

'Did the estate agent advise this?'

'No.'

He looks at me for more.

'It just seemed unfair, to me, that when people come to the house I hide the photo of Gabriel and me in a drawer but Gerry stays on the wall. If I'm putting one man away, I should put them both away,' I say, knowing how ludicrous that would sound to somebody like Richard.

He looks at the photograph of Gabriel on the mantelpiece but doesn't respond, which I suppose I expected. We don't usually have deep and meaningful chats.

Richard gets to work drilling the wall and I do some ironing in the adjoining dining room, where I pile my washing when people aren't viewing the house.

'I met Gabriel for a drink last night,' he says suddenly, unscrewing his drill bit and replacing it with another. His actions are slow, methodical, sturdy.

'Really?' I look at him in surprise.

I don't think Gerry and Richard had ever been for a drink in all the years we were together. Not alone anyway. And even when together, it was my brother Jack that Gerry was drawn to. Jack was my cool brother, easy, affable, handsome, and Gerry looked up to him when we were teenagers. Richard, to Gerry and me, was the difficult, wooden, rather nerdish, boring brother.

After Gerry's death, that changed. Richard stepped up. I was able to identify with him more as he navigated divorce, the loss of his sturdy predictable life, and I counselled him through new life choices. Jack, in comparison, seemed shallow, unable to reach the great depths that I needed or expected. People can surprise you when you suffer through grief. It's not true that you discover who your friends are, but it's true to say that their characters are revealed. Gabriel is always pleasant to Jack, but he's allergic to his smart-suited and booted business friends. He says he doesn't trust a man who carries an umbrella. Richard smells of grass, and moss, and soil, salt-of-the-earth scents that Gabriel can trust.

'Did Jack go too?'

'No.'

'Declan?'

'Just Gabriel and me, Holly.'

He drills again and I impatiently wait.

He stops drilling, doesn't say anything as if he's forgotten.

'Where did you go?'

'The Gravediggers.'

'You went to the Gravediggers?'

'Gabriel likes his Guinness. They serve the best Guinness in Dublin.'

'Who arranged it?'

'I suggested the Gravediggers, but I assume you mean the meeting. Gabriel called me. Quite nice. We'd been meaning to connect since Christmas. He's a man of his word.'

He turns the drill on again.

'Richard!' I shout and he turns it off. 'Is he OK?'

'Yes. A bit going on with his daughter.'

'Yes,' I reply, distracted. 'Was that what it was about? Divorce talk?' Richard's children are nothing like Ava. They sing in choirs, play cello and piano. If you asked them about sambuca, they'd ask what key to play it in. His wife had broken his heart even further when she married an acquaintance of theirs, a professor of Economics. 'Or was it about the car accident? I think he's dealing with it worse than I am.' I want to ask if it was about the PS, I Love You Club, which would be the obvious issue, but in case it's not, I don't want to have to bring it up and therefore discuss it. Richard missed the family conversation at Sunday lunch and to my knowledge it hasn't been brought up again.

'A little bit of all those things,' he says. 'But mostly he's concerned about the club you have befriended.'

'Ah, I see. And what did you tell him?'

'Your shirt is on fire.'

'What does that mean?'

'Your shirt, on the ironing board,' he points.

'Oh, flip it,' I lift the iron from my T-shirt, revealing a burn mark on the fabric. I always do stupid things in Richard's company and use expressions like 'flip it' as though we're in an Enid Blyton book. I don't know whether it's that I always do stupid things and only notice in his company, or if it's his company that brings it out in me.

'You should soak it immediately in cold water for twenty-four hours. Wet the scorch mark with

153

hydrogen peroxide, wet a clean white cloth with peroxide then place it over the scorched fabric and iron it lightly. Should get rid of the burn.'

'Thank you.' I have no intention of doing any of that. This T-shirt is now officially a bed T-shirt.

He notes that I don't do anything he has suggested. He sighs. 'I told Gabriel that it's a very courageous, giving and valiant thing for you to do.'

I smile.

He lifts and removes the picture frame. 'But that's what I told him. I *think* you should tread carefully. Everyone seems to be afraid you'll lose yourself, but you should consider it being *him* you lose as a result of doing it.'

I look at him, surprised by this rare display of emotional intelligence, and then realise conversations about me are being had behind my back. *Everyone* is afraid I'll lose myself. And which is more important, finding myself or losing Gabriel?

The moment has passed and Richard's looking at the wall.

It's covered in deep, ugly holes from where the screws punctured the wall, the paint colour darker than the faded paint that surrounds it. It also seems that my photographer had made several other attempts to get a screw through and failed.

Six ugly scars in the surface.

I place the iron back in its holder and stand beside Richard.

'That looks awful.'

154

'The photographer appears to have struggled. He hit the lath a few times — the wooden strips behind the wall.'

There are four more frames to be removed; in our failure to cull mementos of our magnificent wedding day from the hundreds of options, they cover the entire alcove.

'The holes need filler and then to be sanded and painted. Do you still have the same paint?'

'No.'

'Would you choose another paint for the wall?'

'Then that would be different to all the other walls. We'd have to paint the two rooms.'

'The two alcoves, maybe. Or you could wallpaper over it.'

I ruffle my nose. Too much effort for a house I'm selling for the new people to move in and repaint anyway. 'The buyers are going to want to repaint anyway. Do you have filler in your toolbox?'

'No, but I could get it this afternoon and come back tomorrow.'

'I have a house viewing tonight.'

He leaves it up to me.

I look at the scars on my wall that had been hidden beneath our happy, smiling, wrinkle-free glowing faces. I sigh.

'Can you put it back up?'

'Indeed. But I suggest hanging it on one nail. I don't trust drilling it back into the holes, and I don't want to make new ones,' he says, rubbing his fingers over the enormous gashes.

I give up on the ironing and watch as Richard hammers in a nail and then hangs the photo in

155

the alcove, back where it was. Gerry and me, heads together, beaming. Posing by the sea on Portmarnock beach, across the road from the house I grew up in, beside the Links Hotel where we had our reception. Gazing into each other's eyes. Mum and Dad beside us, Mum grinning, Dad caught mid-blink, the only one where he didn't have his eyes closed. Gerry's parents too, his mum's stiff smile, his dad's awkward feet. Sharon and Denise as brides-maids. The same archetypal photos from so many wedding albums all around the world, and yet we thought we were special. We were special.

Richard steps back and surveys his work. 'Holly, if you're worried about balance, you could leave Gabriel's photograph out on the mantelpiece. It would be considerably easier to make that amendment than the former.'

I appreciate his suggestion. He cares. 'Me cuddling up to two different men, Richard; what would that say about me?'

I wasn't really looking for an answer. It was implied in the question, but he surprises me.

He pushes his glasses up the bridge of his nose with his forefinger. 'Love is a tenuous, rarefied thing. Something to be prized and cherished, displayed for all to see, not hidden away in a cupboard, or to feel ashamed of. The photographs of both men would perhaps say to others — not that you should bother your mind with those thoughts — that you are considerably fortunate to have the indubitable honour of safeguarding the love of not one, but two men in your heart.'

156

He goes to his knees to tidy the contents of his toolbox.

'I have no idea who you are or what you've done to my brother, but thank you, strange being, for visiting us here and departing these wise words from the shell of his body.' I hold out my hand to him, professional, businesslike. 'Please be sure to return him to his original state before you leave.'

He gives me one of his rare smiles, his solemn face creasing, and shakes his head.

★　★　★

Later that night, when I'm in bed, I hear a smash. With Gabriel's phone number ready to dial, terrified the house has been broken into, I grab my crutch, intending to use it as a weapon, and try to make my way quietly downstairs in the dark, which is difficult and turns out to be clumsy and noisy as the crutch whacks against the wooden bars of the banister. By the time I've reached the bottom of the staircase, I'm sure my sleuthing has been audible from the end of the street. Heart pounding, I flick the light switch in the living room.

Turns out the photographer knew what we didn't. His flimsy string wasn't strong enough to carry the weight of his heavy frame and glass. Gerry and I lie on the floor covered in broken glass. Gerry and I are all dolled up, me covered in layers of make-up, posed, with limbs placed at awkward but meaningful angles. My hand on his heart, ring on display, his eyes looking into mine,

157

our family surrounding us. If I was to do it all again, I wouldn't do that. We were more real than that, but it wasn't captured.

Then there's Gabriel and me, relaxed, laughing, hair blowing across our faces, more natural, frown lines and freckles visible. Our photo is a selfie with an indistinct background. I chose to frame it because I liked how happy we look. He beams at me from the mantelpiece, and seems to snuggle me more closely, smug at his win.

19

Of all the areas in the shop, the trinket display is my favourite. It's an old drawer unit that Ciara found, a chunky old-school dresser with three wide heavy drawers and on top stands a discoloured mirror that is so covered in black spots you can't see your face. I love this unit, and chose it specially for the trinkets. The top of the unit contains pieces, the first drawer is pulled out slightly and also displays items, the second drawer a little more and the bottom drawer all the way out, so that it dips because of the weight and sits on the floor. The owner said her mother used the bottom drawer as a cot for her babies. This is the section children are drawn to, but nothing is of any significant value — not that we know of, anyway — and usually items are priced at twenty euros or less. My favourite pieces are the pillboxes, compact mirrors, jewellery boxes and decorative spoons, along with the hair-slides and brooches which are specific to this area and not to be placed in the jewellery section. A new arrival perfect for this trinket display is a jewellery box that I discover wrapped up in newspaper, in a cardboard box. It is mirrored, the lid is embellished with crystals, emerald, rubies and diamonds, of the costume variety. Inside is a velvet insert with sections for individual pieces, where some of the jewels that have fallen off the top sit snugly. I give a gentle tug and the velvet insert lifts, allowing it to be used as a box.

'What you got there, magpie?' Ciara interrupts my thoughts. Today she is dressed as a 1940s glamour puss, all red lipstick and a black-netted head veil, a shoulder-padded dress that squishes her boobs up the V-shaped neck, a leopard-print belt sucks her waist in and sends her hips oozing out. She wears this with floral print Doc Martens.

I lift the box to show her. She examines it, leaving fingerprints where I've already cleaned it.

'Pretty.'

'I'm going to buy it,' I say quickly, before she suggests keeping it.

'OK,' she hands it back.

'How much?'

'Work overtime tonight for free?' she asks hopefully.

I laugh. 'I'm going for dinner with Gabriel. It's been a while, so I'm not cancelling.'

'OK, well if you can't work tonight, you can't have the box.' She pulls it away as I dive clumsily for it.

'Ow,' I wince, hurting my ankle in the process.

She dangles it higher in the air.

'I'm going to report you for employee bullying.'

She sticks out her tongue and hands me back the box. 'Fine, I'll ask Mathew. Good luck with Gabriel, and tell him I'm . . . ' she pauses as I throw her a warning look. She thinks Gabriel is angry with her for making me take part in the podcast, and therefore angry with her for my

160

involvement with the club. I keep telling her to stop apologising, he's not angry with her, just me, but I don't think that's true. He seems to be irritable with everyone these days.

'Tell him you're what?' I ask.

'Nothing,' she finishes her sentence.

'Easy. I tell him you're nothing all the time,' I grin, wiping her fingerprints off the mirror.

★ ★ ★

At one of our regular spots, Cucino, an Italian bistro near his house, I find Gabriel seated outside. It's a cool evening but the gas heaters give it a greenhouse effect and make it feel as though we're in the midst of a balmy Italian summer.

He kisses me and helps me into my chair, laying the crutches on the ground beside us. I scan the menu and choose instantly. I always get the same thing. Gnocchi in burned butter and sage sauce. I wait while Gabriel chooses his dish. He's leaning over the menu, forehead furrowed in deep thought and concentration but his eyes aren't moving over the words. I watch him pretending to study the menu. He lifts his glass and takes an enormous slug of wine, then eyes back to the menu, back to the same place. I study the bottle on the table. Two glasses gone already.

'What do you call a zoo with one dog?' I ask, finally breaking the silence.

'Hmm?' He looks up.

'What do you call a zoo with one dog?'

161

He looks at me blankly.

'A shih-tzu,' I say, smiling.

He has no idea what I'm talking about.

'A shih-tzu. *Shit. Zoo.*'

'Holly, I don't . . . what are you talking about?'

'It's a joke!'

'Oh. OK.' He smiles a little, a vague one, and returns his attention to the menu.

The arrival of the waitress to take our order is the only break in the silence. We order, hand the menus back to the waitress and then he twists his hands and fingers together, fidgeting. And then it occurs to me. He's nervous. I pour his wine to give him a moment to collect himself, but he seems to get worse as he waits, making trumpet-like sounds as he fills his upper lip with air, then stopping to drum the counter un-rhythmically with his forefingers, before resuming his odd in-out lip movements.

The waitress brings bruschetta and chopped tomatoes to the table while we wait for our main course. Seemingly relieved to have a new distraction, he turns his attention to the food, busies himself with balsamic vinegar and olive oil, giving it more attention than he ever has before. He starts playing with his food, separating the chopped tomatoes from the tiny pieces of basil, a wall built from crumbs in between, a precarious structure that rises and stumbles. He studies the increasingly interesting bruschetta. Basil to the left, tomatoes to the right. Crumbs down the centre.

I lean in. 'What's going on, Gabriel?'

He pushes his finger down on the crumbs on

162

his plate, gathering them on his finger, then dusts them off, sprinkling them back to where they were.

'Are you going to act like this the entire time I help the PS, I Love You Club? You don't even know what I'm doing with them. Do you want to ask some questions? You don't even know their names.'

'It's not that,' he says firmly, abandoning the bruschetta and pushing his plate away. 'It's Ava.' He leans in, elbows on the table, hands and fingers pressed together as if in prayer, and rests them over his lips. 'She wants to move in with me.'

'Move in?'

He nods.

'With you?'

Nods again.

'Into the house?'

'Yes.' He looks confused. Of course, where else would she live?

My head races. *I'm* supposed to move into the house.

'She asked me a few weeks ago,' he says, avoiding my eye, and I realise the reason for his distance. It had nothing to do with the accident, silly Holly, nothing to do with the club, he just let you think it was. So that's what all those meetings with Kate and Ava were about.

'Wow. Let me guess, you needed some time to think about it yourself first before telling me? This is familiar, isn't it?' And yet I feel as angry as he did when he accused me of creeping around behind him.

163

He ignores my bait and sticks to the issue at hand. 'You know there's been trouble with her and Kate. They're not getting along.'

'They haven't gotten along for the two years that I've known you.'

'It has gone up a level. Many levels,' he says, shaking his head. 'It's like . . . ' He waves his hands and makes an explosion sound with his mouth.

His eyes still won't meet mine. He's told her yes. It's already been agreed. So he meant it when he said we'd just do our own thing from now on, without discussing it first. Payback for the club.

'Ava living with you means you being home all the time, getting her up and out of bed, getting her to school on time. Getting her to study. Keeping an eye on her.'

'She's sixteen, Holly, not six.'

'She doesn't get out of bed, she wouldn't go to school if she wasn't dragged in every day, you told me that. She'll want to go to a party every weekend. You'll have to speak to parents, get to know her friends, collect her in the early hours of the morning, or sit up waiting for her.'

'I know, I'm not an idiot, I know how to be a dad,' he says firmly. 'I told her I need to speak with you first before finalising everything, but then there was the accident and lately you've been . . . busy every time I call.'

'Sorry,' I sigh. There's so much I have to tell him, about Bert, about Ginika, my secret life that he's had no part of but only because I've felt like it's off limits. Talk of it before angered him.

164

'Look, it's fine with me. She's your daughter, I'm happy for you that this is happening, I know it's important to you. I'm OK with her moving in with us, as long as you know what you're getting yourself into.'

He looks at me then, finally eye contact, his expression soft and apologetic. 'You see, that's the thing.'

It slowly dawns on me.

Ava is moving in *instead* of me.

'She needs me.' He places his hand on my forearm, holds me tightly. I want to spear his hand with my pasta fork. 'I can't turn my back on her after waiting so long for Ava to come to me for help. Kate and Finbar are getting married. She can't stand Finbar. She hates being in the house. She's all over the place, messing up at school, failing exams, partying. I'm afraid I fucked her up and I need to fix it.'

My heart pounds.

He tries a gentler, more apologetic tone. 'Ava and I need space to figure it out and find our way together. If the three of us were living together during this transition, it would be too much for us all.'

'So how long will this *transition* take, do you think?'

He shakes his head and looks to the distance, as if calculating the required transitional days in his virtual mind calendar.

'I don't know. Maybe the best thing would be to wait until she finishes school. I think,' he adds quickly before I bellow, 'that I need to help her through school. And then when she's calmed

165

down and starts university, you and I can do what we like. You and I have lived like this for two years already, we can keep going as we were. It works this way for us, too, doesn't it?' He reaches for my hands, squeezes them.

I free my hands, frustrated by his grip. 'Two years,' I say, looking at him in surprise. 'Two years? I'm selling my house to live with *you*. You've been asking me for the past six months. It was *your* idea!'

'I know, I know.' It's obvious from his pained expression that he doesn't want to do this to me, and I don't want to blame him for this situation. Any dad would do the same; choose their child over everything. But this is really screwing up my plans.

'Maybe two years is too long. Maybe one year is more reasonable,' he says, trying to keep it calm.

'One year?' I splutter. 'What if I get an offer on the house tomorrow, where am I supposed to go? I need to make a plan. Do I search for a new place? Can I even afford one? Should I take if off the market? I mean, Jesus — ' I run my hands through my hair, suddenly realising the logistical nightmare I'm in. And of all the things I think of, I think of the holes in my wall that I now have to fix when I thought they would be someone else's problem. Of all the things, I even have to fix my own mistakes.

'Holly,' he says, his hand brushing my cheek. 'I'm not going anywhere. I need some time to help Ava settle. The rest of my life will be with you.'

I close my eyes. I tell myself he is not sick, he is not dying. Plans change. That's life. But I can't process this.

'I thought you might be a bit relieved to hear this.'

'Why the hell would I be relieved?'

'Because of this club you're involved with. You've barely had time for me.'

The waitress interrupts. 'Are you finished here?'

Oh yes. I am.

She clears the table in a tense silence as we stare at each other, and then she hurries away.

I twist in my chair and lean over awkwardly to pick up my crutches. I can't reach them. I strain my side and my fingers fumble on the ground to feel for them.

'What are you doing?'

'I'm trying to leave very fucking fast, but I fucking well can't,' I say through gritted teeth. I fumble again for the crutches, my fingers brush the handle but I push it away by mistake. 'For fuck sake!' I snap. The table to the right look at me. I ignore them.

Gabriel bends down to help.

'I don't want your help,' I mumble. But I need it. He passes the crutches across to me, but as I take hold of one end, he keeps his grip on the crutch, holding me there, playing tug of war with a crutch.

'Holly,' he says passionately, 'I'm not ending us. I need to hold back on the bigger plans for a while, that's all.'

'What are the bigger plans?' I ask, interested

now, raising my voice louder than I should. 'Are we going to get married, Gabriel? Are we going to have a baby? Just so I know what I'm sitting on my ass and waiting two years for.'

The anger in him rises, but he keeps his voice low. 'The two years, as I said, is open for discussion. I'm trying to be honest with you. I'm trying to deal with the child I actually have. I think we can talk about that another time, don't you?'

It's a funny moment to realise I want a child with him, and that I was hoping for so much more from this relationship. That two years longer places a panicked pressure on me and my body and my mind in a way that I never felt before. I've instantly lost something I didn't even know I wanted. It's being dangled in front of me, all of a sudden, this thing I hadn't previously realised that I want, only to reveal that I may not have it.

I awkwardly manoeuvre my way through the tables and chairs, my crutches getting caught on chair legs, people having to move out of the way so I can get by. It is anything but a graceful exit.

Perhaps he's done me a favour, perhaps we are better off cleaning up our messes alone. Ava back in his life, exactly as he wanted. And in a way, Gerry is back in mine. My life is so full, I think angrily, maybe there's no room for Gabriel any more.

20

I sit with Joy in her kitchen. We are alone, for the first time. Sunlight streams through the patio doors casting light on the table and floor. I'm bathed in scorching sun while the rest of the kitchen is in darkness. The dog lays in the sunlight, hogging the heat, curled in a ball, ears pricked, watching outside, occasionally sitting up and growling when a bird lands on his garden.

'Ginika tells me you've been spending a lot of time with her,' Joy says, stirring the peppermint teabag in the pot.

'We've met four times in the past two weeks. Has she told you what we're doing?' I wonder how secret these letters are supposed to be, if in sharing the concept with the group makes it less of a treasure for their loved ones. Bert had been open and confident to share his 'quiz' with them in the early stages but I don't know if the finalised contents are sacred. I recall how Joy had taken to the altar at Angela's funeral to lead the presentation, but it is unclear to me how involved they wished to be in each other's gestures. I've witnessed the support group as a sharing of ideas, an encouragement and way to lift one another up on each other's shoulders, then they part and think, return and share again. Perhaps my arrival to the club has meant that I am the one who is the sounding board and keeper of the secrets.

'No,' Joy shakes her head. 'Ginika likes her privacy. She's quiet, but formidable.'

'She is,' I agree. 'She chooses her moments and when I least expect it, she lands a clanger.'

'She does,' Joy laughs. 'She's a smart girl. A wonderful mother. I don't think I'd have had the gall to do what she does at sixteen, and alone.'

'I don't think I do now.'

She smiles. 'You've been through it, Holly.'

'Nothing made me feel more like a charlatan than being called a hero for surviving someone else's death. Gerry was the one that suffered.'

'Everyone suffers,' she says gently.

We leave a silence. She tries to grip the teapot to lift it and I see how she struggles. I place a hand over hers to stop her, and take over. Silent, she withdraws her hand and rubs at her wrist, a motion I'm familiar with.

'And you, Joy, how are you?'

'My condition, you mean?'

'I mean everything. You've been so thoughtful at organising everybody else, you make me forget that you are suffering too.'

She takes a moment, and I wonder if it's to decide how much to tell me. 'What do you know about Multiple Sclerosis?'

'I know that it's a neurological condition, but that it's different for everybody.'

She nods. 'MS is a progressive disease of the nervous system. It can cause a variety of symptoms, which may continue or worsen as the disease progresses. Fatigue, walking difficulties, changes in brain function, vision, depression, mood swings. There's no cure. Not currently.

Just palliative care, which helps prepare us for what lies ahead in the end stage.'

'Are you in pain?'

'Muscle spasms, nerve pain. Antidepressants for the neuro-pain spasms. I hate taking drugs, I never even used to take headache tablets. I do physiotherapy for the muscle spasms.'

'You were diagnosed nine years ago,' I say, looking at the dog and remembering how his age represented the time of her diagnosis.

'Yes, and you're right, MS is different for everyone, Holly. Someone can be stable for long periods of time. I was convinced I was fine even after diagnosis, that it was manageable, that my life wouldn't change, but then it advances and comes back with a stronger force. The stick helps me for the time being, but we have that on standby.'

I look across to the folded wheelchair by the door.

I reach out and hold her hand. 'I'm sorry we've lost time, Joy, but I'm here for you now, what can I do for you? How can I help you?'

'Oh, Holly, you being here is a gift to us all. You have re-energised us, given us a goal. Spending time with each of us and listening to us, and guiding us is more precious than you'll ever know, and you wouldn't be human if you didn't need time to think about it. I don't think we considered how life-altering asking you to be involved would be. I hope we haven't up-ended everything for you, have we?' she asks, her brow furrowing.

'Any problems I have are all my own doing.'

171

My smile twists, thinking of Gabriel.

'Angela was a very resilient woman,' Joy says. 'She was convinced she could achieve anything she put her mind to and getting you on board was a mission she took on with gusto. I only hope I didn't take up her challenge too selfishly.'

I agree, remembering how Angela had gripped my arm so tightly at the charity shop, her eyes boring into mine as she urged me to continue telling my story as if her life depended on it.

'The last thing you need to worry about is my life,' I say brightly. 'So, more importantly, have you decided what to write in your letters?'

'I think about them all the time but I'm no closer to knowing what to do. My boys will be OK, they have wives, families. My main concern is Joe. I'm worried about him. He'll be lost.'

I recall him fumbling around the kitchen on the first day I met him, trying to locate simple items, being hit on the head by a broom in search of milk. I try to imagine his home without his wife at the helm; despite his years living here, to him it will seem an alien environment filled with mysterious storage spaces.

'I've noticed he's a little lost domestically,' I say, as tactfully as I can.

Joy surprises me with laughter. 'You've noticed that already in the short time you've spent here. The children always tease him, but I take full responsibility for him being 'lost domestically'. I'm sure we seem very old fashioned to you,' she says, smiling. 'My sons are equal in everything in their homes, and with their children. But Joe and I always liked the way we are. While he was at

172

work, this was my territory. I was never good at sharing. I wash and clean his clothes, iron, make the dinners, do the food-shopping, cook, everything. I never used to let him do anything — not that he tried, because he had no interest. Since he retired, he's been under my feet. He means well, but it takes him a lifetime to find anything.' She grabs my arm, and leans in conspiratorially. 'Don't tell him, but sometimes when the pain is bad and I can't stand it, I ask for things that I know he'll take an age to find just so I can have some peace and to make him stop fussing. God forgive me.'

We laugh, a clandestine pair.

She ponders. 'I've been thinking about what you told us about your letters from Gerry, about them not being reminders of death but about how they enabled you. I want to give Joe a boost after I'm gone. We're not sentimental, Joe and I. I don't think slushy mushy love letters will be what he wants. I've tried to write them . . . ' She shudders. 'It's not our style. If anything, he'll think I must have lost my marbles. I want him to read them and feel as though it's me. But I'm not a writer, Holly,' she shakes her head. 'I don't have the imagination.'

'Gerry wasn't a writer either, believe me, but he was thoughtful. He knew me, he understood me, and that's all you need. I think you need to imagine Joe's life from his perspective and then try to decipher what gesture or words of comfort can make his tough times easier. We'll think of something, don't worry,' I say, mind wandering.

I recall how useless I felt after Gerry's death

173

when the heating broke down in the house or a bulb went. It's not that I was incapable, it's that we all have our duties in a household. We find our niche and we stay in it, and often, in the everyday busy-ness of life, we're unaware of what role the other plays, exactly what it is they do. In the case of Gerry and me, I always felt I was doing more than him, the same internal argument over and over. Only when he was gone did I realise the gaps, the extra things that I had never done and didn't know how to do. The phone numbers I didn't know, the codes, the accounts. Little things, normal, mundane, everyday acts that aided the flow of life. A Rentokil account. The Sky customer password. The phone number for a plumber. We each had our roles and Joy's role is changing considerably, of great consequence to Joe. I sit up, feeling inspired.

'You don't want grandiose declarations of love, so what if your letters were simple but effective? Guidelines for Joe. A map of where everything is in the kitchen. A list of what's in the cupboards. Where the ironing board is, how to iron his shirts.'

Her eyes light up.

'What's his favourite meal?'

'My shepherd's pie.'

My. In control in her home. Her home, her kitchen, her place. No room for Joe. 'How about a recipe and instructions so he can cook your shepherd's pie? A scrapbook to help him get through domestic hell without you.'

'I like it!' she exclaims, and claps her hands.

174

'It's exactly what he needs and it's fun too, he'll have a laugh, as well as being guided. Holly, that's perfect!'

'I think I would have benefited from a few less empowering letters from Gerry and more mundane notes about the day-to-day running of things in our life,' I say smiling. 'Joy's Scrapbook . . . Joy's Guidelines for Joe?'

She thinks, smiling and eyes twinkling, enjoying where her mind is travelling. 'Joy's Secrets,' she says finally.

'Joy's Secrets,' I repeat, smiling. 'We have it.'

We start to make a list of the ideas we have for her scrapbook. Joy begins writing but her hand spasms and she drops the pen, and as she rubs her wrist and arm I take up the gauntlet.

I wander around her kitchen opening cupboards and taking photographs of the contents while she sits at the table quietly, watching me, constantly pointing things out, offering a tip, a trick, a secret. She is territorial about her home, everything has a place, and a reason for the place. If it doesn't fit, it goes in the bin. Not a single bit of clutter, labels all facing front neatly. We're not exactly creating fireworks with Joy's scrapbook idea, but it's tailor-made for her life. Just as every relationship and marriage is unique and individual, the embodiment of two those individuals tangled up together, this service is representative of their union and must be bespoke.

As I move around taking note of everything, I wonder if Gerry did the same thing when thinking of letters for me. Did he observe me and try to figure out what I needed? Was he all the time thinking of his list, enjoying the secret, while I had no idea what was going on in his mind? I'd like to think it calmed him, that in his moments of pain and discomfort he was able to distract himself and go somewhere else, escape into the pleasure of his secret plan.

I notice Joy's been quiet for a while and I stop cataloguing the kitchen and check to see if she's OK.

'I wonder if I could ask one more thing of you,' she says as I meet her eye.

'Of course.'

She reaches into the pocket of her cardigan and takes out a folded envelope. 'I have a shopping list here. I wonder if you could help me. All the money is inside, cash, and there's a list.' Her fingers tighten briefly on the envelope. 'I'm sorry to ask. It's a lot to ask of you. My boys, their wives and our grandchildren. We have a tradition on Christmas Day where Joe and I stand at the head of the room, by the tree and everybody gathers around. Joe pulls a name from a Santa hat and announces the family member and we present them with their gifts. We've been doing it for years, our own family tradition.' Joy's eyes flutter closed, as if she can see it in her mind's eye. 'All the little ones love it. I don't want them to miss that this year. Joe doesn't know the little things that they like.' Her eyes open and with a trembling hand she holds out the envelope.

I pull a kitchen chair out and sit beside her. 'Joy, Christmas is six months away.'

'I know. I'm not saying I won't be here, but I

176

don't know what state I'll be in. You know they say that my brain will be in such decline that I will forget to swallow.' She raises her hand to her throat and squeezes, as if imagining it. 'The palliative care prepares me for the end, but if I'm planning a future with feeding tubes, then I need to plan not just how I feed myself but how I can continue to feed my family too.'

I look down at the bulky envelope.

'I know it's a great imposition, but if you could also wrap and label the gifts for me, I'd like to store them in the attic for Joe to find when he takes down the decorations. As part of Joy's Secrets,' she says, too brightly, trying to make it sound easy when it's not, it's anything but. Perhaps she's trying to screen the sadness that pummels beneath, or perhaps she's genuinely ready for it. I'm learning about this wish for the first time whereas she's thought about it, envisioned it, imagined it, probably lived the very moment when Joe finds the box over and over again in a dozen different ways. Perhaps she's keeping it upbeat for me.

'OK,' I say, my voice coming out as a whisper. I clear my throat. 'But let's make a deal, Joy, if you're able to hand those presents to everybody by yourself, those gifts are coming down before Joe discovers them.'

'Deal,' she nods. 'This is a lot to ask of you and I'm grateful, Holly,' she says, taking my hand. 'I hope it's not too much.'

It's all too much. Everything. All of the time. And then not at all, sometimes, depending on which version of me wakes up.

'Can I ask you something?' I look at her for approval before continuing. 'Why are you doing this?'

She seems confused.

'I know why in theory, but I want to understand exactly why. Is it because you're afraid they'll forget you? Is it because you don't want to feel left out? Is it because you don't want them to miss you?' I take a breath. 'Is it more for you or for them? Asking for a friend.'

She smiles, understanding. 'Everything you said. Everything and more. I can prepare myself for what lies ahead of me, but can't let go before it happens. I can't simply give up. I'm a mother, I've always thought ahead for the little ones. And even though they have little ones of their own, I won't stop thinking ahead. I want them to feel like I'm there with them, and I suppose it's because I won't let go yet. I won't surrender. It's the only control I have over my life. I don't know when my last day of quality will be, or my final day for that matter, but I'm going to make sure I'm around for more than my body could hold out for. I want to live and I'm trying everything; medicine, treatments, care, and now letters and lists. I may have lost control of my body, but I can control what happens in my life, and how life can be for others when I'm gone. It's the last victory I have.'

★   ★   ★

As I make my way home, I ponder Joy's words. *The last victory.*

Death can't win. Life lives on.

Life has roots, and just like a tree in its quest for survival, those roots spread and stretch to find water, they possess the power to lift foundations, uproot anything in their path. Their reach is endless; their very presence has an everlasting effect in some form or another. You can cut a tree down but you cannot kill what it started and all the life that sprung from it.

To most people, death is the enemy, a thing to be feared. We don't see it as the pacifier or sympathiser. It's the inevitable fate we have feared and done our best to avoid by minimising risks, by following the rules of health and safety, and by resorting to every treatment and medicine that might save us. Don't look death in the eye, don't let it see you, don't let it know you're there; head down, eyes averted; don't choose me, don't pick me. By the rules of nature, it is programmed into us that we must root for life to win.

For so very long in Gerry's illness, death was the enemy, but as is so often the case for those dealing with a loved one suffering terminal illness, there came a point when my attitude changed and death became the one thing that could offer peace, that could ease his suffering. When the hope of a cure is gone and the inevitable is inevitable, there are moments in long nights spent listening to short ragged breaths when death is invited. Death is welcomed. Take them away from this pain, guide them, help them, be kind and be gentle.

Even though Gerry was too young to die and

he did everything he could to fight it, when he needed to, he turned to death, saw it as a friend and went to it. And I was relieved, grateful to death for taking him from his suffering and embracing him. In a strange and wonderful way, the thing you have avoided, dreaded, feared is right in front of you and it's bathed in light. Death becomes our saviour.

Life is light, dying is darkness, death is light again. Full circle.

Death is always with us, our constant companion, in partnership with life, watching us from the sidelines. While we are living, we are also dying; every second spent living is a second closer to the end of our days. The balance inevitably tips. Death is there at our fingertips all the time and we choose not to go to it and it chooses not to take us.

Death doesn't push us; death catches us when we fall.

21

'I'm thinking of hiring volunteers,' Ciara declares from the other side of the shop.

'What for?'

'To help us out. Maybe we need security, there's too many things going missing lately, we can't keep an eye on everything and I can't afford to pay somebody else. People are always asking to help out, they know we give some of the proceeds to charity. And it would help me for when you've got hospital appointments, or when Mathew and I are doing collections.'

A customer at the counter picks up a wallet from the discount tray made up of items that are broken, or aged, too bad condition to offer at full price but too lovely to turn away. She turns it over in her hand.

'Is this real leather?' she asks.

'Yes, I think so.'

'For two euro?'

'Yes, everything in the tray is two euro,' I say, distracted, turning to Ciara. 'I've tried to get the hospital appointments on Mondays, Ciara, but they keep insisting on Fridays, I'm sorry.'

'I know, I'm not blaming you. I think it would be helpful for us, that's all. To keep an extra eye on things, have extra hands.'

'I'll take it,' the customer says, happily.

I take the coin and give her a receipt. She leaves the shop.

'And you're a little . . . distracted, with not moving in with Gabriel, or currently on *speaking terms* with Gabriel, not selling your house, helping out with the club, and oh my God I have to sit down, I'm so stressed just thinking about your life right now . . . '

'I'm not distracted, Ciara,' I say, snapping. 'Everything is under control.'

'Well, that's a lie if ever I heard one,' she mumbles.

The bell over the door rings out as a customer arrives. Flustered, she hurries to the cashier's desk. 'Hi, I was in here around fifteen minutes ago and I think I left my wallet by the till.'

My eyes widen.

Ciara throws me a menacing look. 'Find. It,' she says, through gritted teeth.

'I'll be back in a minute,' I say, polite but panicked, grabbing my crutches and hobbling out of the shop. I look left and right, see the woman who bought the wallet disappear around the corner and I yell after her.

* * *

That evening, Ginika sits with me at the dining table for our lesson. True to her word, she has immersed herself in learning how to read and write, and has shown an interest in taking a lesson every single day. And though it's impossible for me to manage a daily meeting with her, she never tires of asking, and I'm inspired by her energy and her desire to learn. She tells me she practises during Jewel's naptime, when Jewel sleeps at night, while waiting for hospital treatments, she has barely watched TV in two weeks and when she does, it's with subtitles. I need to match the strength of her determination.

Jewel sits on Ginika's left knee, moved as far away from the table as possible, chewing on a teething ring between pulling at her mother's pencil, the object that is stealing her mother's attention away from her. Jewel has learned to despise these pencils and papers and knows that in their destruction lies attention from both the women who stop their work to scold her.

Ginika's learning 'OW' 'OU' sounds, along with images. I quickly realised her reading ability sped up when it was accompanied by the visual. Her mind prefers to learn in images, not words, but together they complement each other. All she needed was another way to learn, and more time. Always, more time.

There are four words in the textbook, she needs to identify the word that doesn't have the OU/OW sound and circle it. The options are *Clown, House, Cloud, Cheese.* Cheese is written in yellow with holes through the letters, the 'o' in clown resembles a red nose. Hearing *OW* and *House* in the same sentence trigger my sensitivities. Ow, indeed. I still haven't called the estate agent and put a halt to the house sale. After spending so long putting it on the market, it's taking an equally long amount of time to remove it. Doing so would require focus of thought on my personal life which I'm incapable of right now. My eyes well and I look in the

183

opposite direction, and blink frantically to dispel the tears. When I've managed to chase the emotions away, I turn back to her work.

Ginika and Jewel are both watching me.

'Well done!' I say, jollily. I turn the page.

Ginika looks again at the naked wall scarred with holes where the wedding photo used to hang. She hasn't yet enquired, but I know she's going to. She's not one to hold back, always says what she thinks, seeming not to care about the emotion it will evoke in her companion. She seems to think that holding back is for fake people who 'aren't real'. I tell her it's called being polite.

'What happened?' she finally asks.

'It fell.'

She raises an eyebrow, not believing me.

'What's the foster family like?' I ask tentatively, taking Jewel's little foot in my hand.

She groans and shifts in her chair. 'A woman named Betty takes her for my hospital appointments or when I've no energy. She's got three kids of her own. And a country accent. I don't want Jewel to have a country accent.'

I smile at her. 'You're not sure?'

She shrugs.

'I'm sure nobody is going to feel good enough for you.'

'They have to. Somebody will feel good enough. I'm not going until I've that at least.'

The doorbell rings. I'm not expecting anyone and I don't have the type of neighbours who call by unannounced. I hope that it's not Gabriel. I've avoided his calls, not because I'm being

184

dramatic but because I'm trying to determine how I feel. Sometimes I think the mind is a petri dish of accumulated information, all mushed together, and if I leave it to stew long enough I might find it doesn't actually bother me at all, despite the fact it should. I'm waiting for that to happen. But I don't want to have the conversation with him now and especially not in front of Ginika. Nor do I want to hear his reaction when he discovers that, in addition to guiding people on their letters, I'm teaching them how to write too. It's one thing to help, it's another for it to take over your life. And it's the *taking over my life* that would be the debate, *is* the debate.

I open the door and find Denise, holding a bag wrapped in a dust cover.

'Hey,' she sings. 'Just wanted to return the clutch you loaned me.'

She hands it to me, and steps into the house.

I look inside. 'From last year?'

'You should consider yourself lucky,' she says, going straight into the living room. 'I was going to keep it. Oh hello,' she says, seeing Ginika and Jewel. 'I'm sorry, I didn't know you had company.'

'You didn't ask. Denise this is Ginika. Ginika is a . . . ' I look at Ginika for permission and she nods ' . . . member of the PS, I Love You Club.'

Denise succeeds in hiding the inevitable sadness she must feel on hearing that. She settles on a gentle smile. 'Hi, Ginika. Nice to meet you.' She goes over and hunches down to Jewel's level. 'And who is this beautiful girl? Hello!' She

185

makes all kinds of baby noises and Jewel grins. She offers her teething ring to Denise. 'Oh thank you very much!' Denise takes it and pretends to munch on it. 'Yum yum yum.'

Jewel giggles.

'You have it back,' she hands it back to Jewel. Jewel takes it, slobbers on it and hands it back to Denise. Denise repeats the gesture. And this goes on.

'Are you the Denise who had to be rescued in the sea on holiday in Lanzarote?'

Denise grins and flicks her hair. 'Why yes I am. I was topless in a leopard-print thong. My finest hour.'

'I think I left that detail out of the podcast.'

'She left all the best bits out.'

Ginika smiles. A rare thing.

'Denise — '

'I'd love to hear about the karaoke night,' Ginika continues. 'Was it really as bad as Holly described?'

'Bad? It was worse because I had to listen to it. Holly is as tone deaf as they come.'

'OK, OK,' I clap my hands, trying to get their attention. The only person who takes notice is Jewel, who claps along, her new favourite sport. 'I'm sorry to break you girls up but we're in the middle of something very important here, Denise, and Ginika has to leave in an hour.'

Denise looks at her watch, 'That's OK. I can wait. Will I make you both tea or coffee? Coffee for you, munchkin?' she says to Jewel and tickles her. Jewel dissolves in giggles. 'Do you want me to mind her while you guys work?' Denise eyes

186

the papers on the table.

'Oh no,' Ginika says, tightening her grip around Jewel's waist. 'She doesn't go to anyone but me.'

'Trust me,' I say, backing her up. 'She's all sunshine and light, but as soon as you put her down, the darkness appears.'

'Oh, I don't believe that,' Denise says, back on her knees again. 'Will you come with Denise? Dee Nee? Jewel come to Dee Nee?'

'Dee Nee?' I ask, amused.

'No, it's OK, really,' Ginika says, pulling Jewel away.

'Are you sure?' I ask Ginika. I wink at her conspiratorially. 'Denise really loves babies.' There is only one way to make Denise shut up and back off and that's by her experiencing the full force of Jewel.

'Um . . . OK,' Ginika says, loosening her grip.

'Yay!' Denise says, holding her arms up and cheering. Jewel giggles. 'Yay for Dee Nee!'

Jewel lifts her arms up in the air. The teething ring slams Ginika in the face. Then she lowers her arms again.

'Come to Dee Nee.'

Jewel actually holds out her arms and goes to her, but as soon as she's in Denise's arms she realises what she has done. She looks to her mother uncertainly and the frown appears, the flared nostrils, the obvious distaste and disgust of anyone and anything that is not her mother. The irritated sounds start. Denise stands up. The legs start to kick out, frantically. Socks hang on for dear life off the tips of her toes.

'Look there's Mama. Mama's still there.'

Jewel's sounds of irritation and distress stop, but the face is still on, in full force. She's not sure about what's happening here but she's quite sure she doesn't like it. Maybe.

'Hi, Mama.' Denise waves, and encourages Jewel to do the same. Jewel waves. She brings her on a little walk around the dining room. And then to the TV room. But as soon as she goes to the kitchen out of Ginika's eyeline, the horror movie screaming starts. Ginika stands up.

'Leave her for a moment,' I say. 'Let Denise deal with it.' It pains Ginika to leave her but I'm firm. 'We can finish this section off tonight.'

The screams, the yells, the absolute piercing hysteria echo around the house interwoven with Denise's gentle soothing voice, songs, and chatter, and I can tell that Ginika's barely able to concentrate on what I'm saying or the textbook in front of her. But I continue, push through the wall of noise hoping we can get past it.

I call out some words and Ginika writes them down.

'Where did you and Gerry go on honeymoon?' Ginika asks suddenly.

'I think we need to focus on the work, Ginika,' I say brusquely. But she won't. I have taken her child from her and she is irritated by the lack of control. I push her forward. She pushes back.

'You said in the podcast that Gerry sent you and your friends to Lanzarote because you were going to go there on your honeymoon.'

'Yes.'

She puts the pencil down. 'So why didn't you

188

go there? Where did you actually go?'

'Somewhere else,' I say, handing her back the pencil.

She fixes me with a strange look, unhappy with my response. Here she is raw and vulnerable and I won't answer her questions. I sigh and begin to explain, when she holds her hand up to stop me. She cocks her ear and listens.

'What's wrong?'

'I can't hear anything.'

It takes me a moment to realise that Jewel has stopped crying, that in fact it has been silent for a few minutes. Ginika jumps out of her seat.

'It's OK, Ginika, I'm sure she's fine,' I say, reaching out to her, but she moves quickly, away from the table, through the kitchen and straight upstairs. I follow her, holding on to the banister and hopping behind her as fast as I can. Ginika doesn't wait, she rushes ahead of me up the stairs. I find her standing at the door of the small spare bedroom, blocking my view. Breathless, I peek inside. Denise is sitting up on the bed, against the headboard, her legs out before her, staring out the window, with Jewel fast asleep on her chest, wrapped in a blanket. The room is dark, lit only by the street lamps that shine inside. Denise looks at us, confused as to why we're staring at her.

'Sorry,' she whispers. 'Was she not supposed to sleep? It's late, she seemed tired.' She looks at Ginika and then to me, worried she's upset the mother.

'No, it's great,' I say, grinning. 'Perfect, Denise, well done.'

I go to lead Ginika away, but she doesn't move. She doesn't seem pleased.

'We have to go,' Ginika says loudly and Jewel stirs.

'What? But why?' I ask, whispering. 'We can get a lot of work done now.'

'No,' Ginika says, distressed, and going for her baby. 'We have to go home.' She lifts Jewel from Denise's body, and leaves the room.

22

Despite the awkwardness of Ginika grabbing Jewel from Denise's arms and announcing she'd like to leave, Denise offers to drive Ginika home, and Ginika accepts. It could be for one of two reasons; to further stamp her authority on her place as mother, or because she feels bad putting me out again. Alone, with a frazzled head, I sit on the couch in silence. Ginika's question about my honeymoon stirs my thoughts.

★ ★ ★

'I want to go somewhere relaxing, Gerry,' I say, massaging my temples as he opens another adventure magazine. 'After all the wedding arrangements, after the big day, I honestly just want to go to a beach and lay there all day drinking cocktails and never get up.'

He looks at me, bored. 'I don't want to lie on a beach all day, Holly. We can do that for a few days but not every day. I want to do something. I want to see the world.'

'Look, we're seeing the world right now,' I say, flicking through the pages. 'Hello Iceland, hello Argentina, hello Brazil, hello Thailand. Oh, hi there, Mount Everest, don't think there's a beach near you.'

'I never said I wanted to climb Mount Everest.' He pushes the brochure closed and it closes on my finger.

'Ow.'

He stands up and leaves the table. But there's nowhere really to go, we're in our first flat, a one-bedroom with a small living space. Flat is rather a grand description; it's more of a bedsit. Our bedroom has a wall that doesn't reach the ceiling but separates sleeping from living. Gerry paces the small space there is to walk between the couch and the TV, like a caged lion. I can see he's about to explode.

'Why do you have to be so lazy, Holly?'

'Excuse me?'

'You're lazy,' he says, louder.

'A beach holiday isn't lazy, it's relaxing. Something you don't actually know how to do.'

'We've had five of these holidays already. Five different hotels on five different islands and they all look exactly the same. There's no culture.'

I laugh at this, which makes him even angrier. I should let it go but . . . 'I'm sorry I'm not as cultured as you are, Gerry.' I open a brochure. 'OK, let's go to Ethiopia, live a nomad life in a desert camp and join the local tribe.'

'Shut up!' he roars.

I wait until the veins stop protruding in his neck.

'Look,' I begin again, calmly. 'There's a place in Lanzarote. It's a beach resort but it also does boat trips. You can go see dolphins and whales. They even have a volcano, and you can take a coach tour to see it.'

I hold the brochure up.

'I saw that when I was ten years old,' he

mumbles, but at least he's calmer. 'If you want to see dolphins and whales I'll show you a place that has dolphins and whales.' He leaps over the couch and sifts through the pile of magazines on the kitchen table. He reaches for the Alaska Adventure travel magazine.

'I don't care about dolphins and whales,' I whine. 'That bit was for you. There are no beaches in Alaska.'

He slams the brochure on the table. I jump with fright. Then he picks it up again and this time throws the brochure on the linoleum floor that's burned and bubbling from previous owners' cooking disasters. The magazine makes quite the bang.

'Gerry.'

'Let's look at all the things you don't want to do, and eliminate them, shall we?'

He throws another brochure on the ground, harder this time. 'Iceland. That's boring, is it? Glaciers and hot springs are so shit. No beach. Peru,' he slams another on the floor. 'Who wants to see Inca trails and the highest lake in the world? Not you. Cuba, what a shithole,' he throws that on the floor too.

With each thud, I think of the couple beneath us.

He throws a few more down at the same time. Extra loud. The floor's vibrations rattle the stove.

'But here we go.' He lifts the holiday brochure up in the air like a trophy. 'Two weeks getting drunk and sunburned with a bunch of hen and stag parties, surrounded by English-speaking people and eating burgers and chips. *That* sounds like an adventure.'

He throws it back down on the table.

I look at it, eyes wide, heart pounding at his behaviour.

'I want to do something different, Holly. You need to leave your comfort zone. Be braver, be more exciting! Open your mind!'

I am currently so thoroughly pissed off with everything — the wedding arrangements, the invitations, the RSVPs, the deposits, this shit flat, with Gerry, with getting a mortgage for a new house — that I don't bother holding my tongue. And why should I, my husband-to-be has just accused me of being lazy, and boring.

'I am leaving my comfort zone, Gerry. I'm marrying you, you absolute psycho.'

'Nice,' he says, straightening up.

He leaves the flat and I don't see him for two days.

★　★　★

I'm still daydreaming on the couch when my phone rings and Denise's profile image, wide-eyed, with a chocolate profiterole stuffed halfway into her mouth, fills my screen.

'The package has been delivered,' she says, mysteriously.

'Thanks, Dee Nee, I appreciate it. I hope Ginika was OK with you. She's not comfortable with anyone other than herself being with Jewel. She's at the early stages with a foster family and she's understandably struggling.'

'God love her, it breaks my heart. She seems

194

excited about the lessons though.'

'Really? That's good, but I'm not sure how we're doing, because I don't actually know what I'm doing. I'm following the textbooks but I'd really prefer for her sake if she went to a tutor.'

'Why don't you help her write the words from the letter? Why do you have to teach her from scratch?'

'Because that's what she wants. She doesn't want anybody to know the contents of the letter, and she wants to achieve this herself.'

'The learning is almost as big as the letter itself. It means she has control over something in her life for once. And if, when the time comes and she can't write the letter entirely by herself, you can always help her. Don't feel like this is the only goal here.'

'True.'

Silence, apart from the indicator as she drives.

'Denise?'

'Yep.'

'Do you know why Gerry sent us to Lanzarote?'

'Wow. Your mind is travelling tonight.'

'Ginika asked me something that got me thinking.'

'Well, let me think . . . ' She clears her throat.

It was the July letter. The fifth letter. A simple *Have a good Holly day! PS, I Love You . . .* with instructions to visit a specific travel agent. He'd booked a holiday for me, Denise and Sharon, through a travel agent on 28 November, a day during a time that he should not have left his bed. He had a taxi waiting outside the travel

195

agent. Barbara the travel agent had told me the story, under duress, more than twenty times.

'Didn't you tell us it was where you were both going to go on honeymoon? It was like he was giving you a second honeymoon? Am I right?'

'It's where I wanted to go on our honeymoon.'

'Yeah. That's nice.'

Silence.

'And the dolphins. The next letter was about seeing dolphins.'

The August letter. He'd led me to a spot where you could view them from the beach.

'I can't quite remember the reason for that one, did you always want to see dolphins?'

'No. See, that's the thing. I didn't want to see dolphins. He did.'

'Well, you didn't want to do karaoke again either, as far as I remember.'

'No.'

'I suppose the point of some of his letters was to take you out of your comfort zone.'

The phrase jolts me.

You need to leave your comfort zone, Holly.
Be braver! Be exciting! Open your mind!

I muse on the concerns I've never shared with anyone before, concerns I've always brushed aside until the past few months when I've been forced to re-examine Gerry's letters for the sole purpose of guiding the PS, I Love You Club. The process is making me see his letters differently, in ways that mostly make me feel uncomfortable. 'Do you think that that particular letter, and that

196

trip, was like a 'fuck you'?' *Why dolphins?*

'How could it be?'

'Like a *remember the time you wouldn't do the stuff I wanted to do?*'

'Holly you went to South Africa on safari for him. You slept in a hotel with giraffes. You let him see plenty. He got exactly the honeymoon he wanted in the end.'

'In the end.'

Silence.

'So no, I don't think it was a 'fuck you'. That wasn't Gerry's style. Not the Gerry I knew, anyway. And wasn't it the place *you* wanted to go to? I see it as a gift. Why are you thinking this after all this time?'

We're both silent. I notice her car engine has stopped running, that the background is quiet. I stand and move to the window and I see Denise sitting in her car, outside in my driveway. The car's inside light is on, revealing her.

'I think,' she continues after a long pause. 'That if anything, he was compromising. Maybe he realised he made you do something you didn't want to do and he felt guilty. Or maybe he didn't feel guilty at all but it was like a do-over.'

I lean my forehead against the cold window. 'Denise, why are you staking out my house?'

She looks up and sees me at the window. 'Well, aren't you the spooky sleuth.'

'I'm OK, you know. You don't have to worry about me.'

'I know, Holly, but do we always have to remind you that everything is not all about you?' She gets out of the car with a large bag in her

197

hand. She walks up the drive, looking at me as she speaks into the phone. 'I left Tom. Can I stay with you tonight?'

I rush to open the door. Her eyes are filled with tears and I embrace her.

'On the other hand,' she says, tearful voice muffled, 'life is peculiar. Gerry may very well have had a dark side we didn't know about and he was fucking with you from the grave.'

I hug her tight.

★ ★ ★

Gerry and I moved at different paces. Me, slow and inconsistent, in all directions, few steps forward and then a few steps back; him solid, fast, eager, curious, focused. Mostly I wanted him to slow down, to enjoy the moments instead of rushing through everything with such high energy. He thought I was lazy and was wasting moments. We were the couple equivalent of patting your head and rubbing your belly. A brainteaser, a bimanual interference manifested in a relationship.

I wonder if his body always knew what we didn't: that his moments were more limited than most, that he didn't have the time that I had. His rhythm was in sync with his time. He needed adventure because he wouldn't live to see his thirties. My body had longer, and it took its time to gather momentum, to become curious and adventurous. By the time that happened, he was gone. Perhaps it was his leaving that made that happen.

198

I wonder if he was frustrated with standing still with me when there was a clock inside him ticking and pushing him to move forward. I wonder if I held him back. I wonder, if he'd met somebody else, would he have lived a more fun, exciting, fulfilled life. I wonder, I wonder all these distressing thoughts as a form of self-punishment, but my heart always responds. My heart holds the answer with confidence, firm in the knowledge that we may have had different rhythms but we were always in sync.

23

The bottle of wine is open. Denise and I are on the couch, our feet tucked underneath us as we face each other. Denise's wine glass trembles as it travels to her lips.

'Start from the beginning and leave nothing out. Why have you left Tom?' The words feel alien in my mouth.

The reservoir inside Denise bursts its banks and she goes from being completely in control to losing it completely. I watch her cry but I'm too impatient to wait for answers.

'Did he have an affair?'

'No,' she half-laughs, wiping her eyes.

'Did he hit you? Hurt you?'

'No, no, nothing like that.'

'Did you?'

'No!'

I search for a box of tissues but can't find any so I return from the bathroom with a toilet roll. She has calmed a little but her voice is so shaken and broken I have to concentrate on hearing the words.

'He really wants a baby,' she says. 'Five years, Holly. We've been trying for five years. We've sunk all of our savings into it, we've nothing left and I still can't give him a baby.'

'It takes two people to make a baby, this is not all on you.'

'It is me.'

We've never discussed this before. I never asked, it's none of anybody's business but their own.

'If I step aside, then he could meet somebody else and live the rest of his life the way he wants. I'm standing in the way of his dream.'

I stare at her, my mouth agape. 'This is the most ridiculous thing I've ever heard.'

'It's not,' she replies, turning away from me and crossing her legs. She directs her justification to the fireplace instead of me. 'You haven't lived in our shoes. Every month he was so hopeful. You've no idea what that's like. Disappointment after disappointment. And then every meeting, appointment, every single time we began IVF again, he believed every single time that it was going to happen, and it didn't. And it's not. It never will.'

'It could still happen,' I say gently.

'It won't,' she says firmly. 'Because I'm not trying any more. I'm exhausted.' She wipes her eyes, a definite look in her eye. 'I know that Tom loves me, but I know what he wants, and he can't have that with me.'

'So by breaking his heart and leaving him, you are actually making it easier for him?'

She sniffs in response.

'He wants you, Denise.'

'I know that he loves me, but sometimes that's not enough. The past seven years, since we got married, we've been obsessed with making a baby, making a baby. It's all we talk about. We save and plan, plan and save to make a baby. There's nothing else. And now there will be no baby. So what the hell are we? If we move on, I know what I won't be. I won't be a wife who couldn't make a baby, and he won't be a loyal husband who settled for second best. Does that make sense?'

'Yes.' I finally agree. 'But it's wrong.'

We drink silently. I sip, searching my head for something wise to say, something that will flick the switch and reverse her thinking. Denise takes a huge mouthful of wine.

'Have you had any offers on the house yet?' she asks, changing the subject, draining her glass.

'No.'

'I don't understand why you don't just move in with Gabriel now, while the house is on the market.'

'I'm not moving in with Gabriel.'

Denise's eyes widen. 'You changed your mind?'

'Gabriel's daughter is moving in with him, and he wants to wait until she adjusts before we take the next step. And before you ask, he thinks the *transition* could take up to two years.'

'What the fuck?!' she spits and wine flies from her lip and into my eye. 'Sorry,' she says as I wipe it away. She stares at me, aghast. 'Is he trying to break up with you?'

'He says he's not, but, I sense the future is bleak.' I take a slug of wine.

'But he's the one that wanted you to move in.'

'I know.'

'He asked you for months.'

'I know.'

'This doesn't make sense!'

'I know.'

She narrows her eyes suspiciously at me. 'Has it anything to do with the PS, I Love You Club?'

I sigh. 'Yes, no. Maybe. It probably hasn't helped, all this stuff coming together at the same time.' I rub my face tiredly.

'Maybe you should take a break from the club, maybe it's not healthy for you.'

'I can't, Denise. They're relying on me. You just met Ginika, what would she do?'

'But things were going so well for you before you got involved in the club.'

'Maybe it's helped put everything in perspective for me.'

'I don't know, Holly . . . '

'I suppose I could go ahead with the sale of the house anyway.' I look around. 'I think I'm done with this place. I feel like Gerry checked out of here a long time ago. He's gone,' I admit sadly. Then, as quickly as the sadness arrived, it leaves, and a jolt of adrenaline surges through me. I could do this. Gabriel is making his own plans, taking care of his own life, why should I wait for him?

'Fancy moving in with me?' Denise asks.

'No, thank you.'

She laughs. 'Fair enough.'

'You're going back to Tom and you're going to tell him what you told me. Discuss it like grown-ups. This is only a hiccup.'

'I think I'll need to do more than hold my breath and wait for it to pass.'

True, bad advice. I'm through with holding

my breath. Change needs action. I drain my glass.

'OK,' she sighs wearily. 'I'm going to bed. Can I please sleep in your spare room?'

'You can, but don't keep me awake with your incessant crying.'

She smiles sadly.

'I think you're making a huge mistake,' I say gently. 'Please change your mind in the morning.'

'If we're swapping advice, I know I'm in no position to be handing it out, but you love Gabriel. This club has done something to you, whether you admit it or not. It's brought Gerry back to you, which should be a nice thing, but I'm not sure if it is. Gerry is gone, Gabriel is here, he's real. Please don't let the ghost of Gerry push Gabriel away.'

24

'Paul, if your wife arrives home . . . '

'She won't.'

'But if she does . . . '

'She won't. They're gone for the afternoon.'

'Paul,' I say firmly. 'If for whatever reason, she returns, we cannot lie. I will not take part in deceit, this isn't what I'm here to do. I don't want her to think I'm some nasty other woman. I'm already Bert's reflexologist, and that is disturbing enough.'

He laughs and it breaks the tension. 'I won't ask you to lie for me. I know this is difficult for you, and I, all of us, appreciate what you're doing for us, the sacrifices that you're making after everything you've been through.'

Which then makes me feel awful. My sacrifices are nothing compared to his.

'So what's the plan for today? What do you want me to do?'

'We have a lot to do,' he says, energised. He's a bundle of energy and ideas, he reminds me of Gerry. They don't look alike. He's ten years older. Still so young and yet had ten more years than my husband; the greedy bitter time-comparison monster again.

'I'm only going to write one letter, the letter to them all that explains what I'm doing; the rest, if you don't mind, is visual.'

'Letters are visual,' I say, rather defensively.

'I want to give the kids a sense of who I am, my humour, the sound of my voice — '

'If you write the letters *well* . . . ' I begin.

'Yes, *defender of all letters written ever,*' he teases, 'but my kids can't read yet. I want to do something a little more modern, more in tune with what the kids are drawn to, and they love TV.'

I'm surprisingly disappointed, but I drop it. Not everybody cherishes letters as I do and I suppose Paul is right, his young children, born in this generation, would probably prefer to see and hear their dad. It's another lesson that this process needs to be shaped exactly as the person wishes, for the people they love; bespoke messages from the once living to the still living.

'First things first.' He leads me through the kitchen to a conservatory. 'A piano lesson.'

The conservatory overlooks the back garden. A children's playhouse, swing set, lopsided goalposts, bikes, scattered toys. A doll abandoned in the soil, the head of a Lego man stuck between the cracks of the patio. The barbecue is covered up, unused since the winter, garden furniture needs to be sanded and painted. Colourful birdhouses nailed to the fence. A fairy door by the foot of a tree. The setting paints the picture of their daily life. I can imagine the activity, the mayhem, the laughter and screams. The conservatory feels like it belongs in another home. There aren't any toys, nothing that would link it to the surroundings of the rest of the house. It's an oasis. A light grey marble tiled floor. Light grey walls, a sheepskin rug. A chandelier hangs from the centre of the ceiling, low and hovering just above the piano. And that's it, no other furniture.

Paul is displaying it grandly, proudly.

'This,' he grins, 'was my first baby before the monsters were born. I put it in here for the acoustics. Do you play?'

I shake my head.

'Started when I was five. Practised every morning from eight to eight thirty before I went to school. It was the bane of my life until I left school, started college and then realised being a piano player at parties is a babe magnet.'

We laugh.

'Or at least, the centre of all entertainment.' He starts playing. It's jazz. Free. Fun.

' "I've Got the World on a String",' he tells me, still playing.

He gets lost in his own world, playing along, head down, shoulders up. No despair, just joy. He stops suddenly, and we're plummeted into silence.

I stand up quickly and go to his side. 'Are you OK?'

He doesn't answer.

'Paul, are you OK?' I look him in the eye. Headaches, nausea, vomiting, double vision, seizures. I know what Paul experiences. I've seen it. But he can't be experiencing it now; the tumour is gone. He's in remission, he beat it. This is all precautionary. Of all the people I am spending time with, Paul has the most cause for optimism.

'It's back,' he says, choked up.

'What?' I ask. I know exactly what he means, but my brain can't compute it.

'I had a five-hour seizure. Doctor said it's back with a bang.'

'Oh Paul, I'm so . . . sorry.' It's too weak, the words are not enough. 'Fuck.'

He smiles sadly. 'Yeah. Fuck.' He rubs his face tiredly and I give him a moment, my mind racing. 'So what do you think?' he asks, looking me in the eye. 'About the piano lesson?'

What do I think? I *think* I'm unsure about whether to push him more. I *think* I'm afraid something will happen to him, in my presence, and I'm afraid of that happening and I don't know how I'd explain that to his wife. I *think* that instead of him spending time with me here, he should be with his wife and children, making actual memories, not ones for the future.

'I think . . . that you're right. This works much better on camera than in a letter.'

He smiles, relieved.

I place my hand on his shoulder and squeeze encouragingly. 'Let's show your babies exactly who you are.'

I hold my phone up and begin recording. He looks straight into the camera and the energy is back, a playful look in his eyes.

'Casper, Eva, it's me, Daddy! And today, I'm going to teach you both how to play the piano.'

I smile and watch, zoom in on his fingers as he teaches the scales, trying not to laugh as he jokes and makes deliberate mistakes. I am not in the room. I am not here. This is a man, speaking to his children, from his grave.

208

After basic scales and 'Twinkle, Twinkle', we move to the kitchen.

He opens the fridge and removes two cakes. One is chocolate for Casper and the other is sponge with pink icing, for Eva. He rummages through a shopping bag and retrieves a pink candle; a number three.

'For Eva,' he says, pushing it into the centre of the cake. He looks at it for a moment and I can't even imagine the depths of his thoughts. Perhaps he's making his own wish. Then he lights it.

I press record and zoom in on his face, half-hidden beneath the cake held up in his hands. He starts to sing 'Happy Birthday'. He closes his eyes, makes his wish, then blows the candle out. When he opens them, his eyes are misty. 'PS. I love you, baby.'

I end the recording.

'Beautiful,' I say quietly, not wanting to ruin his moment.

He takes the phone from me and reviews his work and while he's doing that I look inside the shopping bag.

'Paul? How many candles do you have in here?'

He doesn't answer. I turn the bag upside down and everything spills on to the marble countertop.

'OK,' he says, after watching the recording back. 'Maybe zoom in on me and the cake more, I don't want too much of the background.' When he looks up, he sees my face, then the contents of the bag on the counter. Pink and blue numbered candles fill the countertop. I see 4, 5,

6 — all the way to ten. I see an 18, 21, 30. All the years he's prepared himself to miss. He shifts awkwardly from one foot to the other, embarrassed. 'Too weird?'

'No.' I gather myself. 'Not at all. But we're going to need a lot more time to get through this. And we're going to have to mix things up a little. We can't have them looking at you in the same shirt every year. Can you get some different tops? And fancy dress. I bet you guys have lots of fancy dress, let's make this fun.'

He smiles, grateful.

Despite the battle Paul faces, a battle he's had to fight once already, I find that spending time with him feels productive. With Gerry I felt so powerless, we were at the whim of every doctor's decision, following appointments, schedules and treatments to a T, not knowing enough about it ourselves to be able to make clear decisions or take different options. I felt powerless. Now, while I'm obviously still powerless against Paul's tumour, at least I feel that I can do something for him. We have a goal and we're getting somewhere. Perhaps this is how Gerry felt while writing the letters for me. While everything else was uncertain, or out of his control, he had this one thing under control. At the same time I was fighting for him to live, he was making preparations for after his death. I wonder when that began, what moment he submitted to the knowledge, or did it begin as a 'just in case' as it did with Paul.

Spending time with Paul is the ideal remedy to the personal web of confusion I find myself in, because I'm able to discuss these thoughts with him. He wants to know, he wants to hear. The club need me, they want me, and when I tell them stories about Gerry and rehash memories of his letters, I don't need to check myself mid-sentence, I don't have to apologise or stop myself as I do with family and friends if I feel I'm going on, or trapped in a time warp, or moving backwards. The club want to hear about Gerry and the letters, they want to hear about my life with Gerry, they want to hear about how I miss him and of how I remember him. And as they listen, perhaps in their minds they replace him with their own image, and me with their loved ones, envisioning what it will all be like when they're gone. It's my safe place to discuss him, it's my place to bring him alive again.

I can quite happily immerse myself in this world.

25

After a two-hour hospital wait that gives me another insight into my PS, I Love You Club members' lives and how hospital visits, waits, check-ups, tests, results, are so much a part of their lives, I lie back on the hospital bed and watch the nurse draw a line in marker on my cast. Six weeks after shackling me, they're happy with the healing of my ankle revealed in the X-rays. She positions the blade at the start of the guideline, applies gentle pressure and moves the cutter smoothly along the line. Slowly she pulls back the cast, revealing my pale skin, red and sore in places where it reacted to the plaster. Some of my skin comes away with the cast, it looks raw, as if it has been burned.

I wince.

The nurse looks at me, a pained expression. 'Sorry.'

My ankle, shin and calf is distraught, paler in places where it is not flaming red with burns, and it's skinnier than my right leg. It has faced a trauma, is fragile in comparison to the rest of me. It will catch up. I'm relieved.

I feel like an onion, another layer gone. I sting, I am raw, but I feel unshackled and unpeeled.

★ ★ ★

'Hello?' I call, stepping into the narrow entrance

hall, varied art on the walls and a long rug lining the original floorboards. I make my way slowly over the rug wearing a new walking boot to help with the weight placement on my weakened ankle. Though not completely free, I'm grateful to be without the crutches and cast. I breathe in the air of the house I had almost considered my home. Gabriel, not long in from work, wearing his work combats and bomber jacket, is sitting in an armchair tapping away on his phone, and looks up at me, surprised.

'Holly,' he stands. 'I just texted you. How did it go?' He looks down at my foot.

'I have to wear this for a few weeks, then I'm as good as new.'

He comes to me and hugs me. My phone vibrates in my pocket.

'That's from me,' he says.

'Is Ava here?' I pull away, and look around.

'No, not yet, she's moving in on Friday, after school.' He breathes out anxiously.

'You'll be great.'

'I hope so.'

'Can we talk?' I ask, moving to the couch.

He looks at me nervously, then sits.

My heart is pounding.

I swallow hard. 'I don't blame you for the decision you made about Ava — for as long as I've known you, you've told me about wanting to be in her life more — but I can't do this any more. I can't do us any more.' My voice is quivering and I pause to watch his face, see how he's taking it. He's utterly shocked, he's examining me, eyes searing into mine. I'm

213

confused as to why he didn't see this coming, and have to look away in order to continue. I look down at my fingers, grasping each other so tightly, they're white at the knuckles.

'I made a deal with myself some time ago to stop waiting for life to happen. I don't want to put things off for some time in the future, I want to be in it now. I think we've run our course, I think we're finished, Gabriel.' My voice wobbles, but I'm so sure of all the words coming out of my mouth, I've said them to myself over and over. It's the right thing to do. We've lost our way. Some people fight to find their way back together, but not us. We served our purpose.

'Holly,' he whispers. 'I don't want to break up with you. I told you that.'

'No, but you paused us, and . . . ' My mind wavers and I shake out the niggling thoughts of how we could work and stick instead to what I have decided. 'You've other commitments. I know how important it is to you to be a good dad, it's what you've talked about from the moment I met you. Now's your chance. But I can't sit around waiting while you do it. And there are things that I want to do in my life that you don't agree with and I can't do those things if I have to constantly apologise for them or pretend they're not happening.'

He covers his face with his hands, and turns away from me.

I wasn't expecting tears. I place my hand on his back and lean over to study his face.

He looks up then, with a forced smile and wipes his eyes. 'Sorry, I just . . . I'm surprised

. . . Are you sure? I mean, you've really thought about this? Is this what you want?'

I nod.

'Should I try to change your mind . . . could I even convince you?'

I shake my head. I fight the ugly tears that want to fall, and the lump in my throat that's crushing through my skin.

I hate goodbyes, but hating them is never a justification to stay.

26

At home, I shower, relieved to finally be able to wash my entire body. I hiss as the water hits my raw skin and stings. I begin what will become my daily ritual: massaging oils and cream into my skin and gently moving it around, straightening and bending, trying to get used to the new freedom. I still feel incapacitated without the cast, I don't trust my leg to take my full weight without the boot for support. I will be gentle and patient until my muscles regain their tone, trying to be as kind to myself as I would be to others. And when my chest aches with the hurt of losing Gabriel, and the hurt that I've caused him, I think of what he has gained, remind myself that he has Ava. And of course I think of what I have gained this year: my new friends from the club and what, and who, they have brought back into my life.

I never felt that Gabriel and I were forever. I was younger when I met Gerry and perhaps naïvely believed that he and I were soul mates, that he was *the one*, but when he died, I stopped thinking like that. I've come to believe that at different times of our lives we are drawn to certain people for various reasons, mainly because that version of ourselves is connected to that version of them at that particular time. If you stick at it, work at it, you can grow in different directions together. Sometimes you get pulled apart, but I believe there is the right person, *the one*, for all the different versions of yourself. Gabriel and I lived in the now. Gerry and I aimed for forever. We got a fraction of forever. And an enjoyable now and a fraction of forever is always better than nothing at all.

Out of the shower, I discover a missed call from Joy. Bert's health has declined, he's lost consciousness. She adds a panicked, 'Are his letters ready and in place?'

* * *

I choose an Edwardian script font to give Bert's words a more grandiose effect and then wonder if it's too grand, if I should keep it simple, if it's all style and no substance. Other fonts seem too heartless, lacking soul, and even look like ransom letters from a maniac. Once I see that, I can't unsee it. I play around and then go back to the Edwardian script because I think it's the type of writing that Bert was aiming for but couldn't pull off. I print Bert's six notes on gold labels, I stick the labels on to midnight blue textured cards. I decorate the cardboard border with tiny stickers. The theme has meaning to me, Gerry's phrase *Shoot for the moon and even if you miss you'll land among the stars*, though I'm aware Rita will never understand this link. It's just me feeling connected, stamping Gerry's identity to this, though themed or not, it has his essence all over it as he planted the seed. I hope Rita likes stars. I hope Rita doesn't feel this looks like a school project. I chose elegant ones, expensive ones. I slide Bert's notes into gold envelopes, then I print out numbers, experimenting with different fonts. I lean the page of printed numbers against my computer and study them, hoping for one to jump out at me. So much is going on in my sleep-deprived, exhausted mind.

As I sit here, writing the living words of a man taking his last breaths, it is not lost on me that I am writing Bert's letters in possibly exactly the same place as Gerry wrote mine. I stay up all night until the sun starts to rise and sprinkle its hope on the world. By morning, the letters are finished and I hope that dear Bert has managed to cling on through the night.

I am proud of myself for doing this. It is not breaking me as others, and I, thought it might. To look back, to go back, is not to be weak. It is not to reopen wounds. It takes strength, it takes courage. It takes a person who is more in control of who they are to cast a discerning, non-judgemental eye over who they once were. I know without doubt that revisiting me will encourage me, and everyone who is touched by my journey, to soar.

'You've been up all night,' Denise says behind me at the kitchen door, sleepy-eyed and messy-haired. She surveys the table.

'You're still living here,' I reply, catatonic.

'Another time,' she replies. 'Whose letters are these?'

'Bert's. His condition worsened last night. I need to get his letters ready.'

'Oh, wow,' she says softly, sitting down. 'Do you need help?'

'Actually, yes,' I say, rubbing my aching eyes, my head pounding from the tiredness. Denise watches me for a moment, thinking something that she doesn't share and I'm glad of that, then she jumps into action, finding the remaining numbered labels on cards, and sliding them into their corresponding envelopes.

She reads the first one she picks up. 'He wrote poems?'

'Limericks. It's a mystery tour. He hints at a place, his wife goes there, finds the next note and so on.'

'Sweet,' she smiles, reading, before sliding it into the envelope. 'Do you need to deliver these today?'

'It's part of my service. Bert can't do it.'

'I'll help you.'

'You've got work.'

'I can take the day off. We've got enough girls on the shop floor and frankly I could do with a distraction.'

'Thank you, friend,' I say, resting my head on her shoulder.

'How is our man doing?' Denise asks, watching me check my text message.

His family are around him. His grandchildren have sung him hymns. Everyone has said their goodbyes.

I read Joy's text aloud. 'Not long now.'

★　★　★

As I'm locking the front door, I hear a car door slam behind me, followed by heavy footsteps in our direction. Feet on a mission.

'Uh oh,' Denise says nervously.

'I knew it!' Sharon announces.

'Where are the kids?' Denise asks.

'With my mum, I have a scan today.'

'But thought you'd do a little detective work first,' Denise asks.

'I called your house. Tom said you were staying here. Is it true?'

'Denise is having a moment of doubt,' I explain.

'Why didn't you come to me?'

'Because you're highly judgemental and pass-remarkable. And you have no spare bedroom.'

Sharon's mouth falls open.

'But mainly because you have no spare bedroom.'

'I could have put Alex in with Gerard, that's what I always do with guests.'

'Yes, but then I have to share a bathroom and I don't like sharing a bathroom.'

'Holly only has one bathroom upstairs between two bedrooms.'

'Yes, but she has a shower room downstairs.'

I look from Sharon to Denise, to see if this conversation is serious. It is. 'If you two want to continue this conversation, you're welcome to go in and use the house, but I've really got to go.'

'You don't work on Mondays,' Sharon says, narrowing her eyes suspiciously at me. 'The shop's closed. Where are you both going?'

'To deliver some love letters,' Denise sings happily.

Sharon's eyes widen. 'The PS, I Love You letters?'

'Yes!' Denise says, opening the car door and sitting into the passenger seat.

'Why do you tease her so much?' I ask as I pull the driver's door closed.

'Because it's so easy to wind her up.'

I start the engine, lower my window and look at Sharon standing open-mouthed staring at the two of us. She looks exhausted. She could do with an adventure.

'Would you like to come too?' I offer.

She smiles and climbs into the back seat.

'This is kind of like old times,' I reply, looking at the three of us together.

'Can I see the letters?' Sharon asks.

Denise passes them back to her.

'Are you in on this too?'

'I've helped mind a baby while Holly teaches her mum to read and write,' Denise explains.

'You're teaching a person to read and write?' Sharon asks, surprised.

'Trying,' I reply, reversing. I wait for a smart remark. *People get desperate on their deathbeds, don't they?* Something, anything to belittle what I'm doing, but it doesn't come.

'Nice presentation,' Sharon says, sliding out the first limerick to read aloud.

There once was a boy at Chrysanthemum
Who paused for the National Anthem
   He saw a vision in blue
   It was you, always you
Till my heart stops I'll live it verbatim.

221

'How sweet,' Sharon says. 'Where does it lead to?'

'The Chrysanthemum was a dance hall. They met in the sixties, the show band that night was called The Dawnbreakers. But it's too early, the venue won't be open, so we're going to the second location first.'

Sharon flicks on to the next envelope and reads.

There once was a man on a date
Who used a woman's love of poems as bait
*   They sat on the bench*
*   Her lips he did quench*
And the kiss sealed the love-struck fool's
*   fate*

'Their first kiss?' she asks.

'Bingo.'

The place of Bert and Rita's first kiss in 1968 was on Patrick Kavanagh's bench on the north banks of the Grand Canal on Mespil Road, where there's a life-sized statue of Kavanagh sitting on one side of the bench, welcoming a stranger to sit beside him. We stand by the bench and I imagine Bert and Rita here all those years ago, sharing their first kiss, and I feel moved. I look up at the girls, tears in my eyes but Sharon's expression couldn't be more different to mine.

'This isn't where you leave the second envelope.'

'It is.'

'No, it's not. The first limerick leads to the dance hall, then you leave the second envelope there, which leads here. This is where you leave the third envelope.'

Denise and I look at each other, wide-eyed. How the hell did we make that mistake? It's not rocket science.

'I bet you're glad you brought me,' she says, sitting down beside Patrick Kavanagh, with a satisfied look on her face. 'And where are you going to leave the envelope?' she asks, still smug. 'With Paddy here?' She looks at Patrick Kavanagh. 'Paddy, I fear our friend has not thought this through, her grand master plan is turning to poo.'

Denise cackles her dirty laugh again, which irritates me. I throw an angry look at them both and they shut up instantly.

I look at the bench. I consider wrapping the third envelope in plastic and taping it beneath the bench but I know it's not a practical solution. I don't know how long Bert has to live, it could be hours, it could be days. It could be weeks, stranger things have happened. If people can be taken from the world earlier than expected, they certainly can live longer than expected too. I also don't know when Rita will choose to begin the journey Bert has set out for her following his initial note. It could take her days, it could take her weeks, or it could take her months. A suspicious package beneath a famous city centre site visited by tourists, and who knows at night, will not last long.

'I can tell she's thinking,' Denise says.

'Because she's barely blinking,' Sharon finishes.

They giggle, feeling so proud of their poetic hilarity.

'She's got that look in her eye,' Sharon begins.

'And we don't know why,' Denise finishes.

I ignore them. I don't have time to waste. I have four letters to deliver, Bert is dying, beginning his transition as we stand here in a powerful place of his past. I read the inscription and I suddenly realise something bad. Something terrible, and I'm filled with dread.

'Wait a minute. Bert said they had their first kiss on this bench in 1968.'

I look at the girls. They're cosying up to Patrick Kavanagh and taking selfies. Peace signs, and kissy lips.

'This bench was erected in 1991.'

They finish their selfies, sensing the change in mood and stand up to read the plaque. We stare at it in silence.

I frown. My phone vibrates in my pocket. I read the message.

'Perhaps you can check with Bert that he has the right place?' Sharon suggests helpfully.

'It's too late,' I say, looking up from the phone, my eyes filling.

The message is from Joy.

Our dear Bert has gone.

27

I sit on the bench, my head in my hands. 'I'm an idiot.'

'You're not an idiot,' Denise says simply.

'I can't do anything right,' I berate myself. 'People are dying, I've made promises and instead it's like fucking amateur hour. And I broke up with Gabriel.'

'What?' Denise explodes.

'Why?' Sharon asks.

'He wanted to move Ava into the house instead of Holly,' Denise explains.

'What?' she explodes again.

'It was . . . falling apart. We were dangling. So I snipped the wire.'

'Well, actually,' Denise says, turning to Sharon, 'Holly was dangling. She didn't want to have to answer to someone who didn't want her to be part of the PS Club, because it was obvious it's sending her bonkers, and Gabriel was probably afraid he'd lose her, which he has done anyway by not supporting her, and she didn't want to have to face listening to the truth and admit he was right, so she cut him off like she does with most people who don't agree with the way she's living her life, which is probably why she hasn't called you for weeks. Just like when Gerry died, remember?'

Sharon nods, looks at me nervously, then back

to Denise. 'The locking the door thing and not letting anyone in?'

'Exactly, but this time she's locked herself in with a ghost and cut off the real person who loves her, who, granted, may have had a really wrong reaction to all of this, but he doesn't know her like we do, and frankly he's human and none of us are perfect, so who can blame him?'

'Denise,' Sharon says quietly, warning in her voice.

I look at her, stunned. No, distraught.

'Sorry,' Denise replies, looking away, not sorry at all. 'But someone had to say it.'

We sit in silence.

'Flippin' life,' Sharon says. 'I wish we were back in Lanzarote, on a lilo, drifting towards Africa. Times were easier then,' she says, trying to lighten the mood.

I can't laugh, I can't erase what Denise has said. Her words are ringing in my ears, my chest pounding, with a kind of panic that she's right. What if I've made an enormous mistake?

Sharon looks from me to Denise. 'Can you two apologise so we can move on?'

'What do I have to be sorry for?' I ask.

Denise looks ready to blurt out all my faults again but she stops herself. 'I already said sorry but I'll say it again. Sorry, Holly, really, I'm . . . ' she shakes her head. 'Stressed. I may have made a mistake leaving Tom and it's frustrating watching you do the same thing.'

'Did you mean what you said?' I ask.

'Yes,' she says sombrely. 'Every word.'

'Oh for christsake,' Sharon interrupts. 'That is

not an apology. Honestly, you two, I don't hear from you for weeks and you both break up your relationships?'

'Careful, it's catching,' I say, smiling weakly.

'In John's dreams,' she mutters. 'Right, well, one problem at a time,' Sharon says, moving on. 'There must be another bench somewhere. Bert didn't make it up.' She does a Google search. 'A-ha, you're not an idiot. There is a bench that was built by Patrick Kavanagh's friends, weeks after his death. It was officially launched on St Patrick's Day in 1968. That has to be it.'

I try to focus but everything feels like it's falling apart. I'm still berating myself for not helping Bert to think this through properly, but how could I have, if I couldn't even think it through? How could we expect to leave an envelope on a bench?

We walk down the banks of the canal, me using one crutch for my weak ankle, on parallel paths with a line of trees, past the leafy suburbs of Ragland Road and by the canal made pretty with swans. When we reach the south bank at the Lock Gates close to Baggot Bridge, opposite the Mespil Hotel, we find a simple side seat made from wood and granite. We take it in in a respectful silence. The giddiness of the newer Patrick Kavanagh bench is gone, this feels more apt, an old simple bench where Bert and Rita kissed for the first time all these years ago on St Patrick's Day, 17 March 1968, a visit to the new bench celebrating Rita's favourite poet. Different times. Bert is gone but the bench still stands, wood and stone that has absorbed the lives of

227

people who have come and gone, and still observes the changing seasons and the canal water going by. Though we're still faced with the same problem as the last time. Where to put the envelope.

The Mespil Hotel is directly across the road.

'What are you thinking?'

Feeling determined, I cross the road to the hotel. Straight up to reception with the air of someone who means business, and I ask for the hotel manager.

'Just a moment.' The receptionist disappears behind a hidden panelled door in the wall.

'Hello,' a woman steps out of the secret room, hand extended. 'I'm the hotel duty manager, how may I help you?' Her hand is warm, in these days of red tape and paperwork, I hope her heart is too.

She guides me to a seated area and I settle myself.

'Thank you so much for your time. My name is Holly Kennedy and I'm working on a venture called PS, I Love You, which helps terminally ill patients write final letters to their loved ones. I've been sent here by my client Bert Andrews, who unfortunately passed away just moments ago . . . And I need your help.'

And there, we leave his third riddle. When Rita arrives, after a subtle additional hint from me directing her to the hotel, she will receive her safely guarded letter to read in the comfort of a private area and a complimentary afternoon tea.

★ ★ ★

Our second stop runs more smoothly than the first. We visit the dance hall where Bert first laid eyes on Rita. The Chrysanthemum Dance Hall was an iconic venue during Ireland's successful show-band era, the dance mecca of Ireland. Girls on one side, boys on the other. If a boy asked you if you wanted a mineral then it meant he was interested, if you said yes to a dance it meant you were interested. Seemingly more innocent times, when the Catholic Church dominated the country. Thousands of people met their life partners on the dance floors of Ireland's ballrooms.

A security guard grants us entry into the building, and it's empty as they prepare for local school exams. He allows us to wander around and take a look. Gone are the dance floors and mirror balls, rows of desks and chairs take their place, but despite that, stepping inside is like stepping back in time. I imagine the room, hot and sweaty, heaving with people jiving on the dance floor.

As if picking up on my thoughts, Denise says. 'If these paisley walls could talk.'

I explain my mission to the security guard, with more confidence, ease and the insistence that anybody involved is doing a great service to humanity. He agrees to take the envelope and stores it in a safe place with Rita's name on it, where it will take her from the place where she and Bert first met, to the bench where they first kissed. And, thanks to the hint I've added in small print at the bottom of Bert's limerick, across from the bench that marked their future,

229

Rita will find her third letter, which leads us to our next location, the place where Bert proposed.

> There once was a man who did tremble
> There were words his tongue couldn't
>   assemble
>   On bended knee
>   He made his plea
> Of that place he is sentimental

'I'm loving this!' Sharon admits. 'Please let me know when you're doing this again, I'd love to help. Where to next?'

'How much time do you have, I thought you said you have a scan today?'

She looks guilty. 'I made it up. I told my mum that so I could have a few hours off, I'm so tired,' she says, her eyes glistening.

I hug her.

'This is the perfect day, really, I know I wasn't sure about this, Holly, but I'm fully behind you now. There is nothing *wrong* about doing any of this, and if you need me to tell Gabriel all about it, I will.'

My smile instantly fades at the mention of Gabriel, and I remember all over again that I've lost him. I gave him up. 'It's too late for that,' I say, starting the engine.

We travel to Howth Harbour Lighthouse and Martello tower, built in 1817, where Bert proposed to Rita with fish and chips in their hands. The lighthouse caretaker emerges from the small Georgian-style house that is attached to the tower, listens to my story and does me the honour of accepting the letter for Rita. As with the hotel duty manager, and the security guard, I'm discovering that Bert's story, a human story, is one that these busy people make time to listen to. They don't divert me, or stonewall me. I'm not going to them with a complaint, I'm not trying to extort them. I'm just asking them to listen and to play their part in somebody's dying wishes. The kindness of these strangers gives me hope, a faith in humanity: that though sometimes it may feel as though people are shutting down to others, devoid of compassion and empathy, we can still recognise when something is real. We are not altogether numb and unfeeling.

The caretaker takes the envelope containing the limerick:

There once was a fool who got lost
Who was greedy and ignored the cost
I'm sorry my love
From below and above
It's here I felt your hate truly exhaust

'I wonder what he did,' Sharon says, as we walk back along the pier to the car park, eating our own fish and chips.

'I think we can guess,' Denise says, her words thick with cynicism.

'I don't know what you're so angry about, you have a perfect husband who adores you and who stayed by your side through everything,' Sharon snaps. I don't have the energy to agree, after

231

what Denise has thrown at me already today.

'I know that,' Denise says quietly. 'That's why he deserves more.'

We are all quietly thoughtful as we travel to our next destination, Sharon pondering the arrival of a baby into an already chaotic life, Denise pondering the demise of her marriage and a future that is not going according to plan. Me about . . . oh everything.

I park and we get out, looking out at the building Bert has led us to.

'So this is where Rita forgave Bert,' I say, looking up.

Our silence is broken as we break the sombre mood to laugh. It's a hemp shop and tattoo parlour.

'You never know, they might have gotten high and had his and her tattoos declaring their love,' Denise suggests.

'What will I do?'

'You have to follow protocol,' Sharon says, holding out her hand for me to lead the way.

I laugh, take a deep breath and enter.

The staff are the easiest of all the spots we've been at, they're moved by the story and excited to play their part, and they even offer to throw in a complimentary tattoo for Rita on her arrival. It's been a long day, and We're all quiet, eager to finish. The final destination is a house in Glasnevin.

Sharon reads the limerick.

There once was a woman named Regret
Who had a twin who made her fret
  It's time to say hi

To the anger, goodbye
In this place where they both first met.

'A woman named Regret,' Sharon reads. 'Is it all of us a few months from now?'

'It's about Rita,' I explain, again shaking away the horrifying fear Denise has instilled in me. 'The home belongs to Rita's twin sister, where they were born and grew up. They had a falling out when their mother died, something to do with settling the estate. Her sister took everything and they never spoke again, nor do their families.'

'Money makes people crazy,' Denise says.

'I think it's better if you go in there alone,' Sharon says.

I agree.

I limp up the pathway in the colourful neat and tidy garden that has been lovingly maintained. I ring the doorbell. It takes a while for the door to be answered and while I've only ever met Rita a few times, her sister is indeed the image of her, though harder-looking. She looks at me suspiciously through the glass in the side of the door and I realise that she has no intention of opening the door.

'Bert sent me.'

She unlocks the door.

'What do they want this time? My blood?' she grunts, leaving the door open a little and shuffling back inside the house. I step inside and follow her into the TV room.

A TV guide is open on the coffee table, a biro has circled the chosen shows of the day. She slowly sits down in a worn armchair, face twisting with agony as she leans on her cane.

'Can I help?' I move closer to her.

'No,' she snaps.

She takes a moment to catch her breath, pulls her cardigan closed. 'Hip replacement,' she says, and eyes my boot. 'What happened to you?'

'A taxi hit me when I was cycling.'

'They think they own the roads. Are you a lawyer?' she barks.

'No, definitely not.'

'What then? What do they want from me?'

I retrieve the letter from my bag and hand it to her. 'Bert wanted me to give you this. But it's not for you to open. He wanted me to leave it with you for Rita to collect.'

She eyes it warily, as though it's a bomb, refusing to take it. 'Tell him I said he can keep it. I haven't seen her for years. Bert knows that. I don't know what he's playing at. Sick games. Sick people, my sister and her husband.'

'Bert passed away earlier today.'

The anger disappears from her face and her mouth opens in a silent 'oh'. 'I heard a while back that he was in hospital. What happened?'

'Emphysema.'

She shakes her head. 'He smoked forty fags a day. I told him, Bert, those bastards will kill you, but he never listened,' she says angrily. 'God rest his soul,' she adds quietly, blessing herself.

'I'd been spending time with him before he passed. He wanted to leave some letters for Rita, in places of importance.'

'Trying to right his wrongs, is he? Well, isn't

that a fine thing when he's dead? He doesn't have to face it himself. She won't come here,' she says, the anger returning. 'Haven't spoken to her for seven years. Not without it being through a lawyer or nasty letter she'd send. I have them all, you can read them if you want, that'll tell you who the real monster is.'

'I'm not here to take sides,' I say gently. 'I don't know what happened and I'm not judging. He asked me to deliver this to you and I promised him I would.'

'Well, I'll tell you what happened. And unlike them, I'll tell you the truth. I spent every day with our mother when she was sick, brought her to every hospital appointment, bathed her, nursed her, moved in with her to care for her, and they all thought I was doing it to get the house.' She raises her voice as though it was me who accused her. 'What kind of sick people would think that? People who only want the house themselves, that's who. Money, it was all about money to them. I moved in here because the care worker Rita organised was stealing from Mammy. Stole her toilet roll! Have you ever heard the likes of it? Paid for helping an old woman and you steal her toilet roll?! And I save us all the money by doing it myself and *I'm* the thief?' She points her finger at me, poking the air to send home every point. 'They painted me as a con artist, a thief. Spread nasty rumours that the likes of everyone around here was talking about. Can you imagine? I never made Mammy change her will. Never. That was all her own doing. They make it sound like I held her hand and forced

235

her to write. Rita and Bert were fine, Mammy knew I needed it. She left it to me. I couldn't change that.' She sits back, recharging for her next outburst. 'Then when they found out? Ah Lord be God, World War Three broke out. All of a sudden I was a monster. They wanted to make me sell the house. Thought they deserved half of the money. Sent solicitor's letters and all kinds of scare tactics. And for what? So they could go on more holidays? Buy a new car? Pay college fees to bail out their drug addict son who failed all his exams? Oh so high and mighty, everyone knows what that boy was like, but Rita, no, she'd pretend everything was perfect, better than everyone else. She was always like that.' She looks into the distance, her teeth gritted with anger. 'Mammy left this house to *me* and I had nothing to do with putting that in her head.'

'I don't doubt that,' I say, wondering how to extract myself from this.

'They all turned their backs on me. Even the kids, my own nieces and nephews, think I'm the devil. Don't speak to mine either. Cousins who adored each other,' she says, shaking her head angrily. 'Ripped the family apart, Bert and Rita. I'll never forgive them. Mammy wanted me here. Her mind was as clear as crystal when she did what she did. You can't blame the dead. A dying wish is a dying wish.'

I find my moment. I place the envelope down on the opened TV guide where I know it will be seen. 'And this is Bert's.'

★ ★ ★

236

I get into the car with a long sigh, relieved to be out of there, feeling her words ringing in my ears. *You can't blame the dead.*

'What took you so long?' Denise asks.

'I'm exhausted after that. There is some bad blood there.'

'Do you think Bert's letter will work?'

'I have *no* idea,' I say, rubbing my eyes tiredly. 'I hope so.'

It's 6 p.m., it's been a full long day, a fruitful day but a draining one. Going on somebody else's personal journey has brought us back into our own, has made us contemplative, and reflective of our own lives.

'I don't suppose she'll let me use her toilet,' Sharon says.

I laugh. 'I dare you to try.'

'I'll wait,' she says, moving around uncomfortably in the back. 'There's one more envelope left, the first one.'

'Yes,' I say, concerned, unsure how I'm going to pull this one off.

'Do you give it directly to Rita?' Sharon asks.

'Yeah, kind of,' I say, shrugging it off.

'So not exactly,' Sharon says, not letting it go. 'Where do you put the first letter, Holly?'

I clear my throat, nervously. 'Bert wanted the first letter in his hands, for Rita to find.'

Sharon's eyes widen. 'In the coffin?'

Denise cracks up so much, she's doubled over in the back seat.

'How are you going to pull that off?' Sharon asks.

'What are you going to do?' Denise asks,

237

wiping the tears of laughter from the corners of her leaking eyes. 'Crack open the coffin at the funeral?'

'I don't know, I hadn't quite ironed that one out with Bert, but I suppose I'll go to the funeral parlour, so that he has it in his hands when he arrives at the house.'

'They won't let you near him, you're not family!' Sharon says, and Denise continues laughing until she's red in the face.

'I'll tell them it's under his instruction. It's what Bert wanted.'

'Unless you have written instructions from Bert or his family, there's no way they're going to let a random stranger put a letter in a dead man's hands. Holly, honestly, you've some ground rules to iron out before you continue with this.'

'I know,' I say quietly, chewing my fingernails. 'He's having a wake. He'll be laid out in his house for a few days. I'll ask for a moment alone with him and I'll place it in his hands.'

'You were lucky with the security guard, the hotel and the hemp shop, but I don't think a funeral parlour is going to allow you to place a letter with unknown contents in a dead man's hands.'

'OK, Sharon! I get it!'

The girls are quiet. I think they have accepted this plan but out of nowhere Sharon snorts and the two of them dissolve into convulsions again.

I roll my eyes, agitated, not finding this or their laughter at all funny.

I'd laugh along with them but I can't get to

their place. This is serious for me.

Seven years ago Gerry set me on a path of new adventure, seven years later his actions are continuing me on my adventure.

Life has roots, and death, death grows them too.

28

'Oh! Excuse me!' I say with surprise, backing away from the stockroom and reversing to the shop. 'Ciara,' I hiss, finding her cleaning the mirror in the changing room. 'There's a man on his knees in the stockroom.'

'You're always on your knees in the stock-room.'

'Not praying, I'm not.'

'That's Fazeel, our new volunteer — he started today. He's going to cover security. He has to pray five times a day, so don't be in there at dawn, noon, afternoon, sunset or night.'

'Three of those times are not an issue for me, but it's neither dawn nor noon at the moment.' I look at my watch.

'He said he slept it out this morning,' she says, shrugging. 'It'll only be for a few minutes each time. His wife had cancer, he wants to help out.' She eyes the bicycle I've brought through the shop to store in the stockroom. 'Did you cycle to work?'

'No I just thought it would be a pretty accessory.'

'You're not supposed to be cycling.'

'They said I could exercise with the boot. And I really missed it.' I mock cry. 'Anyway, it's great we have a new volunteer because I need to take a few hours off today.' I scrunch my face up and wait for her to holler.

'Again?'

'I know. I'm sorry I've been asking a lot of you for the past few weeks.'

'Months,' she says firmly. 'And that's fine, because I'm your sister and I can tolerate your little meltdown mid-life crisis, but seriously Holly, what is it this time?'

'Bert, a member of the PS, I Love You Club died, and I need to attend his wake. I have to deliver the final letter. Or rather, technically, the first letter.'

Her eyes widen. 'Why didn't you tell me?'

'I'm telling you now.'

'I should have known something was up, you've been so quiet the past few days.'

'Actually, that's because Gabriel and I broke up.' I squeeze my eyes shut again and brace myself for impact.

She slumps in the armchair by the dressing room and tears fill her eyes. 'I knew this would happen. This is my fault. It's because of the club, isn't it? He couldn't deal with it? It's because of the podcast, I shouldn't have asked you. Things in your life were going just fine until I opened this can of worms.'

'Ciara,' I smile, going to her and kneeling down before her. Typical Ciara that I'm consoling her after my own break-up. 'We didn't break up because of the podcast, it had nothing to do with that. We had other problems, which may have been highlighted because of it. It was my decision. As for the club, you played a part in making something wonderful happen. I'm helping people in a way that I was helped. It's a

241

gift. Come with me today, and you'll see. And to be honest, I could do with an accomplice, because what I have to do isn't going to be easy.'

'Mathew!' Ciara calls and Mathew appears in the shop. 'Holly and I have to go out for a few hours, can you take over out here?' She makes her way over to him and kisses him passionately.

'I thought you just hired someone,' he says, wiping his mouth.

'Yes, but he's praying.'

Mathew watches us leave, confused, and I throw him an apologetic look.

★   ★   ★

Joy, Paul and Ginika are waiting at Bert's for me. I introduce them to Ciara, she greets them as though they are royalty and they all look at me, nervous and expectant.

'Rita hasn't found the letter,' Joy whispers.

'I know. I haven't had a chance to deliver it yet.'

'Oh goodness,' Joy says, worriedly, fidgeting.

'Hello,' Rita says, coming from the kitchen to the hallway to greet yet another visitor. 'You're very kind for coming over.' She's dressed in a black shift dress, a black cardigan with a St Bridget's Cross brooch. She takes my hand. 'I'm sorry, I don't remember your name. I'm seeing so many people today.'

'Holly, and this is my sister Ciara. I'm very sorry for your loss, Rita.'

'Thank you, both. These are Bert's book club friends,' she introduces me to Joy, Ginika and

242

Paul. 'This is, was,' she corrects herself. 'Bert's reflexologist.'

Ginika's eyes widen and I see one of her rare smiles form on her lips. She has to turn away and bury her face in Jewel's fluffy crown to hide her smile.

'Oh, how interesting,' Paul says, face lighting up. 'Where do you practise?'

I throw him a warning look and he smiles sweetly. They're all enjoying this. Their little secret.

'I was sent from the hospital.'

'The hospital? Which hospital?' Paul asks, following along as Rita leads me to the living room. Ciara trails behind.

'Bert's hospital,' I reply, throwing him a look over my shoulder. He chuckles.

'Actually, Rita, I was hoping I could have a moment with Bert, if possible,' I ask awkwardly.

If she is unnerved by the foot doctor's request, she doesn't show it. She opens the door and I'm faced with thirty people crammed into the small living room surrounding the open casket in the centre. All eyes turn to me and Ciara.

Ciara, dressed in black like a black widow, wearing a beret with a black net falling across half her face, smiles tightly. 'I'm very sorry for your loss.' She backs away and stands at the wall, leaving me alone.

I catch a glimpse of Paul, Joy and Ginika's anxious faces before Rita leaves the room and closes the door gently in my face, stopping my escape. I stare at the closed door, heart drumming at the impossible task ahead of me.

'What's she doing, Mammy?' a child asks, loudly. The child is hushed, Ciara urges me on, and I slowly swivel to face the room. All eyes are still on me. I smile politely.

'Hi,' I whisper. 'My deepest sympathies.'

Children are sitting on the floor, toys in hand, silently playing together. Closed fists crush tear-filled tissues, everyone is dressed in black, cups of tea and coffee in hands. These, all family members and close friends of Bert's, are wondering who I am and what place I have being here.

Much as I want to, I can't turn around and leave. I'm cringing from the tips of my ears to the tops of my toes. I take the few steps forward and at least most of them have the decency to look away or avert their eyes to give me my moment. The murmuring starts up and the initial tension that greeted me disappears. I feel like an intruder who is about to steal something precious. I am here for Bert, I remind myself. He has instructed me to do something important. I will swallow my fear and pride, and follow through. I need to concentrate on the task at hand. Bert's final request.

Inveniam viam. I shall either find a way or make one.

I self-consciously approach the coffin. My eyes fall upon Bert, so dapper in his best suit, navy blue, crisp white shirt and royal blue tie, with the crest of his cricket club. His eyes are closed, his face relaxed, the funeral home did a good job. I didn't know Bert very well but I know intimate things about him. The few times I met him he

244

was struggling to breathe, now he is calm, serene.

Tears well up. Then I look down at his hands and my eyes widen. He's holding a bible. This was not part of the plan, Bert distinctly told me to put the envelope in his hands. He never mentioned anything about a bible.

I look around to make sure nobody is watching, they've continued their own quiet conversations to give me my moment. With everybody distracted, I place my hand on Bert's hand and give the bible a little tug to see how easily it will move.

'That lady is stealing from Granddad,' a little voice shouts.

I jump, startled, and look down to see a boy beside me pointing right at me.

There's silence in the room again.

'Oh, she's only holding Granddad's hand,' Ciara says sweetly, with a smile, stepping forward to stand by my side.

'Thomas, come here,' his mother says, and he glares at me suspiciously before leaving my side. I look around again and the eyes are back on me. Less trusting now. There may be some truth to peeping Thomas's declaration. I'm starting to sweat; can't they just look somewhere else? I reach into my bag.

The door opens and the arrival of a new mourner steals their attention from me. I use the opportunity to remove the envelope from my bag and place it on top of Bert's hands, but my hands are shaking and its clumsily done. The letter rests uneasily on the bible for a second, then slides down to the side of the coffin where it will never be seen.

'Jesus, Holly,' Ciara mutters in my ear.

I reach in and dig it out. I place it on the top again, trying to balance it where it can be clearly seen. The envelope slides down a second time. I open the Bible and slide the letter between the pages, making sure it can clearly be seen at the top, but I'm not too convinced. Bert wanted the letter *in his hands*.

'She did something to Granddad!' Thomas shouts, standing up and pointing at me.

Thomas is not my friend.

Stunned and completely mortified, I look around at the faces staring at me. The crowd moves forward to peer into the coffin.

'Who is she?' a woman asks quietly, but I hear her.

'This is Holly,' Rita says, behind me. 'Bert's reflexologist.'

I close my eyes.

29

All eyes are on me. I take a deep breath.

'My name is Holly,' I say, addressing the crowd. 'But I was *not* Bert's reflexologist.'

Cue gasp. But that doesn't happen because this isn't a daytime soap, it's real life, despite the ridiculous situation I've found myself in. Ciara immediately reverses to hug the wall.

'I'm sorry, Rita,' I turn to her. 'Bert made that up of his own accord — nothing to do with me, I assure you. He asked for my help arranging a surprise for you, as a symbol of his love for you. I'm sorry I fell at the last hurdle and didn't quite deliver on his wishes in the sophisticated manner he desired. But the envelope I placed on his hands is for you, written by Bert, typed by me, because he said you think he has terrible handwriting.'

She lets out a laugh, a surprised, high-pitched little yelp that escapes her, and her hands go to her mouth. It's as if the handwriting piece of information was a secret code that unlocks her belief in me, and Rita's acceptance causes everyone else to back down.

'What has he done? I knew he was up to something! Oh Bert!' she looks at him with a smile, tears filling her eyes. And then her face crumples.

'Read the letter, Mum,' her daughter says, stepping forward to her side, arm around her.

Daughter of Bert and Rita, mum of peeping Thomas.

I wring my hands, a nervous wreck. The eyes are on me again. I back away from Rita and her daughter, no longer centre stage, and creep towards the door beside Ciara. She takes my hand supportively and holds it tightly, pulling me back from leaving. Joy, Paul and Ginika form a wall at the door, ganging up to block me from escaping. I slowly swivel towards the coffin, a spectator to Rita's new adventure.

Rita lifts the envelope resting on the bible and Bert's hands, runs her fingers over the gold shiny paper.

I'm instantly transported back to the moment I read the first note that Gerry wrote for me, how my fingers traced his letters, looping and swirling, my fingers reliving his words, in an effort to resurrect him.

Gerry's opening words of his first letter come back to me. '*My darling Holly, I don't know where you are or when exactly you are reading this . . .*'

Rita opens the envelope and slides the card out. 'My darling Rita,' she reads.

'Oh Daddy,' a woman gasps from the group. I'm frozen. Frozen in time. Stuck in a memory. *You whispered to me not long ago that you couldn't go on alone . . .*'

Rita continues reading.

'Our adventure together isn't over. Dance with me one more time, my love. Hold my hand and take this journey with me. I've written you six limericks.'

248

'Limericks!' she looks up. 'I hate limericks!' she laughs, and reads on.

'I know you hate limericks,' she continues reading, and everyone laughs.

I am just a chapter in your life, there will be many more.

'Each limerick is a clue. Each clue leads to a place. Each place holds a special memory and meaning in our hearts. Each place contains the next clue.'

Thank you for doing me the honour of being my wife. For everything, I am eternally grateful.

And then, a shiver envelopes my body. A warm feeling, starting at my chest, reaching out to my stomach, my legs, my toes, my head. A wave of something odd *overtakes* me. Not dizziness, but clarity. Not clarity of this moment in this room, but it takes me elsewhere, lifts me up and all I can think of is Gerry. I feel him. He's in me. He's filling every part of my soul. He's here. He's here. He's here in this room.

Trembling, I phase out Rita's words. She's reading the limerick. All eyes are on her, they've forgotten about me. The crowd are smiling, it's happening. Bert's wish is coming true, but I am shaking, my whole body is rattling. Joy, Ginika and Paul have moved closer to Rita. Everyone has moved in, the circle tight and close. Eyes and noses are streaming. Smiles decorate every face. I'm squeezing Ciara's hand as I move away from them all and quietly open the door.

My body is trembling, I can only look at the floor. A burst of adrenaline has shot through me, as though I've had multiple shots of caffeine.

Everything in me is triggered, my senses heightened, connecting me to something else.

I feel a strong arm around my waist.

'Are you OK?' a whisper in my ear.

I close my eyes. It's Gerry, I feel him again.

Suddenly I feel like I'm floating from the room, through the hallway, out the front door. Gerry's arm is firm around my waist, his breath is on my head. He takes my hand.

Gerry. It's Gerry. He's here.

He opens the front door and sunlight hits my eyes and the fresh air fills my lungs. I drink it up.

I realise I'm still holding hands and I look at him.

It's not Gerry.

It's Ciara, of course it's her, but she's doing the same thing as me. Taking deep breaths. Smaller ones.

'Are you OK?' she asks.

'Yeah,' I whisper. 'That was . . . weird.'

'Yeah,' she agrees, seeming shaken. 'Did something happen?'

I think about it. Whatever it was that filled my body, my soul and my mind is gone, but I'm still high from what I experienced.

'Yeah.'

'I was watching you. Your face just changed. I thought you might pass out. You looked like you'd seen a ghost.'

It's as if she knows that Gerry was in the room.

'Did you?'

'Did I what?'

'See a ghost?'

She's not laughing, not teasing.

'No.'

She seems disappointed.

'Why, did you?'

'I felt like Gerry was there,' she whispers. 'I got this . . . feeling.' She lets go of my hand to rub her hand up and down her arm where I can see goosebumps. 'Does that sound crazy?'

'No,' I shake my head. 'I felt him too.'

'Wow,' her eyes widen and fill up. She wraps her arms around me. 'Thank you, Holly, you're right. That was the greatest gift.'

I hold her tight and close my eyes, wanting to relish and remember every single part of that experience. He was there.

★ ★ ★

I'm on a high. Floating on love and adrenaline and peculiar new energies, I feel possessed. Not by Gerry — that feeling is gone — but from the lingering connection to him. Ciara drives us back to the shop and tells me to take the rest of the day off; she's pretty shaken up too. On the way there I receive a phone call from the estate agent. An offer has been made on the house, not for the full asking price, but as close as she thinks we'll get. There is a sign in Ciara's shop, above a gleeful beaming Buddha, that says, 'You can only lose what you cling to.' I can hang on fiercely to the past, to all my things, or I can let go and hold them in my heart.

After a quick consultation with Ciara, I call the estate agent and gleefully accept the offer on

251

my house. I don't need the house to feel Gerry's spirit. I was in a house with no physical link to him, surrounded by people with no physical or emotional link to him, and he was present. This house has acted like a chain around my neck, letting it go gives me power. I can recreate the beauty of us elsewhere, in endless locations in the world, I can take him with me, while I'm creating something new. It's time for me to leave. I've already said my goodbye to it. I was never supposed to stay for so long. It was a starter home for Gerry and me, but then it became the place where we ended.

I get on my bike and speed through the streets, I should really be concentrating on the road but I can't. I shouldn't really be cycling on my newly healed leg at all, particularly not with such gusto, but I can't stop. I feel like I've wings and I'm flying. As I near my house I can't recall the journey to this point. I want to ring somebody, I want to dance, I want to shout from the rooftops with joy that life is wonderful, life is great. I feel drunk.

I cycle up the driveway outside my home. Denise's car is gone, she's at work, or maybe never coming back. I hope the latter. Then as I step down from the bike I feel a searing pain in my ankle. I pushed myself too much. I thought I was invincible. I feel heavy as I lean the bike against the wall in the side passage. My high has come crashing down and my head pounds with the full and immediate effect of a hangover. I step inside the house to silence. I lean my back against the front door and look around.

Nothing.
Stillness.
Silence.
The final words of Gerry's letter.
PS, I Love You.
I come crashing down.

★   ★   ★

I have pushed my ankle too far. It's round, swollen and throbbing, I place it on a pillow, with a bag of frozen peas on top. I lie on my bed and I do not move for the evening, not even when my stomach growls, when it feels empty and hollow, as if it's starting to eat itself, and I'm nauseous. I need to eat but I should keep the weight off my foot. I watch the clouds rolling by, blue to white, large plumes followed by thin stragglers, I watch as the daylight eventually turns to darkness. I don't, *can't* get up to pull my curtains. I am numb, immobile, feeling frozen. I can't move, I don't want to move. My ankle throbs, my head throbs, this enormous comedown after such dizzying heights.

I start to think and I think too much. Of before, of ago, of the very beginning, of old times. Of first times.

★   ★   ★

The front doorbell rings and in my bedroom I pull another dress over my head in absolute frustration and throw it on the floor. My head is so hot my make-up is melting off my face and

253

ruining every item of clothing that smudges against my skin. Even if they were once an option, now soiled, they no longer are. My bedroom floor is hidden by outfits that I've scattered in panic and anger. I can't see the floor for clothes, but I've nothing to wear. I whimper, then, hating how weak I sound, I grunt. I study myself in the full-length mirror, examine my body in my new lingerie from every angle, studying what Gerry will see.

I hear Gerry's voice downstairs and Jack's laughter. The ribbing has probably already begun. *You better keep my sister safe*, the same thing that's been said for the past year since we started going out properly, officially, instead of stealing moments before school, at school lunch and afterwards on the walk home. Two years together, one year full-on, Gerry has become a member of the family, one that my mum and dad keep a watchful eye over.

Dad always says about his favourite brother Michael: 'He's a gentleman but he still cheats at Monopoly.' He uses the same phrase for Gerry.

'Gerry doesn't cheat at Monopoly,' I always retort with a roll of my eyes. 'We don't even play Monopoly.'

'Well you should.'

But I know what Dad means.

Tonight I'm hoping that Gerry will cheat at Monopoly and, as the self-designated bank, I'm ready to aid and abet. I chuckle quietly at my hilarity, giddy with excitement and anticipation, but a knocking at the door silences me. Even

254

though the door is locked, I grab a dress to cover my body.

'Holly, sweetheart, Gerry's here.'

'I know!' I yell back to my mum, irritated. 'I heard the doorbell.'

'OK!' she responds, wounded.

I know that if I'm not careful this night could be ripped from me before it has even begun. It has taken a lot of parent persuasion to allow me to this party tonight. It's the first twenty-first party I'll have been to without parental supervision, and the deal is that I'm allowed to have one drink. The secret unspoken understanding is that this isn't a realistic target for anyone, especially a sixteen-year-old who has a seventeen-year-old boyfriend who is allowed to drink, and so two drinks will be acceptable. I will aim to not have more than four. A fair negotiation, I think.

It's Gerry's cousin Eddie's twenty-first birthday; a disco at Erin's Isle, the GAA club he plays with. And while Gerry's family and extended family will all attend, the rule is that the adults leave at 11 p.m. when the DJ starts. It's Eddie's rule — at twenty-one he does not consider himself among the adults, which says a lot about Eddie's character. Gerry hero-worships Eddie. Four years older than him, he's always been his favourite cousin; he plays for Dublin's under-21s and looks good to reach a senior level. Eddie is cool, and confident. I find him intimidating, the kind of person who'll pick you out in a crowd to make a joke, ask you a question, fire a smart comment, sometimes at your expense if he thinks it's extra-funny. Gerry says it's 'banter', they all talk like that, but nobody as loudly as Eddie from what I see. Everyone always laughs at what he says — and he is funny, a natural comedian — but as a quiet person, not exactly shy, being around unpredictable people like Eddie makes me nervous. Sometimes it annoys me just how much Gerry idolises Eddie, sometimes I think he'd rather be with him than me, because he often chooses to be with him rather than me. Gerry's parents are less strict with him than mine are with me. At seventeen, Gerry is driving his dad's car and he goes to clubs with his older cousin whenever asked. He kind of follows him around, at his heels like a little dog, which is true of most people who like being around Eddie. But then Eddie does make me laugh a lot, he has never said a cruel word to me, he just shines a spotlight on me when I don't want lights shone, and I am jealous of how Gerry spends so much time with him, and Gerry's sidekicky little doggy following around act is so uncool, so I hold it against Eddie.

I survey the bomb site that's my floor, eyes putting together outfits together, locating and mixing, discarding, rearranging the slush piles.

There's another knock on the door.

'I said I'll be ready in a minute,' I yell.

'It's me, hissy fit,' says my little sister Ciara. At eleven years old she has mastered sarcasm, and can buy and sell everyone, including my parents. As she shares this room with me, I'm obliged to unlock the door.

She steps in and quickly takes in the room,

256

and me standing in the middle of it all in my underwear.

'Well, that works.'

She steps over the mounds of clothes, tiptoeing in the cracks where the carpet appears to get to her bed. She holds a tub of Häagen-Dazs, and a large spoon, and sits cross-legged on her bed watching me.

'We were told not to touch the ice-cream. It's Dad's.'

'I told him I have my period,' she says, sucking on a full spoon.

Dad hates period talk.

'A really clotty one.'

I wrinkle my nose. 'Jesus, Ciara.'

'I know, he'd have given me anything to shut me up. You should try it.'

'No thanks.'

She rolls her eyes.

'If you're not careful, he'll send you to hospital. Haven't you had your period for three weeks now?'

She widens her eyes innocently. 'I know, which is why I really need the cookie dough ice cream.' She chuckles. 'So, what's the deal, are you having sex with the Ger-meister tonight?'

'Shhhut up.'

She grins. 'You are. Whoop whoop. Sexy pants.'

I close my eyes. 'Ciara, when I was eleven I didn't speak like that.'

'Well I'm nearly twelve and I do. Come on then, what are the options?'

'All of this. None of this.' I sigh and pick a few

257

things up. 'This. Or this. I actually bought this for the party.' I hold up a denim skirt and a top. Clearly, in this lighting, in reality, the two do not match.

Eleven years old or not, I trust Ciara's opinion, I have faith in her style but I lack the confidence to wear her recommendations.

She puts the ice cream down, lies on her stomach over the edge of the bed to root through the clothes. 'So where are you going to do it?'

'I said, shut up.'

'In the GAA club, up against the Sam Maguire? Or you with your arse *in* the Sam Maguire.'

I ignore her.

'In the toilets, beside a bunch of old men in tweed caps eating egg sandwiches? In the staff room, up against some Tayto crisps?'

That one makes me laugh. The funniest thing about Ciara is how she doesn't find herself funny. She never laughs, even when she says the most hilarious things, and she never seems to run out. She rattles things out one after the other, like her best humour is yet to come, as though she's building it up, practising, trying to improve.

I don't reply to her automatic weapon-like firing off of places I can have sex in a GAA club, but I watch her sorting through my clothes while I think of our actual plans to go to Gerry's house. His parents, along with all the other uncles, aunts, and family members who don't wish to be deafened by music they detest, are leaving Eddie's party to continue the festivities at

Eddie's house — his parents are infamous for their house parties, where the sing-songs go on until the crack of dawn. This means Gerry's house will be empty.

I remember my mum telling me that in a small house of eight siblings she and her brothers and sisters naturally learned to find their hiding places, that in a place so packed with personalities and individuality, it was imperative, a survival strategy, to carve out a space in the world that was theirs, to get lost in their imagination, to play, to read, to be left alone, to be themselves, to find isolation and calm in the midst of chaos. Hers was the space behind the couch where the base of the chair didn't meet the wall. Those siblings who didn't find their own space were, and remain, a little less settled in themselves. The same can be said for my friends. We're always on the hunt for our own space to be with our boyfriends, a free house is a gift to behold and even then, once inside, it's a competitive hunt for your own patch, the end of a couch, a darkened corner or empty room. Finally, tonight Gerry and I can have our own place, our own time, to really be together without prying eyes or people walking in on us, to create some personal chaos in the midst of calm. You can't say that a year of waiting hasn't been long enough. Gerry and I are practically nuns compared to our friends. Tonight is my idea, my persuasion, gentle persuasion. It didn't take much. *I'm ready, are you?* I'd asked him.

Gerry may be wild and fun, but he's also a thinker. Mostly he thinks before his crazy stuff and does it anyway, but he always thinks first.

There's another knock at the door and I feel ready to explode.

'Gerry's waiting,' Dad says, obviously sent up by Mum, who doesn't want to be abused again.

'Rome wasn't built in a day,' Ciara calls.

'It would be built quicker than Holly getting dressed,' he replies. Ciara guffaws sarcastically, and we hear him wander down the hall.

'You're always so mean to him,' I laugh, feeling pity for Dad.

'Only to his face.' She surfaces from a slush pile with a dress. 'This one.'

'That's the one I started with.'

I hold it up against my body and look in the mirror.

'Definitely looks better from the front,' Ciara says, from behind, with a view of my underwear.

It's a little satin spaghetti strap black dress and it's very little.

'The black will hide the blood stains,' she says.

'Ciara, you're vile.' I shake my head.

She shrugs and reaches for her ice cream before leaving.

I go downstairs. Mum steps out of the kitchen to examine me. She gives me a proud but concerned, and at the same time warning, look. All three expressions I recognise and understand. Everything my parents say and do has many meanings. Like when my parents say 'have fun' but their tone suggests they mean to have their idea of fun, that if I actually have the kind of fun I want to have, then there will be repercussions and consequences.

Dad, Declan and Ciara are watching *Beadle's About* on TV and Declan is roaring with laughter. Jack and Gerry are in the den playing Sonic on Jack's new Sega Mega Drive. As well as Eddie, Jack and the Mega Drive are the second addictions to draw Gerry away from me. I've spent countless evenings and weekends in that room up against both of them. The room that usually smells of dirty socks and smelly feet tonight is filled with the smell of aftershave.

Gerry has his eyes fixed on the screen, playing Sonic.

Jack glances at me and wolf whistles in a jeering way. I wait at the door for Gerry to finish and notice me and for more of Jack's smart comments that I'll ignore. I know he likes Gerry, I know that he'd swap him for me any day and that all of his disparaging remarks and stereotypical big brother comments are out of duty, embarrassment and because he thinks it's expected.

Gerry's face is a mask of concentration, pursed lips, serious brow. He's wearing blue jeans, a white shirt. Gel in his hair. His blue eyes sparkle. He's wearing enough CK One for every man at the party. I smile, watching him. As if sensing my desire, he finally removes his eyes from the game. Eyes up and down, quickly at first, then slowly. I've butterflies in my stomach. I wish we could miss the party completely.

'Ah no!' Jack yells, throwing his hands up, giving us both a jolt.

'What?' Gerry looks at him.

'You died.'

'I don't care,' Gerry grins, chucking the control pad into Jack's lap. 'I'm off.'

'Keep your hands off my sister.'

Gerry grins as he makes his way to me. Our eyes lock. He holds his hands up, where Jack can't see them, open palms, spread fingers, squeezing at the air as if about to grab my boobs. The door pushes open beside me.

It's Ciara.

She observes his disappearing spread hands and his quickly reddening face.

'Nice. Is that the foreplay?'

★　★　★

The party at Erin's Isle is everything I imagined it to be, but when I'd imagined it, I was on the outside. It's easier when I'm in it. A room filled with Gerry's cousins, uncles, aunts, we don't stop talking over plates of sandwiches, chicken wings and cocktail sausages. I've finished my permitted one alcoholic drink by 10 p.m. and my secretly understood but not spoken about second drink by eleven. The older guests leave at 11 p.m. as planned, with Eddie starting a conga line to lead them around the venue once before taking them outside to their cars and waiting taxis. And then the DJ starts and the music is so loud there's no more civilised chat. I down a third drink, thinking I'll have time for a fourth, beginning to think that our plans to leave have been scuppered by Eddie's attention on Gerry all night. When Eddie takes to the dance floor to display his comedy breakdancing, I'm sure I

262

should order another drink because Gerry is usually the eager sidekick in this show. But I'm wrong. This time Gerry chooses me.

Gerry leans in to whisper something to Eddie, Eddie grins, slaps his back. I'm mortified, I'm hoping Gerry hasn't told him exactly what we're about to do, but the fact we're leaving early is a giveaway. Eddie drags Gerry across the dance floor over in my direction. Eddie hugs me and squeezes me so tight I can barely breathe. Gerry is so pleased at this meeting of the giants of his heart that he doesn't do anything to stop him.

Eddie, sweaty and drunk, pulls us both close to him.

'You two,' he squeezes us tightly. 'You know I love this lad.' A bit of his spit lands on my lip but I'm too polite to wipe it away. The sweat from his forehead is slick against mine. I think of my make-up being wiped off.

'I love this lad, I do.' He kisses Gerry on the head roughly. 'And he loves you.'

He hugs us both again. Although I know his sentiments are well meaning, and it's a moment, it's also painful. This guy who bashes into grown men on a football field doesn't know his own strength. His shining pointy party shoe is on my toe, it pinches and hurts. I concentrate on making my body as small as possible while he continues.

'He loves you,' he says again. 'And you love him too, don't you?'

I look at Gerry. Unlike me, he seems moved by this messy man display of love and intimacy. He doesn't seem bothered by being squished,

263

sweated or spat on. Or the fact that his girlfriend is having her love for him forcibly squished out of her.

'Yes,' I say, nodding.

Gerry's looking at me with tenderness and large pupils, which tells me he's drunk but that's OK, I'm feeling the buzz too. He has such a silly smile on his face that I laugh.

'Go on, get out of here, you two,' Eddie says, releasing us from his grip, ruffling Gerry's hair with another violent kiss to the head before heading back to the dance floor for a dance battle with a teammate.

We get to Gerry's house as fast as we can, determined not to waste a second of our magic time. Gerry is a sweetheart, Gerry is thoughtful. We both are. We both think about each other, which makes it all the better for ourselves. He lights a candle, puts music on. At sixteen and seventeen we're the last of our group of friends to have sex, and the couple the longest together. I'm smug enough to think Gerry and I will be different and we're smug enough to make sure that it is exactly what we want it to be. I hate the word smug, yet it is how others see us. We are confident enough together to do our own thing, never to follow the crowd, to dance, not march, to the beat of our own drum. It bothers others, cuts us off from time to time, but we have each other and we don't care.

We make love and it's gentle, and deep, and he finds his hiding place in me, and my refuge is wrapping myself around him. We carve our place in the world together. Later, he kisses me gently,

264

eyes searching mine to read how I am feeling, always caring about what's going on inside my head.

'Eddie's hug hurt more,' I say, and he laughs.

I wish I can spend the night with him, wake up in his arms in the morning, but I can't, we're not allowed. Our love is limited and decided by others, the simple but elusive act of waking up together with the sunrise a pleasure for only when 'they' say so. My curfew was 2 a.m. and it is already that time when I wave goodbye to Gerry from the taxi.

I'm barely asleep when my mum wakes me and I think I've been found out, but the early morning emergency wake-up call has nothing to do with us. Gerry is on the phone and he's crying.

'Holly,' his voice is ragged, sobbing. I panic. 'Eddie is dead.'

After his party ended in Erin's Isle, Eddie and his group of friends moved on to a club on Leeson Street. Eddie was falling around drunk and separated himself from his friends in an effort to get a taxi home. He was found lying unconscious on the street. A hit and run. He died before he reached the hospital.

Eddie's death breaks Gerry. He still works, but he's a malfunctioning Gerry and I know he'll never go back to the way he was. I don't lose him, in fact the opposite happens. All the parts of Gerry that were nonsense disappear and the parts that I love and more, become refined.

I'll never know if it is because of the moment we made love around the same time as Eddie was living the last hours of his life, when we melted down our old forms and remoulded into something new together, or if it was Eddie's death. I'm sure it was both. Eddie's death is such a monstrous event in our lives, who's to know which event changed which parts of us. What I do notice is that both events bring us closer together, and what I know about me and Gerry is that the more the world dislocates, the more we come together.

There's the funeral.

And then there's something new.

We are sitting with Eddie's parents, brother and sister in the family room, everyone stunned. Gerry is sorry that he wasn't with Eddie when he was going home; he knows had he been out, he wouldn't have let Eddie go home alone, he would have guided him to a taxi, put him in the back, brought him home. But what we both know is that Eddie knew that we were in love, Eddie loved that we were in love, he pushed us together, squished us together and sent us off. There's no guilt to be felt, only a regret that Gerry couldn't have made it all end better by saving Eddie.

'If I regret not going to the club with Eddie, then I'd regret what happened between us that night,' Gerry reasons when we're alone. 'And I don't regret a second.'

Eddie's mum brings us upstairs to show us the unopened gifts that are still covered in wrapping paper with unopened birthday cards. A pile of wrapped twenty-first presents that Eddie never even had the chance to open. His parents had brought them all home in a bin liner the night of the party.

'I don't know what to do with all of these,' she says.

We look at them. There must be thirty or forty gifts piled high.

'Do you want us to help you open them?' Gerry asks.

'And what will I do with them?'

We look around Eddie's bedroom. It's filled with Eddie's things. Things he touched, loved, things that smell of him, hold his energy, mean something and have a story. Trophies, jerseys, posters, teddies, computer games, college books; the items that carry the essence of him. The unopened presents before us hold nothing of Eddie in them, they never had the chance to absorb his life.

'Do you want us to give them back?' I ask.

Gerry looks at me, aghast that I've said something so wrong, and for a moment I'm afraid I've misunderstood.

'Would you?' she asks.

I kneel down and open a small card tape to a wrapped gift, footballs decorating the blue paper.

'Paul B,' I read.

'Paul Byrne,' Gerry says. 'Teammate.'

'You know them all, Gerry,' his aunt says.

'All of them have cards,' I say. 'We could do it.' I look at Gerry, who seems unsure. 'A gift from Eddie back to his friends.'

I don't know why I say it. I think it's because I'm trying to sell it to Gerry, because I know it's what his aunt wants, but after a while I start to believe it. 'A final gift from Eddie from wherever he is.'

And Gerry clings to that. Over the next weeks we both embark on this mission to return the gifts given to Eddie. To identify the giver, locate them, and return them. And each gift tells a story about the person Eddie was. And the person giving it shares it with us, wants us to know. Why they chose it, the story behind it, and every reason is another moment that Eddie is alive. And even though they're getting back their own present, they're getting a piece of Eddie back. And they'll keep it. It was Eddie's gift, keeping it will keep him alive, whether it's a football jersey, stupid novelty boxer shorts, or whether it's a compass from the uncle for the boy scout nephew so that he'd never again lose his way. Whatever it is, small or big, sentimental or jokey, it represents an acknowledgement of their friendship, and Gerry and I bring it to them, one summer when we're on our school break. We have part-time jobs but we spend every available hour driving around in Gerry's dad's car with Gerry's provisional licence, just me and him, doing this important adult thing with new-found freedom.

We melted and remoulded together. I watched it happen, I felt it happen. He was in my arms. He was in me.

Sex, death, love, life.

I'm sixteen. Gerry's seventeen. Everything that breaks around us, glues us together even tighter, because no matter how chaotic, everyone has to find their hiding place or you can't hear yourself think. Our hiding place is each other. We create our space, and we live in it.

30

The bag of frozen peas defrosted overnight and left a damp patch at the end of the bed. The damp spot pervades my dreams; whenever my feet brush the wet area, I dream of my feet immersed in water, first a gentle walk on a beach, smooth spongey sand and sparkling water lapping in and out, then later poolside, my legs dangling, moving freely beneath the blue. Later, in a deeper darker sleep, I am held by the ankle, a tight grip on my sore throbbing spot, being dipped head first into the water like Achilles. The act is supposed to be making me stronger, but whoever is holding me by the ankle gets distracted, they dangle me for too long. I can't breathe.

I awake with a fright, out of breath. Summer has brought a bright morning, birdsong, and a searing path of sunlight that pierces directly through the glass and on to my face as though a giant is crouched above me holding a magnifying glass. I block my eyes and try to fill my parched mouth with saliva. The sky is blue, a car alarm sounds nearby, a bird begins to echo the car alarm. A wood pigeon responds, a child laughs, a baby cries, a football is pummelled against a garden wall.

It has been a restless night. Thrown by Bert's funeral and by feeling Gerry's presence, I'm once again flattened by loss.

This is the problem with loving and losing, with holding on and letting go, with being held and then released, reconnecting and then disconnecting. There's always another side to the coin, there is no middle ground. But I must find it. I can't lose myself again. I must rationalise, I must locate myself, ground myself, put everything in perspective. I must not make everything about me, my feelings, my needs, my desires, my losses. I must stop feeling so deeply but I must not be numb; I must move on but I must not forget; I must be happy but not reject sadness; I must embrace, but not cling; I must deal with but not dwell on; I must confront but not attack; I must eliminate but not annihilate; I must be gentle with myself but I must be strong. How can my mind be at one when my heart is in two? So many things to be and not be; I am nothing but I'm everything, yet I must, I must, I must.

There's more I can do, more that I should do. Letters are not enough. I must learn from Bert, I can do more for Ginika and I owe it to Jewel. That is where I'll start and this throbbing, this pain from my head to my toe will surely, eventually go. It must, and I must make it so. I am motionless but not powerless. Move, Holly, move.

Denise knocks gently on the door. I wrap the duvet around my neck, pretend to be asleep and hope she'll go away. The door opens slowly and she creeps in. I feel her near me, checking on me. I hear ceramic against my bedside table as she places something down. I smell coffee and buttery toast.

'Thanks,' I speak for the first time and it comes out as a croak.

'Are you OK?'

'Yes. I've had a spiritual awakening.'

'Oh, that's nice.'

I smile.

'I spoke to Ciara, she told me it went well at Bert's wake yesterday.'

I finally open my eyes to study her, to see if she's hiding a laugh, but she's not. She's empathetic, compassionate, considerate Denise.

'My part could have gone better,' I sit up. 'But it was well received, which is the main thing.' I look to the bedside locker and I'm right about the food. Creamy buttery scrambled eggs sit atop the slice of brown bread and my stomach reminds me I haven't eaten since this time yesterday before work. 'Thank you for this.'

'I have to earn my keep.' She smiles sadly.

'Did something happen?'

She picks at her cuticle. 'I went to see Tom yesterday. I told him I was sorry. That I made a mistake, I panicked.'

'And?'

'He told me to go fuck myself.'

I wince. 'Tom is angry, he's within his rights to lash out, but he'll come round.'

'I hope so. I have to woo him. I'm not really a woo-er. I can bribe him with gifts, any ideas?'

My mind has wandered as she spoke. 'Have you ever thought of adoption?'

'You think me adopting a baby will woo him?'

'What? No. I was thinking about adoption, fostering. I know it's not the same thing, it's not

272

a baby born of you and Tom, and that's what you desire, but look how you've been with Jewel, look how loving and caring and wonderful you have been with her. Imagine how many babies are out there, needing the kind of love you are willing to give.' I pause, my mind wandering, as a new thought takes hold. 'Denise,' I say, wide-eyed.

'Don't,' she says, stopping me. 'I know what you're thinking. I already looked into it.'

'You have?'

'It takes eighteen months to do the course and even then, if by some wild miracle I could further topple Jewel's life on its head and traumatise her by removing her from a new home she's settled into after eighteen months, it's not like you can go and pick the child you want. Social services decide who goes where.'

'But if you somehow *could* become Jewel's guardian, would Tom feel the same?' I ask, my mind racing ahead.

'I need him to start *speaking* to me first before a discussion of that magnitude could begin. Or even have him look me in the eye would be a start. Anyway, it's all hypothetical. This would have to be Ginika's decision. I couldn't put it in her head, it wouldn't be right.'

'She may want it too. Wouldn't it be at least worth asking? She's looking for a safe place for her baby to grow up in. You've been nothing but loving and kind to them both. You *want* this so much.'

Denise looks at me.

'And not to put you under any pressure, but

Tom is going to have to take you back, because last night I accepted an offer on the house. We have about eight to twelve weeks before we're homeless.'

'What, really?' Denise tries to sound enthusiastic but I can see the legs pedalling wildly under the calm surface. 'Congratulations. Where are you going to live?'

'I've absolutely no idea.'

'Jesus, Holly, not that I'm in the position to judge, but what is happening to you?' she asks. 'In such a short time, ever since the podcast, it's like the wheels have come off.'

I groan and fall back on the bed. 'Please don't say scary things to me again, I can't take it.' I suddenly notice the coffee mug she has placed beside me. She's drinking from Gerry's *Star Wars* mug. The one that I broke.

'Did you fix that mug?'

'No. It was on the counter when I got in from work.'

Yesterday. I'd been in the kitchen when I got home to get the frozen peas but I hadn't looked around before coming upstairs and falling into bed. I lean forward and study the mug, steam rising from the top. I search for the cracks along the handle and the rim.

'Hold on a minute,' I throw the covers off me and get out of bed, and hurry downstairs to the kitchen. Denise follows me.

I open the cupboard. The broken mug is gone.

'It was right there beside the set of keys,' Denise says, pointing beside the toaster and then I realise what's happened.

They're Gabriel's set of house keys.
He glued Gerry back together.

★   ★   ★

Saturday morning is about restarting the engine but I don't drive, I don't cycle; today I am taking the bus, specifically, the number 66A. Ginika has told me about it, ranted and grumbled about it in her moments of frustration. Her dad, the bus driver, the devil at the helm of the 66 leading his people to Chapelizod, while simultaneously, from afar, driving her insane.

He is not on the nine-thirty shift. I hang back, sit on the concrete steps of a Georgian block in Merrion Square drinking a take-out coffee, lifting my face to the sun and hoping that in channelling my energy directly at it, it will kindly reciprocate and fuel me. At ten thirty, I know it is him. He has Ginika's face. Her big open eyes, her rounded plum-shaped high cheeks.

He opens the doors and I join the queue to step on. I study him intently as people drop their coins in, insert their travel cards and move on. Small nods to those who acknowledge him, a quiet, reserved presence. He is not the picture she painted. There is no arrogant captain of this vessel, just a tired quiet professional man with bloodshot eyes. I sit where I can keep my eye on him and I watch him the entire journey. From Merrion Square to O'Connell Street, he manoeuvres in and out of lanes, raising a hand out the window in thanks to those who make way for him. Patient, calm, careful, smooth, in

275

busy Saturday morning city-centre traffic. Eight further minutes to Parkgate Street, ten minutes to Chapelizod. I turn from the village views to Ginika's dad and back again, examining both with the same interest. Seven minutes to Liffey Valley shopping centre where the majority of people get off. Ten minutes to Lucan Village, a further twelve to River Forest where I'm finally the only person left on the bus.

He looks over his shoulder at me. 'This is the last stop.'

'Oh.' I look around. 'Are you driving back to the city centre?'

'Not for another twenty minutes.'

I stand and move next to him. His photographic ID says Bayowa Adebayo. Photographs and knick-knacks decorate the area around the steering wheel. Crucifixes, religious medals. A photograph of four children. One of them is Ginika. A school photo, a grey uniform and red tie, a beaming white crooked-toothed smile, her chestnut eyes alight with life and mischief, a cheeky dimple in her smile.

I smile at her image.

'Did you miss your stop?' he asks.

'No. Um. I was just enjoying the journey.'

He studies me with discreet curiosity. I may strike him as odd, but it's no odds to him.

'OK. Well, I leave in twenty minutes.'

He pulls a lever and the door opens.

'Oh.'

I step off the bus and look around. The doors close behind me immediately. I take the few steps to the terminus and sit on the bench. He leaves his seat and walks to the back of the bus with a small plastic bag in his hand. He sits and eats a sandwich, drinks a hot drink from a flask. He notices me, sitting at the terminus, waiting, and turns his attention back to his sandwich.

Twenty minutes later he walks up the aisle, opens the doors, steps out, closes them from outside, crumpling his bag in his hand, and places it in the bin. He stretches, pulls up the waist of his trousers over a small belly, and opens the doors. He steps on and closes them again immediately, while he takes his place back in his seat. When he's ready, he opens the doors and I step back on. He nods at me, acknowledging me, no questions, no conversation, none of his business what I'm doing and he's not curious, or if he is, he doesn't show it. I sit in the same seat on the way back. I stand up at the last stop in Merrion Square, allow everyone else off before me. I approach his window at the driver's seat.

'You're going back again?' he asks, amusement in his tired eyes, a small smile on his lips.

'No,' I say, ready this time. 'I'm a friend of your daughter, Ginika.'

His smile doesn't disappear, but the way it freezes on his face says the same thing.

'She's wonderful, very brave, and has inspired me and taught me so much. You should be very proud of her.'

It's really all I have the courage to say. All that I, perhaps, want to say. Because he has a right to know. No, more than that: he *should* know. It is better to know while his daughter still lives and breathes the same air as him that she is

277

wonderful and brave and inspiring. It is not enough to be told after, nor is it good enough to realise it after. I step off the bus quickly before he shouts at me or calls to me or we get further involved than I want to be. That's enough, I think. I hope.

★ ★ ★

It is lunchtime and, buoyed by my brief encounter with Ginika's dad, there is a bounce in my step, a sense of overriding duty to fulfil my next promised task. I have one envelope filled with cash that I have tightly guarded in my bag, one lovingly, carefully written shopping list, and one large desire to continue pushing out the darkening corners of my fragile mind. I must not let the clouds move to the centre, they must drift on, just as I watched the clouds float by my window yesterday. It is the first Saturday in June, and I must begin Christmas shopping for Joy.

Joy has three sons: Conor, Robert and Jeremy. Conor is married to Elaine and they have two children, Ella and Luke. Robert is married to Grainne and they have four small children, twins Nathan and Ethan, Lily-Sue and Noah. Jeremy has a child called Max with Sophie and a baby on the way with Isabella.

Joy has three sisters and one brother; Olivia, Charlotte, Emily and Patrick. Three are married, one divorced, but Joy is close with her in-laws. Collectively they have eleven children, and five of them have children. Joy also has two sisters-in-law and one brother-in-law, all have children and between them make her an aunt to eight more nieces and nephews. Four of these nieces and nephews have a total of seven children. And then there's Joe, her tower of strength, and her two closest friends, Annalise and Marie.

All of these names have been written on Joy's Christmas list, along with a specifically chosen gift. She has asked me to do this, the agent of the PS, I Love You Club, not her children, not her daughters-in-law, or her dear friends, because she wants normal business to resume, nothing to feel out of step, even when life has taken a turn in a direction no one wishes it had. She doesn't want anybody in her life to feel left out; everyone near and dear to her will receive her parting gift.

Delivering Bert's letters, Christmas shopping for Joy and watching her bake and cook Joe's favourite meals, making notes to add to her scrapbook of secrets, being invited into Paul's home and world to film personal messages, getting insights into his private thoughts and memories, has been an intimate welcome into people's precious and private worlds. I feel a sense of purpose, of responsibility to those who have entrusted me with a great duty. While it has undoubtedly distracted me from my own life, it has also gifted me with distraction from my woes. I find myself getting lost in the job at hand. Following Joy's shopping list, buying the gifts according to her budget and then ticking each name and item off the list feels extraordinarily satisfying. I'm busy. I have a purpose, a great one, fulfilling Joy's wish.

When I return home, I sit on the floor of my

TV room, spread the gifts around me in preparation for wrapping. I usually despise wrapping, leaving that task to the wrapping stations in the shops at Christmas. But it's not Christmas and this is my duty. Using craft paper and string, I take greater care than I ever have in ensuring the corners are neat, double-sided sticky tape hidden.

Denise returns to the house at 7 p.m., and Sharon is with her. I feel a flicker of irritation that my isolation has been broken and, even though Sharon is my friend too, that I haven't been asked permission. I'm so used to having my own space, I like being alone. Even when practically living with Gabriel, having our own homes meant we could take necessary breathers for our headspace, and even when together we were good at being separate.

'Are you wrapping Christmas presents?' Sharon asks, watching me from the doorway.

'Yes, for Joy.' I brace myself for a smart retort.

'OK. I won't disturb you, I'll be in the kitchen with Denise.' She swiftly leaves, picking up on my mood. Moments later, I hear music. A stringed instrument leading into the smooth and calming tones of Nat King Cole singing 'The Christmas Song', Sharon's phone the source of the music. She places down a glass of red wine and a bowl of crisps, winks at me and leaves, closing the door behind her.

Each package has a gift card: To Conor, To Robert, To Jeremy . . . to everybody on the list, signed off with *PS, I Love You*. I box them all up in three regular cardboard boxes and label them 'Christmas Tree Lights', the plan being to store it in the attic for Joe to find when he decorates the house for Christmas.

I told Gabriel that my life would return to its normal running, that I would be able to extract myself from these people's lives at the appropriate time when I had fulfilled my obligations. But he was right about me: I can't do that. Where he was wrong, though, was in believing that it was a negative thing. It's not something to avoid, this *is* my life now. This life is giving me life. I drooped yesterday, I crashed, but I'm different now. I've learned from my mistakes and today I picked up the pieces.

31

Unable to take any more time off work, and still feeling revived and enthusiastic a week after my great epiphany, I decide to begin my days earlier. It's 7 a.m. on a Saturday morning, and I'm feeling positive about the next mission with Paul. I wait in the vast empty car park of a retail park, which is the address he's given me. I have no idea why I'm here. I don't have any control over Paul's ideas, I'm merely the camera holder and that's all he wants me to be. I wonder if I should be more, if he will make room for me to be more.

A car finally enters the car park and I can't help but laugh. It's a bottle-green Morris Minor, not Paul's usual car. I film his arrival, keeping my laughter silent and trying to hold my hand steady. I'm not supposed to be seen or heard. He parks beside me and lowers the window, which takes a while as it's a manual roll-down, but adds to the humour.

'Hi, Casper,' he says to the camera. 'You're sixteen. Looking good. I'm sure the girls love you. This here is the car that my dad, Grandpa Charlie, taught me to drive in. It wasn't cool then, it isn't cool now, but today I'm taking you on your first driving lesson in the same car Grandpa Charlie taught me to drive in. Hop in,' he says, winking.

★　★　★

'What's wrong?' he looks at me, uncertainly, when we've finished filming the driving lesson. 'Not good? I'm not sure if you were feeling that one.'

'It's great!' I plaster a smile on my face, but I'm worried. He made quite a few comments that I don't think will be relevant in sixteen years, and I don't think Paul has thought this through entirely. He's acting as though this driving lesson is about to happen to his two-year-old son tomorrow, mentioning friends his son has now, referencing everything from now, or things that it is impossible to predict in fifteen years' time. I don't say anything because I don't want to spoil Paul's mood. His wishes are my command and it's uplifting to be with him when he is in such a cheery mood. Preparing the letters and films doesn't steep us in darkness as one would imagine, as Gabriel feared; it's all positive and fun and forward-thinking. I'd like him to see me as I am at this moment; laughing and smiling, enjoying time with someone he assumed would drag me down into a deep depressive state.

'Are we still good for Eva's videos tomorrow?' he asks, high-energy, anxious, worried as if I'm going to say no.

'Everything is organised.'

'Great,' he says. 'Then we're almost finished. I need to have it all complete by next week.'

Once I'm finished with Paul, there's only one person left. What will I do then? 'Why next week?'

'The craniotomy is scheduled.'

Without a doubt, brain surgery of any description is probably the most dangerous surgery you can undergo. A craniotomy is the most common type of brain surgery to remove a brain tumour, where the surgeon cuts out a part of the skull to get to the brain. Often it's not possible for the surgeon to remove all the tumour so they remove as much as they can; this is called debulking. The risks are infection, haemorrhage, or bleeding in the brain, blood clots, brain swelling, seizures, some patients can develop a stroke due to low blood pressure.

'My husband had one.'

'It will be my third. The surgeon has suggested there may be left-sided paralysis.'

'They have to give you the worst-case scenario.'

'I know. But I want to have all the messages ready, just in case. I've written the letter for Claire, and we've dozens of videos, you'll have them all ready, won't you?' His legs bounce nervously beneath the steering wheel.

'I've been sending them to the email address we set up for Casper and Eve,' I say calmly, trying for my tone to be an influence.

'My letter will tell Claire what to do for the kids,' he says.

I nod. I hope Claire will think it's a good idea, otherwise she will be burdened for the rest of her life delivering emails to her growing children. I wonder if I should ask him this, but instead I ask, 'Paul, should you even be driving?'

He's irritated by this question.

'I ask only out of concern.' For almost four

years my days revolved around what Paul is experiencing. I know about the double vision, the seizures, the immobilisation. Gerry's licence had been suspended.

'After next week, I won't be. After next week, I won't be doing a lot of things. Thanks for your help, Holly.'

It's blunt and I know it's my cue to get out of the car.

A tap on my window gives me a fright.

Paul looks up and curses.

I look out and see a young woman, around my age, with a yoga mat bag over her shoulder, glaring angrily through the window.

'Shit,' I whisper. I look at Paul, who's white in the face. 'Is that Claire?'

He paints on a wide grin and gets out of the car.

'Paul,' I hiss, my heart pounding with nerves.

'Just go with what I say.' He smiles at me through gritted smiling teeth.

Claire backs away from my window.

'Hi honey,' I hear him say warmly, oozing with charm and in my opinion lies.

'Fuck, fuck, fuck,' I whisper to myself before taking a deep breath and opening the door.

Claire won't embrace her husband, her body language is cold.

'What the hell are you two doing?' She looks at me. 'Who the hell are you? What are you doing with my husband?'

'This is Holly, honey,' he says in a warning tone. 'Look at me. This is Holly. She's a friend of Joy's, she's a member of the book club.'

285

Claire looks me up and down, and I can't look her in the eye. This situation is awful, it's what I feared. I even hate me. If I had found Gerry sitting in a car with another woman, a week before a big operation, after giving my life to his care, I'd have wanted to strangle them both. This is not good.

'You said you were getting toys for the kids in Smyths,' Claire says. 'You're not even supposed to be driving, but I let you go. I've been so worried, I've been calling you. I have a class now, I had to call Mum to mind the kids. Jesus, Paul what are you doing? And why have you got your dad's old car?'

The frustration is steaming from her. I'm on her side.

'I'm sorry, I forgot about your class. I'll go straight home and mind the kids, your mum can go home. And you're right, I shouldn't have driven. I met Holly in Smyths, I didn't feel well and I asked if she'd mind driving me home. Nothing serious, just a headache and a little dizzy, but I didn't trust myself to get behind the wheel so I was showing her how it works, that's all.'

He speaks too fast, it's hard to believe but also difficult to interrupt and argue with. Claire looks at me. I take a step away, ready to leave.

'She was helping me out, that's all.' Paul looks at me. 'Doing me a huge favour. Isn't that right?'

I look at him. 'Yeah.'

There's no way that Paul is out of the woods yet but I'm not sticking around for it. I will not be made a liar, or a cheat.

286

'It was nice to meet you, Claire,' I say apologetically, feeling self-conscious about my tone, my words, my expression, my stance. 'Make sure you get home safely, Paul,' I say stonily.

I signed up to this to help, not to be the lie, not to be the punching bag. Even if that does help him, each hit bruises me.

★   ★   ★

By the end of my work day, I feel like I've reached the point of exhaustion as I sit at the table with Ginika. We're blending, running all the sounds together to make the word. I set up a sun umbrella so we could sit outside with bees dancing noisily around us feasting themselves on Richard's colourful additions. The garden furniture has been dusted off, sanded and varnished, in time for the two-week heatwave that's upon us. Denise is on a blanket with Jewel, rolling around, singing and laughing, pointing out birds and bees and flowers, while Jewel's tiny pudgy forefinger is in constant pointing mode.

Her favourite word is 'wow' and right now, the whole world is wow.

'Look, Jewel, an aeroplane!' Denise says, lying on her back and pointing up at the sky, at the lone airplane streaking across the blue sky, leaving a trail of white behind it.

'Wow,' says Jewel, ready with her pointing finger.

While Denise opens Jewel's eyes to the world around her, I am grateful for the equally attentive Ginika, who has been seriously keeping her side of the bargain. Whatever reckless kind of student she claims to have been in school, she certainly isn't that now. Dedicated, punctual, prepared, she is pouring her heart and soul into her literacy like her life depends on it.

'S-h — '

'Those two letters go together, sound them together.' I put my finger over my lips to give her a hint.

'Sh,' she says, and I grin, happily, proudly.

'Sh-i-t.' She sounds them out separately. She frowns and says it again. 'Shit,' she says suddenly, realising, then looks up at me. 'Shit.'

I grin.

'I wish my school had been more like this,' she says, laughing.

'Next word.'

'F-u-ck. Fuck. Fuck!' she laughs.

'Next one.'

'P-ai-n. Pain.'

'Yes!' I punch the air. 'A and I go together, you didn't separate their sounds.' I hold my hand up for a high-five.

She rolls her eyes and gives me a weak high-five, embarrassed by the praise. 'You are such a dork. Shit, Fuck and Pain,' she reads. 'What kind of shitty mood are you in?'

'Some words have an irregular spelling and can't be read by blending,' I continue, ignoring her question.

Ginika tuts.

'I know, there's always something to throw at us just as we're getting the hang of it.'

'Like cancer.'

'Ginika!'

She laughs wickedly.

'Unfortunately, many of these words are common words and we call these *tricky* words.'

Ginika rolls her eyes. She rolls up her sleeves. 'Right. Let me at the bastards.'

I smile. 'For example. This word,' I write it down. 'Normally we would read this as . . . '

'L-a-u-g-h,' Ginika sounds it out with the *g* and *h* sound. 'What the hell does that mean?'

'Perfect,' I smile.

'I got it right?'

'You got it right and wrong. It's a tricky word so it's actually pronounced laugh. The *GH* has an *f* sound.'

'Ah for fuck's sake, then why don't they give it an 'f'? How's anybody supposed to learn this stuff?' She tosses her pencil up in the air and it lands on the table. The pointed lead dents the fresh varnish. I pretend her outburst never happened; it's certainly not the first time.

'Ginika,' Denise says. 'Sorry to interrupt you guys.' She has a peculiar tone, she sounds nervous. 'A friend of mine was getting rid of some baby stuff recently — her kids are older now, and she was going to throw out a buggy. I took it, thinking it might be good for Jewel. You don't need to use it if you don't want . . . '

'She hates buggies, you know that. She likes to be held,' Ginika says firmly, not looking up from her page.

'Of course, you're her mam, you know best. But I thought I'd take it instead of letting it go in the skip. I'll show you.' She dashes into the house, while we watch Jewel lying on her stomach and focusing on a blade of grass, her finger pointing, gently touching it, and then . . . grabbing and pulling. Denise returns to the garden with the buggy.

It doesn't look old at all. It's brand new.

I steal a glance at Ginika, who's staring at the buggy blankly, with a million things going through her head.

'I could bring her out for a walk, just around the streets, we won't go far,' Denise offers, keeping her voice light and airy. 'For a change of scenery.'

I stay out of it. Head down, continue my prep.

Ginika is silent. When she's pushed, she's the explosive kind, particularly when it comes to her daughter. Her response, when it comes, surprises both of us.

'OK.'

Jewel kicks up a lot when placed in the buggy, but then is quickly distracted by the — also new — range of toys that Denise places on the bar. She also attaches her favourite book and Jewel is happy.

Ginika is quiet after they're gone. She turns away from the workbooks and to the empty play mat on the grass. She seems tired. She is tired. Dark rings around her eyes, she's lost a lot of weight, with the cancer extended to her liver, bowel and groin. She reaches down to her bag with great effort and I get it for her. She rummages in a package and takes out a lollipop, but I know that it's nothing sweet. It's a fentanyl lollipop, for sudden bursts of severe pain.

'Let's take a break,' I say. 'Do you want to go inside? Maybe it's too hot.'

'I don't want to take a break,' she snaps.

'OK. Can I get you anything?'

'No.'

Silence.

'Thank you,' she adds, more gently.

Giving her time, I move my chair out of the shade and finally relax, I sit back in the chair, close my eyes, lift my face to the sky, listen to the birds singing with delight, the bees all around me, scrunch my toes into the hot grass. My crap day begins to dissipate.

'Did your husband use these?' she asks.

I open my eyes and see her waving her lolly in the air. 'No. He was on morphine. Intravenously.'

'This is stronger,' she says, sucking. 'Morphine was making me sick.'

The change from when I met her is startling, but not in the obvious ways. Yes, her body is changing, but so too is her mind. Her body is thinner but her mind is broader. She speaks more personally, when she's not concentrating on keeping the wall up, and we have proper conversations. She is more confident, self-assured, she knows what she wants. Of course, she always knew that, but she delivers her opinions and emotions differently. She admitted her joy at being able to read the instructions on the medicine label for Jewel's cough medicine. She reads her a bedtime story every night. Being able to read has made her feel more confident and less lost and confused by the world.

'I think your house is haunted. Your photographs keep moving.'

I follow her gaze, through the opened patio doors through the dining room and into the living room. I assume she's referring to the mantelpiece where the photo of Gabriel and me in happier times is gone, replaced by the fallen photograph of Gerry and me, in a smaller frame. I saw her notice it when she arrived, was waiting for the question as soon as her eyes landed on it, but to my surprise she held back.

'Gabriel and I broke up.'

She looks at me in surprise. 'Why? Did he cheat?'

'No. He has a daughter who needs him, she took priority in the end.' My immediate guilt for painting Gabriel as the bad guy tells me that I know Ava wasn't the real reason for our break-up. The denial potion is wearing off.

'What age is she?'

'Your age,' I say, connecting this for the first time. Ginika seems light years older.

'So why does she need him, is she sick?'

'No, I'd say troubled. In trouble at school, she acts up. Drinking, smoking, partying. Doesn't get along with her mum and step-dad-to-be. Gabriel thought it would be best if she moved in with him.'

'Instead of you?'

'Basically,' I sigh. 'Yes.'

'So because she's a brat, he dumped you?'

'She needs stability.' I try to hide the cynicism from my voice. 'And he didn't dump me. I ended it.' I'm tired of feeding her tidbits, it's what she does with me and if we keep this up we'll never get anywhere. I lean in, elbows on the table, face in the shade. 'I got tired of waiting for him, Ginika. And he wasn't supportive of me doing this.'

'Jealousy,' she nods understandingly, looking at the empty blanket where Jewel's toys still lie.

'No.' I frown, confused. 'Why do you say jealous?'

'It's obvious. Your husband did something amazing that other people are now trying to imitate. He started something pretty big. Your fella can't compete with a dead husband, can he? No matter how good he is at chopping down trees or anything else. So he says to himself, if she's gonna spend time with her ex-husband, I'll move my daughter in instead of her. See how she likes it.'

I look at Ginika in surprise. This is a perspective I had perhaps foolishly not considered.

Could Gabriel have been jealous of Gerry? It makes sense, because isn't that exactly how I felt about his reunion? 'Ginika, you're one of the wisest people I know.'

'I can't even spell wisest,' she mutters, uncomfortable with the praise.

'I don't think that's the definition of wisdom.'

'What is the definition of wisdom?'

'I don't know,' I smile wryly.

'Five minutes with me and I'd put his daughter straight,' Ginika says, defensive of me. 'I might not have the energy I used to have for a good scrap, but I could ram this lollipop up her arse.'

'Thank you, Ginika, that's very moving, but stop trying to be teacher's pet.'

She winks. 'I've got your back, *miss*.'

'And it's thoughtful. It would both hurt her *and* relieve the pain.'

She laughs loudly, a real belly laugh, and her face lights up.

'Can I ask you about Jewel's dad . . . again?' I probe, feeling we're having a moment.

'I just want to write a letter.'

'Sorry.' I reach for the book.

'That's not what I mean,' she says, hand on top of the book to stop me from opening it. 'What I mean is, I want Jewel to have a letter, from me. I don't need you to do any of that reuniting stuff for me like you did for Bert's wife and her sister.'

'OK.' It's like she's seen right through me. Does she know? Is she testing me? Was her dad in contact? I can't let it lie. 'Ah, about that, Ginika,' I say nervously. 'I saw your dad at the weekend.'

Her eyes narrow and I feel the sting of her sharp stare. 'You what?'

'I felt as though I wasn't doing enough, that I — '

'What did you say? Where did you meet him?'

'I took the bus. The 66A. You told me that was his route. I sat on the bus, I went all the way to the end and back,' I explain. 'Then, as I was getting off, I told him that I know you, that you are wonderful, incredibly brave and one of the most inspiring people I've ever met and that he should be immensely proud of you.'

She frowns, examines me to see if I'm telling the truth. 'What else?'

'Nothing else. That's all, I promise. I want your parents to know how amazing you are.'

'What did he say?'

'Nothing. I didn't give him time to speak. I just got off the bus.'

She turns away and absorbs this and I hope I haven't ruined everything, jeopardised our relationship, which I now realise is a friendship, and one I don't want to lose. I have definitely overstepped the mark, I can only wonder if she will forgive me for this. There's not doing enough, as with Paul. And then there's doing too much, as with Ginika. I need to find the middle ground.

'When did you see him?'

'Saturday morning. Ten thirty route.'

'What did he look like?' she asks quietly.

'He was quiet. He was busy, working. He was concentrating. He . . . ' I shrug.

She looks at me, then really studies me. 'Are you OK?'

'No, I'm actually shitting myself that you're going to kill me.'

She smiles. 'I might. But no. I mean, are you actually cracked? You spent your Saturday morning sitting on a bus with my dad, for what? For me?'

I nod.

'Jesus.'

'I'm sorry.'

She's quiet. 'Thank you for telling him that. I don't think he's ever heard that about me from anyone before.' She sits straighter, prouder. 'Did you speak to my ma as well?'

'No,' I hold my hands up in defence. 'You didn't tell me where she works.'

'Thank fuck for that.'

We smile.

'He has a photo of you at his steering wheel. A school photo. Grey uniform, red tie, cheeky little smile on you.'

'Yeah,' she says, disappearing a little. 'He prefers her.'

'Which version of you do you prefer?'

'What?' she asks, frowning.

'I've been thinking this year that Gerry doesn't know me now, he never met the person I've become. I prefer this version of me, yet I became this way because I lost him. If I ever had the power to undo everything, I wouldn't want to unravel who I've become.'

She ponders that. 'Yeah, I know what you mean. I like me better now.'

And what Ginika has been through to get to this version of herself.

'I'm sorry if I did the wrong thing. I promise I won't contact your dad again.'

'You did the wrong thing,' she agrees, sucking her lollipop. 'But it was a nice thing, if not a bit fucking pointless.'

Before the wall goes up, I continue. 'I was thinking of Jewel, of her future, of where she'll live and who will provide a life for her. I know you have a foster family, but perhaps there are guardians you know who could care for her. You're fully in control of that, you know, you'd just need to add it to your . . . '

'What?'

'Your will.'

Her eyes narrow. 'Have you anyone in mind?'

'I mean, I . . . ' I stall. It's a vulnerable time in her life, I don't want to be accused of undue influence, not over something as important as this. I sidetrack. 'Well, her dad for one. Does he know about what's going on? About Jewel? That you're sick?'

She glares at me.

'Sorry.' I back off. 'I thought we were having a moment.'

'You're having a flippin' breakdown moment, is what you're having. Let's get back to work.'

We open the books and pick up where we left off.

'Do you ever wish your husband wrote you different letters?' she asks suddenly in the middle of writing the word *love* over and over. I'm choosing words that I know she'll need for her letter to Jewel.

I tense up. 'What do you mean?'

'What I said,' she says bluntly.

'No.'

'Liar.'

Irritated, I let her comment pass.

'Do you know what you're going to write in your letter yet?' I ask.

'I'm working on it,' she says, head down and concentrating again on her cursive writing. Now it's: *dear, dear, dear, dear, dear, dear.* 'I know I don't want it to be anything like Paul's though,' she adds when the line is complete.

'Why not?' I ask, surprised.

'Are you serious?' She eyeballs me again. 'Paul has every second of his kids' lives all sewn up, by the sounds of it. Their birthdays, their driving lessons, their weddings, their first days of school, the first day they wipe their own arses. It's like he thinks he can see exactly who they're going to be. But what if they're not that person? I know Jewel better than anyone in the whole wide world. But even I don't know what she'll do five minutes from now, never mind tomorrow. It'll be weird for them, you know?' She shudders at the thought of their futures., 'So that's why I asked you about your husband's letters. Maybe he got something wrong, that didn't suit you after he died.'

She's looking at me again. Her words have hit me with impact and my mind is racing.

'Because if there's a letter you didn't like or something, you should probably tell Paul — not that he'd listen, Mr I Can Do This All By Myself. What is it with the men? Him and Bert. If they wanted their letters delivered, they should've hired a courier service. Me? I really need your help.'

'I don't know, Ginika,' I sigh, everything unravelling again. 'I sometimes wonder who's teaching who here.'

32

The next day I have another session with Paul, our final one before his surgery. I'm not in the best of moods, particularly after how yesterday's driving lesson ended. I'm missing a Sunday roast in my parents' house and I'm a little resentful of that despite the fact I'm relieved I don't have to answer to them about my break-up with Gabriel and my involvement in the club, about how I'm ruining Paul's marriage, as opposed to cherishing it. I can only imagine what Ciara is telling them. I've chosen to be here but still feel contrary about missing out on my life, as though Paul should know what I'm sacrificing for him.

He's sheepish when he arrives. 'I'm sorry about yesterday. Claire believed me, if that makes you feel any better.'

'It doesn't,' I snap. 'I didn't even want to come here today.'

'I was afraid you wouldn't.'

'What happened yesterday goes against everything that I'm trying to achieve. I don't want to lie to your wife. I don't want her to hate me. I don't want to ruin anything, the object is to give her a gift, not a nightmare. I'm supposed to be invisible, not the cause of a problem.'

'I promise, Holly, it won't happen again. I won't lie; if anything, I'll tell her the truth.'

'If you don't, I will,' I say firmly.

'Understood.'

I breathe out, feeling a little better. 'OK, let's finish this.'

The 'PS, I Love You initiative' as I phrased it in our communications, managed to come to an agreeable decision with Donard Castle, a fifteenth-century castle that was family-owned until fifty years ago and is now a popular event venue. Today they are hosting a wedding reception and while the couple are in a nearby chapel saying their vows, Paul and I have permission to utilise their fully furnished and decorated reception room to film his pieces for Eva.

His father of the bride speech.

When he shared the idea with me some time ago I was moved, but today, standing at Eva's faux-wedding, I'm agitated. After Ginika's pearls of wisdom yesterday, I haven't been able to shake the question about Gerry's letters. Were they all helpful? Did he get anything wrong? Alarm bells are ringing. Am I getting it wrong? It's not just about holding the camera, making a film; I was put into this position by the PS, I Love You Club because of my own personal experience. I can offer Paul more and I haven't been.

During an illness, especially one such as his, there are few moments of light, and I didn't want to be the one to block it out. I didn't interrupt or interfere in his excited plans because I didn't want to spoil his vision. Yet in staying quiet I certainly put his loved ones last. Just as I've done with my own. I check the time. They're probably sitting down to eat. I've no idea what Gabriel is doing with Ava. Perhaps they're sitting around for dinner with Kate and Finbar, and the idea of them playing a happy united family without me saddens me.

'What do you think?' he asks, modelling his black tuxedo. 'It's Murphy. Paul Murphy.'

I smile and adjust his crooked bowtie. 'Most youthful father of the bride I've ever seen.'

He surveys the wedding reception room, impressed. 'Holly,' he grins, 'You have surpassed yourself.'

The bride and groom's choice of decorations are pink and silver themed, with pink peonies at the centre of every circular table of ten. The table linen is white and the chairs are covered in white fabric with pink and silver bows on alternating chairs. The head table is long and laid out banquet-style, facing the room, behind it is a stage where the band recently completed their sound check then left to give us our designated thirty minutes. It was the most time I could negotiate for no fee whatsoever.

'You ready?' I ask Paul, snapping him out of his trance, as he studies the room, absorbing the fantasy set-up of his daughter's future wedding. Drinking it in and adding it to his memories, as though he was there.

'Eh, yeah,' he says, perhaps surprised by my brusque tone.

'The head table is here.'

He follows me, slowly walking along the table, reading the names, perhaps imagining who will be seated at Eva's wedding.

'Father of the bride is here,' I interrupt his thoughts. 'I brought you a bottle of champagne. Non-alcoholic, because I know you're not allowed to drink with your medication.' I remove the bottle from my bag. I pop the cork, no nonsense, fill a glass that was also in my bag and hand it to him.

He watches me, silent.

'It's for your toast.

'Is everything OK, Holly, you seem a little . . . '

'What?'

'Nothing,' he says, backing off. 'If it's because of yesterday, I apologise. Again.'

'Thank you. We only have twenty minutes left before the bridal party arrive.'

'Right. OK.'

He takes his place at the father of the bride's position.

'How much of the table do you want me to capture?' I ask. 'Zoom in on you and we could be anywhere, which defeats the purpose of this room. Zoom out and I capture the table and it's obvious you're at a table by yourself.'

He blinks. Looks lost.

I decide. 'I can get the flowers in this way. On one, two . . . ' I give him the nod.

He lifts his champagne glass and grins. 'Hello, Monkey Face. My darling Eva. I'm honoured to be here with you on your special day. You look so beautiful. And this man — '

I must make a face because he stops. 'Did I say something wrong?'

I stop filming. 'No. Why?'

'You made a face.'

I shrug. 'Ignore my face. Concentrate on your speech. Go again.'

'My darling monkey face Eva. I'm honoured to be here — '

'OK.' I obviously did make a face because the same thing annoyed me the second time. I lower the phone. 'Eva is a one-year-old now, I get that you call her monkey face, but do you think you'd be calling her that on her wedding day?'

He thinks about it. 'It's funny?'

'She might not — remember — that you called her monkey face. This is going to be at least twenty years away.'

'Right.' He clears his throat. 'My darling Eva, I'm so happy to be here on your special day. You look so beautiful in your dress — '

'What if she's not wearing a dress?'

'Every bride wears a dress.'

'In 1952 they did.'

He looks at me, confused.

'She could be wearing a bikini on a beach, or in an Elvis suit in Vegas. You've no idea what she's wearing. You're probably going to appear on a screen in a room. People are going to be shocked. Moved. Confused. Imagine how Eva will feel. You sharing your sentiments is enough, don't be too specific because if you get it wrong it will feel . . . off.'

'OK. Yeah. Good point.'

He starts again. 'Hello, my darling Eva. I'm delighted to be with you on your special day and even though I can't be with you in person I'm raising a glass to you from the best seat in the house. I'd like to congratulate the groom. I hope this guy knows how lucky he is — ' His smile fades. Irritation. 'What now?'

I stop filming again.

'What if she doesn't marry a guy?'

He rolls his eyes.

'Think about it. She's one and she may seem terribly heterosexual to you,' I say sarcastically, 'But she will change. If she's marrying a woman, you saying this will actually spoil the entire wedding.'

I'm irritating him but he gathers himself and starts again.

It's all going well until. 'As the father of the bride, on behalf of me and Claire.'

I stop recording. 'Paul,' I say gently.

'What?' he snaps.

I walk towards him. We're running out of time. Time for me to speak.

'Please allow me to speak freely.'

'Jesus, haven't you been? The guests are going to arrive soon and we've got nothing! I should have run this speech by you before.' There's sweat on his upper lip, beads on his forehead.

'I offered and you said no. You wanted to do it on your own. Now hear me out.'

He calms.

'I haven't been honest with you. This whole time I've been going along with your enthusiasm, swept along by your mission, but I'd be doing you a disservice if I didn't stop this.'

One jab to the heart, and he readies himself for more.

'Your ideas are wonderful. They're exciting. They're moving. They're filled with love . . . but mostly they're for you.' I pause to see how he'll take it and it's not looking good. I continue.

'They're so you feel included in the moments. And also so that they'll feel you're there, but you will already be in their minds in these moments. If you don't do all this, it doesn't mean that you disappear.'

He looks downward, emotion gathering and bubbling around his jaw.

'What if Casper doesn't want to drive? What if he does and Claire wants to teach him? What if Eva never gets married? What if she marries a woman and what if Claire wants to make the speech? You can't decide their futures for them.'

'I hear what you're saying,' he says, voice shaking. 'But I don't want them to feel like they're missing something. Growing up empty, like there's a hole in every place in their life. An empty place at the table where their dad should be.'

I think about whether to say it or not. Even Gerry thought about what Paul hasn't, his final letter paved the way for his space to be filled. 'What if the seat isn't empty?'

'Oh wow. Holly that's just . . . Jesus. You saved that one for a good moment,' he says angrily. 'This is bullshit, I'm done. I'll record my own message.'

He storms out of the room.

I chase after him, afraid. My aim was to fill the PS, I Love You Club with hope, but now I've broken his heart even further, a man who's facing the end of his life. Well done, Holly. I race out of the conference room, through the bar, past the photo booth and a box of silly clothes ready for the party festivities, and out the door of

305

the bar. He's sitting outside, at a picnic table decorated with pink and silver balloons, looking out at the view. I'm sure he would rather be left alone but I'm not finished yet. I'm not finished until he understands. I approach him and my heels crunch over the pebbles. He turns around to check on his company, then back to the view again.

'Go away, Holly, we're done.'

I sit opposite him anyway. He looks out, still ignoring me but at least not challenging me. I take this as positive encouragement under the circumstances.

I take a deep breath. 'Halfway through my husband's letters, I wished he'd stop.'

That gets his attention. 'Now you're being honest. You think you could have told us all this a few months ago?' he asks, but the anger is gone.

'When Gerry died, I was in a dark miserable fucking slump that I couldn't get out of. That's how it is. Just shit. I was angry, I was sad, everything was unfair. Why and how did the world keep turning without him in it? Poor me, that's what I honestly kept thinking. I wasn't strong. I wasn't wise. I didn't handle it well. I gave up. The letters gave me purpose. Companionship. More of *him* that I craved. His letters forced me to get up and get out. He got me moving, and then, when I was back to life again, I felt that waiting every month for another letter held me back. Every new letter was a reminder that he was gone, that everyone around me was moving on. Friends were getting engaged, pregnant, and I was still waiting for more letters, for direction from my dead husband, afraid to do anything for myself in case it clashed with the next mission. I loved them, but resented them at the same time. After a year, the letters stopped and I knew that was the end. Closure.

'The right letter can be a blessing; the wrong one can be dangerous. It can be a setback, it can trap you in a dangerous place where you're living in between. My husband got my letters right because he knew me, he thought about me. If he'd continued writing letters for my whole life . . . it wouldn't work, because he doesn't know me now. If we had children, maybe he wouldn't know that somebody helped raise them, loved them, maybe even called him dad or walked them up the aisle. You can't replace people, Paul, you'll *never* be replaced, but you can replace roles.

'By writing your letters, or filming your videos, you can't write others out. I know you can't see into the future, nobody's asking you to be perfect, but if your wish is to be there for your family — for Claire, for Casper and Eva — then you can't decide their futures for them. You won't always get to be a part of their every day. But the memory of you will.' I think of how I felt Gerry fill my body with his energy at Bert's funeral. 'And maybe you will get to be there in another way, maybe they'll feel you in ways that you can't plan or imagine. I believe that now.'

I stop speaking and stare straight ahead at the fields that surround the castle. I wait for him to stand and leave, but after a moment he's still there. I sneak a look at him and he's rubbing tears from his cheeks.

I hurry around to him and sit beside him, and wrap my arms around him. 'I'm sorry, Paul.'

'Don't be sorry,' he says, voice trembling. 'That's the best advice anybody ever gave me.'

I smile, relieved, but I feel his aching sadness; a pressing weight on my chest. 'I should have said it a long time ago. To you all.'

'I probably wouldn't have listened.' He wipes his eyes. 'I'm dying,' he says, finally. 'I'm just trying to do everything to give them more of me.'

'I know, but you have to leave room for them to remember you themselves.' A thought strikes me, clear and vivid and it's directed at myself. 'And they can't allow the ghost of you to take someone else's place.'

★   ★   ★

After meeting with Paul, I give up on the idea of gathering with my family and go home. I take Gerry's letters from my bedside locker, never far from me after all these years, and I open the one that I need to examine with a different pair of eyes.

Gerry's fourth letter was one I treasured and was grateful for. In it, he encouraged me to rid myself of his possessions — not everything, of course, but he guided me as to what to keep and what to lose, what to give away and to whom. He told me I didn't need his things to feel him with me, that he'd always be there wrapping his arms

308

around me, guiding me. Gerry was wrong. At the time I did need his things to feel him with me. I smelled his T-shirts I refused to wash and hugged myself in his sweaters to fool myself into believing his arms were around me. This letter was one of my favourites because it kept me busy, it wasn't a one-off event, it took me one month. It was weeks of work, gathering items, reminiscing, holding on then letting go as I allocated homes for them.

I wish I'd taken more time before following Gerry's instructions. I wish I'd thought about my life more carefully and about what I would need. Instead he instructed me based on the woman I was when he knew me, instead of the woman I became when he was gone, and there are items that I gave away that I wish I'd kept and, most importantly, there are precious belongings of his that he told me to keep that I know I shouldn't have. I kept them because he told me to, and I used him as my excuse for my own needs and greed.

It was delivering Bert's letter to Rita's sister that has played on my mind for some time. *You can't blame the dead*, Rachel had blasted, respecting her mother's final wishes, as though the final decisions of the dying are the correct ones, sacred and untouchable. I used to agree with her, but perhaps we're wrong. Perhaps the ones who leave us behind don't always see the bigger picture, but instead place it in our hands with trust in us to make better decisions.

I enter Malahide village, and take a left at the church, down Old Street and towards the marina and the boat-repair facility where his dad still works. After Gerry's death, I used to meet with his parents a few times a year; they were still family to me, I was still their daughter-in-law, but over time as the middle-man to our connection had passed, so too did our relationship. Conversation was sometimes forced, sometimes awkward, hard work and draining because though we were joined by love, it was impossible to avoid the fact we were also joined by loss. As time is no one's friend, and in my effort to move on and let go, to face the light, I suppose that fraction of my life got bumped. Christmas cards, birthday presents, at first were hand-delivered and then mailed, and so we drifted further from one another.

Gerry's dad isn't expecting me; even when married to Gerry I never visited his workplace, but it must be done and it must be done today. Being involved in the PS, I Love You Club has given me new insight into why Gerry wrote his letters, and part of that lesson has been in discovering that Gerry wasn't always right, and I wasn't always right to follow them.

I arrive at the boatyard and, naturally, the steel gates are shut. Behind the barrier men are busy at work cleaning, repairing, maintaining boats of various sizes mounted on steel legs. I finally catch the attention of one bare-chested worker, sweating in the sun, and I wave at him.

'I'm looking for Harold,' I call. 'Harry?'

He opens the gate and I follow him in. Harry is fully dressed, thankfully, hard at work by the propeller of an enormous vessel.

'Harry!' my guide yells, and Gerry's dad looks up.

'Holly,' he says, surprised. 'What brings you here?' He puts down his tool, and walks towards me, arms open.

'Good to see you, Harry,' I say happily, examining his face for a trace of his son, the Gerry I knew and a glimpse of the aged Gerry he never became. 'Sorry to drop in unannounced.'

'It's great to see you. Come to the office for a tea?' He places a hand on the small of my back and starts to guide me.

'No thanks. I'm not staying long.' I feel the emotion gathering, as it does anytime I'm with a physical reminder of Gerry. His dad brings him to life, his life emphasises his death, and an actual acknowledgement of his death is always crushing.

'What is it, love?'

'I've taken on a new project this year. Something inspired by Gerry.'

'Go on,' he urges me, fascination in his tone.

'I've been helping terminally ill people write letters to their loved ones. They call it the PS, I Love You Club.'

Unlike the majority of my family who hated the idea, he immediately grins, his eyes dewy. 'What a wonderful idea, Holly. And a lovely honour to Gerard.'

'I'm glad you approve. They've got me thinking about his letters again, about what was right, about what was wrong.'

The PS, I Love You Club has been a treasure trove of valuable lessons for me. I guarded the experience of the letters with my life for the past six years, but as soon as I said the words aloud for the podcast, holes appeared and questions surfaced. Were his letters for me as I assumed, or were they for his own benefit? Did I always want them to continue? Did he always get them right? Were there any letters that I would have changed? In order to help the club curate their own, I had to be honest about what worked for me and what didn't, and that didn't mean being disloyal to Gerry as I'd feared it would.

'Anyway.' I reach into my bag and retrieve a box, which he recognises immediately. A pained sound escapes from the back of his throat. He takes it from me and opens it. It's the watch he gave Gerry on his twenty-first birthday; a valuable timepiece Gerry wore every day.

'Gerard left this to you,' he says, and his voice cracks.

'He made the wrong decision,' I say. 'It was a gift between father and son. Father should get it back.'

He pauses then nods his thanks, eyes filled, head lost in I don't know what, but perhaps the memory of him giving it to his young son, the great moment, and all the moments they spent talking about it, huddled over it, the bond that connected them.

Gerry left it to me because it was valuable, but it's worth more to his dad.

Harry takes the watch out of the box, hands the box to me and slides the watch onto his wrist, securing it closed. He wipes the tears from his eyes.

312

I remember the moment the watch stopped, two days after Gerry's death. I had it on the nightstand, I was hidden beneath the duvet, in the dark world, eyes peering out to the other world, not wanting to be involved but keeping an eye out anyway, listening to his watch tick, watching the hands go round, the face I saw on my husband's wrist every day of our lives. And then just like that, it stopped.

Harry turns the crown a few times and it starts again.

33

'Pull in here,' Ginika says suddenly, sounding panicked, as I drive her home from a lesson.

I indicate quickly, and swing into a hard right on Drumcondra Road, thinking she's ill, that she needs to vomit, or pass out.

I stop the car. 'Are you OK? Have some water.'

'I'm fine,' she says quietly, distracted. 'Drive down the lane.'

I hadn't even taken notice of where we were, I didn't think it mattered, but as we continue down the long drive I realise that we're at HomeFarm FC, a soccer club. Confused, I turn the car into the space she's pointing at, in front of a soccer pitch, which is busy with a team being taken through their drills. I look at her, waiting for an answer but none comes. She watches the boys playing and, realising she needs some time, I sit back and give her space.

'I used to play here,' she says.

'Really?' I ask happily, glad she's opening up. 'I didn't have you down as a soccer player.'

'I was a striker,' she says, while her eyes don't move from the guys on the pitch.

'Of course you were.'

This brings a small smile to her lips.

Jewel cries out from the back seat, I turn around and reach for the rice cake she has dropped. She takes it from me with a gentle 'ta

314

ta' and shoves it in her mouth to continue sucking. One hand on her rice cake, another on her big toe, which she is pulling at and lifting to her mouth, deciding which she prefers the taste of.

'That guy there?' Ginika points out a tall handsome assistant coach. 'He's Jewel's dad.'

'What?' I shout so loudly I give Jewel a fright. 'Sorry, baby, I'm sorry.' I rub her foot and calm her. Her bottom lip trembles for a moment, and then she concentrates on her rice cake again.

'Jesus, would you shut up? He'll hear you!' Ginika slaps my leg.

'Sorry. I just can't believe that . . . you're telling me. That's him.' I lean over the steering wheel and examine him. 'He's gorgeous.'

'Yeah well. His name's Conor. You wouldn't shut up asking me about him, so, there.'

I didn't ask her that often but she's changing, she's thinking, she's planning for the end. Transitioning. My heart twists.

'We can leave now.' She nods at the steering wheel to hurry me up, perhaps panicking that I'll cause a scene.

'No, wait. We're not going anywhere yet.' I continue watching him, this mysterious character I've wanted to know so much about for so long.

'Well, we're not getting out of the car.'

'I know. OK. We won't. But,' I watch him, running through drills with younger kids. 'What age is he?'

She thinks. 'Eighteen. Now.'

I look back at Jewel and at Conor. She's so

close to her dad. Possibly the closest she's ever been.

'Don't,' Ginika warns. 'I knew this was a mistake.'

'It's not, I won't do anything,' I say firmly. 'Just tell me, does he know? Does he know about Jewel?'

She shakes her head. 'I couldn't, didn't want him to get into trouble. Didn't want to fuck up his life. Conor's nice, you know? I found out I was pregnant, then that I was sick. I dropped out of school. I couldn't tell him.'

'I understand, Ginika, it's OK.'

'Really?' she seems surprised. Relieved. 'I thought you'd judge me.'

'Who am I to be the judge of anyone?'

'You just, you know . . .'

'What?' I ask.

'Your house, your life, you're so perfect.'

'Ginika,' I look at her in surprise. 'I am far from perfect.'

'Not what it looks like from here.'

'Well, thank you, but . . . I'm very fucked up.'

She actually laughs. And then I join in too. The two of us, emotional and delirious, share this moment.

'So why are we here?' I ask gently. 'What do you want me to do?'

'I don't know,' she shrugs. 'I don't know. Maybe after, maybe when I'm, you know . . . whatever. Maybe he can know then. Maybe he'll want to know, maybe he won't. But I'll be gone and whatever happens, happens.' She looks at me. 'No one knows he's her da. I thought I should tell someone. I trust you.'

'Fuck,' I say, breathing out.

She looks at me in surprise, and laughs again. 'I've never heard you swear before and you've done it twice.'

'OK,' I try to get a handle on the situation. 'Let's think. Seeing as we're talking, can we really talk now?'

She braces herself. 'Sure, but can we get out of here first?'

We settle in Ginika's basement flat and I discreetly survey the connected bedroom and kitchen, the single bed and cot. A pink lamp beside the bed, pink cushions and duvet cover, pink fairy lights twisted around the rail of the headboard. I didn't have Ginika down as a pink girl. It is young and feminine and makes who Ginika and Jewel are and their situation all the more sorrowful. I peek out through the drawn curtains and see a long garden with grass that hasn't seen a lawnmower in years. It makes a great place to hide the sodden ripped mattress, old stove, and rusty broken bicycle and car parts that previous tenants or even the landlords themselves have discarded.

'It's not exactly a palace,' Ginika says, self-consciously, watching me take it in.

It's not for Ginika's lack of trying, it's the lack of maintenance that's responsible for the decay, the mould and musty smell. There's more in this home for Jewel than for Ginika, another giveaway sign of her character. Every sacrifice has been for her daughter. Ginika places Jewel in a high chair and reaches for one of the many

317

baby food jars on the open shelf.

'Can I feed her?' I ask.

'Sure, but watch out, she'll grab the spoon.'

As warned, Jewel reaches for the incoming spoon of food. We struggle over it, Jewel's pudgy grip stronger than I thought, while food splashes around. Finally, I win. I'll be faster next time.

'So,' Ginika says nervously, twisting her fingers around each other, waiting for me to pick up where we left off in the car park.

So focused on this impossible task of feeding feisty Jewel, who despite already ingesting three rice cakes is eating faster than I can reload my spoon, I'm reminded of why we came here.

'I have avoided this conversation for a long time, probably too long, because I felt it was absolutely none of my business. But now it's different. As your friend — and I consider you my friend, Ginika — I wouldn't be doing a good job if I didn't share with you what I think, or at least hear what you think. I don't want to put ideas in your head, or confuse your thought process or — '

'Jesus, quit with the disclaimers, I get it,' she interrupts, rolling her eyes. 'Go on, spit it out. You think Conor should get custody of Jewel.'

'No, actually,' I say, surprised. 'Well, it's not that I *don't* think that, but I had something else in mind. Some*one* else. I wondered if you'd considered Denise.'

'Denise!' her eyes widen and she thinks for a moment. 'Denise,' she says softly. 'You like Dee Nee, don't you, baby?'

Jewel has her mouth wide open and is leaning

forward to the filled spoon I paused in the air while I spoke. I grin and feed her and quickly follow it up with another, giving Ginika some time to think.

'Actually, Denise and Tom,' I add.

'Aren't they split up?'

'It won't last.' I wonder how much to share or how much Denise has already shared with her. 'They really want a baby, but they're struggling. To conceive, I mean.'

'Oh,' she seems interested, focused.

'That's probably all I should say about it, it's up to you to discuss with them. And your social worker, and foster family, and whoever else you'd need to speak with. I just want you to know that it's a possibility, it's worth thinking about. And at least Denise doesn't have a country accent,' I add, with a smile.

'No,' she replies, seriously. 'But does her fella?'

I laugh and continue feeding Jewel.

'I'd have to meet him first.'

'Of course.'

'I thought you were going to say you wanted Jewel.'

'Me?'

From the way I snap my surprised response, she realises she's off by a long shot.

'I adore Jewel, but . . . ' It feels terrible having this conversation in front of her, I'm pretty sure this wise little one is taking everything in. 'I'm not . . . I wouldn't . . . I don't know how to . . . '

'You'd be a great ma,' she says softly.

I don't know how to respond to that. I

self-consciously spoon another mouthful into Jewel's mouth.

'You're around the same age as my ma. And look how good you've been with me. I'm not saying, like, that I think you're my ma, but you know what I mean. You've been there for me, you're helping me in a way a ma would. I bet you were really good with your fella's daughter.'

I wasn't. I should have been. I realise I could be.

'Jesus Christ, are you crying?'

'Just got some food in my eye,' I say, blinking back the tears.

'Come here, you softy,' she says, and we embrace.

While my back is turned, Jewel has grabbed the jar of food and the spoon and she's shaken them both ecstatically up and down in the air, so that it's splashed on her face and hair and all over the table.

'Actually,' Ginika adds in her usual dry tone, 'you are a bit shit.'

I laugh.

'What are you going to do when we're all gone?' she asks, removing the food from Jewel's hair.

'Ginika,' I say softly, shaking my head. 'I don't want to talk about that. You're here now.'

'I'm not talking about me, I'm talking about you. What are *you* going to do when the three of us are gone?'

I shrug. 'Keep working at the shop. Sell the house. Find a place to live.'

'Move in with your fella.'

'No. That's over. I told you.'

She studies me. 'Nah,' she says, nudging me. 'It's not. He's a tasty one. Just tell him,' she laughs, 'tell him to think of you like you're a tree. He works with broken ones, doesn't he?'

'Kind of.'

'Tell him to climb your branches and instead of cutting you down, to give you a bit of mending.' She chuckles. 'I've been watching that fella Dr Phil every morning, I think it's catching.' She looks at me. 'Full of shite, isn't he, most of the time. But, sometimes, there does be *kernels* of knowledge,' she says grandly, waving the spoon around. 'Call him, ye eejit.'

I laugh. 'We'll see, Ginika.'

★ ★ ★

On the drive home it pains me to think about Ginika's question, to imagine a world without Ginika, Paul and Joy being in it, for them not to be a constant consideration. I tell myself that there is lots of time before I need to worry about that. But Ginika's illness is choosing its own pace and a mere two weeks after sitting in her kitchen, giddily laughing and joking, and talking about the future, her future decides to slow down, to come and take a closer look at her.

I sit with Ginika at her bedside in hospital. If she was fire, now she is embers, but she continues to glow and give out heat, proof of fire, symbol of life.

'I wrote my letter last night,' she says, dark rings around her eyes.

321

'Did you?' I take her hand.

'It was so quiet here. Nurses were around but it was calm. I FaceTimed Paul. Have you seen him?'

I nod.

'He looks like shit. All bloated. Says he can't see out of his left eye. I couldn't sleep after that, thinking about him, about everything. The sentences came into my head and I couldn't get them out so I started writing.'

'Do you want me to read over it for you?'

She shakes her head. 'Your work is done. Thanks, *miss*,' she attempts a joke, but it lacks her usual zest.

My eyes fill and overflow, and this time she doesn't tell me to stop. She doesn't tell me I'm an idiot or a softy, because she's crying too.

'I'm scared,' she whispers so quietly I can just about make the words out.

I wrap my arms around her and hold her tight. 'I know. I'm here for you. Joy is here. Paul is here. Denise is here. We're all here for you. You're not alone.'

'Was your husband scared, in the end?' she asks, tears streaming from her face. I can feel them soaking my neck.

'Yes,' I whisper. 'He wanted me to hold his hand, the entire time. But then something happened, he slipped away. It was calm. It was quiet.'

'Peaceful?'

I nod and cry. 'Yes,' I manage. 'So so peaceful, Ginika.'

'OK,' she says, and pulls away. 'Thanks.'

I reach for the tissues beside her bed and hand her one, take one for myself.

'Ginika Adebayo, you are a precious amazing woman and I have nothing but respect and love for you.'

'Ah, thanks, Holly. I feel the same about you,' she says, firmly taking my hand, to my surprise, and squeezing it. 'Thank you for everything. You did more than any of us ever asked you to.' She looks at the door and her face changes. She lets go of my hand. 'Fuck it, they're here and I look a mess.'

'You don't.' I grab another tissue and dry her face.

She straightens her turban, smooths down the bed blankets and slowly, painfully adjusts her position. She reaches to the drawer in the locker beside her and retrieves an envelope. I recognise it as the one she and Jewel chose on the day I set up the stationery in Joy's home. My eyes fill again, I cannot control my emotions. She hands it to me and our eyes lock.

'Now you have to go. Go, leave, goodbye,' she says, shooing me away.

'Good luck,' I whisper.

I have to remember, for every goodbye, there's been a hello. And there's nothing more wonderful than a hello from one person to another. The sound of Gerry's voice each time he picked up the phone. When he opened his eyes in the morning. When I came home from work. When he watched me walking to meet him and made me feel like I was everything. So many beautiful hellos, only one real goodbye.

Ginika is busy today, fixing what she can, preparing the world for the gap she will leave, preparing for the biggest goodbye to the most important person in the world to her.

Jewel's foster mother has arrived with Jewel, and Ginika has asked for Denise and Tom to attend. They wait outside the room with their solicitor. Ginika has a will to write, with Jewel's guardians to add. The rules usually only allow two visitors at a time but for Ginika, in these circumstances, they allow for all necessary parties to be present. For their privacy, I step out of the room as soon as they all arrive, but I do procrastinate. I stay to watch as Ginika uses every bit of the dying energy from her body to take Jewel from Betty's arms, and place her in Tom's arms. A great hello.

If only Gerry knew what he'd started.

Of course I'll never know what Gerry was thinking when he wrote his ten letters for me, but I am learning one thing. It wasn't all for me as I'd believed at the time, it was his own way of trying to continue his life when life had exhausted all avenues, and death was moving closer to catch his fall. It was his way of saying not just to me but to the world, *remember me*. Because ultimately, it's all anyone wants. Not to get lost, or left behind, not to be forgotten, to always be a part of the moments they know they'll miss. To leave their stamp. To be remembered.

34

'You've got to crack a few eggs to make an omelette,' I say aloud, surveying the disaster site that is my bedroom as I try to pack up for my move.

'Eggs give me the squirts,' Ciara shouts from further away than I thought. She's in the spare bedroom next door.

'Ciara!' I warn.

She appears at my bedroom door, wearing a peculiar collection of clothes that I just bagged for the shop. All at once, together, mismatched.

'You're supposed to be helping me fill the bags, not empty them for dress-up.'

'But if I did that, I wouldn't look like *this*.' She poses provocatively against the doorframe. 'I think I'll wear this outfit on Friday night.'

'Which one?' I ask. 'You're wearing about three.'

Putting ten years of clutter into refuse bags, or boxing them to create further clutter in my new home, is taking longer than expected as each letter, receipt and bottom of every pocket of every pair of jeans or coat *tells a story* and draws me into a memory. I'm used to doing this with great efficiency at work, and yet because it's personal, every single item is a wormhole and sucks me into another time of my life. Despite feeling suspended in time, one hour becomes two, daylight becomes night. I'm more ruthless with clothes, shoes, handbags and books that don't hold any sentimental value. Anything I haven't worn in the past year and can't believe I ever bought in the first place goes straight into charity bags.

It's stressful at first. Everything scattered in piles around me, I'm making more of a mess than I had in the first place, every item is being pulled out of its hiding place, its unnecessariness revealed.

Triage, Ciara had called it.

'I don't know how anything actually makes it to the shelves of your shop.'

'That's why it's your job to empty the bags and boxes. I have a habit of wanting the things that people don't want,' she says cheekily, 'which Mathew says is a curse but I know it's a gift, because that's exactly how I married him and I told him so.'

I laugh. I sit on the floor, back against the wall. Time for a break.

'I'm so glad you're doing this,' she says, relaxing on the floor, legs out, pop socks over a pair of tights. She puts a pair of strappy sandals over the socks and tights. 'I'm proud of you. We all are.'

'Everybody must have very low expectations of me if selling a house induces pride.'

'It's more than that and you know it.'

I do know it. 'What if I told you it was less about an emotional willingness to mature and more about the fact my kitchen needs an overhaul, the windows need to be replaced, there's something wrong with the heating and the floors are lifting in the dining room so I hid it with a rug so house viewers wouldn't notice.'

'I'd say I'm proud of you for not going down with the ship.' She smiles, and she tries to hold it but it wobbles. 'I've been so scared for you over the past few months.'

'I'm OK.'

'Now all you have to do is find a place to stay,' Ciara says, singing, twirling a tulle scarf around, as though she's doing ribbon acrobatics.

'Everything I've looked at is so bleh. The last one I looked at had an avocado-coloured bathroom suite from the seventies.'

'Retro is cool.'

'Forty years without other people's bum bacteria is cooler.'

She chuckles. 'I think you're making excuses. I think you know where you want to live.'

I feel the torn part of my heart letting me know it's still there, it's not going away. No matter how much I try to focus on everything else, it has no intention of healing without my attention. I look around my bedroom. 'I'll miss the memories.'

'Gross,' she says, teasing.

'I don't want to forget everything, or *anything* really, but I want . . . ' I close my eyes. 'I want to go to sleep in a room where I don't have an aching longing for someone who's gone and will never come back. And I want to wake up in a room where I haven't had the same nightmares.'

Ciara doesn't reply and I open my eyes. She's rummaging through another bag.

'Ciara! I'm baring my soul here.'

'Sorry, but,' she whips out an old pair of

knickers, 'I'm beginning to get a sense of the painful memories you need to forget. How old are these and please tell me nobody ever saw them.'

I laugh and try to grab them from her. 'That bag is for the trash.'

'I don't know, I think I could fashion these into a new hat.' She squeezes them onto her head and poses. I pull them off her head.

'Roots and wings,' Ciara says, suddenly serious. 'I was listening to you, by the way. Mathew and I went to collect some things for the shop from a woman who was selling her childhood home. Her mother passed away and it was difficult for her to sell. She asked me if it was possible for something to have both roots and wings. Keeping it helped her to hold on to her mother and their memories, selling it was giving her financial security and other possibilities. Roots and wings.'

'Roots and wings,' I repeat, liking it. 'I hate goodbyes,' I say with a sigh, and then add more as a mantra to myself, 'But hating goodbyes is not a justification for staying.'

'And fearing goodbyes is also not a justification for leaving first,' Ciara finishes.

I look at her in surprise.

She shrugs. 'Just saying.'

As we're hauling the bags into the van, my phone rings inside the house. I run inside but still miss a call from Denise which makes my stomach churn with dread. I take a moment to calm myself and I call her back. She answers immediately.

'I think you should come over.'

'OK. God.' My throat tightens.

'Her parents just left. She wasn't responsive but I think she knew they were there.'

'I'll be there as fast as I can.'

★ ★ ★

Denise's home is calm. The main lights are off, lamps and candles light the hallways and rooms. It feels hushed, but calm, no urgency or sense of immediacy, and we all keep our voice down. Now that Denise and Tom are the official guardians for Jewel, Ginika and Jewel have been living with Tom and Denise for the past four weeks, receiving care in their home, and it has been good for Ginika, even in the condition she is in, to be in the space where her daughter will grow up, to be breathing the same air. Holding on and letting go. Tom guides me to Ginika's bedroom, where Denise is by her side, holding her hand.

Her breathing is slow, barely there. She hasn't been conscious for days.

I sit at her bedside and take her other hand, her right hand, her writing hand. I kiss it.

'Hello, sweet girl.'

A mother, a daughter, a striker, a fighter. An inspiring young woman who only got a fraction of the whole, but gave me and us so very much. It doesn't seem fair because it isn't fair. I held Gerry's hand as he left the world and here I am again, saying goodbye to somebody I love, and I *love* this girl, she got inside my heart. Witnessing this transition, saying goodbye, never gets easier, but preparing myself and helping her to feel prepared has eased the suffering, the anger, the rage that spikes when confronted with the brutal reality. They say easy come, easy go, but not in this instance. Arrival into this world is a marathon for both mother and child, life pushes to get into this world, and leaving it is a fight to stay.

Denise and I stay by Ginika's side for the remaining hours, a gentle departure from this world as she knows it. After hanging on to her breath for so long, she takes a final inhale, and there's no exhale as life lets go and death catches her. Though the illness was a painful one, the passing is peaceful as I promised her it would be, and as she lays still on the bed, no more fluttering eyelids, no more rise and fall of her chest, no more laboured breathing, I imagine, I hope, I wish, that the fun-filled soul that inhabited her body now has the freedom to drift and dance, swirl and soar. Ashes to ashes, dust to dust, but my God, *fly* Ginika, *fly*.

A moment like this, as tragic and overwhelming as it is, is an honour to witness and, perhaps selfishly, in time it will help that I was with her for the end. I will always remember how Ginika and I met, I will always remember how we parted.

As if she knows, as if she senses her own greatest loss, from the other room, Jewel awakes from her sleep with a cry.

★   ★   ★

Around the kitchen table, red-eyed and exhausted, Tom, Denise and I regroup. I retrieve a keepsake box from my bag and place it on the table.

Ginika's letter.

'This is for you, Jewel. From Mama.'

'Mama,' she says, grinning. She grabs her pudgy toes and pulls at them.

'Yes, Mama,' I try to smile, wiping a tear. 'Mama loves you so much.' I turn to Denise. 'This is your responsibility now.'

Denise lifts it and runs her fingers across the lid. 'Beautiful box.'

It's the mirrored jewellery box I found at the shop. I glued the loose crystals found inside back to the lid, and I slid out the inside so it is perfect as a keepsake box, which contains the envelope, Jewel's first pair of socks, babygro and mitts, and a lock of hair, both Jewel's and Ginika's first cuts braided together.

'She wrote the letter herself,' I explain. 'I didn't read it and she didn't tell me what she was going to say. She did it all by herself.'

'Brave girl,' Denise says softly.

'Open it.' Tom encourages her.

'Now?' Denise asks, looking from him to me.

'I'm sure Jewel would love to hear it, wouldn't you?' he says, kissing her head.

Denise opens the box, takes out the letter. Unfolds it. The sight of her handwriting, her hard work and effort makes me cry again.

Dear Jewel,
You are thirteen months old.
You love sweet potato and stewed apples.

Your favourit book is the hungry caterpillar and you chew the cornurs.

The map song from Dora the Ixplorir makes you laugh more than anything.

You love popping bubbles.

Your favourit teddy is Bop Bop the bunny.

Sneezeing makes you laugh.

Paper being ript makes you cry.

You love dogs.

You point at clouds.

You get hickups when you drink too fast.

You love the song ABC by The Jackson 5.

Wunce you put a snail in your mouth and sucked it out of its shell. Yuk. You don't like snails.

You love sitting on my knee and don't like to be put down. I think you are skared of being left alone. You are never alone. You will never be alone.

You can't see the wind but you hold your hands out to catch it. It makes you confyoused.

You call me mama. That's my favourite sound.

We dance every day. We sing incey wincy spider in the bath.

I wish I could see you grow up. I wish I could be beside you all the time forever. I love you more than anyone or anything in the hole world.

Be kind. Be smart. Be brave. Be happy. Be careful. Be strong. Don't be afraid of being afraid. Sum times we are all afraid.

I love you forever.

I hope you remember me forever.
You are the best thing I have ever done.
I love you Jewel.
Mama

35

I lean my bicycle against the red-bricked wall and take the few steps to the front door, my legs heavy and my trainers feeling like lead. I've had a long cycle to clear my head but I can barely remember the route here. I press the doorbell.

Gabriel answers and looks at me in surprise.

'Hi,' I say, quietly, shyly.

'Hi,' he says. 'Come in.'

I step inside and follow him down the narrow corridor to the internal main room, the familiar smells intensifying the butterflies in my stomach. He checks behind him to make sure I'm still there, in case I've changed my mind and left, or I'm not real. He has something jazzy playing on his record player, and there's a large plasma screen on the wall.

'You're healed,' he says, noting my boot-free foot.

'You got a TV,' I note. 'A big one.'

'I bought it for you. I had it stored in the shed for months,' he says, a little awkwardly, nervously. 'I was going to surprise you when you moved in. Surprise,' he says weakly, joking, and I laugh.

'Tea? Coffee?'

'Coffee please.' I've been up all night with Denise and Tom, crying, sharing stories of Ginika, discussing her funeral arrangements,

334

wondering when in Jewel's future would be an appropriate time to contact Jewel's biological father. The big conversations and the small rolling softly into, over and under each other. All the ifs and buts. We were all exhausted but none of us could sleep. I don't envy them the busy day ahead with Jewel, but I know that they will treasure every second of the gift Ginika gave them.

Coffee vapours fill the room as Gabriel pours water over the ground coffee. I wander away and into the conservatory, drawn by the morning light. Nothing has drastically changed, apart from the home office in the corner, which used to be in the spare bedroom, now Ava's. I wouldn't have thought it, but surprisingly it fits; buildings bending effortlessly to owners' desires. I should take a leaf out of this house's book. I look out at the cherry blossom tree, green leaves turning to gold. I recall last year waiting impatiently for it to bloom in spring, only for its petals to blow away practically overnight in a storm, at first coating the stones with a plush pink carpet before turning to slippery slush. How I'd like to watch it flower again.

Gabriel joins me and hands me a mug of coffee. Our fingers touch.

'Thanks for fixing my mug,' I say. Instead of sitting, he stands. Mug in one hand, the other pushed into the pocket of his jeans.

He shrugs it off, embarrassed perhaps at having done it. 'You mean Gerry's mug. I know you're not a *Star Wars* fan. You said you'd throw it out, but I know you're more inclined to keep

335

things that are broken. Maybe I should have left it as it was. Maybe you wanted to fix it yourself. Maybe I was overthinking the mug.'

I smile. He's right, I do keep things that are broken, but I also never fix them. I kept it there in the cupboard, a self-inflicted punishment, a reminder of what I had and what I'd lost. People not things, that's what I should hold on to.

'Are you still involved with the club? he asks.

I nod.

'How are you doing?' his blue eyes search me intensely, like an X-ray of my soul.

All of a sudden I want to cry. He sees it coming and puts the mug down, comes round to me, down on his knees and hugs me tightly, rubs his fingers through my hair as I let it all out and let it all go. The utter exhaustion takes over me and the months of work, worry, highs and lows, unleash themselves through my tears.

'I was so afraid of this happening, Holly,' he says, whispering into my hair.

'It has been one of the best experiences of my life,' I say, in an unnatural high-pitch, through my badly timed sob.

He lets go, pulls back and studies me, fingers still running hypnotically through my hair. 'Seriously?'

I nod emphatically, through tears, though the sentiments may be hard to believe while he's looking at me in this state.

'I lost a friend yesterday. Ginika. She was seventeen years old. Her daughter is one. Denise and Tom are her guardians. I taught Ginika how to read and write.'

336

'Wow, Holly,' he says, wiping my tears. 'You did that?'

I nod. Bert is gone. Ginika is gone. My time is finished with a diminishing Paul, I'm lingering with Joy despite her scrapbook of secrets for Joe being complete. 'I don't want it to end.'

He considers this, considers me, then lifts my chin gently with his fingers so that we're looking each other in the eye, so close. 'So don't let it.'

'How?' I wipe my wet face.

'Find more people. Keep it going.'

I look at him, surprised. 'But you said getting involved was a mistake.'

'And I was wrong. I was wrong about a lot of things. If you say it's the best experience of your life — '

'One of.' I correct him, with a smile.

'I was only trying to protect you. You told me not to let you do anything more, and I honestly thought I was doing the right thing. I didn't even wait to see.'

'I know, and you were right. A little bit. I can't hold you responsible, Gabriel. I did lose myself. I put the club first, when I should have put you first.'

'I didn't give you much of a choice,' he says wryly. 'I think we both made the same mistake. We chose one part of our life over us. I miss you so much,' he says.

'I miss you too.'

We smile, and he looks at me hopefully, but I'm not ready yet. I reach for my coffee and take a sip, try to compose myself. 'How's it going with Ava?'

337

'Good,' he says, pulling out the chair beside me. He turns it so he's facing me, our legs touching, his hand on my thigh, all so familiar. 'She's calmed a lot. We're figuring it out. But I made a really bad decision, a really big mistake losing you, Holly.'

'I overreacted,' I admit.

'I didn't support you. Can you give us another chance? Will you move in here? With me, and Ava?'

I look at him and wonder, but I'm tired of thinking, I only know what feels right and forgiveness is a gift. I feel so utterly relieved to be offered a second chance with him.

'We have a TV,' he offers, weakly.

I smile, and rest my head on his shoulder, and he covers me in gentle kisses.

I want to tell Ginika what has happened, that she was right, again. The tears roll. Bittersweet ones.

36

I lock my bike to the railings on Eccles Street, having cycled there directly from work on a bright Friday evening, inhaling the sunshine, the fresh summer air, vibrant and busy with people attending the Mater hospital and the Mater private. My destination is on the opposite side of the street; a line of grand Georgian buildings, once grand homes, then tenements, the home of Leopold Bloom in *Ulysses*, and currently a row of consultants' offices, clinics, doctors and outpatient facilities. There is a positive air in the city on a Friday, the promise of the weekend, a relieved celebratory mood that we all made it through another loaded week. The weather is looking hot for the weekend, our Indian summer; the Met Office has given the thumbs up for barbecues. Supermarkets will be ambushed for burger patties and sausages, coast roads to the seaside will be gridlocked with top-down cars vibrating with music, ice-cream vans with hypnotic tunes will be prowling housing estates to lure customers, dogs will be walked, parks will be heaving with displayed flesh and dehydrated drunks. Monday morning may be filled with regret and sick-days, but this hour, today, Friday at 6 p.m., the air is ticklish with anticipation and scheming, a world of possibilities open ahead of everyone.

'Hi, Holly,' Maria Costas says with a

professional warmth, greeting me at her office with a solid handshake.

She closes the door behind us and leads me to twin armchairs by a Georgian window. The room is calm and filled with light; a safe place for people to bear their souls. If these walls could talk . . . they'd owe a fortune to psychologist Maria. There's a cactus on the table in the centre.

She follows my gaze. 'That's Olivia. My sister gave her to me,' she explains. 'I find that if I name plants, I'm less inclined to kill them. Kind of like what people do with kids.'

I laugh. 'I had a plant once named Gepetto that died. It turned out he needed water more than he needed a name.'

She chuckles. 'How can I help you, Holly?'

'Thanks for your time. As I explained to your PA, it's not a personal visit.'

She nods. 'I recognise your name. I'm familiar with your podcast interview, I recommended it to some of my clients, those in grief and those who are terminally ill.'

'I've been working with some of your clients: Joy Robinson, Paul Murphy, Bert Sweeney and,' I swallow hard, still grieving my friend, 'Ginika Adebayo. I recently discovered that they learned about my story in a group therapy session with you. My story inspired them to write letters for their loved ones, and they came to me asking for my help, to guide them.'

'I apologise for that imposition,' Maria says, frowning. 'Joy responded so positively to you sharing your experience, and came into the group session bursting to discuss it. It triggered a great discussion, of how they could best prepare themselves for leaving their loved ones. I encouraged them to keep in contact with each other throughout their shared experience; some did, some didn't. It wasn't until Bert's wake that I learned about him leaving letters, and I thought it was a one-off until I spoke with Joy recently.'

'You were at Bert's wake?' I ask, horrified.

'Yes,' she says, smiling. 'That little boy didn't make your job very easy for you.'

My cheeks heat up. 'That was a botched job.'

'It was a lot to ask of you, to place the envelope in his actual cold dead hands, but I'm not surprised by Bert.'

We laugh and when we calm, she says. 'I was sad to hear of Ginika's passing recently. She was a young woman with great spirit. I loved hearing her opinions, she cut through everything. I wish the world had more Ginikas.'

'Or just the original would do.' I smile sadly.

'And her little girl?'

'In the loving arms of her guardians. Friends of mine actually, I saw her last night.'

'Is that so?' She studies me. 'Is this letter-writing still continuing?'

'That's why I'm here. The letter-writing has a name.' I smile. 'It was named The PS, I Love You Club by its founding member Angela Carberry, and I want to honour her and the other four original members by continuing the club. I'd like to continue assisting and guiding the terminally ill with their PS, I Love You letters and I'm hoping you could introduce me to others that I could help.'

Spurred on by Gabriel's support and his encouragement to grow the club, I found out about Maria Costas from Joy. As the doctor is the root of all of this, I thought it would be natural for it to bloom from here.

'Is there a financial gain for you in this club?'

'God no,' I say, insulted. 'Not at all. I work full-time, this has all been done in my free time. I'm not looking for money, just more people to help.' Feeling misunderstood, I continue my passionate plea. 'I realise that this concept of letters isn't for everyone, but I've learned that there are those who feel compelled to leave something behind. My husband was one of those people. In the beginning, seven years ago, I thought my husband's letters were all about me, but throughout this process, I've learned that it was as much for him. It's part of the journey in saying goodbye, preparing for the journey to end. Part of keeping house, part of wanting to be remembered. I don't work from a template; everybody's letters need to be individual, and in order to figure out how their letters would best assist their loved ones I've had to spend some time with them and observe their relationships. Ginika was with me up to three times a week, sometimes more. If you're concerned about my intentions, I'd like you to know that they are completely honest and well-meaning.'

'Well,' she says brightly, 'you certainly come from an honest and passionate place. Look, you don't have to sell the idea to me, I encouraged

Joy to share it with the group, remember? How to live knowing your time is limited is the terminal palliative phase that you're addressing here, and I believe that it's an imperative part of their journey. I can see that you're thinking of the needs of both the patient and their loved ones, and while there are obvious privacy issues with me sharing my client list with you, I have no issue recommending your podcast to people I counsel,' she says.

'But.'

'But,' she says, 'terminally ill patients are vulnerable, faced with the threat of early death. Patients with dysfunctional mindsets are sensitive and need to be dealt with sensitively.'

'I've spent the past six months dealing with terminally ill patients sensitively, I'm aware of their mindsets. If you had any idea what I've been through with them, not to mention, the experience I have with my husband, who I cared for throughout his long illness — '

'Holly,' she says gently. 'I'm not attacking you.'

I breathe in and let it out slowly. 'Sorry. I really don't want this to end.'

'I can understand that. To move forward with this, I think it would be advisable to have a clearer strategy. Find a structure for the club; you need rules, you need guidelines. For yourself, and for them. You need to be in control of how you help these people,' she says firmly. 'Not just for them, but for yourself. I can't imagine what it was like this year, helping four people through this journey on your own. It must have been overwhelming.'

My defences fall. 'Well yes.'

She sits back, and says with a smile, 'Before you help more people, make sure you're in a secure position yourself.'

I leave her office feeling like I've been squashed. I'm deflated, but I also feel reflective; have I made mistakes with Paul, Bert, Joy and Ginika? Have I counselled them badly? Did I damage them or their loved ones? The journey certainly wasn't perfect but I think I did a damn good job. My motivations couldn't have been more honest either. I'm not looking for a cent from anyone. I'm doing this for those who I believe will benefit, but I'm also, without a doubt, doing this for me.

A car beeps loudly as I veer out of the cycle lane. It gives me such a fright, I pull over and stop. I lay my bike on the ground and walk away, as though it's a ticking bomb, my heart pounding in my chest. I wasn't concentrating; I was almost hit again.

'Are you OK, love?' A woman standing at the bus stop, who witnessed the entire thing, asks.

'Yes, thanks, just catching my breath,' I reply, sitting in a chair outside a café, feeling shaken.

I can become defensive about my role in the club this year, and never fix a thing and run it and myself into the ground, or I can be realistic and take advice. Maria Costas is right. My personal life came out of it battered and bruised and I can't afford to do that again.

The ghost of Gerry back in my life, or the real Gabriel?

I choose Gabriel.

37

'In here,' Gabriel calls, as I enter the house. Our bedroom is the first right off the corridor as soon as you step into the house, Ava's is on the left, both look out over the tiny front garden, which is paved, with no planting, overlooking a busy main road. I wonder if Richard could get his hands on the front garden, start bringing it to life. The bedroom door is wide open and Gabriel is lying on our bed.

'Why are you in here?'

'The TV's too loud,' he says. 'I brought my music in here but I've nowhere to put it with all the clothes and shoes, and make-up and perfume, and bras and tampons that have moved in.' He pretends to cry. 'It's like I don't know who I am any more.'

'Poor Gabriel,' I laugh, climbing onto the bed and on top of him.

'I'll get over it,' he says, kissing me. 'How did it go with the therapist? I'd say it's like quicksand in there. Did she get stuck?' He screws my temple with his finger and whispers in my ear. 'Maria, are you in there? Should I send for help?'

I roll off him. 'She's not on board.'

'That's OK, you can try something else,' he says optimistically. 'Contact cancer charities. Tell them you've got a beneficial service to offer.'

'Yeah,' I agree, flatly. 'Or I could just not do it.

345

I don't need to do it.'

'Holly, snap out of it. You didn't need that therapist to get started, you don't need her now to continue. You know, at times like this I think it would be helpful for you to stop and close your eyes and think . . . ' He squeezes his eyes shut, with a smile threatening to form on his lips, ' . . . What would Gerry do?'

I laugh.

'I do it sometimes,' he says, a mocking tone. 'You should try it.' He closes his eyes, and whispers, 'What would Gerry do? What would Gerry do?' All of a sudden his eyes fly open.

'Well? Did it work?' I chuckle, needing his good humour.

'Yes, thank you,' he says, saluting the sky. 'He says he'd do . . . ' He flips me onto my back and lands on top of me. 'This.'

I yelp out of fright and dissolve into laughter. I smile and run my fingers across his face. 'You should always just do what Gabriel would do. That's what I want.'

'Yeah?'

I examine him. Though he'd been speaking in a playful tone, perhaps Ginika had been right about Gabriel's jealousy of Gerry.

'You're not competing against him,' I say.

'I was, but you can never win against a ghost,' he says. 'So he and I had a chat, and I told him that, with all due respect, he and I have a common goal, i.e. loving you, so he needs to take a step back and trust me. Too many chefs and all that.'

'That sounds a bit weird. But lovely.'

346

He laughs, and kisses me gently.

'Gross,' Ava says, and we stop kissing immediately and look to the door to find her watching us, her face all twisted in disgust. She closes our door, and the TV gets louder in the other room.

Gabriel rolls off me and pretends to cry again.

★   ★   ★

The meeting with Maria Costas was important. I went there looking for new members of the PS, I Love You Club but I left with a larger idea, a broader perspective of how I should be approaching this. She was right: I need to set boundaries for myself, so that I don't allow every single person's story to live in my heart and affect my life. I can't have every member in my home three times a week, and I can't spend full days traipsing across the city on treasure hunts. I can't miss Sunday roasts and I can't take time off work. The year of the meltdown, as Ciara calls it, is over.

I stand in the Magpie stockroom. One wall has floor-to-ceiling shelving, full to the brim, there's a rail of clothes waiting to be washed, steamed and ironed. A basket of clothes and a box of items we won't sell and will instead send to charities. There's a washing machine, a tumble dryer, a steam iron. It's the busy but organised control room of the shop, but if I just . . . I pull a chair across the floor to the back of the room, facing the door. I sit down and imagine a desk before me, with a chair facing me. I imagine a couch, perhaps by the washing machine and tumble dryer. I close my eyes. Imagine.

There's a rap on the door and I open my eyes. Fazeel steps in with his mat rolled up under his arm.

'It's noon,' he says, with a smile.

I grin and jump up from my chair. 'Volunteers! Yes! That's it!' I go to him and hug him.

'My, my, you are happy today,' he says, laughing, hugging me back.

'Ciara!' I yell. 'Ciara, where are you?' I enter the shop.

'Yes, yes, yes,' she says. She's lying on her back beneath a mannequin, head hidden under the skirt.

Mathew is sitting on a stool, arms folded, watching her.

'What are you doing?' I ask.

'Her leg fell off,' Ciara responds, voice muffled.

'Is it wrong that I'm turned on by this?' Mathew asks.

I laugh. 'Ciara, get up, get up, I have news. I have an idea!'

★   ★   ★

'So,' I say excitedly to my family, who are seated around my parents' dining table tucking into their Sunday roast. Gabriel and Ava have joined us this week and Ava hasn't stopped laughing at Declan and Jack's childish antics, which they've played up for her. 'I'm going to turn the Magpie stockroom into a PS, I Love You office.'

348

'Yes!' Ciara says in a celebratory high-pitched tone, fist-punching the air. 'Though perhaps not the entire stockroom!' she adds in an equally celebratory tone, smile frozen on her face.

'I'll meet people there. *Clients.*'

'Yes!'

'Then, because there's only one of me and hopefully there'll be lots of people who require my services, I will employ *volunteers* to help me carry out the physical tasks, and there we have the all-new PS, I Love You Club!'

'Yes!' Ciara squeals, clapping her hands excitedly.

Ava laughs.

'Hold on a minute,' Mathew interrupts Ciara's celebration. 'You were dead against this at the start of the year, why are you now all, 'Yes'' He imitates her high-pitched tone.

'Because,' she says, widening her eyes at everyone as if I can't see or hear her, 'because nobody wanted her to do it last time and she did it anyway, and had a psychological crisis, so let's support her.'

'Ah, come on, so you don't think it's a good idea?' I ask.

'It's wonderful,' Mum says.

'Good for you!' Dad says, mouth filled with potato.

'I'd like to volunteer,' Ava says suddenly, and Gabriel looks at her in surprise. 'Well, you said I needed a job. This sounds cool.'

'But I can't pay you, sweetie,' I say sadly, so honoured she'd offer.

'You can pay her if you get funds,' Richard

says. 'If you register the PS, I Love You Club as a foundation or charity, then you can fundraise for the resources you need. You should also gather a team, for example, an accountant, a business adviser to help with the paperwork and legal obligations. Everybody would have to give their time on a voluntary basis.'

'Really? You really think I should?' I look around the table at them all.

'I could do the bookkeeping for you,' Richard offers. Before he began his landscaping business, he was an accountant.

'I would love to help with fundraising,' Abbey says.

'I say a raise of hands for yes,' Ciara declares.

They all raise their hands. All apart from Gabriel.

'It's a big undertaking,' he says.

'She can do it, Dad,' Ava says, nudging him.

'Yeah, Dad,' Jack says, imitating Ava.

'Yeah, Dad,' the rest of them say in unison, and crack up laughing.

As the conversation turns into the usual noisy brawl, Gabriel wraps his arm around my shoulder and leans close. 'I know you can,' he whispers, and kisses me gently.

Excitement builds inside me. All this time I was thinking of it as a club, but it could be more. With enough support, we could help more people. I could dedicate more time to the people who need me to properly observe their life and help construct and distribute their letters. The PS, I Love You Club could become a nationwide foundation or a charity, helping those who are terminally ill finally reclaim their goodbyes. And all because of Gerry.

My phone rings; I don't recognise the number. 'Hello?'

'Hi, is that Holly Kennedy?' a young male voice asks.

'Yes. This is Holly.'

'Uh, I got your number from, er, Maria. Maria Costas? She told me about your club.'

'Yes, this is the PS, I Love You Club,' I say, standing up to leave as everyone hushes around the table.

'Ssh,' Jack starts, childishly, to Declan.

'Ssh,' Declan replies.

'Ssh,' Mathew continues it, nudging Ciara, who's not saying anything at all.

I press a finger into my ear and leave the room.

When I end the call, I see Gabriel standing at the door, watching me.

'I have a client,' I say happily, then wipe the smile off my face, uncertain that my happiness is fair to Philip's predicament. 'But don't say anything, you know what they're like.'

'I won't,' he whispers conspiratorially.

As soon as we walk back to the dinner table, he grabs my hand and lifts it high in the air. 'She has a client!'

They roar in celebration.

★   ★   ★

'Hello, Holly,' Maria Costas says, greeting me at the main door of St Mary's hospice. 'Thanks for

351

coming at such short notice.'

'No problem, I'm glad Philip called.'

'He told me he wanted to leave something behind for his friends but couldn't think what. That's when I told him about you and the club. I wasn't sure if you were going to continue it, after our chat.'

'You gave me a lot to think about after we talked, but it was always about growing it, not ending it. Since we last met I've been implementing plans to develop the PS, I Love You Club, with more of a structure, and a team. If you have time after this, we can talk about it?'

'I'd like that.' We stop walking. 'This is Philip's room.'

'Tell me about him.'

'He's seventeen, he was diagnosed with osteosarcoma, which is a type of bone cancer. He's been through a lot, he's had limb salvage surgery to replace his left femur, he's had three cycles of chemo, but the cancer is aggressive.'

We enter Philip's room and he looks younger than seventeen. He's tall and broad but shrunken in his own body, his skin has a yellowish tinge. His brown eyes are deep, large in his shrunken sockets.

'Hey, Philip,' Maria says coolly, going to him with a hand held up for a high five.

'Hey, Maria, the Greek goddess.'

Maria laughs. 'I'm a Cypriot, actually, and no royal blood in my veins, unless you count my granddad's home-grown olive oil. I brought a present for you. Holly, this is Philip. Philip, this is Holly.'

'I prefer a boom,' I say, holding my fist out.

'Oh, she's a boom-type girl,' Maria says, smiling as Philip and I tap fists.

I sit beside him and notice the inside of his locker is covered in photos of friends. Boys his age, groups of them messing, laughing, posing, in rugby gear, a rugby team. A group holding a trophy. I recognise Philip instantly, a broad, muscular young teenager before the cancer took hold.

After spending an hour brainstorming with Philip, we part and Maria and I leave him alone. 'Well?' I ask, feeling that I was auditioning in there for her.

'For your club to work, you'd need a therapist who can have the psychological needs of your clients in mind, particularly one who understands the natural course and treatment of the illness, and has a flexible approach in accordance with the medical status of the patient.'

'Where could I find one of those?' I muse.

She looks in the window at Philip and takes a moment. 'I'm in,' she says.

38

Two months later, I sit on stage alongside teachers of Belvedere College, a secondary school in Dublin, while the principal makes a speech to the leaving cert students who will be sitting their final exams in the summer. He's motivating them to study harder, believe in themselves, give themselves one big push, because it means something. It's their future. I scan the faces of the young men of seventeen and eighteen years of age, I see hope, determination, I see stifled yawns, mischievous private jokes. All kinds.

'But there's another reason why we're all gathered here today.'

Silence. Intrigue. They murmur amongst themselves, trying to guess, but they won't.

'Today is Philip O'Donnell's eighteenth birthday. We want to remember our student and friend, who we sadly lost a few months ago.'

A cheer goes up, louder in the middle section. Philip's friends.

'We have been joined by a special guest, Holly Kennedy, who will introduce herself and tell us why she is here. Please welcome Holly Kennedy to the podium.'

Polite applause.

'Hello, everybody. I'm sorry to have dragged you away from your classes, I'm sure you all want to get back as quickly as possible so I won't

354

take up too much of your time.'

They laugh, delighted to be called from class.

'As Principal Hanley said, my name is Holly and I work with a new foundation called PS, I Love You. Our work is to help those who are terminally ill write letters for their loved ones, to be delivered after they've passed on. It's something I have personal experience with, and something that I've learned is very important and precious to those who are ill, ensuring that the people they have left behind know that they are not alone, that they will be guided, and also to ensure that they themselves will be remembered. I appreciate Principal Hanley allowing Philip to carry out this wish, and gathering you all here today. I have a letter here, from Philip. It was his wish that I read this aloud to his special friends, Conor aka Con-Man, David aka Big D, and Michael aka Tricky Mickey.'

Despite the moving context, the audience *jeer* the nick-names.

'Philip wanted me to ask you three very special friends of his to stand.'

I look out at the sea of faces, every one of them looking around for the three young men. Slowly Philip's best friends get to their feet, and already one is crying. Arms around each other's shoulders for support, as though standing on the rugby pitch for the national anthem. These three teenagers helped carry his coffin at the funeral and they still stand side by side. I take a deep breath. I need to hold it together.

'Dear Con-Man, Big D and Tricky Mickey,' I read. 'I'm not going to make this morbid, I'm

355

sure you're all morto enough, standing there in front of everyone.'

Somebody wolf-whistles.

'Everyone in this room knows you three are my best mates. I'll miss you, the only thing I don't regret about all of this is missing out on my exams this year. At least I got away with not having to study.'

A cheer breaks out and they applaud him.

'Today is my eighteenth birthday, I'm the youngest and you lot never let me forget it. Respect your elders, you always used to say, Tricky Mickey. Well I do. I wish I was there to do this with you, but you can finish off what I've started. On December twenty-fourth, Christmas Eve, you'll be doing the twelve pubs of Christmas.'

An eruption of cheers and applause. I wait for the rowdiness to die down with help from the principal.

'Twelve pubs. Twelve pints. And they're all on me, lads. Bring a puke bucket for Big D.'

Retching, vomiting sounds circulate the room, and the teenager in the middle of the trio gets a ribbing from the people sitting behind him. I have located Big D.

'You'll be starting in O'Donoghue's, where there'll be a pint from me waiting for you. When you finish your pint, the bartender will give you an envelope with a note from me, telling you where to go next. Because Hanley is listening, and he wouldn't agree to this being read out otherwise, I have to add the condition that you'll accompany each pint with a glass of water.'

356

The audience cheer at the mention of the principal, and I turn in time to see Principal Hanley wiping his eyes.

'Enjoy the night, have an extra pint for me. If I can, I'll be watching. PS, I love you, lads.'

The three friends gather in a group hug while the rest of the auditorium applaud respectfully and arise in a standing ovation, chanting Philip's name. Two of the three friends are crying, Big D in the centre, and the third is seriously struggling but is keeping it together, manning up, the very serious daddy one of them all, keeping them together.

You can't know anything for sure but I wonder, if Philip had lived, whether they'd have eventually gone their separate ways. Now, though, in Philip's death, they'll be bonded together always. Death rips people apart, but it also has a way of stitching those left behind together.

★ ★ ★

I push open a garden gate, which squeaks at the hinges, and step on to the path leading to the cottage. I ring the doorbell and when I hear footsteps make their way to the door I nod to Mathew, who's standing at the back doors of his van. On my nod, he opens the boot and takes out half a dozen red balloons in each hand. He's followed by Ciara and Ava, who are also carrying a dozen red balloons. As the cottage door opens, Mathew hands me his red balloons and hurries back for the rest.

The woman isn't much older than me. 'Hello,' she says, smiling, but confused.

'From Peter,' I say, handing her a card that reads,

Happy Birthday, Alice,
Red Balloons Go By,
Love, Peter
PS, I Love You

She takes it in shock.

I press play on my iPhone and the song '99 Red Balloons' by Nena begins, the first song they danced to together. She steps aside and watches the procession of ninety-nine balloons enter and fill her home as the song fills the house.

★   ★   ★

I sit at the kitchen table of a widow who is holding her new gift of a charm bracelet in her hand, tears running down her cheeks.

'Each charm has a story,' I explain, handing her the eight envelopes with her wife's messages. 'She chose them especially for you.'

★   ★   ★

I sit with a dad and his three young children in their home. They are looking at me wide-eyed.

'Mam did what?'

'She started her own YouTube channel,' I repeat. 'How cool is that?'

'So cool!' the eight-year-old punches the air.

'But Mam *hated* us watching YouTube,' the teenager says, stunned.

'Not any more,' I smile. I open their mother's laptop and turn the screen around to face them. They crowd around, elbowing each other, fighting for space.

The music starts and the voice of their mother calls out in a tone she's stolen from the YouTubers her children idolise. 'Hey, guys, it's me, Sandra aka 'Bam-It's-Mam!' and welcome to my YouTube channel! Have I got some cool things to show you guys, and I hope you have fun watching at home. PS, I Love You *so* much, guys. Now, let's get started! Today we're gonna make slime!'

'Slime!' the children shriek, and their dad sits back in his chair, covers his mouth to stifle his sudden swell of emotions. His eyes fill but the children are so engrossed in their mother's video they don't notice.

★   ★   ★

I wake with a start. There's something I need to do urgently, I wanted to do it last night before I went to bed but it was too late. I sit up and grab my phone from the bedside table.

'Hello?' Joy answers.

'It's December eighth.' The unofficial start of Christmas. It's a holy day, apparently, the feast of the immaculate conception. People from all around the country used to travel to Dublin to do their Christmas shopping, before their towns

359

grew, before travel became easier, before society and culture changed. These are old traditional beliefs, not followed by all any more, but one thing hasn't changed, it's also the day that many traditional people decorate their homes for Christmas.

'Holly, is that you?'

'Yes,' I laugh. 'Joy, it's December eighth!'

'Yes, I know, you said so, but I don't understand.'

'Is Joe going to buy a Christmas tree today? Is he going to decorate the house?'

'Oh,' she realises, and lowers her voice to a whisper. 'Yes, he is.'

'He can't go up to the attic,' I say, quickly getting out of bed, and hurrying around naked, looking for clothes.

'Oh dear, what am I going to do? I can't get up there.'

'Of course not. That's why I'm calling: I put them up there, now I'm going to take them down.' I pause, smiling. 'Joy. You made it.'

'Yes,' she whispers. 'I did.'

39

The family solicitor who handled the purchase of our house ten years ago retired, transferring all my paperwork to a new firm that I've had no business dealings with since. I visit the office to finally finalise the paperwork for the sale of the house.

'Nice to see you today, Holly. I've spent time familiarising myself with your property and the deeds. I came across something unusual and I contacted Tony about it. He told me all was correct and in place.'

'Please tell me there's nothing wrong, it's taken so long to get to this point. I just need to sign the paperwork,' I say, exhausted from the experience.

'There's nothing wrong. A personal note was attached to the files. It was given to Tony Daly with a note explaining that this letter should be handed to you *in the event that Holly Kennedy sells the property.*

Instant palpitations. My hope surges but I know it's stupid after all this time. It's been eight years since Gerry died, seven years since I read his last note. There were ten letters, I read them all. It would be greedy to hope for more.

She reaches into the files and slides out an envelope.

'Oh my God,' I say, hands to my mouth.

'That's my late husband's handwriting.'

She holds it to me but I don't take it. I keep looking at it, held by her in the air, his writing. She eventually places it down on the desk before me.

'I'll give you some time alone,' she says. 'Would you like water?'

I don't answer.

'I'll get you some water.'

Alone with the envelope, I read the words on the front.

One for the Road.

★   ★   ★

It's late Saturday night, early Saturday morning. The crowds are leaving the pub, being shouted out and abused by the doormen. The lights are on full, the smell of bleach is strong as the staff attempt to flush the crowds out. Others are going home, or are continuing on to a club. Sharon and John are practically eating each other's faces alive, as they have been all night, but what seemed mildly unappetising in the dark is far uglier in the harsh bright lights.

'One for the road?' Gerry says to me, looking bleary-eyed, with a charming grin. Eyes always smiling, with devilment, with life.

'They're throwing us out.'

'Denise,' Gerry calls. 'Work some magic, will you?'

'Already on it.' Denise salutes him and heads directly to a handsome young bouncer.

'Stop pimping my friend.'

'She loves it,' he grins.

Denise turns and winks, already successful at securing a last round.

'Always one more,' I say, kissing him.

'Always,' he whispers.

★ ★ ★

My alarm sounds. It's 7 a.m. I roll onto my side and turn it off. I need to get up, out of bed, go home, shower, get to college. I feel Gerry stirring beside me. His hand reaches across the bed to me, warm like a furnace. He moves his body and presses up against me, full, wanting. His lips brush the nape of my neck. His fingers find me, just where he needs to to convince me to stay. I press back against him, responding.

'One for the road,' he says, sleepily.

I feel his words against my skin. I hear the smile in his voice. I'm not going anywhere else but to him.

'Always one more,' I whisper.

'Always.'

★ ★ ★

I stare at the envelope on the desk before me, in shock. How did I not consider this, in all the analysis and calculations since his death? One for the road, he always said it. There's always one more. Always. Ten letters, it should have been enough, but seven years since I read the final one, here's one for the road.

Dear Holly,

There's always one more. But this is the last.

Five minutes for me, but who knows how long for you. Maybe you'll never read this, maybe you'll never sell the house, maybe it will get lost, maybe somebody else is reading this. A beautiful daughter or son of yours. Who knows. But I'm writing this with the intention of you reading this.

I could have died yesterday, it could have been decades ago. You could be putting your teeth in a glass beside your bed at night, I'm sorry I didn't get to grow old with you. I don't know who you are in your world right now, but here in my world, at the time of writing this, I'm still me, you're still you and we're still us.

Let me take you back there.

I'm sure you're still beautiful. I'm sure you're still kind.

You'll always be loved, from here and away, from near and from far.

I have experience in loving you from afar, remember? It took me a year to ask you to go out with me.

I've no doubt it will ever change, all I know is that the less life I have in me, the more I love you, as if love is filling the spaces. When I'm gone, I think I'll be filled with nothing but love, made of nothing but love for you.

But on the off chance I do hook up with somebody on the other side, please don't

get mad, I'll drop her as soon as you arrive.
If you're not looking or waiting for someone
else.

Good luck with your new adventure,
whatever it is.

I love you, beautiful, and I'm still glad
you said yes.

Gerry

PS — I'll see you later?

Inside the envelope is a note that, despite it sitting in an envelope for eight years, has a crumpled, wrinkled appearance. I smooth it out on the desk and, seeing the handwriting, I realise it's the first letter Gerry wrote to me when we were fourteen years old.

His words bring me back in time and take me forward with renewed hope for my future; they plant me in the earth, grounding me in reality, and they lift me up so that I feel like I'm floating.

His letter gives me roots and wings.

★　★　★

Tuesday morning. I hate Tuesdays because they're worse than Mondays. I've already been through a Monday and the week still isn't even half over. My school day begins with double Maths with Mr Murphy, who hates me as much as I hate Maths, which is a lot of hate in one room on a Tuesday. I've been moved right up to the front row in front of Mr Murphy's desk so he can keep an eye on me. I'm quiet as a mouse, but I can't keep up.

It's lashing rain outside, my socks are still wet from the walk from the bus stop to school. I'm freezing cold and to add to it Mr Murphy has opened all the windows to wake us up because one person yawned. The boys are lucky, they get to wear trousers, my legs are goose-pimpled and I can feel the hairs standing up. I shaved them up to my knee but cut my shin and it's stinging through my grey woollen uniform sock. I probably shouldn't have used Richard's razor but last time I asked for my own razor, Mum said I'm too young to shave my legs and I can't be bothered going through the mortification of asking her again.

I hate Tuesdays. I hate school. I hate Maths. I hate hairy legs.

The bell rings at the end of the first period and I should feel relief as the halls outside are flooded with students going to their next class, but I know we've another forty minutes to get through. Sharon is out sick and so the seat beside me is empty. I hate when she's not beside me, it means I can't copy her answers. She was moved beside me because she kept laughing, but she's good at Maths so I can copy her. I can see the hallways through the glass panel beside the door. Denise waits until Mr Murphy isn't looking and she presses her face up against the glass, opening her mouth and pressing her nose up like a pig. I grin and look away. Some people in the class laugh, but by the time Mr Murphy looks over, she's gone.

Mr Murphy leaves the classroom for ten

minutes. We've to finish a problem he gave us. I know I won't reach the solution because I don't even understand the question. X and Y can kiss my arse. He'll come back into the class stinking of smoke like he always does, and sit in front of me with a banana and a knife, looking at us all in a menacing way like he's a badass. Someone slides into the seat beside me. John. I feel my face go red with embarrassment. Confused, I look over my right shoulder to the wall where he normally sits, with Gerry. Gerry looks away and down at his copybook.

'What are you doing?' I whisper, even though everybody else is talking, probably finished their work. Even if they're not finished, it won't matter, Mr Murphy will always ask me.

'Me mate wants to know if you'll go out with him,' John says.

My heart thuds and I feel my mouth dry up.

'Which mate?'

'Gerry. Who'd you think?'

Thump, thump.

'Is this a joke?' I ask, annoyed and mortified at the same time.

'I'm serious. Yes or no?'

I roll my eyes. Gerry is the most gorgeous guy in class — correction, in the year. He can have anyone he wants and this is most likely a joke.

'John, it's not funny.'

'I'm serious!'

I'm afraid to turn around and look at Gerry again. My face is full on flaming red. I much preferred sitting in the back row where I could always stare at Gerry whenever I wanted.

Everyone likes him, and he's gorgeous, even with his new train tracks, and he always smells nice. Of course I fancy Gerry, most girls — and Peter — do. But me and Gerry? I didn't think he even knew I was here.

'Holly, I'm serious,' John says. 'Smurf will be back in a minute. Yes or no?'

I swallow hard. If I say yes and it's a joke then I'll be mortified. But if I say no and it's not a joke, I'll never forgive myself.

'Yeah,' I say, and my voice comes out all funny.

'Cool,' John grins and hurries back to his seat.

I wait for jeering, for everyone to laugh and tell me it's a joke. I wait to be humiliated, afraid to turn around, sure that everyone is silently laughing at me. There's a bang on the open door and I jump with fright. Mr Murphy is back, with his banana and his knife, stinking of smoke.

Everyone goes quiet.

'Everyone finished?'

There's a chorus of yeses.

He looks at me. 'Holly?'

'No.'

'Then let's go through it, shall we?'

I'm so self-conscious that everybody's eyes are on me that I can't even think. And Gerry, he must be thinking I'm an absolute dunce.

'OK, take the first part,' Mr Murphy says, unpeeling the banana and slicing the tip. He never eats the tip, he hates the black pointy part. He cuts a thin slice of banana and eats it off the knife.

'John has thirty-two chocolate bars,' he says slowly, patronisingly, and a few people laugh. 'He eats twenty-eight. What does he have now?'

'Diabetes, sir!' Gerry shouts out, and everybody cracks up laughing.

Even Mr Murphy laughs. 'Thank you for that, Gerry.'

'No problem, sir.'

'Since you think you're so smart, finish this off for us.'

And he does. Easy as that. I'm saved. I'm grateful but too embarrassed to turn around. Something hits against my leg and lands at my feet. I look down and see a scrunched-up piece of paper. I pretend to be leaning down to get something from my bag and while Mr Murphy has his back turned and is writing on the board, I open the ball of paper and smooth it open on my lap.

It wasn't a joke. Promise. Wanted to ask you for ages.
Glad you said yes.
Gerry
PS, see you later?

I grin, my heart pounding, my stomach alive with butterflies. I shove the letter into my bag and as I do, I sneak a glance behind me. Gerry is watching me, big blue eyes, kind of nervous. I smile, and he smiles. Like a private joke only the two of us are in on.

Epilogue

I'm in Magpie, at my favourite area with the trinkets and the chest of drawers, polishing and sorting, kind of playing, when Ciara interrupts my thoughts. She's standing in the window dressing the mannequins.

'I'm thinking of naming the mannequins. The longer I spend with them, the more I'm certain they each have a personality.'

I laugh.

'If I listen to them, I can utilise them to their best advantage. Maybe sell more. For example, this here is Naomi.' She turns the model around and waves her hand at me. 'She's a window girl. She likes being centre of attention. On stage. Unlike . . . Mags over there, who hates the attention.' She jumps off the raised platform and makes her way to the mannequin in the accessory area. 'Mags likes to hide. She likes wigs, sunglasses, hats, gloves, bags, scarves, you name it.'

'That's because Mags is on the run,' I say.

'Yes!' Ciara's eyes widen and she studies the mannequin. 'You're not shy at all, are you? You're *on the run*.'

The bell rings as the door opens.

'Who are you running from, Mags? Is it something you've seen or something you've done? Let me look you in the eye.' Ciara lowers her glasses and stares at her. She gasps. 'What have you done, you naughty thing?'

The customer clears their throat and we turn our attention to the door, where there's a young man standing, with a half-filled black bin liner in his hand.

My heart pounds wildly. I hold on to the chest of drawers. Ciara looks at me in surprise and then back to the man. I know by her reaction that she sees it too; he's the image of Gerry.

'Hello,' Ciara says. 'I'm sorry . . . you've caught us . . . we're talking to . . . my goodness, you look very like somebody we know. Used to know. Know.' She tilts her head, and examines him.

'How can I help you?'

'I'm looking for Holly Kennedy,' he says. 'From the PS, I Love You Club?'

'I'm Ciara. This is Mags. If that is in fact her real name,' she says, smiling. 'She has a dark history. Oh, and that's Holly.'

I try to snap myself out of it. It's not Gerry. It's definitely not him. Just a young, handsome, incredibly similar guy, so similar he managed to take both Ciara's and my breath away. Black hair, blue eyes, a common Irish look, but my God, he's cut from the same cloth.

'I'm Holly.'

'Hi. I'm Jack.'

'Nice to meet you, Jack,' I say, shaking his hand. He's so young, I'm guessing ten years younger than me now, but the way Gerry was, before the end. 'Come this way.'

I lead him to the stockroom that I've renovated to include an inviting space for the

371

club, and we sit down at the couch area. He looks around. I've framed photographs on the wall of the original members of the PS, I Love You Club: Angela, Joy, Bert, Paul and Ginika. I added Gerry to the group, as seemed fitting, considering he's the original founder. Jack's eyes settle on Gerry. I wonder if he sees the resemblance too. I hand him a bottle of water. He nervously downs half of it immediately.

'How can I help you?'

'I read about the PS, I Love You letters in a magazine — while I was waiting at the hospital, ironically.'

I know the magazine piece he saw; we're a new foundation, not many profile pieces to be confused about. It was in a health magazine, complete with a photograph of Gerry and me. Perhaps it was Gerry who drew him to the club.

'I have cancer,' he says, his eyes filling. He clears his throat and looks down. 'I want to do something for my wife. We only got married last year. I read about your story. I want to do something fun for her, every month for a year, like your husband did.'

I smile. 'I'd be honoured to help.'

'Did you ... did he ... was it ... ' he struggles with the question. He sighs. 'You obviously think it's a good idea or you wouldn't have started this. Will she like it?' he eventually asks.

There's so many levels to this experience, so many layers to explain. His wife will feel so many things about these letters and tasks that her husband will surprise her with, I find it difficult

372

to put it into words. She will feel loss, and grief, but also connection and love, spirit and darkness, black and anger, light and hope, laughter and fear. Everything in between, a kaleidoscope of emotions that shine and flicker from one moment to the next.

'Jack, so much of what's to come will change her life forever,' I say eventually. 'These letters, planned in the right way, will ensure you're by her side every step of the way. Do you think she'll want that?'

'Yeah. Definitely.' He smiles, convinced. 'Good. Let's do it. Look, I told her I'd only be in here for a minute, that I was dropping off some old stuff for my mum.' He glances down at the bin liner by his feet. 'It's old newspapers, sorry.'

'Well, best not leave her waiting.' I stand and lead him back to the shop. 'We can meet again soon, and you can give me more of a sense of her personality. What's her name?'

'Molly,' he says, with a smile.

'Molly.'

'Bye, Jack,' Ciara says.

'Bye, Ciara, bye, Mags,' he says with a grin.

The door closes and Ciara looks at me as though she's seen a ghost. I rush to the window and watch him get into a car beside a pretty young woman. Molly. They're chatting while he gets his keys ready.

Molly catches sight of me, and she smiles. In that look, that quick connection we make, she transports me back, so far back, I feel like I'm speeding through a black hole and my heart can barely keep up with the travel. I feel protective of her, like a parent, like a friend. I want to mind her, reach out to her, embrace her. I want to tell her to squeeze him, hold him tight, breathe him in, treasure every single second. I want to leave her alone and give her the space she so desires, let her build a wall around herself while patiently listening from the other side. I want to help her build that wall, I want to help her tear it down. I want to warn her, I want to give her hope. I want to tell her to keep going, I want to tell her to turn around and go back the other way. I feel like I know her so well. I know who she is and where she is now, the journey she is about to embark on and the distance she will go. And yet, I know I have to step back and let her get there on her own.

I may envy her a little at this moment, watching them together, but I don't envy the journey ahead of her. I made it, I did it, and I'll be rooting for her and waiting for her on the other side.

I return the smile.

And then they drive away.

Acknowledgements

Thank you Lynne Drew, Martha Ashby, Karen Kostolynik, Kate Elton, Charlie Redmayne, Elizabeth Dawson, Anna Derkacz, Hannah O'Brien, Abbie Salter, Damon Greeney, Claire Ward, Holly MacDonald, Eoin McHugh, Mary Byrne, Tony Purdue, Ciara Swift, Jacq Murphy and the wonderful innovative teams at Harper-Collins UK and Grand Central Publishing US. Andy Dodds, Chris Maher, Dee Delaney, Howie Sanders, Willie Ryan, Sarah Kelly. Thanks to all at Park and Fine Literary and Media especially Theresa Park, Abigail Koons, Emily Sweet, Andrea Mai, Ema Barnes and Marie Michels. To the booksellers far and wide. To the printers. To the readers. To the sources of my inspiration; the divine and the everyday.

My parents, my sister, my family, my friends, my David, my Robin, my Sonny.

We do hope that you have enjoyed reading this large print book.

Did you know that all of our titles are available for purchase?

We publish a wide range of high quality large print books including:
Romances, Mysteries, Classics
General Fiction
Non Fiction and Westerns

Special interest titles available in large print are:
The Little Oxford Dictionary
Music Book
Song Book
Hymn Book
Service Book

Also available from us courtesy of Oxford University Press:
Young Readers' Dictionary
(large print edition)
Young Readers' Thesaurus
(large print edition)

For further information or a free brochure, please contact us at:
Ulverscroft Large Print Books Ltd.,
The Green, Bradgate Road, Anstey,
Leicester, LE7 7FU, England.
Tel: (00 44) 0116 236 4325
Fax: (00 44) 0116 234 0205